A Kiss and a Promise

JESSICA STIRLING

A Kiss and a Promise

**HODDER &
STOUGHTON**

First published in Great Britain in 2008 by Hodder & Stoughton
An Hachette Livre UK company

1

A CIP catalogue record for this title is available from the British Library

ISBN 978 0 340 96249 7

Typeset in Plantin Light by Hewer Text UK Ltd, Edinburgh
Printed and bound in the UK by CPI Mackays, Chatham ME5 8TD

Hodder & Stoughton policy is to use papers that are natural, renewable
and recyclable products and made from wood grown in sustainable
forests. The logging and manufacturing processes are expected to
conform to the environmental regulations of the country of origin.

Hodder & Stoughton Ltd
338 Euston Road
London NW1 3BH

www.hodder.co.uk

To Lyn
With Love

CONTENTS

PART ONE

A Kiss and a Promise

I

Most girls in Hayes regarded Tom Brodie as a catch worth having, though a few well-bred young ladies adamantly declared that he was far too coarse for their taste and his sugary compliments nothing short of vulgar. Such slanders did not concern Betsy McBride who felt just as entitled as any girl in Ayrshire to nurse a fancy for the farmer's son.

What drew her to Tom Brodie was not his gift of the gab but the strut of him, half bashful, half arrogant, and the sprig of dark hair tied with blue ribbon that protruded from under his bonnet when he sauntered to church of a Sunday. She had exchanged not a word with him, though, until the day Mr Rankine sent her up to Brodie's farm to help the old man out of his difficulties.

Betsy was not by nature timid and did not lack experience. Mr Rankine had stuck his hand up her skirts before she had turned fifteen and, when she had grown a bit, a lot more than his hand. If her mother guessed what dirty old Johnny was up to, she kept it to herself, for Mr Rankine was a man of influence and brought work their way. Besides, old Johnny popped in and out of her quick as a sparrow and slipped her a kiss and a few brown pennies, and in spite of his fat belly and red cheeks, Betsy was quite fond of him.

When Mr Rankine informed her that he had loaned her to the Brodies as a live-in for part of the winter she made no complaint. She ran home to pack her belongings and tell her mother and father that she was leaving home at last.

In the middle of the afternoon, she headed along the old toll road to the track that led up to Hawkshill. She had never set foot on the hill track before, though old Mr Brodie's farm was only a mile from the house where she had been born and raised and not much further from Mr Rankine's place where she'd entered day service as soon as she was old enough to lug a milk pail.

It was already coming down towards dusk. Black clouds threatened more rain and the track was muddy. Mr Brodie's rigs were hidden by rising ground and the farm buildings tucked into a fold close to a stagnant hill loch. In the gloomy afternoon light the place seemed sullen and remote. Snow had lain late into April and rain storms in August had all but trashed the harvest. Poor seed and failed crops had ruined many an Ayrshire tenant, for the landowners showed no mercy when it came to clawing in rent. She wondered if bad weather was the cause of old Mr Brodie's difficulties and recalled some market gossip about him being under summons for debt.

Three years ago her brothers had bought a calf from Mr Brodie and back in the spring of 1780 her sister, Effie, had been sent to deliver a small parcel of material that their father had woven on his hand-loom. Effie had been paid on the spot and had been given a bowl of warm milk by the lady of the house and had her head patted by old Mr Brodie himself. He had asked her if she studied her Scripture, a question Effie had been too shy, or too stupid, to answer. I'd have answered him boldly enough, Betsy thought. I can read and write a bit and can chant a psalm just as loudly as any of Mr Brodie's brood; all of whom, bar Tom, hunched, cowed and surly, in church as if they were more afraid of their father's disapproval than the preacher's threats of damnation.

She was still some way short of the ridge when the first spots of rain splashed her cheek. Hastily gathering her skirts, she entered the farmyard just as the first great sheets of rain rattled across the causeway.

She drew up, unsure which way to go. Then a voice called out, 'Come in here, you daft creature, afore you drown,' and with her bundle bobbing on her head, she scampered for the shelter of the barn.

Tom Brodie looked different in work clothes, smaller, thinner, less cocksure. His hair was plastered to his brow, his shirt open at the throat and loose at the waist. He had been flailing sheaves of green corn and sweating hard. He grinned, showing white teeth and, screwing up a fistful of shirt-tail, swabbed his wrists and forearms.

'You're Rankine's lass, I take it?'

'Aye, sir. I am.'

'Weaver McBride's daughter?'

'Aye.'

She felt his eyes upon her, sizing her up.

'I've seen you in kirk, have I not?' he asked.

'Aye, Mr Brodie,' she answered. 'In the gallery.'

'Have I not seen you at the dancin' school too?'

'Nah, nah. The dancin' school's not for the likes o' me.'

'Why not?' he said. 'From what I can see you've the leg for it.'

'But not the manners, Mr Brodie, nor the features.'

He tossed the flail aside and before she could stop him touched the scar that was not quite hidden by a curl of soft fair hair. It was not much of a scar, a little crescent of raised flesh that encroached an inch or two on to her temple, but she was embarrassed by it and believed, wrongly, that it set her apart from other girls. She flinched and tried to draw away but he was too quick for her. In spite of his black, broken nails his fingers were as soft as thistledown as he brushed back her rain-wet hair.

'Who did this to you?' he said. 'Some bully?'

'No bully, no.'

'Is it a legacy of birth?'

'No, Mr Brodie. I was kickit.'

'Horse or cow?'

'Horse – when I was a bairn.'

'By God, it could have killed you.'

'It might have been better if it had.'

'Why do you say that?' Tom Brodie asked.

'It's an ugly thing to have to carry all your life.'

Stooping, he lifted her bundle. 'Well, you don't look ugly to me an' it's our good fortune you survived. If what I hear from Johnny Rankine is true then the world would be the worse off without you. What do I call you?'

'Some call me Lizzie,' she said, 'some Betsy.'

'Which name do you prefer?'

She had never been offered the choice before. She shrugged.

'I'll call you Betsy,' he said. 'Betsy sounds right to me.'

'An' you, Mr Brodie, am I to be callin' you Master?'

'Thomas will do, or Tom. Now, rain or no rain, I suggest we make a cut for it. My sister will find you a bed an' show you what needs to be done.' Then, locking her elbow in his, he led her across the yard to the door of the cottage where his sister Janet watched, scowling, as her brother and the sturdy young servant lass came scurrying out of the rain.

The old man was up that afternoon, shuffling about the smoky room. He had been out pulling turnips in the plot behind the house, it seemed, and the labour had drained his strength and shortened his temper.

Tom pushed her forward.

'This is the girl, Dad,' he said, 'the lass we told you about.'

Matthew Brodie knew less of her than she had been led to believe. He might once have patted her wee sister's head but he was far past patting heads now. He was hardly more than a rack of bones.

Chin drawn down to his chest, eyes glassy, he studied Betsy at some length, then said, 'Is this another o' your harlots, Thomas? Is it not enough for you to have them in the dark o' the night, now you have to flaunt them before us in broad daylight?'

'I'll thank you not to shame the girl with your insults. She's here because we need an extra hand to help us through the winter months,' Tom said thinly. 'She's Jock McBride's lass.'

'Aye, an' Rankine's harlot.'

'Indeed, an' I am not, sir,' Betsy piped up. 'If you're goin' to call me names I'll be makin' my way home again. I'm not indebted to you.'

He seemed surprised by her indignation. 'You've a bold tongue in your head, I'll say that for you,' he told her. 'But you've also got right on your side. I was o'er hasty in makin' judgement. I am well aware of the sort of man your master is, however, an' that he an' my reprobate son have more things on their minds than obeyin' the will of God.'

'It's not the will o' God fetched me here, Mr Brodie,' Betsy said, 'not unless you prayed for a strong pair o' shoulders to help gather your corn. If that's the case then your prayers have been answered.'

'Perhaps they have, lassie. Aye, perhaps they have. Do I have you to thank for this, Thomas? Have you been tradin' on Rankine's friendship again?'

'I spoke to him at the lodge last fortnight,' Tom admitted. 'Johnny's crops are well in hand an' his calves close to weaned. Miss McBride is superfluous to his needs – at least until spring.'

'We'll think about spring when Martinmas is past,' Matthew Brodie said. He gripped Tom's arm, inched round and steered himself towards the bed. 'Janet will show you what's to be done, lassie. An' you, Thomas, had best get on wi' your work.'

'It wants but a half-hour until dark, Father,' Janet said.

'Then he'd best take advantage o' what light's left to him,' the old man said, 'for there's more light left to him than there is to me,' and, grunting, seated himself on the bed by the wall and closed the sackcloth curtain.

The Brodies' cottage was smaller than Betsy's father's house in Hayes and much smaller than Mr Rankine's spacious two-storey farmhouse with its whitewashed walls, black-painted window sills and fine big kitchen. There was no separate parlour, the ingle was as deep as a cave and the flue so wide that it not only sucked up smoke but let in rain. In a room to the left of the fireplace Janet slept in a narrow bed that Betsy would be expected to share.

On the far side of the ingle a vertical wooden ladder gave access to the loft where the boys slept. Mr Brodie's sickbed occupied an alcove screened by a curtain, and a thin vertical opening in the plaster wall allowed a peep into the stable so that, in the old style, the Brodies lived cheek by jowl with their horses.

When the brothers returned, drenched, from their day's labours there was hardly room to turn round. Betsy found herself tripping over Tom's feet and Henry's knees. Tom's sister, Janet, was not welcoming. She tisked, tutted and darted black looks in Betsy's direction until Tom told her to hold her scolding tongue and get on with serving supper.

He pulled a warped old chest from beneath the table to serve as a chair. Betsy mounted it as if it were a saddle. Janet, not chastened by Tom's reprimand, sniggered. There was no tea or small beer to wash down the salty soup and not so much as a sliver of butter to flavour the dry bread but Betsy was hungry and ate without a word of complaint.

Tom and Henry watched her with interest.

The brothers were not alike in character or appearance. Tom was dark and brooding, quite a different fellow from the devil-may-care gamecock who swaggered about the village. Henry, on the other hand, was courteous and self-effacing. He had a long, oval face, wispy fair hair, piercing blue eyes and, Betsy thought, a poise that would not shame a gentleman.

'No need to skimp, Miss McBride,' he said. 'There's not much variety but there's no paucity. Barley broth and pease-meal are nourishing an' filling.'

'I've supped on both often enough, Mr Brodie.'

'Then eat up, lassie,' Tom's mother, Agnes Brodie, said. 'You'll need all o' your strength tomorrow to reap the last o' our corn.'

'When the crop's brought in, what then?' Betsy asked.

'There's the stubble to rake,' Tom answered.

'An' the cattle to see to,' said Agnes Brodie.

'Do you winter your beasts in the byre?' Betsy asked.

'Only if there's feed enough,' Henry told her. 'We might have to sell half the herd just to pay the rent if the winter brings early snow.'

'We're down to skin an' bone as it is,' Tom said. 'Would you leave us without horn or udder an' every damned, miserable acre left bare?' He tapped the table with his spoon as if he were calling for order at a lodge meeting. 'We know you're an advocate of conciliation but I tell you, Henry, if the case goes against Daddy conciliation will equate wi' starvation. There's only this much' – he held up his hand with forefinger and thumb a half-inch apart – 'this much between us an' the poorhouse.'

Matthew Brodie pulled back the curtain and swung his feet to the floor.

'In God's name, Thomas,' he snapped, 'what's this talk of the poorhouse? There'll be no mention of the poorhouse while

I still have breath in my body. I'll not bow down to Neville Hewitt. The man is a villain, a thief an' a liar. I'll not have you makin' a settlement with him.'

'All or nothing, Daddy,' Henry said. 'Is that the way of it?'

'Aye, all or nothin',' Matthew Brodie said. 'Right is on our side.'

'When did right equate wi' justice?' Tom said.

Janet spoke up. 'Why don't we abandon this dung-heap before the Sheriff's officer arrives wi' a warrant?'

'Every farthing we have is sunk in Hawkshill,' Tom said. 'Would you have us lease another place, Janet, just to dig ourselves a deeper hole?'

Betsy had heard enough talk in Mr Rankine's milking-shed to know that Mr Brodie's farm was owned by Neville Hewitt, a flax manufacturer from the town of Drennan, three miles down the Ayr road. She had also heard Mr Rankine say that Hawkshill had been a bad bargain from the beginning and Brodie a fool to take on a lease on the strength of a handshake.

'If only we could persuade Hewitt to deliver a few loads o' lime,' Henry said, 'we could sweeten the meadow an' give the beasts an early bite.'

'Hewitt will pay for nothin' until we pay him,' Tom said. 'Besides, if we do make improvements he'll only increase the rent.'

'He can't increase the rent until the first day o' November,' Matthew Brodie said. 'We've a bindin' agreement.'

'A bindin' agreement,' Tom said, 'without a scrap o' paper to back it.'

'He gave me his hand on it,' Matthew Brodie said.

'A handshake will not hold up in law,' Tom said. 'Hewitt was livin' fat when he let us this place but if rumours are to be believed his flax mill is workin' on half shuttle an' he's in financial straits himself now.'

'I'll wager Mr Hewitt's not sittin' down to sup on barley broth an' pease puddin', though,' Janet said, 'no matter how poor he claims to be.'

'I have no fear o' Neville Hewitt,' Matthew Brodie said. 'If I had air in my lungs an' more flesh on my bones I'd tackle him face to face.'

'He's threatenin' to have our stock sequestered an' your name called round the parish as a debtor if we don't pay him the full year on the due date in November,' Henry said. 'If he does so then we're finished here on Hawkshill an' no land-owner in his right sense will grant us another lease.'

Matthew Brodie crept back into bed. 'I've heard enough argument for one night. If Hewitt becomes insistent we'll put the matter up for judgement an' that will gain us a few more months.' He tugged the blanket across his chest. 'But not yet. Do you hear me, Henry? No conciliation. Not yet.'

'I hear you, Daddy,' said Henry softly.

'An' you, Thomas, do you hear me too?'

'I do, Dad,' Tom said. 'I do.'

Betsy was not used to going to bed early. Her father seldom finished work on his loom much before nine after which the family gathered at the table in the kitchen to eat supper. When she'd been younger her brothers and her slump-shouldered daddy would invent some silly piece of nonsense to keep them all amused while Mammy clapped her hands and laughed until tears formed in the corners of her eyes. Her mammy was a perfect match for her father; a quick wee person whose outlook on life was as rosy as her cheeks. But thirty months ago her brothers had abandoned the weaving trade and had leased a small farm in the Border country and only Effie remained at home to help Daddy at the loom.

An elbow dug into the small of Betsy's back.

'Are you snivellin'?' Janet Brodie asked.

'I've a bit o' a cold, that's all.'

'Are you pinin' for some man?' said Janet.

'I'm not pinin' for anyone.'

'So it wasn't a man gave you that scar?'

Betsy sniffed up her tears, fluffed her hair to hide the shameful mark and wriggled away from the edge of the mattress.

'No.' She hesitated, then said, 'I was knifed.'

Janet sat up. 'Knifed?'

'Aye,' said Betsy. 'In a fight.'

'Who was fightin'?'

'I was,' said Betsy. 'In Souter Gordon's tavern.'

'Souter Gordon's?' said Janet. 'Only bad girls go there.'

'What makes you think I'm not a bad girl?' said Betsy.

'You're a weaver's daughter, an' I've seen you in church,' Janet said sceptically. 'You were never stabbed wi' a knife.'

'Oh, have you not heard the story? Come to think o' it, I don't suppose you have since it was all hushed up at the time.' Betsy inched into the middle of the bed and Janet retreated towards the wall. 'I was drinkin' wi' the Irish tinkers after harvest three years back. One o' the men – a handsome devil, he was, too – took a fancy to me. His lassie resented it. She came for me in a jealous rage brandishin' a blade.'

'You fought wi' a tinker in a quarrel over a man?'

'Aye.'

Betsy claimed half the bolster, punched it with her fist and, with a sigh, settled her head in the hollow.

At length, Janet said, 'What happened to the tinker girl?'

'I strangled her,' said Betsy.

Silence for a moment, then, 'How?'

'Wi' my bare hands,' said Betsy.

'An' – an' the body?'

'Carted off in my cousin Connor's boat.'

'Carted off where?'

'To the Isle o' Man,' said Betsy, 'in dead o' night. The tinks wanted no trouble. The body was slipped o'er the side in the deep channel an' there was nothin' to show for the murder but my scar.'

'I don't believe you,' Janet Brodie said.

'Believe what you like.' Betsy gave the bolster another thump. 'My cousin Connor knows the truth. Ask Connor next time you see him.'

'An' when will that be?' asked Janet.

'When he comes to fetch me for his bride,' Betsy answered and with a dark little laugh that sent shivers down Janet Brodie's spine, tugged the blanket over her shoulders and settled down to sleep.

2

At first she thought rain dripping from the eaves over her bedroom window had wakened her, then, when the scratching became louder, that a rat had crept into her room to sink its teeth into her throat and that blood – her blood – would spurt on to her breast and she would be dead before she could cry out.

Heart thudding, she sat up and stared at the window which was faintly outlined by light from the lantern that hung outside the surgeon's shop on the opposite side of the row.

She tried not to think what Dr Glendinning might be doing at that hour of the night and if the sound that had wakened her was related to the grisly mysteries that Dr Glendinning unravelled with his saw and sharp knives. Mrs Prole had told her that Dr Glendinning and his hunchbacked assistant were fond of cutting up bodies in the long room behind the house and especially fond of cutting up wicked young girls who had been cast out by their families for misbehaving with boys.

'Who – who is it? Who's there?' Rose whispered.

Flint and candle were on the stand in the corner. She did not have the courage to leave the bed to fetch them before a muffled voice called out, 'Rose, Rose, my love, it's me. It's Tom.'

'Tom?' She frowned. 'Tom who?'

'Tom Brodie, of course.'

She got up and padded across the room to the window which was open at the bottom by an inch or so, a gap, it

seemed, sufficient to accommodate young Mr Brodie's fingertips by which, Rose guessed, he had obtained enough
leverage to hoist a leg on to the narrow ledge.

Shivering in her flimsy nightgown, she glanced round at the
door.

Soon after Mama had passed away Papa had transferred
Mrs Prole to the bedroom behind the kitchen and for the sake
of convenience – so Papa said – had banished Rose to the attic.

Holding her breath, she waited for her father to charge in,
bellowing for blood, but when he did not, she knelt by the
window and whispered, 'What are you doing here, Thomas
Brodie? What do you want?'

Cheek squashed against the glass, he begged her to open the
window.

'I will not,' said Rose.

'Please, my love, please.'

She glanced over her shoulder again then lifted the frame
three or four inches. With a grunt and a gasp, Tom Brodie
stuck his arms through the gap and with his knees bent to his
chest squatted on the ledge like a monstrous crow.

'More,' he said.

'No,' said Rose. 'That's far enough.'

'Will you not let me enter your sanctuary?'

'I most certainly will not,' Rose said. 'If you don't go away,
I'll summon my father – and you know what he'll do to you.'

'Are you afraid of me, Rose?' Tom Brodie asked. 'Are you
afraid you might yield to the passion that lurks within your
breast?'

'What are you blathering about?'

'Reciprocal passion.'

'Beg pardon?'

Rainwater dripped from his hair, nose and ears. His high-
collared coat was black with rain and droplets from his sleeves
pit-a-patted on to the floorboards. 'Reciprocal,' he said, with a

hint of impatience. 'Mutual. Shared. Or is it the word "passion" you do not understand, my sweet, innocent Rose?'

He spoke in a clipped tone like a minister reading from the Bible. She was not flattered by the affectation.

She had conversed with him only once, a brief unmemorable exchange about the weather when he had encountered her upon the green. She hadn't even flirted with him as she had flirted with the foreign gentleman who had visited her father with a view to selling him a machine that would break up flax stalks cleanly and quickly. Her father hadn't purchased the machine but he had detected the attention that the handsome young man had lavished on her over supper and how eagerly she had responded. He had packed her off early to bed and had locked her door with an iron key. Next morning, after the foreign gentleman had left, Papa had whipped her with a withy as a punishment for making eyes at a stranger.

'I know what passion means,' she said.

'Do you?' Tom Brodie said. 'Do you know what a fire you have started in me, dear Rose? How that fire rages when I contemplate your beauty. Let me in.'

'*No!*'

'A kiss then, one kiss, an' floatin' on wings of ecstasy, I'll be gone.'

'Do you promise?'

'Upon my word, I promise.'

She squeezed her knees together, covered her breasts and, leaning forward, rested her chin on the frame.

'I can't.' Tom Brodie scrambled again. 'I can't reach you.'

'Try flapping your wings of ecstasy,' Rose suggested.

And Tom Brodie suddenly vanished.

She waited for the crunch of bones as he struck the cobbles but then his head reappeared over the window ledge and, labouring hard, he brought his face to the aperture again. 'You,' he said, 'promised.'

'Oh, very well.' Rose pursed her lips.

The stubble on his upper lip was rough. His breath, sweet with wine, mingled with hers. He stroked her lips lightly with his tongue. Then, with a little whoop of surprise, he vanished once more.

Rose threw up the window and leaned out just in time to see him land on a pile of old straw which had evidently been placed there for the purpose of breaking his fall. He was up and running almost before he touched the ground.

A horse clattered out of the lane by Dr Glendinning's house, the rider wrapped in a cloak, his face hidden by a floppy-brimmed hat. He reached down and hoisted Tom into the saddle behind him and just as Rose's father threw open the front door, spurred the horse to a gallop and rode off down Thimble Row in a haze of spray.

Her father, in nightshirt and nightcap, looked up.

Rose looked down.

'Who is it, Papa?' she heard herself say. 'Who's there?'

'Drunken ruffians,' Neville Hewitt growled. 'Did their antics waken you?'

'Yes,' Rose lied. 'I was fast asleep.'

'Did you catch sight of their faces?'

'No.'

'Well, they've gone now,' her father said. 'Go back to bed.'

He stepped into the house and closed the door.

And Rose, shivering, returned to bed to consider the significance of Tom Brodie's silly compliments and, of course, his kiss.

The fire had all but gone out. Janet had carelessly covered the embers with green twigs and damp straw and had applied the bellows so vigorously that the kitchen was filled with acrid smoke that Betsy reckoned did Mr Brodie's lungs no good at all. The curtain over the old man's bed remained closed but she could hear him coughing, a rasping, tearing sound that set her teeth on edge.

Breakfast, like supper, was meagre: watery porridge and dry bread. She longed for a tasty strip of bacon and a beaker of tea to warm her before she set off for the fields. Back to the hearth, she supped her porridge and listened to Janet's attempts to wring answers from Tom.

'She says she throttled a tinker lassie. Haven't you heard the story?'

'Nuh,' Tom grunted.

'She says her Irish cousin threw the body off a boat.'

'Nonsense!'

'Listen to me when I'm talkin' to you, Tom Brodie,' Janet persisted.

'I am listenin',' Tom said, 'but you're just talkin' rubbish.'

'Is it rubbish I've to share a bed wi' a murderess?'

'You might share a bed wi' worse before you're done,' said Henry. 'Who told you this bloodthirsty tale?'

'She did.' Janet pointed at Betsy. 'An' she stole all the bedclothes.'

'Oh, a hangin' offence, that is,' said Henry.

'All very well for you,' Janet said. 'You're not sharin' a bed with her.'

'Not yet,' said Tom, and chuckled.

When breakfast was over Betsy settled her shawl about her shoulders, tucked the ends into her broad belt and followed Tom into the yard. He had already run out the smaller of the carts and harnessed the horse to it. Tom climbed into the cart and hoisted her up.

'Are we harvestin' two-handed?' Betsy asked.

'We are,' Tom answered. 'Mammy has her work cut out attendin' my father. Janet will see to the cows an' Henry's gatherin' sheep.'

He turned up his collar, tapped his cap down and with a flick of the reins urged the horse forward. The cart swung on to the track.

'Why did you send for me?' said Betsy.

'I didn't send for you,' Tom said. 'Johnny offered your services.'

'What did Mr Rankine say about me?'

'He said you were fond o' throttlin' tinkers.'

Betsy laughed. 'I had to tell your sister somethin'.'

'Nosy bitch,' Tom said. 'You can hardly blame her, though. There's precious little here on Hawkshill to keep her entertained.'

'An' you, Mr Brodie?' Betsy said. 'How d' you entertain yourself?'

'I read,' he said, shrugging.

'An' dance at the school?'

'When I've sixpence to spare.'

'An' drink at Souter Gordon's?'

'Moderately, moderately.'

'An' attend lodge meetin's wi' Mr Rankine?'

'A man has a duty to participate in the life o' the community – within the limits o' his purse,' Tom said. 'Are you scoldin' me, Betsy McBride?'

'I wouldn't dare,' said Betsy.

'Why didn't you tell my inquisitive sister the truth?'

'Knives an' tinkers make a better story,' Betsy said.

'Now she's afraid of you; is that it?'

'Perhaps she'll treat me wi' a wee bit more respect.'

'I don't believe fear an' respect go hand in glove,' Tom said.

'Do *you* always tell the truth, Mr Brodie?'

'I do or I try to. I regard myself as an honest man.'

'Then,' Betsy said, 'how did you come by that limp overnight?'

'I tripped gettin' out o' bed,' Tom said, and steered the horse to the lip of the cornfield and, rather harshly, Betsy thought, reined the poor beast to a halt.

Unlike the parlour behind Souter Gordon's, the room above the saddler's shop had a certain shoddy dignity. Printed notices announced lectures on various topics related to farming and a large board recorded the names of past chairmen of the Hayes Agricultural Society. Matthew Brodie had been a member at one time but had never been elevated to the chair and had relinquished his ties when the annual subscription was raised to five shillings. Matthew Brodie had never attended a meeting of the Bachelors' Club, however, for that privilege was reserved for the matrimonially uncommitted.

Proceedings were informal; the rules, proposed and drafted by none other than Mr Thomas Brodie, were too high-flown to be taken seriously. Meetings were held on the second Friday in the month with a lull for spring sowing and autumn harvesting. The October gathering was the first of the winter season and there was much to discuss, not least the amorous adventures of the summer.

The first of several bottles began its tour of the table.

There were a dozen, mostly young, men in the room. Muscles racked by labour in the fields relaxed, backs bowed by too many hours at desk or bench straightened, and the chat grew loud and lively.

Tom thumped the table with his fist. 'Gentlemen, gentlemen, to order, to order, if you please.' The buzz died down. 'The subject proposed for discussion this evenin': Is it better to have loved an' lost than never to have . . .'

The topic was anything but original. It had been done to death less than a year ago. A groan went up.

'Sir, sir, Mr Chairman, sir,' cried a tea-dealer's clerk from Drennan. 'With respect, sir, are you not bein' a wee bit hasty in shovin' such a shop-worn subject down our throats?'

'Hasty?' Tom said. 'By God, haste is not a thing I'm often accused of, not by the ladies at any rate.'

'Which beggars the question, Mr Chairman,' said another young man. 'Or, on consideration, draws us closer tae the very marrow o' the matter.'

'Does it now?' Tom said. 'An' what is the marrow to which you refer?'

Several voices called out in unison, 'In the minutes. Read the minutes.'

Mr Chairman contrived to look puzzled. Peter Frye, the club's secretary, leaned across the table, whispered in Tom's ear and placed an index finger on a passage in the minutes book.

'Ah!' Tom said, nodding. 'Ah, yes. The wager.'

'The wager it is, Tom, the wager it is,' said Mr Ogilvy, the oldest member. 'Are we not to be told if the terms o' the wager have been fulfilled?'

'Can't have been,' said the clerk, 'or he'd have been grabbin' his guinea from the kitty before now.'

'A guinea, was it?' Tom said, apparently without guile. 'Aye, I do believe it was – an' the terms o' the wager?'

'Hoh! You rascal!' said Mr Ogilvy. 'Coyness doesn't become you. Stop playin' the fool an' tell us – did you, or did you not, fulfil the conditions made in good faith an' by general consent last July?'

Tom frowned. 'Will a guinea pay for the claret?'

'Aye, with a shilling or two to spare,' Peter Frye informed him.

'Then,' Tom said, 'I will pay for the claret.'

'You had her!' Mr Ogilvy cried. 'By God, you had her!'

'Did you mow her?' the tea-clerk asked.

'Nah, nah,' Tom replied. 'The terms o' the wager were a kiss, a single kiss upon the lips. No more, no less. I confess, though, it was only with great difficulty I restrained myself from unsheathin' my scythe.'

'A stolen kiss isn't worth a guinea,' someone complained.

'The kiss was freely given,' Peter Frye put in.

'How can you be sure, Peter?' Mr Ogilvy asked.

'I witnessed it,' Peter Frye said. 'I'll swear an oath to that effect if you require it. Tom invited her to kiss him and she complied.'

'On the lips?'

'On the lips.'

'Neville Hewitt's daughter?'

'Neville Hewitt's daughter.'

'The virginal Rose?'

'The one and only daughter of the ogre of Thimble Row, clad, I might add, in a short nightgown that left little to the imagination,' Peter said. 'Now, gentlemen, dwell on that picture while I extract Tom's well-won guinea from the funds and order us – what? – another half-dozen bottles.'

'Where did this momentous event take place?' Mr Ogilvy asked.

'At her house,' Tom answered.

'Was her daddy not at home, or that hag he dandles?' the clerk said.

'Oh, indeed!' said Tom. 'They were both at home, busy wi' their own – ah – affairs, no doubt, for it was dead of night an' rainin' like the devil.'

'Did you enter her room wi' Hewitt sleepin' below?' Mr Ogilvy said in amazement. 'God, but you're a brave fellow, Tom Brodie.'

'I'm not as brave as all that,' Tom admitted. 'I confess I played the Romeo an' climbed up to the damsel's window. Peter was mounted close at hand, for however much I might desire a taste of the young lady's rosy lips I'd no intention of givin' up my life for it.'

Ogilvy nodded. 'Hewitt would have shot you without a qualm.'

'Aye,' Tom said, 'an' nailed my cods to his lintel, too.'

'But she did kiss you?' came a voice from the end of the table.

'Opened the window at my request, parted her lips, sucked my tongue, an' sighed like a zephyr.'

'Is this all true, Peter?' Mr Ogilvy enquired.

'Every word,' Peter Frye answered.

'What else did you do to her?' someone asked slyly.

'Sir,' said Tom haughtily, 'how dare you impugn my honour. Now, I ask you, would I take advantage of an innocent maid clad only in her cutty?'

'Aye,' came the answer from all quarters. 'Aye, damn it, you would.'

Tom rose to his feet and raised the glass that Peter had thoughtfully filled for him. 'An' aye, damn it, I *will*, gentlemen. On my word as a gentleman an' a bachelor, I will have the cutty off Miss Hewitt's back before the barley shows a hint o' green.'

'An' mow her?' the clerk called out.

'An' marry her,' Tom said, so soberly that no one took him seriously.

Betsy tilted her chair against the breast of the ingle and stretched out her legs. Janet had gone to bed. Agnes lay by her husband's side, snoring. The fire glowed red. The big, black kettle released little puffs of steam. On a shelf close to the door a battered old bracket clock wearily ticked out the minutes.

'Away to your bed, lass,' Henry told her. 'It's near eleven an' we have an early rise tomorrow.'

'I'm not one needs much sleep.' Betsy rocked a little on the creaking chair. 'You're waitin' up for Tom, aren't you?'

Henry paused. 'What if I am?'

'Is it a special meetin' o' the lodge tonight?'

'The Bachelors' Club, I believe.'

Betsy had heard from the girls at Rankine's what went on at the Bachelors' Club, which was less offensive to female sensibilities than what went on in the back room of Souter Gordon's and a deal less mysterious than Masonic initiations.

'Are you not inclined to join him, Mr Brodie?' she asked.

'I'm not Mr Brodie. Mr Brodie is my father. I'm Henry, plain an' simple,' he said. 'To answer your question, Betsy, no, I'm not inclined to seek membership o' that particular society. They're Tom's cronies, not mine.'

'You are a bachelor, though?'

'Of course I am,' said Henry. 'Do you suppose I've a wife hidden away upstairs? Look around you, Betsy. What sort of girl would have me when all I have to offer is a life of servitude an' a dung-hill of debt?'

'What you mean is no proper young lady. All men are the same when it comes to pickin' a wife. Ploughboys set their sights on house servants. Farmers on landowners' daughters. It's the way o' the world.'

'What do dairymaids set their sights on?' Henry asked.

'Anythin' they can get their hands on,' Betsy answered, and laughed.

'Doesn't love enter into it?'

'Love?' said Betsy. 'Love's what you make o' it, Mr Brodie.'

'Henry.'

'Henry then,' Betsy said. 'Love's just another arrangement.'

'Have you no notion to marry?'

'Aye, I'd marry in the blink o' an eye,' said Betsy. 'But who'd have the likes o' me? Nah, nah. The pretty ones get courted an' the rest o' us just get . . .' She shrugged.

'Betsy, how old are you?'

'Nineteen come the New Year.'

'Have you never had a beau?'

'A beau?'

'A suitor?' said Henry. 'A lover?'

She thought of Johnny Rankine slapping his fat belly against hers before he hitched up his breeks and trotted off to sup with his wife.

'Nah, I've never had a lover.'

'Has no one ever taken your fancy?'

'Connor,' she said quickly. 'My cousin, Connor McCaskie.'

'Would he not make a good husband?'

'Connor – a husband?' said Betsy. 'God, no! He's Irish.'

Tom was careful never to drink so much that he couldn't cling to the saddle of his trustworthy old mare as she picked her way home. He led the animal into the stable and took off her saddle. He filled her rack with hay and her bucket with water then through the slit in the plaster caught sight of his brother and Betsy seated knee to knee in the kitchen. His arrival had cut off their conversation and – he laughed to himself – had probably put paid to any notion Henry might have harboured of stealing a kiss, or more, from Rankine's handsome servant.

Still chuckling, he rested his cheek on the mare's rump and studied the girl who had landed in the family's lap. At that hour, she seemed almost as desirable as Rose Hewitt or, for that matter, any of the other bonnie lassies he had fallen in love with.

'Whoa!' he said aloud. 'Whoa!'

Staggering from the stable, he untied his breeks and relieved himself against the wall. When that need had been taken care of, he tottered to the cottage door and fell rather dramatically into Betsy's arms while Henry danced anxiously up and down and hissed at Tom to hold his noise lest he waken their father and spark an ugly scene.

Tom clung to the buxom Miss McBride, head on her bosom, hands cupping her buttocks and let her steer him into the room. 'Och, now,' he crooned, 'are you not a grand armful, Betsy, m' love.'

'Pay no heed,' Henry said. 'He's drunk.'

'I am not drunk,' said Tom indignantly. 'I've had worse skinfu's at the communion table. Och, Betsy, give us a cuddle.'

'Here.' Henry grabbed his brother by the shoulder. 'Come here an' I'll give you a cuddle. I'll cuddle you up to your bed.'

'Jacob's ladder won't lift me to heaven.' Tom massaged Betsy's flanks. 'Lyin' with this lovely creature, though, would surely transport me to—'

He let out a yelp as a small, hard fist clipped the side of his head and he was dragged, still yelping, away from the servant.

'Mam,' he cried out. 'Mammy, you're hurtin' me.'

'I'd take a stick to you if one was handy,' Agnes Brodie said. 'Is drinkin' not enough for you? Now you have to shame us by pawin' a young lassie sent to help us. It's just as well your daddy isn't fit to thrash you, Thomas, grown though you are. Henry, get him out o' my sight.'

'I will, Mother.' Henry snagged Tom's arm, guided him to the ladder and pushed his feet on to the wooden rungs. 'He'll suffer for this tomorrow,' Henry promised. 'Goodnight, Betsy.'

'Goodnight, Mr Brodie,' Betsy said.

She would have gone to her room at once if Agnes Brodie hadn't barred her way. 'You mustn't think ill o' him, Betsy,' she said. 'Our Tom has the devil boxed within him. There are times I think there's not one man but two wrestlin' inside his head. He means no harm.'

'No, Mrs Brodie.'

'For all that,' the woman said, 'you mustn't encourage him.'

'No, Mrs Brodie,' Betsy said and with a chaste little curtsey, and never the hint of a smile, took herself off to bed.

3

If Betsy McBride's arrival at Hawkshill did not change the Brodies' fortunes at a stroke at least it coincided with a spell of settled weather that enabled them to harvest the last of the corn crop.

Betsy soon discovered that the seventy acres of Hawkshill were rented from Neville Hewitt on a twelve-year lease with a breaker at the six-year mark – a mark that fell on the first day of November. If the Sheriff's officer showed up with a writ for sequestration before then he would have damned little to lay claim to. Old Mr Brodie's stock amounted to four horses, two ponies, thirteen cows, six calves, two yearling bullocks, fourteen sheep, a plough, two carts and a harrow. The bullocks and four fat lambs were to be sold at Drennan market and Betsy was invited along to help the young Brodies on the drive.

She had already accompanied the family to church and had met with her mother and father and assured them that she was well treated at Hawkshill. She had also bumped into Mr Rankine who had merely winked by way of greeting.

Church-going in Hayes was one thing, however, market day in Drennan quite another. The town boasted a market square, a school, two churches, three corn mills, two lint mills, and a mill for the beating of flax. There was also a handsome brick-built poorhouse, an inn, three ale-houses, a Freemasons' lodge and a long, low wooden building that housed a modest library of improving literature and, whenever Mr Arbuthnot came to town, the dancing school.

The mart was held in a field a quarter-mile from the centre of town. For once, the ground was not awash with mud. Every dealer, breeder and butcher in the shire had turned out in search of bargains, for a late spring and wet summer had meant poor grazing and many tenant farmers who could not afford to winter their beasts were forced to sell them off before they starved.

The Hawkshill bullocks were already big and rambunctious. It took Tom and Henry all their time to tether them to the stake on the rented pitch. Sheep were easier to deal with and Janet soon had the fat lambs penned in a triangle of wicker where the poor bewildered creatures barely had room to stamp their hooves or make water.

All across the field farm animals were similarly penned and tethered. The uproar was deafening. Dust clouds billowed over the cottages, fell like fine sand on the awnings of the stalls in Market Street and made the traders and their customers sneeze and spit and those boozers who were at it early cover their tankards with their hats.

Drennan mart was no great tryst like the annual gathering at Falkirk. Buyers and sellers were known to each other and deals struck with a nod and a handshake. Hardly had the Hawkshill bullocks been roped than a potential buyer sauntered up to inspect them.

'Aye, Brodie, is this the best you have to offer?'

'It is, Mr Fergusson, the very best.'

'Watered in yon foul pond you call a loch?'

'Nah, nah,' Tom answered. 'You'll find no leeches in the nostrils o' my cattle. Look into their eyes, sir, an' see the gold there. They'll grow faster than you can throw hay into the rack.'

'Fathered by Braystock's old bull, I take it?'

'Braystock's bull may be old, but he's reliable,' said Henry.

'Why don't you give them another summer on the grass?' Fergusson said. 'If they're as fit as you claim, they'll make ten times the price in a year's time.'

'We had a good drop o' calves this spring,' Tom lied. 'We haven't byre space to rear them all.'

'In other words Hewitt's bitin' your arse for his rent?'

'Hewitt's bitin' everybody's arse, Mr Fergusson,' said Tom.

'That may be, but you're not givin' away young cattle out o' the goodness o' your heart. Better a few shillings in your fist than handin' them over to the Sheriff's man to raffle. Am I not right?'

'What about our lambs, sir?' Janet piped up.

'I don't waste good grass on sheep, girl,' the grazier said. 'Tell you what, Brodie, I'll give you a guinea the pair for the calves, cash in hand.'

Betsy saw Henry's fingers curl into his palms.

Tom, nonchalantly studying the horizon, shook his head.

'Tom?' Janet said, then again, 'Tom?'

'Ah!' said Tom. 'What a mild day it is for October. I've a bite o' bread an' cheese in my pocket an' my sister will fetch me a stoup o' ale from Caddy Crawford's, so I think I'll just sit back an' wait for somebody wi' more sense to come along. Good day to you, Mr Fergusson.'

'A guinea will square your doctor's bill,' the grazier said, 'or buy your daddy a decent mort-cloth when his time comes – unless you plan to bury him naked in your dung-heap.'

Tom stepped up to the big-bellied grazier and placed his hand on his collar. The grazier was too long in the tooth to be intimidated. Thrusting out his gut, he stood his ground.

Tom grinned, brushed a speck of dust from the grazier's coat. 'Is it greed drives you to slander my old daddy, Mr Fergusson? Well, I tell you, my old daddy will see you out, sir. He is a man made of iron an' will not meet his Maker until he an' his Maker are good an' ready for the encounter.'

'I spoke in haste,' Fergusson said. 'No offence intended.'

'An' none taken,' said Henry.

'I'll go as high as twenty-four shillings,' the grazier said.

'You can go as high as the spire o' St Giles,' Tom said. 'I wouldn't sell my daddy's beasts to you now if you were to offer me twenty guineas. Put it down to pride, if that's your wish, but I'd as soon butcher those bullocks myself as yield to your suggestion that my father will die a pauper's death if we don't snatch your miserable offer.'

'Twenty-six, the pair,' Fergusson said.

'No,' Tom said. 'No, damn it, no.'

'Tom, please,' Henry murmured. 'Don't be hasty.'

A ring of eight or ten men had gathered round the Hawkshill stake. Walter Fergusson had deep pockets and a hundred and sixty acres of the best grazing in the shire. He bought cheap, always cheap, and knew to the penny just how much each desperate tenant owed his landlord.

Betsy watched Henry shake his head and step forward to intervene just as a huge, brown paw clasped her shoulder.

'Connor,' she said, looking round. 'What are you doin' here?'

It wasn't easy for Rose to escape the vigilant Mrs Prole. She was well aware what form her punishment would take if she strayed from the woman's side to exchange words, however casually, with any male under the age of eighty.

Her first encounter with Thomas Brodie had occurred on one of the few occasions when she had been allowed out alone. Mrs Prole had returned to bed after breakfast that morning and she, not Dorothy, the day-maid, had been sent across the green to fetch bread from the town bakery.

Why Tom Brodie had been mooching about Drennan on a Tuesday forenoon was a mystery to which Rose had given no thought at the time. In the light of what had happened since, however, she had reached the conclusion that Mr Brodie had tramped the miles from Hawkshill for the sole purpose of accosting her. Try as she might, though, she couldn't recall anything in the conversation that had encouraged the fellow to climb to her window in the dead of night and beg for a kiss, a kiss that had opened a window into all sorts of things that she could not rationally explain.

'*Rose? Rose Hewitt?*'

She pressed herself into the muslin screen that protected the cheeses that the stall-holder had set out on little painted dishes; soft white cheeses too delicate to appeal to rustic palates, though, so Rose had heard, lairds and their ladies loved the stuff and bought it by the tub. The stall-holder was a hand-some woman not much older than Papa. With her back to the screen at the rear of her stall she looked out into the curve of Market Street in search of stewards or housekeepers brand-ishing orders for her dainty fare.

When Mrs Prole arrived, agitated and angry, Rose hardly dared breathe for fear that the cheese-maker's wife would give her away.

'Cheese,' the woman said. 'Ripe an' brimful o' flavour.'

'I'm lookin' for my – for my charge,' Mrs Prole said icily. 'Mr Hewitt's daughter. Has she passed this way?'

'Not that I've seen,' the woman said. 'Perhaps she's with her daddy?'

'She is not with her father; she's with me,' Mrs Prole declared.

'But she's not with you,' the woman pointed out. 'Did you send her to buy one o' my fine cheeses?'

'No, I did not,' said Mrs Prole. 'The wilful child has run off. When I lay hands on her, I'll teach her a lesson she'll not forget.'

'How will you do that, Mrs Prole?' the woman asked.

'I – I'll reprimand her appropriately.'

'Quite right!' the woman agreed. 'I've daughters o' my own so I know how skittish young girls can be.'

'Have you not seen her?'

'No.'

'*Rose? Rose Hewitt?*' Mrs Prole moved away. '*Come here this minute or it'll be the worse for you.*'

Crouched in the narrow aisle between the back of the cheese stall and the gable of an ale-house, Rose let out a sigh of relief.

'Are you still there?' the stall-holder whispered.

Rose answered, 'Yes.'

'She's gone. You're safe now. Why are you hidin'?'

'I have something I must do on my own.'

'Ah!' said the cheese-maker's wife. 'Is a man involved?'

'What?' said Rose. 'Certainly not. I'm looking for Tassie Landles. Do you happen to know where she might be found?'

The cheese-maker's wife laughed.

'I see,' she said. 'Is it your fortune you're after, Miss Hewitt, or is it a love potion? Well, Tassie Landles'll take your sixpence an' deliver whatever you require. I should warn you, though, the old witch doesn't always live up to her reputation.'

'Where can I find her?'

'On market days she's usually in her shop at the bridge end.' Rose jumped back as the muslin was drawn aside and the woman looked down at her. 'Be careful, Miss Hewitt. Old Tassie's not a person to meddle with. Who told you about her?'

'Our day-maid, Dorothy.'

'I hope for your sake whatever you receive from Tassie Landles will be worth the beatin' you'll get when you get home.'

'I hope so too,' Rose said, and with a weak little smile by way of thanks, slipped out from behind the cheese stall and headed downhill to the bridge.

★　　★　　★

The curly brown beard had gone and with it the best part of ten years. He looked much younger without the whiskers, Betsy thought. He had also shed the big silver ring that usually dangled from his ear and the spotted silk bandana that kept his unruly locks in place. He still sported the blue flannel trews that her mother had sewn for him and, in lieu of a coat, the moulting goatskin vest that lent him his unique odour. Even without the beard and earring, he was still unmistakably her Irish cousin, Connor McCaskie, broad-shouldered, barrel-chested and as tall as a tree.

'Twenty-six shillings,' Connor said. 'Is that the bid?'

'This isn't an auction, sir, whoever you may be,' Mr Fergusson told him.

'I'm Connor McCaskie, sir, whoever *you* may be. Sure now, if this is a private transaction between you and the owner o' these fine beasts, I'll step aside an' watch you kiss.'

'No kisses, Connor,' Betsy spoke up. 'No handshake neither.'

'Is that a fact?' Her cousin stuck his thumbs into his broad leather belt, a match of her own. 'So no bargain has been struck?'

'It has not,' said Tom.

'Emphatically not,' said Henry.

'I'll rise to thirty,' said Mr Fergusson, rather too hastily.

'Thirty shillings for these beauties,' Connor said. 'God, man, any fool with half an eye can tell they're destined to provide a hundred good dinners in a year or two's time.'

'Are you a dealer, sir?' Fergusson enquired.

'I'm a connoisseur o' good beef, sir, an' sufficiently patient to defray the pleasure o' sinking my teeth into a slice or two o' these young fellers till they're big enough to be introduced to the butcher's axe.' Her cousin, Betsy thought admiringly, was even more eloquent than Tom Brodie. 'It seems to me a shrewd dealer like yourself would not be making an offer o'

thirty shillings if the beasts were not worth twice that sum. Mr
Brodie – it is Mr Brodie, is it not now . . .?'

'It is,' said Tom and Henry in unison.

'Mr Brodie, would fifty shillings per head be acceptable?'

'Indeed, it would,' said Henry. 'By God, it would.'

Connor McCaskie spat on his hand and held it out.

'Done then?' he said, and shook Tom's fist.

Then, dipping into his pouch, he produced a handful of
silver coins and counted out five pounds.

'Will you take the calves with you, Mr McCaskie?' Tom
asked.

'Nah, nah.' Connor turned to Betsy. 'Are they honest, these
farmer friends o' yours?'

'Honest as the day's long,' Betsy said.

'I'll pay you an extra guinea, Mr Brodie, and leave my
beasts in your care until they reach a suitable age to be
butchered. Will a guinea be enough for winter feed an' a
summer's grazing?'

'A guinea,' said Henry, 'will be fine.'

'Then,' Connor said, 'let's repair to the nearest hostelry to
seal our bargain with a dram. Would you care to join us, sir?'

'Damned if I would,' Walter Fergusson snarled and, thoroughly defeated, stalked off through the crowd to find another
victim.

The Drennan was a lively little river that tumbled out of the
Carrick Hills but by some quirk of contour wound, serpent-
like, round upon itself before, gaining depth and breadth, it
rolled into the sea near Port Cedric four miles away.

The shop on its banks below the Ramshead bridge was not
really a shop at all, just a one-room cottage so small and beetle-
browed that Rose had never noticed it before, though she had
often crossed the bridge in Papa's pony-carriage when he had
driven Mama and her to Ayr to listen to preaching in the

church of St Quivox or buy fish on the harbour wall. After
Mama had died and Mrs Prole had been promoted house-
keeper, the outings to Ayr ceased, for, Rose gathered, Mrs
Prole was not a widow and still had a husband of sorts living in
Ayr and did not wish to create 'awkwardness' by bumping into
him.

Rose tiptoed down the path to the cottage with one eye on the
river as if afraid that something might jump out of the swirling
brown waters and gobble her up like a trout with a mayfly.

A painted signboard, much weathered, hung above the half-
open door. She peered up at the crooked letters and the faded
image of some strange creature for several seconds before she
realised that the letters spelled out nothing more sinister than
'Eggs for Sale' and that the strange creature was meant to
represent a hen.

'Come awa' in, dear. Dinna be frighted,' said a voice from
within.

Rose was tempted to turn and run but she was afraid of
giving offence.

'One foot,' the voice advised, 'an' then t'other. That'll do it.'

According to Mrs Prole, Tassie Landles was the great-
great-granddaughter of a notorious Renfrew witch who had
flown about the shire like a rook and had commanded the
spirits of the dead. In Mrs Prole's view, which she vented by
way of rant, old Tassie Landles was tarred with the same foul
brush as her ancestor, and if the law had not turned lenient in
recent years would have been ducked in the Drennan or,
better yet, burned at the stake on Pendicle Hill.

Sucking in a deep breath, Rose stepped over the threshold.

'So,' said the voice, 'it's a lady, a pretty, young lady come to
visit Tassie on this lovely autumn morn. It'll not be a basket o'
eggs you'll be wantin', I'll wager, but a wee peek at the future
or maybe a cake o' my special marzipan to soften some man's
hard heart.'

'His heart,' said Rose, with more confidence than she felt, 'is soft already – or so he claims – although I suspect his head is hard enough.'

Tassie Landles was seated on a stool by the side of the hearth. The room was crammed with bric-à-brac and odd bits of furniture. Light came from a little window in the rear wall. Through it, clear as a crystal, Rose saw the fragment of a garden gaudy with autumn, the crown of a well and the corner of a wooden roost upon which several pigeons were perched.

Tassie Landles chuckled. 'A false lover, is it?'

'He is not my lover.'

'But he wishes to be, does he not?' said Tassie.

The woman was clad in a shawl with teardrop tassels, her greying hair covered by a spotless linen mutch, her complexion dusted to a shade that reminded Rose of cinnamon biscuits. She was not much older than Mrs Prole and did not look in the least like a cohort of the devil.

'Yes, I suspect he would,' Rose replied.

'Has he said as much?'

'He has.'

'Many times?'

'Just once,' Rose answered. 'Very fulsomely.'

'Do you believe him?'

'I'm not sure I do,' Rose said. 'I hope you might be able to advise me how I should respond to the fellow's advances – and what the outcome may be.'

'Fellow?' said Tassie Landles. 'I notice you don't call him a gentleman?'

'He's not a gentleman, not by birth or upbringing.'

'But you, Miss Hewitt, you're a lady, are you not?'

'Oh!' said Rose. 'You know my name?'

'Neville Hewitt's daughter, aye,' the woman said. 'Now, come closer. Sit here on the chair next to me an' we'll see what the cat has to say.'

'The cat?'

'Pussy's very experienced in matters o' the heart.'

Reaching down by the stool, Tassie brought up a brown earthenware cat. The pose was upright, alert and inquisitive, the figure a good eighteen inches tall. Tassie handed it to Rose who found it so heavy that she had to prop it on her knee.

'Shall I stroke him?'

'It's a female,' said Tassie.

'How can you tell?'

'Sexin' is another o' my many gifts.' Tassie chuckled mischievously. 'Since you're not carryin' Tam Brodie's bairn, though, we'll not be needin' that one today.'

'What?' said Rose, astonished. 'What did you say?'

'I never said a word,' Tassie Landles told her. 'It was her who let it slip.'

'Do you mean our day-maid, Dorothy?'

'Nah, nah, not Dorothy. Her.'

Rose's eyes widened. 'The cat told you about Tom Brodie?'

'No secret's safe from pussy,' the woman said. 'She told me that Rose Hewitt would be droppin' by today an' that young Tom Brodie's not far away.'

'Is Mr Brodie here?'

'I've trouble enough conjurin' up the spirits o' the dead wi'out tryin' the trick on those still livin',' Tassie said.

'The spirits of the dead?' Rose clutched the cat in both hands. 'My – my mama is dead. Can you . . .'

'Enough o' that,' said Tassie sternly. 'You've troubles enough in this world without seekin' more from the next. Put your left hand on pussy's head an' ask your question.'

Gingerly, Rose cupped the head of the cat and, feeling just a little foolish, addressed it. 'Does Mr Brodie love me? If I submit to him will he marry me?'

'Submit to him?' said Tassie. 'What do you mean by that?'

'Let him do to me whatever it is that men do to women.'

'An' what is it men do to women?'

'I mean' – Rose blushed – 'let him enter my – my body.'

'You've never been wi' a man, have you?'

Rose shook her head. She was thoroughly disconcerted by the fact that Tassie Landles knew so much about her. She had told no one of Tom Brodie's midnight visit, not even Dorothy. 'No, I've never been with a man,' she said, snappishly. 'Will you please answer my question? I have money here; see – a sixpence. If you require a larger sum, I've an extra shilling in my pocket.'

'Money stole from your daddy's box?' said Tassie.

'No,' Rose lied. 'He gave it me to spend at the market.'

'However you came by it, give me your sixpence,' Tassie said, 'an' puss will give you answers.'

Rose fished in the pocket of her skirt, brought out a coin, placed it in the woman's palm and watched it disappear.

'Now,' she said, 'my answer, if you please.'

'Not my answer, but your answer,' Tassie told her. 'The answer's in you, Rose Hewitt, if you but knew it.'

'This is nonsense!' Rose made to rise. 'You're nothing but a swindler.' The earthenware cat seemed to leap a little under her hand and Rose quickly seated herself again. 'How did you do that?'

'Do what?' said Tassie Landles. 'Ask awa'.'

'Will Thomas Brodie marry me?'

Tassie closed her eyes and placed a hand to her ear as if she were listening to distant music. She held the position for several seconds and Rose, in spite of her scepticism, found herself listening too. There were no sounds, though, other than the gurgle of the river and, far off, the faint, faint thump of a drum from somewhere in the heart of the town.

'Marriage,' Tassie said. 'There will be a marriage. I see you standin' tearful at Tam Brodie's side.'

'Tearful?'

'Weepin' tears o' joy,' Tassie went on. 'There's a chest overflowin' with silver an' a grand big house with many windows.'

'My house? Our house?'

'Children; three, four – five bairns.'

'Five!' Rose exclaimed. 'Five children!'

'Sorrow, too, some darkness, a shadow that willna' lift.'

'Do you mean that I won't make my husband happy, that he'll be disappointed in me?'

Tassie Landles opened one eye. 'This is your fortune, not Tam Brodie's.'

'Oh, yes! Quite!' said Rose contritely. 'How soon will I be married?'

'Soon,' said Tassie. 'But perhaps not soon enough.' Then, before the girl could blurt out another question, she opened her eyes.

'Wait,' said Rose. 'Please. I'll give you a shilling to go on.'

'Nah, nah,' said Tassie Landles. 'Poor puss is tired.'

Rose glanced down at the earthenware cat but Tassie plucked it from her hands, rubbed it with a corner of her shawl and put it away by the side of her stool. 'There,' she said. 'That's us done.'

'No. Please. No.'

Tassie rose from the stool. She was taller than Rose had supposed her to be and the linen mutch all but brushed the blackened beam above the hearth.

'Now, Rose Hewitt, you must go an' tak' your medicine.'

'Medicine?'

'Go home.'

Rose got shakily to her feet, dropped a polite little curtsey, murmured her thanks and went out into the sunlight.

She rested against the stonework of the bridge and, looking back, saw that the door of the cottage was still ajar and the sign 'Eggs for Sale' still creaked in a non-existent breeze.

She did not know whether or not to believe the witch woman. Had she or had she not been given a glimpse of a future, or, she thought, was the future really just written on water, like scribbles of foam? Then, as two young, giggling farm girls came skipping, arm-in-arm, down the path, she slipped away and headed into town to hand herself over to Mrs Prole and a beating she probably deserved.

4

When word got out that Tom Brodie and an Irishman with more money than sense were drinking in the garden behind Caddy Crawford's ale-house they were soon joined by Peter Frye and Mr Ogilvy, two of Tom's bachelor friends who happened to be in Drennan that day.

Henry and Janet had remained in the field in the hope of selling the sheep and to stand guard, as Connor put it, on his beautiful hairy babies, but Betsy had no qualms about sharing a spot of dinner with four gentlemen and, leaning against Connor's shoulder, felt as safe as a ship in harbour.

Caddy Crawford's pot-boys were run off their feet fetching food and drink to the tables in the garden while the men talked of failed crops, iniquitous taxes, what was going on in France and what had gone on in America. Betsy noticed that her cousin made no mention of his encounters with the King's cutters or his narrow escapes from customs officers and presented himself as nothing more colourful than a short-seas trader who ferried small cargoes between Ireland, Scotland and the Isle of Man. She had a feeling that Peter Frye, the lawyer's son, might have guessed what Connor really did for a living but if this was so Peter kept his mouth shut.

Peter's father was a Writer to the Signet who owned a modest estate on the seaward side of Hayes, not far from Port Cedric. Peter, Betsy gathered, was presently employed in clerking for his father but would eventually be despatched to Edinburgh to study at the university there. He was better educated and better dressed than anyone else in the garden and had a quick wit that only Tom could match when insults flew and arguments became heated.

It was Peter Frye who spotted her first. Glass in hand, bonnet tipped over one eye, he appeared to be engrossed in a debate about land taxes and forfeitures, when, cocking his head, he peeped over the low wall that separated the ale-house from the lane and said, 'By God, it's her, Thomas. It's the fair maid of Thimble Row.'

Tom dumped his glass on the table and shot to his feet. 'Is Hewitt with her?'

'No, she's alone.'

'Alone?' Tom said. 'Without that damned Medusa in tow?'

'Quite alone.'

'Oh-hoh!' Mr Ogilvy exclaimed. 'See what you've done, Brodie? She'll be on the prowl in search o' more o' the same.'

Connor frowned a question at Betsy, who shook her head.

'Miss Hewitt,' Peter Frye called out. 'Miss Hewitt, a word if I may.'

'No,' Tom said. 'No, Peter, don't.'

'Too late,' Peter said over his shoulder, then with a smile that would charm the birds from the trees, greeted a pretty young woman who Betsy had never seen before. 'Miss Hewitt, what a coincidence. My friend Mr Brodie has just been singing your praises and would, I'm sure, appreciate a word.'

'Mr – Mr Brodie?' the young woman said shrilly.

'Tom Brodie,' said Peter Frye. 'Have you forgotten your last meeting with the gentleman from Hayes?'

The young woman came to the wall and looked over into the garden.

In other circumstances, it might have been comical, the farmer and the lady, tongue-tied and awkward, both on toe-tip, but Betsy found no humour in the situation.

'M-m-m . . . Mr Brodie.'

'M-m-m . . . Miss Hewitt.'

'If you have nothing better to do, please join us,' Peter Frye said. 'See, we are a mixed company and you will not be thought forward.'

Rose Hewitt said, 'If that is your wish.'

'It is, it is,' Tom Brodie said. 'Most fervently, it is.' Then nimbly vaulting the wall he took the girl firmly by the arm and escorted her through the little wicket gate and into the garden.

Rose thought: *What is it Mr Fergusson says: one may as well be hanged for a sheep as a lamb? The old woman warned me Mr Brodie was close at hand. I cannot escape my fate, it seems, even if I must pay for it later.* When Tom Brodie touched her arm she felt as if she were floating above herself, more spirit than flesh.

'Tom?' Peter Frye said. 'Make a place for the lady.'

'Sit here by me, Miss Hewitt,' said Mr Ogilvy.

'She will sit with me,' Tom said. 'Miss Hewitt is my guest, gentlemen, an' you'd do well not to forget it. Betsy, shift up an' make room.'

Tom ushered Rose into the narrow space and seated himself beside her. The young woman, Betsy, seemed almost, if not quite, as large as the man at the end of the bench. Rose tucked in her skirts and her elbows and glanced at Tom who was signalling to one of the pot-boys to fetch clean plates and glasses. She trained her gaze on the roast beef and cold mutton on the platter before her but was too much of a lady, and too nervous, to help herself.

'Here.' Betsy slapped meat on to a none-too-clean plate. 'Eat.'

Rose looked round for a fork. Betsy dug her in the ribcage and, lifting a strip of mutton between finger and thumb held it up, dropped it into her mouth and, chewing, said, 'Like this.'

Rose experienced a little wave of revulsion at what they expected her to do and then, abruptly, her fastidiousness evaporated. She peeled off her gloves and tossed them behind her on to the grass.

Picking up a slice of beef, she tore it into small pieces and stuffed the fragments into her mouth. She glanced at Tom to see if her bad manners had shocked him but, apart from a raised eyebrow, he gave no sign of disapproval. He lifted a glass, wiped the rim with his shirt cuff, poured wine from one of the bottles and held it out to her.

She took it, tipped up her chin, drank the warm, harsh, heady stuff in a swallow and, struggling not to cough, held out her glass for more.

'A woman after your own heart, Tom,' said Mr Ogilvy.

'Aye, a woman of good appetite.' The Irishman let out a bellow of laughter. 'More o' that claret's in order, I reckon, since we have the makings of a proper carousal and the day's still young.'

Tom poured.

Rose drank.

Her father and Mrs Prole were partial to a glass or two after supper but she had been allowed only a sip of sweet sherry or a thimbleful of the vinegary German wine that Papa bought cheaply in Ayr. Even as she downed a second glassful, she realised that this rich, red liquid was strong enough to melt her inhibitions as swiftly as fire melts ice. She placed the empty glass on the table and reached for another slice of beef.

A number of local folk occupied the benches in the garden, and more were clustered about the back door of the smoky little ale-house. The women were not trulls or harlots, as Mrs Prole would have it. She recognised the miller's wife, and twin sisters who had worked in her father's manufactory until diminished business had caused him to let them go. Seated on a chair by the door, nursing a tankard of ale and smoking a clay pipe, was an old, old woman, widow of the notorious bard of Copplestone who had slipped into obscurity and an early grave almost forty years ago.

She was no more a stranger to these men and women than they were to her. Even a glimpse of the surgeon's assistant, resting his crooked spine against the ale-house wall and munching on what appeared to be a pig's foot, gave her no pause. She smiled, raised the glass that Tom had refilled and called out, 'Hoh, Archie,' a greeting that the hunchback either did not hear or chose to ignore.

'Miss Hewitt,' Betsy said, 'I think you've had enough.'

'Nonsense!' Defiantly, she extended her empty glass. 'Thomas, if you please.' When Mr Brodie put an arm about her waist she wriggled her hips and nudged him with her knee under cover of the table. For a second he appeared nonplussed by her friendly gesture then with considerable aplomb, she thought, poured a stream of the luscious red liquid into her glass without spilling a drop. He wiped the neck of the bottle and with a fleeting glance across the table at Mr Frye, offered her his hand.

Undaunted by the silence that had descended on the table, she looked Tom dead in the eye and with the tip of her tongue licked the drops of wine from his calloused fingers.

'Good God!' Mr Ogilvy exclaimed.

'Well, well, well!' said Peter Frye.

Rose threw back her head. 'You did not expect that, did you, Mr Brodie? If you wish to make fun of me will you at least be straightforward about it?' She caught his wrist and drew his hand to her mouth once more. 'Your fingers, sir, are a deal less hairy than your chin and, I confess, a deal less tasty than your tongue. Would you care to kiss me, Tom, or are you so bashful that you will only kiss a lady in dead of night with a horseman standing by?' She spread a hand across her breast, blew out her cheeks and before anyone could say a word, swung round. 'Now, Mr Irishman, where is the wine you promised me? Is there no more wine to be had?' Before the Irishman could answer, she swayed again. 'Well, Tom, will you not kiss me before witnesses or, Tom, are you afraid to declare yourself in daylight when you cannot escape the consequences?'

The Irishman craned forward. Peter Frye and Mr Ogilvy sat bolt upright. Her little speech had drawn the attention of the farmers at the ale-house door and a pot-boy bearing a laden tray poised in mid-stride.

'Well, Tom?' Betsy said quietly. 'Answer the girl.'

Tom paused for a moment then brought his face forward and kissed her mouth. He did not pull away but let his lips linger, his breath upon her cheek. She closed her eyes and with cheers and applause ringing around her, felt the world go round and round and, fearing that she was about to faint, let her head drop until her brow rested on Tom Brodie's chest.

'*You filthy pig, take your hands off her.*'

Mrs Prole stooped over the wall, bent like the blade of a jack-knife. She screeched Rose's name and sought to grab the Irishman's hair as if he, not Brodie, had been caught in the act of defiling her charge.

'*Let her go, let her go, you – you . . .*' Mrs Prole shouted. '*Rose, come here to me this minute or by everythin' I hold holy I'll send for the soldiers.*'

'The soldiers?' Connor McCaskie said. 'What soldiers?'

Rose wiped her greasy fingers on her sleeves, smoothed down her skirts, adjusted her bonnet and with an unsteady little bow to the company, said, 'Thank you for your hospitality. It appears my presence is required at home.'

She planted a kiss on Tom Brodie's brow and with as much dignity as she could muster in her tipsy state, tripped to the wicket gate and, like a pouting child, allowed herself to be dragged away.

On the eve of the American war the Caledonian Bank had foundered with debts of over a hundred and forty thousand pounds. The crash had wiped out not only several of Glasgow's wealthiest tobacco lords but also a hatful of Scottish lairds, Sir Adam Pendicle among them. The old boy had somehow managed to hang on to a few hundred acres of woodland and his crumbling baronial castle on the west side of Pendicle Hill but all his parks and policies in and around Drennan had been sold off in small parcels to local merchants who had money to spare and ambitions to rise in society.

Walter Fergusson had picked up one hundred and sixty acres of best grazing for not much more than a song. Neville Hewitt, with his friend's encouragement, had borrowed against his manufactory to purchase three small farms. He had promptly replaced the sitting tenants with families willing to sign leases just this side of usurious. Two of Mr Hewitt's new tenants had already gone to the wall, stock and chattels sold off, their farms leased out at once to a fresh batch of optimists, of which there seemed to be no scarcity in Ayrshire.

Only Hawkshill remained in possession of the original tenants; seventy sour acres occupied by Brodie and his clan whose hand-to-mouth existence offended Mr Hewitt's sensibilities and whose stubborn refusal to break their backs improving his ground ate like a canker at his soul.

The death of his wife had affected him less than the downturn in his commercial affairs, for the flax mill was not the gold mine it had been a decade ago. Distracted by a slipping market and the not unwelcome demands of his housekeeper, he had failed to realise that his prime asset was not the pitted retting-tanks in his flax shed but his beautiful daughter, Rose.

'Why,' said Mr Fergusson, 'I'd marry her myself if she came with a dowry. Indeed, Neville, I might even be willin' to forgo a dowry. Your daughter is a jewel among women and, I assume, unspoiled?'

'I can vouch for her innocence,' Mr Hewitt said uncomfortably.

'She can read and write, I take it?'

'Of course she can read and write,' said Mr Hewitt. 'I've employed a number of tutors over the years. She can speak in French, too, if called upon and, after a fashion, play upon the harp.'

'The harp?' Mr Fergusson raised an eyebrow. 'Now wouldn't that be a talent to delight a man, to have such an angel play the harp for him when he comes home weary of a winter's eve? How large is her instrument?'

'Quite small,' said Neville Hewitt.

'To suit her dainty fingers, I expect.'

'Walter,' Neville Hewitt said, 'I'd be only too happy to fall into an arrangement with you in respect of my daughter. There is, however, one fly in the butter dish that we can't ignore.'

'My wife, you mean?' Walter Fergusson said. 'Aye, that's an impediment no amount of wishing will remove. In any case I expect you've a husband for Rose already in your sights, a gentleman with refined tastes an' the wherewithal to support them.'

'In fact,' said Hewitt, 'I do not.'

'You do not?' said Fergusson, raising his brows again. 'My, my, you surprise me! Is the lass not inclined to marry?'

'She will marry when she's told to marry, not before.'

'Then,' Walter Fergusson said, 'you'd better be quick.'

'Had I?' said Neville Hewitt. 'Why?'

'There are plenty of young men in this shire who'd think nothing of robbin' your daughter of her virtue.'

Neville Hewitt glanced at the assorted ruffians who were drinking at the inn's long tables or lurking furtively in corner booths. He shuddered at the thought of such coarse hands roving over his daughter's body.

Mr Fergusson refilled Mr Hewitt's glass.

'Young men like Tom Brodie,' he said.

'Brodie?' Neville Hewitt exploded. 'My daughter has no acquaintance with Brodie, nor he with her. This is naught but spite on your part, Walter, 'cause Brodie sold his cattle to a stranger.' He paused. 'Unless you've heard something I haven't?'

'Nothing of any weight.'

'Nah, nah, if there are rumours, they're false rumours. My Rose is seldom out o' my sight. When I'm engaged in business Eunice makes certain no harm comes to her.' He shook his head. 'Rose an' Tom Brodie? Never!'

'Ah, Neville, Neville,' the grazier said, 'how forgetful we've become now we're approaching our dotage. Don't you recall the all-consuming fire that burned in our loins when we were Brodie's age? There's not a bachelor in Drennan, not to mention Hayes, who wouldn't sell his soul to bed a gem like your daughter. Do you suppose they don't indulge in filthy fantasies when the drink flows freely? Do you suppose they don't lie on their sacks of a night with their heads full of beautiful creatures an' their hands full of—'

'Enough, enough,' Neville Hewitt interrupted. 'You're right, of course. It probably is time I picked out a husband for Rose before she becomes too headstrong.'

'What age is she now?'

'Sixteen.'

Walter Fergusson sighed. 'Well, if you heed my advice, Neville, you'll seek out a suitable gentleman an' marry her off before she loses her – shall we say – charms.'

'That will not happen.'

'I wouldn't be so sure, if I were you,' the grazier said.

The four fat lambs fetched little enough but one poor sale did not dampen the Brodies' spirits. Tom and Betsy returned from Caddy Crawford's in time to take charge of the bullocks and allow Henry and his sister a run at the market. With a light heart and a shilling in her pocket Janet scurried off to buy pies and ginger beer and poke about the stalls that sold ribbons, lace and small trinkets and, not incidentally, to give the eye to any handsome man who happened to stray across her bows. She had been disappointed to learn that Betsy's strapping cousin had already left Drennan to return to Ayr where his boat was awaiting a cargo. There would be time enough, she thought, to interrogate Betsy on the Irishman's 'intentions', to discover if any firm promises had been made and if there was any hope at all that she might steal him away.

Henry had more pressing business on hand. He ate Tom's packet of cheese and oatcakes as well as his own, sank a mug of ale at the door of one of the houses then, wasting no time, set off in search of Dr Glendinning who, as luck would have it, had just returned from visiting a patient and was about to sit down to a belated dinner. The conversation took place on the doorstep of the doctor's house in Thimble Row.

'A guinea?' the old doctor said. 'Do you have a guinea, young man?'

'I do, sir. See, here it is,' Henry answered.

'It's your father again, is it not?' the doctor said. 'Is he worse?'

'Much worse.'

The doctor sighed. 'I fear, Mr Brodie, you may be throwing good money after bad. Your father was almost beyond my aid at the back o' last winter.'

'Will you come for a guinea?' Henry said. 'It's all I have.'

The doctor hesitated, then, with another small sigh, accepted the coins that young Brodie offered.

'Of course, I will.'

'When, sir?'

'Tomorrow, in the forenoon.'

'Tomorrow it is then,' Henry said and after shaking the doctor's hand, returned to the market square to round up his companions and drive McCaskie's high-priced bullocks safely back to pasture at Hawkshill.

The light in the west had all but faded, though soon there would be a moon to light the way. Mindful of his charges, Tom drove the bullocks from the turnpike to drink at a pebbly stream that trickled out of Johnny Rankine's field. Grass was sparse but weeds still flourished and the beasts were young enough to munch on whatever green stuff they could find.

It was peaceful in the windless evening, the insects that hovered over the stream not bothersome. Betsy sat close to Tom and nibbled the sugar stick Henry had bought her. Janet lay on the grassy bank, too worn out by excitement to prattle, while Henry, standing above her, stared through a gap in the trees towards the distant sea.

From the corner of her eye Betsy noticed Tom take something from his pocket and lift it to his nose. She turned her head a little and in a voice not much above a whisper asked, 'What's that you have there?'

Tom displayed the gloves.

'Oh, you rogue,' Betsy said. 'You stole her gloves.'

'Not I,' said Tom. 'I found them on the grass behind the table.'

'No doubt you'll also find an opportunity to return them,' said Betsy.

'I might at that.'

'Hewitt's daughter will not be an easy catch even for the likes o' you.'

Tom tucked the gloves into his coat and propped himself on an elbow. 'The likes o' me?' he said.

'It's as plain as the tail on Donnelly's donkey what you're up to.'

'What might that be?'

'Marryin' that young girl to be shot o' your debt to Hewitt.'

'Now you're just bein' daft,' Tom said. 'She's locked up like a prisoner.'

'But you still managed to kiss her – an' not for the first time.'

'A kiss isn't a courtship,' Tom said. 'Besides, I'm o'er young to marry.'

'But not o'er young to mow her.'

'That's a coarse way o' puttin' it.'

'I'm a coarse sort o' person,' Betsy said, then added, 'but I'd never kiss a man on the lips in broad daylight.'

'What about in the dark, Betsy? Wouldn't you let your Irish cousin kiss you in the dark if he asked it of you?'

'Connor would never ask it.'

'So he's not your beau?'

'No,' Betsy said. 'An' never will be.'

'Pity,' Tom said. 'He struck me as a fine big fellow an' it'll take a fine big fellow to keep you in hand. What about me? Would you let me kiss you, if I asked polite?'

'Not if you went down on bended knee,' said Betsy and, unable to hide her irritation with her arrogant master, called out to Henry to get the cattle back on the road.

He had made one deal with a flax grower and another with a linen merchant but neither transaction had been satisfactory. With Walter Fergusson's warnings ringing in his ears Neville Hewitt was in no mood to receive the news that greeted him when he returned home.

'Brodie?' he barked. 'Are you telling me she ran off to meet Tom Brodie?'

'I caught her,' Eunice Prole said, 'drinkin' with Brodie an' others of his ilk outside an ale-house. There's no sayin' what might have happened if I hadn't found her.'

'How did you lose her in the first place?'

'I turned my back for a second an' she was off like a hare.'

'How long was she missing?'

'An hour or two, that's all.'

'That's all!' Papa Hewitt slapped a hand to his brow. 'Where is she now?'

'In her room.'

'She must be punished.'

'She – ah – she's already been punished.'

'Then she must be punished again.'

'No.' Eunice Prole put a hand on Neville's shoulder. 'Leave her to stew.'

He paused, one foot on the stairs. 'Did you whip her?'

'I did.'

'Soundly?'

'I gave her no more than she deserved. She's uttered not one word o' apology an' shows no signs o' remorse. I tell you, Neville, she's proud o' the dance she led me.' Eunice continued to grip his shoulder, her bony fingers tightening their hold. 'You might think it's all that farmer's fault, that he turned her head somehow, but how did Rose know he'd be in town today?'

'Have you asked her?'

'She won't tell me.'

'Well, by God, she'll tell me,' Papa Hewitt said and tearing himself from the housekeeper's grasp charged off upstairs.

Brandy was Tassie Landles' favourite tipple. When Peter placed the bottle on the table, she thanked him by kissing his cheek. She had done fair business that market day. The little enamelled box that lived below her armchair was half filled with brown pennies and silver sixpences. She had sent off the last young lass, a dairymaid, with a cheerful prediction and a packet of herbs to rid her of the itch that troubled her. After that, she had coaxed the hens into the roost, had drawn water, built up the fire and put on a fishy sort of stew, rich with onions. Then, just before nightfall, her 'nephew' had turned up bearing a bottle of brandy as a reward for a job well done.

'The cat,' Peter Frye said. 'You used the cat again, I suppose.'

'Pussy is seldom found wantin',' Tassie said. 'How could you be sure the lass would come to me?'

Peter perched himself precariously on the three-legged stool. 'After you dropped a hint to Hewitt's little day-maid, I trusted curiosity to do the rest.'

'A low trick,' Tassie said, 'one that'll bring grief in the end.'

'Is that a prophecy, Auntie, or guesswork?' Peter said. 'It seems that less than divine hand of yours gave Miss Hewitt a shove in Brodie's direction. She found us in the garden behind Caddy Crawford's house and consented to join us for a bit of dinner and a glass of wine.'

'She'll pay for her pleasure, you know.'

'I'm certain she will,' said Peter, 'but we all have to pay for our pleasures one way or another.'

Tassie stooped over the pot on the fire and stirred the stew. 'Do you need fed?'

'No, thank you all the same,' said Peter. 'I'd better show my face at the supper table at home tonight. I've been absent all day and you know how concerned my mother can become when I stay out late.'

'How is your mother these days?'

'Well, she's well,' said Peter. 'She's asks after you.'

'She does not,' Tassie stated.

'No,' Peter said. 'She does not.'

In fact neither his mother nor his father ever mentioned Tassie Landles' name. Tassie was the black sheep of the family, a stain that the passage of years had not erased. Only David, his brother, and he had truck with her. They had been nudged into serving as go-betweens as soon as they were old enough to saddle a pony and ride from Copplestone to Drennan.

It was not just Tassie's strange gifts or her mode of life that set her apart from the Fryes. She had been the product of an illicit union between Peter's grandfather and a wild young woman from the shire of Renfrew who, so it was told, had put such a powerful spell upon the man that he was willing to surrender his marriage to couple with her. Tassie had been the consequence of that long-ago affair. Abandoned, quite literally, on the doorstep of Copplestone as an infant, she had been fostered to a woman in Drennan to be reared and almost, if not quite, forgotten.

Over the years bits and pieces of money had been ferried to the foster mother, Alice Landles, who had three boy children of her own but no husband. Peter's mother and his 'Auntie' Tassie had never met face to face. On the few occasions when they had passed each other on the road not so much as a nod had been exchanged. But after the Landles boys had grown and were gone and Alice died, Margaret Frye had insisted that the family connection with Tassie be preserved through David and Peter if only to deter the woman from wreaking a belated revenge – a notion that Tassie found hilarious.

She held out the spoon.

Peter licked a blob of blue-grey gravy from the tip, closed his eyes and, as was expected of him, said, 'Delicious!'

'Stay then,' said Tassie. 'I've a walnut cake, too, all hot and spicy.'

'No, Aunt Tassie,' Peter said, rising. 'Don't tempt me. I really must head home before Mother has fits.'

'Where's your horse?'

'In Caddy's stable.'

'Has Brodie gone home too?'

'He has cattle to trail – and his sister is with him.'

'So he'll not be up to mischief tonight?'

'Not this night, no.' Peter glanced at the door.

'Tell me this afore you gallop off: what does Tom Brodie want with Hewitt's lassie?'

'What any man wants from a pretty girl.'

'Is he in love with her?'

'Tom falls in love with every girl who takes his fancy. Unfortunately, he's incapable of separating lust from love.'

'Rose Hewitt will only bring him grief.'

'Her father will, you mean?' said Peter.

'No, the girl,' Tassie said. 'I mean the girl.'

'Rose Hewitt's nothing but a weak little thing.'

'All the more dangerous for that,' Tassie said and, holding the spoon at arm's length, kissed him once more on the cheek.

She knelt by the bed wearing nothing but a chemise. He could see the shape of her beneath the linen, hips and bottom womanly, her breast, crushed by her arm, plump and puffy. Her petticoat and stockings as well as her frock had been flung about the room as if by a furious draught of wind. The water jug lay shattered on the floorboards. The bolster, beaten shapeless, almost tripped him as he entered the room. He stepped over it, his rage frozen at the sight of his daughter bowed and silent like a nymph at her orisons.

At first he assumed that the pattern on her chemise was an elaborate piece of embroidery then, stepping closer, he realised that it was blood.

He wondered what she had done to herself, if petulance had turned to violence, or if – the thought struck him like a blow – Brodie and his gang had stripped and raped her in broad daylight or in the filthy back room that Caddy Crawford hired out to lovers.

'Rose?' he said under his breath. 'Rose, what have they done to you?'

She did not move, not a muscle, not a hair.

For a single terrifying instant he thought she might be dead.

He leapt forward, caught her by the hair and wrenched her head up. Her eyes were wide open, staring and blank, then casually, almost diffidently, she twisted her head and spat a little gout of blood on to his trouser leg.

'Is it your turn now, Papa?' she said.

To Betsy's surprise old Mr Brodie was up and dressed and seated in the wooden chair by the side of the fire. Clear skies meant a cold night and there was already a touch of frost in the air. The old man had a blanket draped over his shoulders. His feet, in thick stockings, were so close to the fire that the wool was in danger of scorching. He looked not pale but flushed, too flushed. Sweat dripped down his face and his head shook as he raised himself and asked, 'Did you make a sale, Henry? Are the calves gone?'

'No, Daddy, the calves are back in the pasture.'

'An' the sheep?'

'Sold for pennies,' Janet told him, 'just pennies.'

The old man sank back. There seemed to be nothing of him but sagging features and big, long, skinny hands, hands, Betsy thought, like Henry's. Hovering behind her husband's chair, Agnes Brodie adjusted the blanket over his shoulders.

'He was countin' on money from the calves,' she said.

Brodie's children gathered round the chair, smirking and smug. It was a cruel trick to play on a sick old man, Betsy thought, payment for all the cruel tricks he'd played on them over the years, perhaps.

'Aye, Daddy,' Tom said, 'the bullocks are where they belong, snickin' dry grass in the loch field.' He put his hat on the floor and dipped a hand into his coat pocket. 'But they're not our beasts now. Nah, nah. We're grazin' them for a fee till they're full grown.'

The old man's nostrils flared as if he were sniffing for the smell of drink on Tom's breath or perfume on Henry's handkerchiefs.

'Sold to a sailor, an Irish sailor,' said Henry.

'Her cousin.' Janet jerked her thumb at Betsy.

'How much did they fetch?'

Spreading the blanket to cover his father's knees, Tom dropped the silver into his father's lap. 'Four pounds, Daddy, four pounds – an' one extra for feed.'

That, Betsy knew, was a lie. She had watched Connor pay out the money. She wondered where the balance had gone, not the few shillings Henry, Tom and Janet had spent on small luxuries but almost two whole guineas.

'Hah!' Matthew Brodie said. 'You've done well, for once.'

'We've Betsy to thank for it,' Henry said. 'If she hadn't told her cousin we'd be at the mart today—'

'I didn't tell Connor anythin' o' the sort,' Betsy said.

'Someone did,' said Henry. 'Your mother, perhaps?'

'Aye,' said Betsy. 'Perhaps.'

Connor had always been a bit of a jack-in-the-box, popping up without warning. But now she thought of it, it did seem odd that he'd shown up at a cattle mart miles from Ayr harbour just in time to throw money at the Brodies.

'However he came to be there,' Tom said, 'he saved our skin. Sooner or later Fergusson would have had the beasts for half their worth.'

Janet had bought a packet of soft cheese for her mother. When that gift had been handed over and duly sampled, Janet went into the back room to gloat over her purchases while old Mr Brodie, invigorated by his sons' success, urged the boys to tell him all about the day's events and, to Betsy's astonishment, discuss how best the windfall could be spent before the landlord could lay his hands on it.

It was a blessing, Eunice Prole thought, that she had passed the age of child-bearing. In fact, she had never been fertile. In spite of her husband's countless attempts to render her pregnant she had been unable to conceive. Had her fish-merchant husband but known it, Eunice was delighted as the years went by with never a sign of a swollen belly. She was utterly devoid of maternal instinct and had nothing but scorn for those wives who meekly turned themselves into breeding manufactories.

While loudly professing disgust at the 'sinfulness' of others, Eunice had used the period of her marriage to indulge an immoderate liking for coupling. It had come as something of a shock when, nine years ago, her husband had impregnated not one but two of the callow young fisher-hands who gutted herring on the quays and had brought them and their squalling infants to share room and board with Eunice and him.

Soon after that – very soon, in fact – Eunice had abandoned her husband and his fecund fisher-hands to weather the censure of the kirk and the opprobrium of the community and had applied for employment in the household of Mr Neville Hewitt. With an ailing wife and young child to look after, the wealthy flax merchant had advertised for a competent housekeeper to manage his domestic affairs. Mrs Eunice Prole, next best thing to a widow, had filled the bill admirably and long before the fragile Mrs Hewitt had gone to meet her Maker, Mrs Prole's skill in the kitchen had been topped by her skill in the bedroom.

Age had not withered Eunice's allure, not much at any rate. She was still adept at twisting her employer round her little finger and keeping his pretty daughter, Rose, firmly in her place. Her authority had rarely been challenged until now.

The last thing Mrs Prole needed to appear trim and slender was a corset. She'd had the garment since her bridal night and used it now not to keep any fleshy bulges in but to make sure they stuck out, a function that the faded silk stays performed quite effectively, particularly when coupled with a sleeveless under-bodice and a gown that was nothing much but décolletage.

In spite of his simmering anger, Neville Hewitt could not keep his eyes off the soft and only slightly wrinkled display.

Seated on his knee, holding a wine glass to his lips, Mrs Prole said, 'Did she eat anythin' of the supper I sent up?'

'Not a bite.'

'Did she bathe herself?'

'She washed the blood – bathed her limbs an' put on the lotion.'

'A very good lotion,' said Eunice Prole. 'I've used it myself.'

'Have you?' Neville said. 'Does it sting?'

'Only if carelessly applied to delicate female parts.'

'Quite!' Neville said. 'Will it avert scarring, do you think?'

'Scarring?' Eunice wriggled guiltily. 'She won't scar, will she?'

'Eunice,' Neville Hewitt said, 'you almost killed her.'

'I did, I confess, lose my temper.'

'Well, my dear, you mustn't lose your temper again. Indeed, you mustn't punish her again, not with the withy at any rate. Come to think of it, I forbid you to lay a finger on Rose from now on.'

'But Neville! After what she did . . .'

'What Brodie did, you mean.'

'Brodie, aye. Without doubt Brodie lured her on. But Rose must share the blame. How's she to be disciplined – I mean, protected – if I'm not allowed to punish her?'

'She's too valuable to be punished.'

'Valuable?'

The flax manufacturer slid his housekeeper from his knee and got to his feet. He was shorter by several inches than Mrs Prole and might, if he had chosen to do so, have rested the tip of his nose in the cleft of her bosom.

Instead, he stepped away, put the oval table between them and leaned upon it. 'My daughter is sixteen years old, Eunice, an' the most beautiful creature this side of paradise.'

'She's pretty enough, I suppose,' Eunice conceded.

'She's a beauty, a pearl, a jewel among women.'

'Neville, what are you sayin'?'

'I'm sayin' Rose is an asset, a valuable asset,' Neville Hewitt went on. 'My friend Walter Fergusson has made me see the light. Isn't it obvious by her rebellious behaviour these past months that what Rose needs is not a jailer but a husband?'

'Fergusson? He's already married, isn't he?'

'Of course, he is. Not Fergusson.'

'Who then? Brodie?'

'Don't jest with me, woman,' Neville Hewitt said. 'I'd see her dead before I'd let her go to Tom Brodie. No, we must find Rose a husband, a man endowed with good taste and, shall we say, a fiery spirit.'

'An' money?' Eunice put in.

'An' money,' Neville agreed.

Eunice seated herself, sipped wine from her master's glass, cocked her head first one way then the other and unselfconsciously plucked at her bosom to give it air.

'Prime catches don't grow on trees,' she said.

'I'm well aware of that,' Neville said. 'We must apply ourselves to seekin' out such a man and, in the meanwhile, ensure that Rose is not scarred.'

Eunice nodded. 'Since she's been with Tom Brodie, though, she might wish to be with him again. God might not guide me to her quite so opportunely.'

'Brodie an' his brood must be squashed. God isn't goin' to do it for us.'

'But you can do it, dearest, can you not?'

'Oh, aye,' said Papa Hewitt. 'I can do it.'

'While I take care o' Rose.'

'Without the whip,' said Neville.

'Without the whip,' Eunice Prole agreed and to thank him for forgiving her leaned over the table and kissed his wet little mouth.

5

Betsy had been ten when her Grandmother McBride had died. She had been shocked less by her glimpse of the old woman's corpse than the vast quantities of whisky, cake and tobacco the mourners had consumed in the course of the wake. On the evening after the burial, she had found her daddy seated at his loom and weeping as if his heart would break. He had stroked her hair and told her tearfully that no right-minded person ever begged burial money from the Kirk Session or called for aid from the poor-box and had made Betsy promise that when his time came she would see him off 'properly', no matter the cost. She had been too young to understand the nature of family pride in those days and was not entirely sure that she understood it now. She was certainly not prepared for Agnes Brodie's unctuous hand-wringing when Dr Glendinning and his assistant arrived in a pony-cart the morning after market day.

Henry was summoned from the hill, Tom from the long field, but by the time the boys reached the cottage the doctor had completed his examination and old Mr Brodie lay prone upon the bed, chest bare, arms by his sides, breathing so shallowly that it seemed he was not breathing at all. He did not open his eyes when the surgeon cut into a vein in his arm and tapped several ounces of blood into a porcelain dish which the hunchbacked assistant then took outside and poured away. From a scuffed valise the doctor then unpacked three blue jars, a small bottle and a measuring glass. He put the glassware on

the table and with everyone watching intently, measured a
small quantity of liquid from each jar into the bottle which he
stoppered with a piece of cork and shook vigorously before he
passed it to Tom.

'Six drops measured into clean water,' Glendinning said.
'Administer four or five times each day, as necessary.'

Tom looked up. 'Will this mixture cure him?'

'It will ease his pain and render him less restless.'

'Make him well again, you mean?' said Agnes brightly.

'It will not cure, Mrs Brodie,' Glendinning said. 'No cure is
possible.'

'No cure?' said Tom. 'Will my daddy always be an invalid?'

'He will . . .' Glendinning hesitated. 'He will not be an
invalid for long. He is beyond my aid.'

'Why did you bleed him then?' said Janet.

'To relieve the pressure of blood in his lungs,' the doctor
answered.

'An' this?' Tom held the bottle aloft. 'Is this medicine
naught but a sop?'

'It's a tincture of strong narcotics to ease—'

'Help him die, you mean?' Tom said.

'A peaceful death is all one may hope for,' the doctor said.
'You must prepare yourself for the worst.'

'No,' Tom shouted. 'No,' and rushed out into the yard.

The harp was little more than a toy. It was shaped like the
Celtic harp that graced the tomb of a forgotten Ayrshire bard
on the back side of Pendicle Hill and the harps that the angels
clasped to their bosoms in the engravings in the big, black-
bound volume of *Prayers and Sermons* that her father had
picked up at a roup sale as a substitute for a family Bible. He
had written his name, her mother's name and her name too on
the speckled flyleaf but to Rose's knowledge had never opened
the book again.

She, on the other hand, had pored over the illustrations whenever an opportunity came her way. She was fascinated by the depiction of angels in nightgowns welcoming worthy souls into the vault of heaven. She had once asked Mrs Prole if it never rained in heaven and had had her ears boxed for her impertinence which, in Mrs Prole's opinion, almost amounted to sacrilege.

The harp had also come from a sale, from one of the big houses south of Girvan. Her father had told her it had once belonged to the small daughter of a fine gentleman before she had been called away to join the angels in paradise. Rose had wondered why the small daughter of a fine gentleman had not been required to take her harp with her but she thought it best to remain in ignorance rather than risk another cuffing for questioning the ways of the Lord.

The harp had a single row of strings. The frame was made of varnished wood that had recently begun to warp in the damp atmosphere of the attic. Mr Cameron, who had been employed to tutor Rose in French, had told her it was an imitation lyre or, possibly, a clarsach, upon which instrument Tristan had taught music to Isolde.

Bushy-browed, threadbare and not a day short of sixty, Mr Cameron had been foolish enough to recount the tragic tale of Tristan's passion for his uncle's wife and, being a bit of a pedant, had outlined the story's origins in Pictish history and its development as a medieval romance. He had even loaned Rose a small, precious volume of the story in French to encourage her reading but Papa had snatched the book from her, hurled it at Mr Cameron's head and had dismissed the old fellow then and there for peddling filth to an innocent child.

Although Rose's lessons in French had been discontinued she still had the harp and, warped or not, could conjure from it a few simple melancholy tunes that might even resemble the songs that Tristan sang to his lovely Isolde. She would make up words and croon them softly to herself while the strings throbbed beneath her fingertips and the reek of steeping flax and the raucous sounds from the town's ale-houses melted away.

In spite of the ointment that Mrs Prole had provided, her wounds continued to leak. She bathed them with the warm, salty water that Dorothy brought up in a bowl from the kitchen.

'Did you get whuppit for what Tassie telt you?' Dorothy asked.

'Tassie telt – told me nothing of any consequence,' Rose answered.

'She's fair mad at you,' Dorothy said. 'Old Prole, I mean.'

'I gave her good reason, I suppose.'

'Did you meet him, then, your man?'

Rose dipped a swab of lint into the bowl and, flinching a little, painted her thighs with salty water. She was leery of the little day-maid, who was not as dimwitted as she pretended to be, but she had no one else to talk to and Dorothy at least pretended to be an ally.

'Yes, I met him.'

'Tassie brung him tae ye?'

'Well,' Rose said, 'perhaps she did.'

'She did, I know she did,' said Dorothy. 'Tassie can dae all kinds o' things beyond the nat'ral. She sent me Loon Leach.'

'Who's Loon Leach?'

'The midden man's son. He catches the rats an' gets paid a farthin' a tail. He's got plenty o' money.'

'Tassie sent you to him, did she?' said Rose.

'Sent him tae me, more like.'

'Has he kissed you yet?'

'Aye,' said Dorothy. 'He cuddles me tae.'

'My, my!' said Rose. 'Do you like being cuddled?'

'Aye, I do. There's better tae come, Loon says, when we're wedded.'

Dorothy was a foundling who had been reared by the parish, a snubnosed, brown-eyed girl, who breathed through her mouth. Mr Fergusson had found her employment in the Hewitts' house, though, being barely twelve, she returned each night to the orphanage. She had confided in Rose that one day she intended to serve in a grand mansion and marry a laird's son, an ambition that Rose considered impractical.

'Would you rather marry Loon than a laird's son?' Rose asked.

'Tassie tells me Loon's tangled in ma future an' there's nae escape.'

'No escape!' Rose exclaimed. 'Doesn't that prospect frighten you?'

'Nah, nah,' said Dorothy soberly. 'If Loon's for me, he'll dae fine.'

Rose picked at the edges of the wounds that marred the smoothness of her thighs. She was bruised across the ribs and buttocks too and could not sit down properly or find a comfortable position in which to lie. She had spent last night kneeling by the window with a blanket over her shoulders.

She lowered her head and murmured, 'If Tom's for me, he'll do fine.'

She brought the harp from the bedside, propped it gingerly upon her knee, strummed a chord and called out loudly, '*If Tom's for me, then he'll do fine,*' and, laughing, heard Eunice Prole slip away from the attic door and creep downstairs to report, no doubt, to Papa.

The long field was an awkward shape and had been used these past four years for grazing. It was tough ground, bristling with thistles, alive with wireworm and poorly drained. To tackle it with the heavy plough was Tom's intention. Given that, come spring, they might no longer be the tenants of Hawkshill, Henry saw no sense in making improvements. Tom was sick of Henry's reasonable arguments. A portion of the Irishman's money might be spent on the purchase of good seed and the long field was the natural place to sow it.

That morning, very early, he had harnessed the horses, carted the plough to the head of the field and had driven the cows to the infield where Janet would find them handy for milking. It had barely been daylight when he'd grasped the stilts, dropped the coulter and had given the cords a tweak. The horses had needed no further instruction. Trace-chains had rattled, swing-trees tightened, the share had bitten into the earth and with the first furrow folding back from the mould-board, the team had plodded off up the slope.

There was more to ploughing than breaking old ground. His control over the horses had taken his mind from his father's illness, the looming threat of eviction, and his yearning to hold Rose Hewitt in his arms.

Conquest might seem to be all for the blades in the Bache-lors' Club but there was not one among them who didn't long to find a girl in whom all the virtues were combined, a lady whose conversation would not pall, who would not only raise the flag upon the flagpole but make the heart swell and the head spin – and if she came attached to a dowry so much the better.

Tom had roamed far and wide in his quest for true love and had set his sights high. The summer before last he had courted Mrs Craven's middle daughter – mainly, it must be said, by letter – until Mrs Craven's steward had called upon him, shown him a brand-new mantrap and quietly warned him to watch his step. Tom, not being entirely besotted, had penned a final flowery letter to the young lady and thereafter had put away his quill.

To console himself he had taken up with a kitchen maid from Pendicle who, he discovered, was not only willing to be wooed but was even more willing to be mowed. Only a false alarm concerning motherhood had melted his resolve to marry the cunning wee creature and had sent him, mildly chastened, back to the dancing school in search of another true love.

The seduction of Rose Hewitt had been a challenge, a dare, but after he had kissed her and she had returned the favour in the ale-house garden his intentions had changed, for Miss Rose Hewitt had put a halter round his heart.

Now he was back in the long field with pale sunshine glistening on the furrows, the gulls wheeling noisily overhead and Glendinning's pronouncements ringing in his ears and no thoughts of Rose Hewitt, no annealing fancies could save him from the certain knowledge that his daddy was close to death.

'Tom,' Betsy said. 'Oh, Tom!'

The horses had pulled the plough out of the furrow and were cropping weeds on the verge. The gulls had floated up, screaming, when Betsy appeared but the rooks and crows, more circumspect and sly, had only hopped away and were soon feeding greedily again.

Tom was seated on the damp grass at the head of the field, knees drawn up, his head in his hands. He looked up at her bleakly, dry-eyed.

'Has Glendinning gone yet, him an' his hunchbacked butcher?'

'They're takin' tea,' Betsy told him. 'Your mother insisted.'

'Aye, she would,' Tom said. 'She'd give hospitality to Satan himself if he rode up to the door wi' a smile on his face. Have you been sent to fetch me?'

'No one sent me. I came because . . .' Betsy shrugged.

'Well, you'll not catch me weepin' o'er some rancid old man's lies. Mark my words, my daddy'll be cuttin' capers in the corn rigs come summer, bright as a rainbow.' Denial drained away. He let out a little sob. 'God! God! What'll I do, Betsy, what'll I do without him to guide me? What can I do, Betsy? Tell me, what can I do for him now?'

She had nothing to say at first, no comfort to offer until she heard her father's voice, faint and tearful, somewhere inside her head.

'Bury him decent, Tom,' she said.

He laboured all day in the long field. He was weary to the bone by nightfall and hungry too but it seemed wrong to sit at supper and stuff his face while his father lay dying behind the curtain.

Henry put up the horses while the women took turns on the stool by the bed to watch over the old man. He was too weak to talk but Glendinning's medicine had eased his agitation and Henry said it had been worth every penny of the doctor's fee.

Tom did not argue.

There was no conversation at the supper table. It was so quiet that the clicking of knives and rattle of spoons sounded as loud as musket fire. For once there was meat to eat, a joint of boiled brisket. Agnes had sent Janet down to the butcher's shop in Hayes to buy something special, though just what there was to celebrate no one cared to enquire. The choice cut, doused in gravy, that Agnes took behind the curtain to tempt her husband's appetite came back untouched.

Tom's eyelids were drooping. It seemed as if he might fall asleep at the table. Henry took two blackened clay pipes and a pouch of fresh tobacco from the shelf above the fireplace, filled both pipes and lit them with a taper, then, tapping Tom on the shoulder, jerked his head towards the door. Tom sighed and followed his brother out into the clear, crisp starlit night. They seated themselves on the shafts of the small cart. Tom was not much of a one for tobacco but Henry was fond of the weed and felt its need when the pouch on the shelf was empty which these past months had been most of the time.

'Do you know why I've brought you out here?' Henry said.

'To enjoy a good smoke,' said Tom.

'We might've smoked indoors, might we not?'

'Aye.' Tom nodded. 'So if you've somethin' to get off your chest, Henry, get on with it for I'm in sore need o' my bed.'

'What will we do when he – when Daddy dies?'

'Bury him,' Tom said. 'Bury him decent.'

'I mean about the farm.'

'Keep it.'

'How can we keep it when it's saddled wi' debt?'

'We'll find a way to pay the debt,' Tom said.

'Or declare the debt paid by death an' move on?'

'So that's what's bitin' you, is it?' Tom said. 'Well, I'm not movin' on. I'm not movin' anywhere.'

'In that case Hewitt will have to be paid.'

'Hewitt will be paid,' Tom said.

'How?'

Tom took the clay from his mouth and poked the stem at his brother.

'Look,' he said, 'I know what's on your mind, Henry, an' I'll have none o' it. Aye, we can lay the debt down wi' Dad's body, for the lease is in his name an' the debt with it. We can walk away wi' our tails between our legs if we choose.'

'An' some o' the stock,' Henry reminded him.

'No stock,' said Tom. 'Hewitt'll have it all bar McCaskie's calves.'

'Under the law—'

'Damn the law!' Tom said. 'It's true what you say: we can bury the debt wi' Daddy an' walk off without a mark against our names. We'll be at liberty to acquire a lease on another piece o' ground an' scrounge enough cash to stock it.'

'Rankine might lend us somethin'.'

'Rankine might,' Tom agreed.

'There's a lease comin' up on a place not too far from Port Cedric, so I've heard. You have influence, Tom, you've friends who understand what happened here on Hawkshill wasn't our fault.'

'Whose fault was it then? Daddy's?'

'I didn't say that.'

'Aye, an' you'd better not,' said Tom. 'Daddy took on this wicked lease for our sakes, an' broke his back to keep it.'

'Hawkshill's not worth keepin'. We can shake out clean if we want to an' start afresh,' Henry said. 'Daddy wouldn't grudge us that.'

'Then we'll ask him,' Tom said. 'He's not dead yet.'

'No,' said Henry in alarm. 'Don't ask him, Tom. Don't tell him what's on our minds. He'll only fret.'

'Then,' Tom said, 'we won't ask him. We'll tell him.'

'Tell him what?'

'That we'll look after Hawkshill when he's gone.'

'Would you lie to him on his deathbed, Tom?'

'I'd cut off my arm afore I'd lie to him.'

Henry paused. 'What about the girl?'

'What girl?'

'Hewitt's daughter.'

'Oh, you've heard about that, have you? Who told you? Was it Betsy?'

'Janet had it from the butcher. It's the talk o' the town,' Henry said. 'What came over you, flirtin' with Rose Hewitt in the ale-house garden? We're in too deep wi' Hewitt as it is. Did the Irishman egg you on?'

Tom grunted and spat a little globule of tobacco juice over his shoulder, as if he were throwing salt to the devil.

'I need no man's encouragement to court a beautiful lassie.'

'Hewitt's daughter?' said Henry again. 'Were you drunk?'

'Sober,' Tom said. 'Stone cold sober.'

'Dear God, man, you're playin' with fire.'

'What if I am?' Tom got to his feet. 'Hewitt's intent on seein' us out whatever happens. Courtin' his daughter can't make matters much worse. Besides, my intentions are honourable.'

'Honourable?' Henry said. 'You don't know the meanin' o' the word.'

'I intend to marry Rose Hewitt,' Tom said, 'if she'll have me.'

'What!' Henry shouted, leaping up. 'Hewitt will never stand for it.'

'Hewitt will have no choice but to stand for it.'

'Don't tell me she's carryin' your bairn?'

'Not yet,' Tom said, 'not yet,' and, handing the pipe to his brother, went quickly back indoors.

Few things in life gave Walter Fergusson as much pleasure as watching calves being fed. However tight-fisted in his dealings with stock traders, he was not niggardly when it came to attending his herd. He took endless pains to ensure that feeding routines were adhered to and milk kits warmed to blood temperature. He did not tether the little animals in sunless sheds or feed them artificially and he was most meticulous about the weaning process; a pluck of sweet hay, a pint of hay-tea mixed with the milk or, best of all, a dollop of linseed jelly invariably smoothed the way to grazing on rye grass and red clover. He was no less attentive to 'bought-in' beasts and by careful management turned a pretty penny on his purchases.

All his profits were ploughed back into improving his herd and it was said that his byres, barns and milking sheds were cleaner and more comfortable than the dwelling he shared with his wife, Flora, and son, for the farmhouse on the out-skirts of Drennan was little more than a hovel with a sagging roof, peeling walls and a smoky chimney.

Mr Fergusson's son, Lucas, was nothing much to write home about either.

For a man who had devoted his life to breeding, Walter Fergusson had singularly failed to produce a winner. Only one child had been dropped by Fergusson's dam, after which the lady had become barren, a condition no amount of dosing with pills and potions had been able to reverse. Consequently, Fergusson was stuck with a solitary heir, a chap who even his doting dad had to admit was not a prime example of rugged young manhood and was more often than not an absolute pain in the arse.

'Looo-kuss,' the dairymaids would call out when they thought the old man was out of earshot. 'Aw, Looo-kuss, gi'es a kiss then. See, wee Jenny's got her bubbies out for you tae play wi'. Whaur are ye gaun, Looo-kuss? Are ye gaun tae clipe tae yer daddy?'

Four years of schooling had failed to educate the Fergusson boy. Horseplay with stable lads had failed to toughen him. The taunts of the rough-and-tumble lassies his father employed reduced him not to awareness of his sexual powers but simply to tears. He was forever weeping was Fergusson's lad. He wept when he stumbled upon the first snowdrop cowering under a hedge. He wept when a pigeon fell from the rooftop or one of the dogs came home with a rabbit dangling in its mouth. He wept when his father raged or his mother chided and wept most of all when the milk tally would not add up and he was forced to take off his mittens and count on his fingers, as if a pickle of wool made a blind bit of difference to faulty arithmetic.

He had been twelve years old before he had learned to tell the difference between a heifer and a bull and had paid dearly for the experience with three cracked ribs and a swollen kneecap. At fourteen he had fallen through the soft crust of the dung-heap trying to rescue a duckling and, stinking to high heaven, had been hauled out by the head cattleman with the aid of a rope and a pony. At seventeen he had nicked himself shaving with his father's cut-throat, had tried to staunch the bleeding with a dab of horse glue and had lain at death's door for a fortnight with a sepsis of the blood.

The following August, hay-making, some wag had spiced his water bottle with whisky and only prompt action by one of the collies had saved him from being bisected by the wheels of the hay-cart.

Aged nineteen, almost to the day, he had been set upon in the corn rigs by a gaggle of not quite sober girls, had had his trousers removed and his parts fondled and, shocked by their intimate attentions, had slid into a melancholy state that did not lift until Martinmas.

Now twenty, he rarely ventured out after dark and even in broad daylight preferred to keep Dad well within hailing distance.

Dad was certainly within hailing distance that morning.

Father and son leaned side by side on the gate of the stockyard while the girls trotted about with buckets of warm milk and the soft cloth teats from which the calves were being taught to suckle. Mouth closed, cap pulled down to keep his ears from sticking out and sunlight shining on his long fair lashes, he looked, Mr Fergusson thought, almost intelligent.

He gave Lucas a nudge. 'Which one do you fancy then?'

'The Galloway's no' very pretty but she's got girth.'

'The Galloway?'

'That one.'

'Oh, the Ayrshire. Nah, nah, Lukie, not the calves, the girls. Have you no eye for the lassies?'

'Mean, they are, mean bitches.'

'What happened was an accident. They were just frolickin'. Are you still sulking 'cause I didn't send them packing?'

Lucas lifted a shoulder and let it fall.

Walter sighed. 'Good dairy hands are hard to come by, son. Besides, they're not wicked. They just got carried away. Is it not time to put it behind you an' start thinking about takin' a sweetheart?'

Lucas frowned. 'A sweetheart?'

'A wife then.'

'What would I want wi' a wife?'

Walter sighed again. 'A wife to cook your dinner . . .'

'Mam does that already.'

'A wife to share your bed an' bear you children.'

The frown deepened. 'Children?'

'Sons o' your own,' said Walter. 'Heirs.'

'Hairs?'

'Heirs, heirs – inheritors.' Walter lowered his chin to his chest and counted to five before he went on. 'You're a grown man, Lucas. Your mother an' I are agreed it's time you took a wife.'

'Why, but?'

'Because that's what men do.'

Lucas was not ignorant of the processes of procreation. He had witnessed so many copulations and births over the years that even he had eventually put two and two together and concluded that men and women were anatomically akin to bulls and cows and that the thing between his legs had a purpose other than making pee-pee.

'Now, there's McAllan's daughter. She's a fine, sonsy lass, Lucas. She'd make any man a good wife.'

'Ugly.'

'Is Jenny more to your taste?'

'She swears.'

'They're country girls, for heaven's sake, not genteel ladies. Look at Biddy. See how nicely she tends that calf. She's a gentle creature is Biddy, even if she is a wee bit long in the tooth.'

'Long in the shank, an' all,' said Lucas.

Walter draped a paternal arm over his son's shoulder and drew him close enough to whisper into his ear. 'They say she has a treasure tucked between her legs an' she's fair fussy who has sight of it.'

'Treasure?' said Lucas. 'What sort o' treasure?'

Closer still, Walter imparted a detail or two.

Lucas pulled away. 'That's disgustin'!'

'Oh, for God's sake, Lucas!' Mr Fergusson exploded. 'What do you want from a woman? There's no such thing as a rose without a thorn.'

'A what?'

'A rose, a rose, damn it, a . . .' Walter Fergusson's eyes widened, his mouth dropped open, then, leaving Lucas propped on the gate, he rushed off to find his wife.

6

If Betsy had been in the yard that morning she would surely have stepped up and told Neville Hewitt that he had no right to barge into the house of a dying man. Betsy was out in the field when Hewitt rode up, however, and handing the reins of his horse to Janet strode into the kitchen without invitation or apology.

'Where is he?' he called out. 'Where's Brodie?'

Drugged and sleepy, Matthew struggled to untangle himself from the sheets. 'He's here.'

'Not you, you fool,' said Neville Hewitt.

'If it's Tom you want, he's in the field,' Matthew said, 'but if you have business to discuss then discuss it wi' me. I'm still head o' this household.'

'I'll not talk business with a cripple.' Hewitt looked about the room. 'What about the other one – Henry, is it? Where's he?'

'He's gone to Hayes to buy seed,' Agnes blurted out.

'Seed, is it?' Hewitt said. 'Where, tell me, did he find cash to buy seed when there's rent owing?'

Matthew hoisted himself from the bed. 'You'll have your rent as soon as I'm on my feet again.'

'Look at you, Brodie. You'll never be on your feet again. I'm astonished you're on your feet now. Lie down, for God's sake,' Hewitt said. 'I'll not have you dyin' in front o' me.'

Matthew braced his hip against the edge of the mattress. Neither his wife nor daughter moved to assist him for they were less in awe of the landlord than the old man's stubborn pride. Hewitt shifted closer to the bed.

'Come the first day o' November you'll owe for a year an' that's more licence than any sane man will allow. Next time I show my face it'll be with the Sheriff's officer or the bailie.' He lifted his hand to poke a finger into Brodie's chest then thought better of it. 'Is it your hope you'll be taken before then? Is it your hope you'll be took an' the debt will go with you, leavin' me with this ill-worked bit o' land while your idle brats skip away to prey on another poor landlord?'

'I'll pay my debt before I go, never fear,' Matthew Brodie said.

'What, with dung and spittle? You've precious little else.' Hewitt dragged a stool from beneath the table and perched a foot upon it. 'Fergusson tells me you sold two calves at a fat profit. What happened to the cash?'

'It's gone to buy seed,' the old man said, 'to sow spring wheat an' start the rotation on a proper footing. Wheat, barley, oats an' peas, then—'

'Yes, yes,' Hewitt said. 'Are you ploughin' the long field at last?'

'Tom is, aye.'

There was something indomitable about old Brodie. He was pared to the bone by a devouring disease yet he still had a sullen fire in his eyes at the mention of land, not even his land, but mine, Neville Hewitt told himself. If Brodie died before the first of November he would take the debt with him and he, Neville Hewitt, would be out of pocket. On the other hand if Brodie hung on past the first of the month he would be cried as a debtor and every implement, every cow, sheep and fowl that Brodie possessed would be sequestered and the old man and his family, including Rosie's seducer, would be flung on the mercy of the parish.

'Plantin' a few bushels o' seed,' Hewitt said, 'will not stay my hand.'

'It's not intended to stay your hand,' Matthew Brodie said. 'It's intended to feed sour ground an' make it bear a crop.'

'Do you expect me to wait for my arrears until you sell wheat that isn't even sown yet?' Hewitt kicked the stool away. 'I've been patient, Brodie, far too patient with you an' your whelps. You're six months – soon to be twelve – behind in the rent. I'll not be drawn into conciliation. You've no case to plead before the Sheriff, no leg to stand upon. If I'm not paid the full sum on the first o' November I'll have you cried as a debtor an' see you carried out o' this cottage on a litter.'

'Unless I die first,' Matthew Brodie reminded him.

'If that's God's will,' Hewitt said, 'so be it. But if you don't die you'll be buried in a pauper's grave, your wife an' daughter will be driven to the poorhouse an' your precious sons left without a pot to piss in. It's no more than you deserve, you an' that cocky brat o' yours who thinks he's good enough to court my daughter.'

'So that's it,' Janet said. 'It's a punishment on Tom.'

Hewitt swung round. 'No, that's not it, girl. I'm not the blackguard here. I want what's due me, no more, no less, but I'll wait no longer to get it.' He turned again to Matthew. 'Two weeks, Brodie, two weeks an' I'll be rid of you an' your brood an' Hawkshill will be leased to a better servant o' the land than you turned out to be.'

'You starved us,' Matthew wheezed. 'You promised us lime an' you promised us seed an' we got neither.'

'Excuses will serve no purpose now.'

The old man tried vainly to raise himself up but racked by a fit of coughing he toppled sideways on the bed and buried his face in the bolster.

Hewitt stepped to the door and, discarding any shred of pity for his tenant, called out, 'Two weeks, Brodie, fourteen days.' Then he trotted out into the yard to find his horse and beat a retreat before one of the boys came scurrying home to lay him by the heels and blame him for all their misfortunes.

Betsy found it hard to believe that Henry could curse so foully or conjure up so many hideous punishments for the flax manufacturer. He might have carried out his threats, too, have taken a scythe from the hook in the barn and have ridden off to rip out Neville Hewitt's guts if Tom hadn't pulled him from the stable, pinned him against the wall, shouted into his face and, with Betsy and Janet watching helplessly, pummelled him with his fists.

Henry did not attempt to defend himself and after a minute or so Tom stopped hitting him and steered him back into the stable. When they emerged a half-hour later Tom returned to the long field without a word to anyone and Henry, pale and trembling, entered the cottage.

Still greatly agitated, the old man was stretched out on top of the bed. He beckoned Henry to his side. Father and son remained deep in conversation while Janet prepared a thick slice of bread and cheese for Tom's dinner, wrapped it in paper and gave it to Betsy to take out to the field, together with a flagon of beer.

It was a still, grey morning, the sky lidded with cloud. Now the trees had shed their leaves Betsy could make out the sea. For a second or two she had the impression that it was not sea at all but ice and the peaks of the islands that lay off the coast were already coated with snow, though sense told her it was nothing but a layer of cold white cloud.

When she reached the field gate she called out to Tom.

Elbows cocked, head bowed, he ignored her and continued ploughing. Betsy leaned on the post of the gate until at length he reined the horses at the head of the field. He was meticulous in his method and showed no sign of rage as if, she thought, he had reconciled himself to ploughing this field or another like it for the rest of his days.

He signalled. She went to him and handed him the packet of bread and cheese, and the flagon. He was smeared with earth, his boots clay-clogged; his hair, untied, stuck out from under his cap like a hedgehog's spines – and yet, Betsy thought, he had never looked manlier than he did at that moment.

'What are you starin' at?' he said.

Betsy nodded at the sacks that she had brought out early that morning. 'Do you want me to give the horses their hay-bags?'

'Oh, aye,' Tom said, 'the horses must be fed. I'll do it.' He looked at her at last. 'What are you standin' there for? Have you no work to keep you busy?'

'Plenty o' work,' said Betsy. 'Don't you want me to stay?'

'Did Henry send you to look after me?'

'No.'

'Where is he?'

'In the house.'

'Talkin' to my father, I suppose?'

'Aye,' said Betsy.

'Is he bad, my daddy?'

'Aye, he's bad.'

'An' Henry?'

'Calmer now,' said Betsy.

Tom wiped his mouth with the ends of his scarf. 'If he'd gone harin' off to murder Hewitt I'd have lost my opportunity.'

'Opportunity?' said Betsy. 'What opportunity?'

'To marry Rose Hewitt,' Tom said. 'Rose wouldn't look favourable on a man whose brother had slaughtered her father, would she now?' He opened the packet and toyed with the bread. 'Do you think I stopped Henry from runnin' off in a temper because I've a conscience? Nah, nah! I'd gut that bastard Hewitt myself if he wasn't Rose's father.'

'Are you in love wi' Rose Hewitt?' Betsy asked.

Tom pursed his lips and lifted his chin. 'Indeed, I am,' he answered, 'but I'll have to wheedle her out o' that ogre's clutches afore he crushes her.'

'Run off wi' her, you mean?'

'If that's what it comes to, aye.'

'Your mammy, your sister: what will become o' them?'

'Henry'll take care o' them,' Tom said.

'Damned you are, Tom Brodie,' Betsy told him, 'to skip off wi' a girl you hardly know an' leave your brother to clear your daddy's debts. Is that why you're so keen to sow this field – to salve your conscience? Aye, well, I'm thinkin' your daddy's right to fear for you.'

'My daddy won't last the month,' Tom said. 'I'll bury him decent, like you said, but then' – he shrugged – 'then I'll be free to make my own way in this miserable world.'

'An' take her, Rose Hewitt, wi' you?'

'She's what I want.'

'Is that all that matters – what you want?'

With a flash of temper he tossed his dinner to the ground.

'By God,' he snarled, 'are you too damned stupid to see what's in front o' your nose, Betsy? Did that kick from a horse when you were a bairn addle your brains completely?'

'Stop it,' Betsy said. 'For pity's sake, Tom, stop it.'

'That ruined man, my daddy, that withered bundle o' bones is hardly fifty years old – he slaved all his days for others' profit. He worshipped God, praised His name an' begged forgiveness for sins he never had a chance to commit. Where's it got him? A bed in a hovel in the back end o' nowhere, spewin' out his life's blood while some snot not fit to wipe his arse duns him for money. Where's the prize for my daddy? Where's his reward? Tell me that, Betsy McBride. Well, I'll not be caught in that trap. What I want, I'll take.'

'An' pay the price?' Betsy said, barely holding back tears.

'What *is* the price? Twenty shillin's an acre for ground so sour it struggles to bear weeds? A nod from God's administrator in the kirk on Sunday? The good opinion o' men who care not a fig whether you live or die? Where's the dignity in that, tell me? Nah, nah! I'll have my prize now, thank you. I'll snatch my own reward.'

'An' burn in hell for it,' Betsy said.

She spun on her heel and stumbled over the furrows to the gate. She ran across the infield while Tom shook his fist at the sky and roared, 'This *is* hell, you stupid bitch! Don't you see it yet? *This* is hell.'

He was still roaring when Betsy reached the top of the hill track, and with her hands clapped over her ears set off for Hayes and her father's house, leaving Tom Brodie and Hawkshill behind.

The visit was announced by card which in Mrs Prole's view marked it as something special from the beginning. Only gentlemen used cards and only gentlemen thoughtfully indicated that they would require tea. She sent Dorothy to buy fresh bread and a pound of boiled ox tongue which, she recalled, was a cold cut much favoured by Mr Fergusson, then, rolling up her sleeves, she reached for the flour bin and greased up the griddle to bake scones.

If Neville had been at home he might have indicated that the rather formal tea-taking had a purpose other than mere social intercourse, but the master had ridden out to Hawkshill and it was almost one o'clock in the afternoon when he returned. He went at once to the cupboard in the parlour to pour a tumbler of whisky which he drank in two swallows before he came into the kitchen with the card in his hand.

'When did this arrive?'

'About ten o'clock,' Eunice told him. 'I've brought in bread and meat an' I'll serve bramble jelly with the scones. Did things go well with the Brodies?'

'Well enough,' Neville said grimly. 'The old man will die soon.'

'An' the sons?'

'I didn't encounter the sons.' He paused. 'See that she's washed an' combed an' wears her prettiest dress, then bring her down about half past three.'

'Is she to take tea with us?' Eunice said.

'Mr Fergusson will expect her to be present.'

'Will he?' Eunice raised an eyebrow. 'Why will he expect such a thing?'

'She's been a prisoner upstairs long enough. It's time she learned how to behave in company.' He pulled a watch from his vest pocket and squinted at it. 'If we're takin' tea at four I'll do without my dinner. I've business at the manufactory but I'll be back in time to welcome our guests.'

'Our guests?' said Eunice. 'Is Mrs Fergusson comin' too?'

'Somehow I doubt it,' Neville said and before she could interrogate him further, headed out to find his horse and ride the short distance to the works.

'Mr Fergusson!' Rose exclaimed. 'My, my! How can I contain my excitement at being invited downstairs to take tea with Mr Fergusson?'

'Sarcasm does not become a lady,' Mrs Prole said. 'See, I've brought warm water so you can wash afore you dress. I'll send Dorothy up to attend to your hair presently. Your father wants you to look pretty.'

'Is it really so long since you've seen me that you've forgotten how pretty I am? Now, what shall I wear, I wonder? Shall I wear my short frocks so that Mr Fergusson might admire the scars on my legs?'

Eunice Prole did not rise to the bait.

'Or,' Rose went on, 'shall I accoutre myself in an apron and a robe without a breast knot so that Mr Fergusson may judge for himself just how much I have swelled since you locked me away up here?'

'I did not—'

'Of course you did not, dear Mrs Prole,' Rose interrupted. 'I've been in voluntary retreat, enjoying a period of quiet contemplation, and I am the better for it.' Lifting a piece of sponge from the water basin, she dabbed each cheek in turn. 'I am reformed in my ways, you see. I'll associate no more with coarse farmers and servants in the gardens of ale-houses. I'll await whatever fate Papa has chosen for me with perfect equanimity.'

'Have you finished wi' your dinner?' Mrs Prole enquired.

'Yes, see, I have eaten every morsel. You may, if you wish, remove the plate. Will meat be provided for our illustrious visitor?'

'Ox tongue.'

'Fit for king,' said Rose approvingly.

Mrs Prole raised her arm then lowered it again. She did, however, point her forefinger and in a tone that mingled caution with command told her master's daughter that she'd do well to guard her tongue.

'Or what?' said Rose, smiling. 'Or what, dear Mrs Prole?'

The housekeeper had no ready answer to that question, and thoroughly flummoxed by Rose's knowing tone retreated downstairs to bake another batch of griddle scones.

'Why, Lucas, what a pleasant surprise.' Rose offered the young man her hand but he did not seem to know what to do with it. She bestowed her winsome smile on Daddy Fergusson instead. 'How thoughtful of you to bring Lucas to visit us, Mr Fergusson. It's been many a year since last your son and I met face to face – at a preaching in St Quivox, if memory serves. If I may be pardoned for remarking upon it, he has grown exceedingly handsome.'

'Has he?' Walter Fergusson shot a glance at his one and only in the vain hope of catching him blushing. 'Aye, Miss Hewitt, I suppose he has.'

'Come now, Mr Fergusson, let's dispense with formality. Do, please, call me Rose as you have done since I was a tiny girl and you visited with Mama when Papa was not at home and, as I recall, pinched my cheek and gave me sweetmeats.' Rose waved in the direction of the door. 'Speaking of Papa, I must offer an apology on his behalf. I assume he has been detained at the manufactory – or, perhaps, that you were early in arrival.'

'Perhaps a wee bit,' Walter Fergusson conceded, 'a minute or two.'

'A quarter-hour, I believe,' said Rose. 'However, what does time matter when old friends are brought together?'

'Aye, old friends,' Lucas grunted in response to a dig in the ribs from his father. 'Right you are, Miss – ah . . .'

Rose wondered if Lucas had already forgotten her name or if he did not quite know into whose parlour he had been dragged, let alone the reason for it.

It had not taken her long to conclude that with a ragged lover lurking in the wings, her father would attempt to marry her off to the first available suitor with any sort of pedigree and that Fergusson's numbskull son was precisely the sort of fellow Papa would choose, given that expediency was the watchword and the idiot boy so handy.

In repose Lucas Fergusson's features were unremarkable. His lashes were a shade too fair and his mouth a trifle too girlish but she'd seen worse-looking young men round and about the town. It was only when you caught sight of his eyes, pale to the point of transparency and as vacant as an empty house, that you realised that young Mr Fergusson's head was not occupied by much in the way of intelligence.

'Shall we wait for tea?' she said. 'It wants but five minutes to four o'clock and I expect Papa to come bounding through the door at any moment. If you are famished, though, I'll instruct the housekeeper to serve at once.'

'Tea?' Lucas licked his lips. 'Is there cake, but?'

'Scones with bramble jelly,' Rose said. 'Do you like scones, Lucas?'

'I like cake.'

'Well, perhaps there will be cake too,' said Rose. 'Tell me, Mr Fergusson, what is the nature of the business that brings you here by prior announcement? Does it concern flax or corn, or cattle perhaps?'

'No, it – ah . . .'

'Does it concern me?'

'Now why would it concern you?' Walter Fergusson said. 'Has your daddy been talkin' out of turn?'

'My daddy has not been talking at all,' Rose said. 'In the absence of your wife, I thought you'd taken it upon yourself to act as an intermediary.'

'To intermediate on what?' Walter said defensively.

'To ensure that everything is square and above board,' said Rose. 'I find such caution admirable. One cannot be too careful in fostering virtuous intercourse between young people.'

'Intercourse?' said Walter.

'I may be just a simple country girl, Mr Fergusson, but I am familiar with the manner in which such delicate matters are handled by gentlemen of quality.'

'What delicate matters?' said Walter.

Rose placed a hand on the grazier's knee and looked at him with an expression that baffled the already bewildered dealer.

Softly, she said, 'I will be only too pleased to accompany Lucas – properly chaperoned, of course – to the dancing school on the Friday after next.'

'The dancing school?' said Walter.

'Oh!' Rose sat back. 'I'm sorry. I thought it was your intention to encourage a friendship between your son and I by allowing us – properly chaperoned, of course – to test the waters with an evening of instruction at Mr Arbuthnot's dancing school?'

'Lucas isn't trained in the dancin'.'

'No more am I,' said Rose. 'Indeed not, but with a suitable partner – properly chaperoned, of course – I am anxious to learn.'

By now Walter Fergusson knew he was being manipulated. Under other circumstances he would have resented it, particularly as the manipulator was a sweet-faced sixteen-year-old. But he could not deny that if the girl had moved swiftly she had at least moved in the right direction.

'Lucas.' He nudged the boy again. 'Miss Hewitt is keen for to learn to dance. If you ask her, I'm sure she'd be willin' to have you as her partner.'

'Dance?' said Lucas; then loudly, pitifully, 'Dance!'

At that moment, to Walter's relief, the door opened and Neville Hewitt, full of apologies, bustled into the parlour.

Before he could so much as remove his hat to mop his brow Rose threw herself into his arms, crying out in great excitement, 'Oh, Papa! Guess what?'

And within five minutes the matter was settled.

It was after ten o'clock when Henry arrived at the weaver's house. Mr McBride had been on the point of raking the fire and snuffing out the candles and was a little too slow in calling out a warning to his youngest who, without caution, flipped the latch and flung open the door.

Lit only by the lantern in his hand, the figure in the doorway appeared threatening and Jock McBride's first thought was that it was a robber. He caught Effie by the shoulder and pulled her back, then, squinting, recognised the late-night caller.

'I've come to offer an apology,' Henry said.

'An apology for what?' said Weaver McBride.

'For the way my brother treated your daughter.'

'Oh!' said Mr McBride. 'An' what way was that?'

'He lost his temper an' said things that should not have been said,' Henry explained, 'least of all to a lass who came to us out o' the goodness of her heart.'

'Did your brother strike her?'

'Betsy? No, no,' said Henry. 'If he had struck her, my mother would have laid him out wi' a stick. Besides, it's not in Tom's nature to lift his hand to the fair sex. Is Betsy asleep?'

'She is, fast asleep.'

'I'd be obliged if you'd waken her.' Henry took off his hat. 'I wish to have a few words with her, but I'll not keep her long from her bed.'

'You want her back,' Mr McBride stated.

'I do,' said Henry. 'We do. My mother was fair offended by Tom's behaviour an' insisted I approach wi' an olive branch.'

'Is our Betsy that useful to you?'

'Most useful,' said Henry, 'especially at this sorry time.'

Jock looked down at Effie who had been standing just behind him, all agog. 'Go an' waken your sister,' he said, 'an' your mammy.'

Then he ushered Henry into the kitchen.

Drowsy and a little confused, Betsy pulled on an old canvas smock to serve as a robe and padded barefoot and blinking into the kitchen to find Henry already seated at the table with a glass of her father's whisky in his hand.

He looked up and gave her a small, tight smile.

She was not entirely surprised to see Henry, nor was she displeased. She was not embarrassed by her tousled appearance; she had lived cheek by jowl with the Brodies for weeks and did not have much to hide. Betsy nodded, pulled out a chair and seated herself.

Henry came straight to the point. 'Tom shouldn't have spoken to you as he did, Betsy. I'm here to apologise for his ill-considered remarks an' ask if you'll return with me to Hawks-hill.'

'Does Tom want me back?'

'He does.'

'Why didn't he come with you?'

'He's too ashamed,' said Henry.

'So he should be,' said Betsy. 'Did he tell you what was said?'

Henry shook his head. 'Only that he swore at you.'

'I've been swore at before,' said Betsy.

'What was it then?' Henry asked. 'What did he say to offend you?'

'Aye, lass, tell us what was said,' her mother urged.

Betsy doubted if Henry had any inkling of what was on Tom's mind. Whatever secrets the brothers shared, Tom's plan to cast aside his responsibilities and desert the family was surely not among them. How could she explain that she had been cut to the quick by Tom's admission that he was in love with Rose Hewitt? She didn't know if he was moved by desire, by greed or by a need for revenge – and she doubted if Tom quite knew himself.

'It isn't Tom or what he said,' she heard herself say. 'It's just that I've never seen a man die slow before.'

'Why didn't I think of it?' Henry said. 'Poor old Betsy, havin' to put up with our hardships an' our tears for no reward worth the mention.'

The truth was that while she felt sympathy for the old man she was not repelled by the trappings of death. In fact, she felt more alive on gloomy Hawkshill than she had ever done in Johnny Rankine's cowsheds. There was a raw edge to the Brodies' reckless confrontation with defeat, and their refusal to be humbled by failure struck more of a chord with her than she cared to admit.

'Mr Rankine pays her,' her father said. 'She's still John Rankine's servant, not yours, Mr Brodie.'

'That's true,' Henry conceded. 'If it was within my power I'd offer Betsy twice what Rankine pays her but we're poor, Mr McBride. There's no skatin' round the fact. I have my seven pounds a year, an' Tom the same. My sister works for keep. Five hands for seventy acres might seem excessive but before he was struck down my father put in work enough for two men.'

'No need to explain your situation to me, Mr Brodie,' her father said. 'For you it's the ploughshare; for me, the loom. I know only too well the difference an extra pair o' hands can make. If Betsy has the stomach for it then by all means let her go with you. But it's not for me to tell her what to do.'

Betsy looked directly at Henry, eye to eye.

'When Mr Brodie dies, what then?' she asked.

'It's a fair question, Betsy, but not one I can answer.'

'If you lose Hawkshill . . .'

'We will not lose Hawkshill.'

'Mr Hewitt'll try to take it from you.'

'He'll not succeed,' Henry said.

'How will you stop him?'

'God knows!' said Henry. 'But we will, Betsy, with your help we will.'

'What difference can I make?'

'Who will I have to talk to in the late hours if you desert us?' Henry said lightly. 'Who will Tom have to lean on?'

'Betsy,' her mother said, 'give the young man an answer.'

'Aye,' Betsy heard herself say. 'I'll come by again tomorrow.'

To her surprise, she heard Henry sigh, then, still without embarrassment, he reached out for her hand and kissed it.

7

If Rose expected a setting fit for a celestial entertainment and Mrs Prole had anticipated something closer to the last days of Gomorrah both were disappointed. Drennan's little assembly hall was lighted not by glittering chandeliers but by a dozen tapers stuck to a cartwheel that dangled perilously close to the dancers' heads, and it smelled not of perfume and powder but of old sweat mingled with the odour of the piggery that, rather unfortunately, backed on to its outer wall.

On a small crescent-shaped platform three fiddlers in stained trousers and leather vests greased their bows while Mr James Arbuthnot, tall and stooped, welcomed eager students of Terpsichore to his travelling academy and relieved them of sixpence at the door.

Once, long, long ago, the venerable gentleman had taught the steps of the *Allemande* in the ballroom of Copplestone House. Before that he had served as an instructor to several grown men in Edinburgh who were anxious not to trip about like fools at royal assemblies. Since those glory days, however, Mr Arbuthnot had fallen on hard times. He earned his living now by travelling about the country setting up 'progressives' for a peasantry who had no patience with intricate French steps or insipid English formations and turned every dance, circular or linear, into a wild Scotch romp.

Rose entered the hall on Lucas Fergusson's arm, Mrs Prole a bare half step behind. Lucas parted with a shilling willingly enough but a brief altercation about the entrance fee for chaperones followed.

It had been many a long day since Mr Arbuthnot had encountered a chaperone let alone had his nose bitten off by one but with a crowd of lads and lassies clamouring in the narrow corridor just outside, he admitted the woman at no cost but with a murmured warning not to place one foot upon the floor or he would personally wrestle her to the ground to extract his tutor's fee.

Mrs Prole smirked at the notion of being wrestled to the floor by the elderly dancing master but he spoke so quietly and with such refinement that she elected to treat his threat as a joke and, with a flip of her gloved hand and a flutter of her eyelashes, led her charges into the crowded hall.

She steered them to one of the wooden benches that flanked the dancing floor and barked at a clutch of young ruffians who were furtively sipping whisky from a leather flask. The ruffians prudently beat a retreat and Mrs Prole commandeered the bench.

She was the oldest person in the room, apart from the dancing master and possibly one of the fiddlers. She recognised two or three faces without being able to put names to them and was appalled at the number of girls and young men who had managed to beg or borrow a sixpence to take instruction in this pointless pastime. Where was the poverty, she asked herself, where was the hardship one heard so much about? And why, come to think of it, did Neville's scheming daughter need protection from Fergusson's unassuming son?

Unassuming was not the word that sprang to Rose's mind in respect of Lucas Fergusson. He was clean enough, polished almost. His father had tricked him out in a dress coat, a florid waistcoat and a pair of brand-new, very fashionable long-toed shoes with gleaming buckles and medium-high heels.

She could not decide if Lucas was fascinated by his new footwear or had some unsuspected defect in the bones of his neck, for he had hardly raised his head from his chest from the moment he had arrived to collect her in the ponytrap. If Lucas did not care to gaze upon her beauty, she consoled herself with the thought that every other eye in the room was upon her as she was not only the prettiest girl present she was also the only one who might, without conceit, lay claim to being a lady.

'Miss Hewitt.' Mr Ogilvy delivered a courtly bow. 'What an unexpected pleasure to see you at our modest gatherin'.'

Mrs Prole had not forgotten him from their brief encounter in the ale-house garden. She placed an arm across Rose's midriff as if she feared that the not-so-young man intended to haul the girl from the bench and ravish her.

'And who might you be, sir?'

Mr Ogilvy adjusted his wig, a simple toupee with small side curls.

'Robert Ogilvy, coal merchant, presently resident in Drennan.'

'How, if I may ask, are you acquainted with Miss Hewitt?'

'Through a mutual friend,' Mr Ogilvy answered, not quite as tactfully as Rose might have wished.

'Does this "mutual friend" have a name?' said Mrs Prole.

Rose managed to catch Mr Ogilvy's eye without being too obvious about it. He cleared his throat. 'Frye, madam. Peter Frye.'

'Is Mr Frye here this evening?' Rose enquired.

'He is expected,' Mr Ogilvy answered.

'Alone,' Rose said, 'or in company?'

'In company.'

'Not, I trust, in company wi' that blackguard from Crawford's yard?' Mrs Prole said.

'No, madam,' said Mr Ogilvy. 'That blackguard has gone back to sea.'

'To sea?' said Mrs Prole, puzzled.

'To Ireland,' Mr Ogilvy explained. 'If that's the blackguard you mean?'

'Oh, you are all blackguards to me,' said Mrs Prole.

'Some blacker than others, though,' said Mr Ogilvy, with a twinkle, then wandered off to wait by the door to warn Tom Brodie what to expect.

Tom said, 'She made no mention of fetchin' along with a partner.'

'What do you want from the poor girl?' said Peter. 'I imagine it was difficult enough for her to smuggle out a note through that half-witted maid of hers without rambling off into fine details.'

'I'd hardly call yon housekeeper a fine detail,' Tom said. 'Who's the boy? Is it Fergusson's son – or am I mistaken?'

'No,' said Mr Ogilvy, 'you're not mistaken.'

'God, will you look at his shoes?' Tom said. 'Does he think the Drennan dancin' school carries the same prestige as a ball in Auld Reekie?'

'Does he think at all? that's the question,' said Mr Ogilvy.

The men huddled at the door. Now that they had paid the entry fee they were free to come and go as they pleased.

Mr Arbuthnot had closed the inner door and, with his takings secured in a pouch in his trouser pocket, had jingled his way to the centre of the room and was busily organising the first dance of the evening, a longwise introductory 'For as Many as Will' which would lure all but the shyest on to the floor and spark the first of the evening's innumerable flirtations.

He demonstrated a few simple steps, male first then female, and as the fiddlers struck up with 'The Lads o' Dunse', grabbed one startled lass and swept her up and down the length of the hall while the students cheered and applauded.

He broke and peeled most elegantly, then swiftly organised four long lines and, with his hands above his head, brought the fiddlers in on the beat.

'Where is she?' Tom said, on tiptoe. 'Is she in the line?'

'Nah,' said Mr Ogilvy. 'See, she's still planted on the bench.'

'What's wrong wi' droopy Fergusson?' Tom said. 'Has he no gumption? How can he sit there stiff as clay when the music plays? Well, damn it, if he won't make a move, I will.'

'Wait.' Peter Frye clasped his friend's arm. 'Bide your time, man. The Medusa will strike you dead if you rush at her headlong.'

With his father close to death and the threat of eviction hanging over him, Tom had abandoned the idea of attending the dancing school until, that is, Rose had persuaded her maid to deliver a note to Peter Frye at his father's chambers, indicating that she would be taking her first lessons in the art of dance from Mr Arbuthnot and hoped that she would find friends there.

'Look,' Tom said, through his teeth. 'See how she watches. She's waitin' for me, you know. That lumpkin Fergusson's just a diversion.' The lines went up and down, pairing, setting, bumping, skipping and peeling away. 'I don't know how Rose got here,' he went on, 'but I know she's come for me.'

Then, still muttering, he plunged from the huddle at the door and, to Mr Arbuthnot's chagrin, locked on to the end of the gentlemen's line, clapping and setting to a non-existent partner in full view of the pretty lass from Thimble Row, her surly beau and her chaperone.

Betsy clung to Henry's waist with both arms and hugged the horse's flanks with her thighs. She had never been on a horse before, let alone shared a saddle with a man. She was not entirely sure she liked the sensation, particularly when Henry spurred the animal to a trot as soon as they struck the toll road.

It was very dark and there was nothing to guide them but a bobbing lantern strapped to a wooden frame above the horse's collar, a lantern that seemed to Betsy to scatter light in all directions save the right one.

She leaned her chin against his shoulder and yelled. 'Henry, are you sure about this?'

He turned his head, the brim of his hat brushing her cheek. 'Certain.'

'What if he's not there?'

'Oh, he'll be there.'

'Did he say somethin' to you? He said nothin' to me.'

'He doesn't have to say anythin',' said Henry. 'I can read his intentions like a book. I'll wager a year's wages he's gone dancin' in Drennan.'

'Why not leave him to it?'

'She might be there,' said Henry. 'The Hewitt girl.'

'Rose?'

'Aye, Rose.'

'She'll not be there,' said Betsy. 'Her daddy won't let her go.'

'Daddy or no daddy' – Henry wrenched on the reins – 'if she's as mad in love wi' our Tom as he claims she is, she'll find a way.'

'Is she mad in love wi' Tom?' said Betsy.

'He says she is,' Henry said. 'For once I think he may be right.'

'But why?' Betsy's teeth rattled against Henry's shoulder. 'Why do we have to go there? Can't Tom take care o' himself?'

'Hoh!' Henry exclaimed, wrenching the reins again. 'When it comes to women Tom's never been able to take care o' himself.'

'Is it because she's Rose Hewitt?'

' 'Course it is,' said Henry. 'By God, Betsy, if you give my brother the sniff o' a skirt, next thing you know there's a female at the door wi' a bairn in her arms cryin' out to be married.'

'Has that happened before?'

'Twice,' said Henry. 'Twice the lassies had to be bought off.'

The horse picked up speed. Betsy bobbed up and down. Her rump hurt and the insides of her thighs felt as if they were on fire.

Henry craned back and shouted, 'No wonder my daddy has no faith in him. I tell you, Betsy, my brother's led us all a merry dance these past seven years. He's contrite one minute an' the next he's glowerin' an' stubborn an' blamin' the poor girls for leadin' him on.'

Betsy swallowed several mouthfuls of cold night air.

'Does – does Tom have children, then?' she asked.

'Hah!' Henry yelled. 'He says not. He says there's not a word o' truth in any o' the accusations made against him. He says he's a victim o' several misunderstandings, though he accepted his reprimand from the Kirk Session an' repented in front o' the whole congregation. My daddy was filled wi' black burnin' shame. It was the best part of a year afore he spoke civil to Tom. If my mam hadn't stood up for him Tom would have been flung out o' the house.'

'When did it all take place?'

'Seven years since,' said Henry. 'The last time was just before we leased Hawkshill. Tom's the reason we had to clear out o' our family holdin', a fine, neat wee farm o' fifty-five acres near Ballantrae where my daddy settled after marriage. It was like tearin' up a root for Dad to leave there – an' excuse it how you will, it was all Tom's fault.'

'What age was Tom then?'

'Seventeen,' said Henry. 'Seventeen years old an' all he had to do was squint at a female out o' the corner of his eye an' she fell pregnant.'

'Were they ladies?'

'Nah, nah,' said Henry. 'Tinkers in for to help wi' the harvest, both of them. If they hadn't been tinkers Tom would never have got away with it. With tinkers there's always doubt.'

'What happened to the lassies?'

'Daddy sold our stock to pay them off an' they went away.'

'An' the babbies?'

'Gone too.' Henry rocked in the saddle. 'Now do you see why we're headin' for Drennan before Tom can do more damage?'

'But why have you fetched me along?'

'To help me lure him away.'

'Like a goat does wi' a randy ram, you mean?' said Betsy.

'Aye,' said Henry, 'that's it exactly.'

In a flutter of sleeve-ribbons and handkerchiefs, she was on her feet and gone before Eunice Prole could raise a finger to stop her. One moment she was seated quite demurely between the chaperone and Fergusson's lad and the next she was hand in hand with Tom Brodie, setting and stepping with her head tossed back. He looked into her eyes, grinning, turned her with a flick of his wrist, cupped her slender waist and they whirled around quite out of sequence while Mr Arbuthnot cried, 'No, damn it, Brodie, no, no, no.'

He reached for Tom's shoulder.

Tom shrugged him off.

When Eunice Prole shot up and squirted towards him, he executed a simple reverse and swinging Rose on his arm, hop-skipped to the tail of the second line and, splitting, followed the trail to the head of the set and met his love again with an expression so sunny and surprised that the quick little kiss they exchanged beneath the arch of hands and arms seemed as natural as daybreak.

Tom was on the floor, Tom Brodie! The fiddlers picked up

the tempo and the clapping became louder. The young men cheered and the girls giggled as Tom elevated his partner and spun her round and round, her feet hardly touching the floor, round and down and back into the tail of the line again while the skinny old woman vainly ran after them and the dancing master ran after her in a comical variation of pursuit before punishment which every mischievous labourer and butterfingered scullion understood.

They knew Tom Brodie, they knew him well. The lads envied him the dainty piece from Thimble Row who was as untouchable as communion plate and as precious as crystal glass. And the lassies envied her because she had captured Tom, their stack-yard hero, and would soon have what they had only dreamed about, a good stiff ploughing from the golden boy who, as all but the dullest among them could plainly see, had fallen in love again.

'You.' Eunice kicked young Lucas on the shin. 'Get up an' do somethin'.'

'Do what?' said Lucas.

'Catch her. Stop him. Strike him down.'

'That's Tom Brodie, but,' Lucas said.

'I don't care if it's Moses descended from Sinai.' Mrs Prole nabbed the young man by the ear. 'Stop him before he does somethin' terrible.'

'Terrible?'

'For God's sake, are you more mouse than man?' Eunice Prole hoisted him up by his most prominent feature and ignoring his cries of 'Ow, ow, ow,' projected him into the skein of dancers. Then, wheeling, she confronted the outraged Mr Arbuthnot and howled, 'Sixpence, sixpence for this – this hooley. You'll get not one farthin' from me, sir.'

'Tush!' said Mr Arbuthnot. 'You are a fiery one, are you not, madam?'

Trapping her bony hands in his, he tugged her on to the floor and throwing order to the winds, broke into the line and dragged her up the corridor of clapping hands, up and down again, then with an arm about her middle, danced her towards the half-open door where with a cheerful cry of, 'Out, madam? Out or in?' he pinned her against the wall.

'Unhand me, sir,' said Eunice Prole, 'or I'll have your pillock threaded on a string.'

'You may do as you wish with my pillock,' Mr Arbuthnot said, '*after* you've paid me my sixpence. Now, old lady, what's it to be? Out,' – he nudged her with his pelvis, – 'or in?'

'I – I do not have sixpence,' said Eunice, oddly subdued.

'Shall I take my fee in kind then?' said Mr Arbuthnot.

Mrs Prole had no need to ask the gentleman what he meant by 'kind'. She was tactful enough to consider his offer for a moment before, with a simpering smile, she said, 'How generous of you, sir, but if you turn around you'll see I've a gallant of my own – an' that, I believe, is a sixpence in his hand.'

'Here, Mr Arbuthnot,' Robert Ogilvy said. 'Here's your fee.'

Mr Arbuthnot released the chaperone and, more relieved than disappointed, accepted the coin. He knew Ogilvy by name as well as sight, for the ageing bachelor had been a student of the dance for many years.

Slipping the sixpence into his pouch, Mr Arbuthnot stepped away from the half-open door and with a final deep bow to the woman, said, 'Welcome to Arbuthnot's school of dance, madam. Since you've had a taste of my technique at no cost, do you wish further instruction now it's been paid for?'

'No,' said Eunice Prole curtly. 'I do not.'

With a little tap on Mr Ogilvy's sleeve and a whispered 'Good luck,' the dancing master went off up the side of the hall to signal a change of tune.

With a final rasping flourish the fiddlers finished the round. They laid their instruments across their knees and reached for their kerchiefs to mop their brows while the dancers, many already paired off, waited, chattering excitedly, for the next dance to begin.

'Thank you,' Mrs Prole said, 'for your timely intervention, Mr Ogilvy.'

'It's the least I could do,' said Mr Ogilvy. 'It's not often we have the pleasure of entertainin' a woman of more – of slightly more mature years at our gatherings. There's no obligation for you to do so, but I'd consider it a great honour if you'd join me in the next dance which is, I believe' – he held a hand to his ear as the fiddlers struck the opening chord – 'a Strathspey.'

'I'm not here to dance, Mr Ogilvy,' said Eunice Prole. 'I'm here to provide an escort to Miss Hewitt an' Mr Fergusson an' see they don't—'

'Don't?' said Mr Ogilvy. 'Don't what, Mrs Prole?'

'Where is he? Where's Brodie?' She raised herself to her full height with a hand on Mr Ogilvy's shoulder. 'An' where's Rose?'

'I'm afraid,' said Mr Ogilvy, trying hard not to smile, 'they've gone.'

'All right, Peter,' Henry said, 'where are they?'

'I really have no idea,' Peter Frye said. 'His mare's still tethered at the rail so they can't have gone far.'

'Unfortunately, Tom doesn't have to go far,' said Henry grimly. He turned to Mr Ogilvy. 'I thought better of you, Robert. Have you no sense?'

'I did no more than was asked of me,' Mr Ogilvy said. 'If it hadn't been me, Tom would have found another conspirator. He has no shortage of friends ready to join him in a prank.'

'Prank!' said Henry. 'This is no prank – an' well you know it.'

'Henry,' Betsy put in, 'are you sure he's taken the girl with him?'

'Of course he has,' Henry answered. 'How did he know she'd be here? Peter, did you have somethin' to do with it?'

'She sent me a note,' Peter admitted, 'which, in effect, was intended for Tom. What choice did I have but to pass the information on to him?'

'How did she get here, though?' said Betsy.

'She brought a sweetheart with her as well as the house-keeper,' Mr Ogilvy explained. 'A clever manoeuvre on her part, don't you think?'

'A sweetheart?' said Betsy. 'Where's he now?'

'There, sitting on the bench.' Peter nodded. 'I question if he's even aware of what's going on let alone what it means.'

'An' Prole?' said Henry. 'Where's she?'

'She rushed out, presumably to scour the streets for the errant child,' Peter said. 'Won't you concede there's a degree of humour in all this, Henry? Tom may wish to tweak Hewitt's nose, but he's no fool. He'll bring the girl back none the worse for wear.'

'Unless . . .' Betsy bit her lip.

Henry rounded on her. 'Unless what?'

'Unless he's run off with her,' said Betsy.

She was too young to favour hoops and too slender to require tight lacing. She shook out the ringlets it had taken Dorothy so long to arrange and when Tom slid his knee between her thighs, tilted forward and, crushing her skirts and petticoats into her lap, rode upon it as a child might ride a rocking-horse.

He rubbed his tongue across her lips and she stuck out the tip of her tongue and teased him with it. Reaching between her legs she dragged up her skirts and felt the long, hard muscle of his thigh against her flesh. He put his free hand under her and hoisted her higher, her breasts crushed against his forearm, and the length of him pressing against her belly.

'*Rose, Rose?*' The voice grew louder. '*Rose, where are you?*'

Together they listened to the thudding music from the hall and the woman's strident cries. 'She won't find us here, will she?'

'No one will find us here,' Tom said, 'not until we're ready to be found.'

'And when,' Rose whispered, 'will that be?'

'Never,' he said and laughed.

There was no furniture in the library save a table, a wooden chair and an unlit lamp. An old man from the Agricultural Society opened the place for a couple of hours on two or three evenings a week but the door was rarely locked.

'Have you brought other girls here?' Rose asked.

'No,' Tom answered. 'I'm not the opportunist you take me for.'

There were noises outside, horse sounds and voices, the clatter of the hall door opening and closing again.

'I do not take you for anything,' Rose said.

'You've heard the slanders about me, I suppose?'

'I care nothing for slanders,' Rose said. 'I love you.'

'More fool you, Rose Hewitt,' Tom said.

She said, 'Do you not love me?'

'Aye,' he said. 'Aye, Rose, that's my predicament.'

'Don't you of all people know what to do with a girl who loves you?'

'Damn it, Rose, I'd know what to do if I *didn't* love you.'

'Then do it.'

'I can't.'

'Kiss me.' She nuzzled him. 'Put your hand on me. I'm ready for it.'

'It's not what you want, though, is it?'

'Yes, my dearest, it is what I want.'

'Well, it's not what you deserve,' he said.

'Who are you to say what I deserve?' she asked.

'Is Fergusson the fellow your father's chosen for you to marry?'

'I expect he is,' she said. 'But I'll not marry him, not to please my father – and certainly not to please you.'

'It wouldn't please me,' Tom said. 'It'd be wasteful to see you squandered on such a weak-kneed fool as Lucas Fergusson. He wouldn't know what to do with you.'

'Would you?'

'Indeed, I would,' Tom said.

'Then show me.'

'I'll show you only when I'm deservin' of it.' He reached out and drew her to him. 'Make no mistake,' he said thickly, 'I've wanted you since the moment our lips touched that night in the rain, but I want you for my wife not my lover. You're too good for that.'

'Are you afraid of my father?'

'I'm not afraid of your father, Rose, I'm afraid of you.'

'Afraid of me,' she said, 'but why?'

'Because I know you'll break my heart,' Tom said, then, to her astonishment, he took her hand and led her back out into the hall.

Although Janet had never been to the dancing school she had heard talk in the village that it was a grand place to catch a man. She could not understand why she had not been invited to accompany Henry to Drennan and why he had taken Rankine's bitch with him instead. There were many things Janet did not understand, or preferred not to understand. She had a natural gift for separating cause from effect and ignoring everything that did not contribute to an inner life composed mainly of grievances and day dreams.

Tonight, for instance, she nurtured an irrational notion that her father might pass away in time to let her tie up her skirts, throw on her shawl and hare along the road to Drennan to join in the last reel or two. But when she peered down at her daddy, stretched out in bed, she knew he would not die this evening and was inclined to believe that he would not die at all.

She retreated, sulkily, to her room, peeled off her clothes, kicked a bolster into shape, punched the straw-filled mattress, pitched herself into bed and pulled the covers over her head.

'Agnes,' Matthew Brodie whispered, 'has Janet left us?'

'Aye, dearest. She's gone to her bed.'

'Are we here alone?'

'We are, Matthew, we are.'

'Come closer. I can hardly make you out.'

Agnes Brodie was too small to kneel by the bed, too frightened of hurting her husband in his frail state to lie by his side. This past fortnight she had slept on a chair by the hearth. Henry had offered her his bed and Tom had told her he would build her a little nest out of canvas and straw, but she was happy enough to drowse in the chair or when Matthew's cough slackened to ease herself gently on to the bed and stretch out at his feet, like a cat.

She carried a chair to the bedside, knelt on the seat and rested her chin on her arms. Look at you now, Matthew Brodie, she thought, with your bones poking through your skin, your eyes staring out of your head and your mouth sunk like a heel-print in sand. You were a fine catch once, my love, but only a fool would have you now. And when he opened his eyes, she kissed him, once upon the cheek and once upon the brow.

He spoke so faintly that she had to stoop to hear him.

'What day is this?'

'Tuesday,' Agnes answered.

'Is it dark outside?'

'It is.'

Three days,' he said, 'to the month's end. We must do it soon?'

'Do what, dearest?'

'Take me to meet my Saviour.'

'Oh, Matthew, Matthew!' she said. 'Jesus will call you when He's ready.'

'I canna wait for Him to be ready,' her husband said. 'I'd do the thing myself if I had the strength. How much o' the doctor's medicine is left?'

'Only a drop or two. We'll purchase more tomorrow.'

'No,' he said. 'No more. Now we're alone, just the two o' us, take the bolster an' put it o'er my face.'

'Stop it,' the woman said. 'I'll have no more o' this talk.'

A sudden, shocking surge of energy brought him upright. He caught her by the nape of the neck. 'Where's Tom?'

'Gone to Drennan.'

'Dancin'?'

'Aye.'

'Henry?'

'Gone to fetch him.'

'Hawkshill's a poor bit o' ground but it's all I have an' it must serve as Tom's anchor. Grand it would be if he married the big lass Rankine sent us. She's a worker, you say, an' she has his measure?'

'It seems so, aye.'

'Then there's some hope for him, I suppose.' He released his hold. 'Do it now, Agnes. Take up the bolster an' put it o'er my face. My debts'll go wi' me to the grave an' you can get on wi' your weepin' free o' Hewitt's clamour.'

She stepped back from the bed, tipping over the chair in her haste. She swung round and glanced at the door of her daughter's room. She was afraid that Janet would come rushing out and that Matthew would instruct his daughter to do what she, his wife, could not do, not to save Hawkshill, not to spite the greedy landlord, not even out of love.

'Agnes,' her husband said. 'Agnes, please.'

She lifted the chair and placed it by the table, as far as possible from the curtain, the bolster and the dying man. Then, because she could no longer bear to be alone with him, she threw open the door and ran out into the yard to watch for her boys coming home.

When Eunice Prole eventually made her way back to the hall she was so relieved at finding Rose apparently unharmed that she wouldn't have cared if the girl had been dancing with the devil.

The floor was crowded, the benches empty. Lucas Fergusson had been kidnapped by Nancy Ames, a flouncy young thing from his father's cowshed. He was clumsily following the girl's lead while trying to protect his new shoes from damage. Tom Brodie, his brother Henry, Peter Frye, the weaver's daughter and old Mr Ogilvy were all on the floor, spinning like tops in a great stramash that rendered Mrs Prole quite dizzy.

Out of breath, red-faced, and thoroughly demoralised, she sank down on the bench with not enough bile left to create a scene and when Mr Arbuthnot invited her to accompany him into the Reel of Tulloch she was too weak to resist. She soon found herself setting to Tom Brodie who grinned when he grasped her arm and, high-cutting, lifted her as if on springs until they broke to face new partners. She had learned to dance long ago, before she was old enough to realise what a sin it was, and to her amazement she discovered that her feet had not forgotten how to execute the steps.

She threw herself into one reel after another with never a thought for the effect on her shanks, or her soul, and the hours flew past until, close to midnight, the fiddlers broke their bows in one last sweeping chord and, amid much moaning and sighing, the dancing school closed and the lads and lassies gathered their boots and shawls and headed out into the streets.

'Madam,' Tom Brodie said, 'I have your young lady, I believe.'

Rose clung to the ploughman's arm, her face dewed with perspiration, her eyes shining.

Eunice Prole looked from her lofty height at the child whose wickedness had tried her temper for so many years and with something that may or may not have been a whimper capitulated to the memory of what it was like to be young.

'Thank you,' she said. 'Thank you, sir,' then catching herself teetering on the brink of sentiment, pivoted on her heel and yelled for Lucas Fergusson to fetch the blessed pony-trap and bring it to the door.

Betsy had assumed that Henry would attempt to separate Tom from Rose Hewitt and the brothers would quarrel and might even come to blows. Soon after Tom had reappeared with the Hewitt girl on his arm, however, Henry's mood had changed and he had abandoned the challenge of protecting Rose Hewitt's chastity and what was left of the Brodies' honour.

He had led Betsy on to the floor and, with more enthusiasm than skill, had partnered her through several reels and two Strathspeys in the course of which, as was the manner of Scottish dances, she had also danced with Tom and, putting herself out, had skirled and whooped and shaken her hips, though she had known that his mind and his eyes were elsewhere and she was no more to him then than an arm and a hand and might have been any lumpy girl from any broken-down farm.

Now they stood by the horse-rails, watching the Fergusson boy negotiate the pony-trap through the thinning crowd. She saw how the girl waved, her face pale in the moonlight; how

Tom raised his arm in a lofty salute and called out, plain for all to hear, '*Au revoir, au revoir,*' and how he remained motionless even after Peter Frye patted him on the shoulder and, accompanied by Mr Ogilvy, went off to find the horses.

At length, puffing out his cheeks, Tom released a whistling sigh and, glancing round, said cheerfully, 'Betsy, will you ride with me?'

Henry said, 'Nah, nah. She'll ride with me.'

And a few minutes later they were off along the road to Hayes. Tom followed on his mare while she clung to Henry's waist, sweat drying under her skirts and the night air cool upon her cheeks.

Cloud crossing the face of the moon threw strange shadows on the cobbles. She smelled the earth of the fields in the darkness and heard behind her the laughter of labourers and girls as they wandered homeward or, she thought wistfully, found shelter in pockets of shadow to kiss and cuddle. She shifted her weight, clasped Henry's narrow hips with her thighs, and rested her head on his shoulder. She was not quite awake, not quite asleep when they passed through Hayes, not quite asleep and not quite awake when the horse pulled on to the slope of the track. Soon, she thought, soon I'll be snug in bed.

Then Henry cried out, '*Mammy, what's wrong?*' and she felt a rush of air beside her as Tom galloped past on the mare.

'What?' Rose said. 'Have you come to whip me?'

'No, I've not come to whip you,' Eunice Prole said. 'I've come to talk.'

'Is Father asleep?'

'Dead to the world.'

The woman set the candle-holder upon the night-table. Rose, already undressed, covered her breasts with her hands as if she had something to hide.

'I trust you aren't going to lecture me,' she said. 'I'm very tired.'

'I'm not goin' to lecture you,' said Mrs Prole in a smothered tone. 'I'm here to help you.' She pushed Rose on to the bed and clasped her hand. 'If you have clothes in need o' launderin', give them to me right now. He need know nothin' about it. For good or ill, we're in this together.'

'In what together? I don't understand.'

'If there's blood on your clothes . . .'

'Blood? No, no.'

'Neville – your father must be kept ignorant of any . . . any change in you,' Eunice Prole said in a hoarse whisper. 'He mustn't find out that Brodie was there tonight or that you went off with him. Whatever harm Brodie did you—'

'He did me no harm, no harm at all.'

'You're a glib liar, Rose Hewitt,' Eunice Prole said, 'but I require the truth from you now, the whole truth, however sordid.'

'Unless I'm mistaken, my dear Mrs Prole, you're not concerned with what "harm" may have befallen me at Tom Brodie's hands; you're concerned you'll be blamed for it and my father will send you packing.'

'Aye, I'm afraid he might,' Eunice Prole admitted. 'He values you above all things, even above my – my services. If you're no longer pure then you must tell me. You'll need a woman by you when your time comes.'

'My time, what time?'

'When your bleeding stops.'

'Oh!' Rose got to her feet. 'Do you think he mowed me? Tom did not *mow* me. He did not attempt to *mow* me. In fact – since we're being honest with each other – I may as well tell you that he *refused* to mow me. Unfortunately for me, it seems that Tom Brodie is more of a gentleman than any of us imagined him to be.'

'God save us!' Eunice Prole exclaimed. 'He loves you.'

'He does,' said Rose smugly. 'And I love him.'

'Awww,' Mrs Prole groaned, rocking forth and back. 'Awww, this is bad, so bad, worse than I'd supposed. Not a word now, not a word to your father.'

'Not a word will pass my lips,' Rose promised, 'but what if Lucas Fergusson tells his father and his father tells Papa?'

'Lucas Fergusson's the man you're supposed to marry.'

'I'm well aware of it,' Rose said. 'On the other hand, a prolonged courtship with young Mr Fergusson will give me ample time to devise a plan to marry Mr Tom Brodie.'

Eunice Prole sniffed. 'Well, if you're hell-bent on throwin' your life away on this worthless farmer I'll do nothin' to hinder you. In the meanwhile . . .'

'I know,' Rose said, 'not a word to dear Papa.'

8

The ploughing of the long field was finished at last. With Betsy as his 'boy', Tom went out to clear the ditch at the bottom of the slope. It was hard, dirty work. With very little sleep behind them neither Tom nor Betsy was much in the mood for conversation. Betsy worked barefoot and bare-legged, skirts pouched about her waist. The mud was clotted with decaying leaves and coated with an oily blue scum. It was cold too, so cold that Betsy's breath caught in her throat when she first stepped into it.

'You've no call to be doin' that,' Tom told her gruffly.

'Have I not?' said Betsy, equally gruffly. 'Is it not the best way?'

'Aye, I'll grant you that much.'

'An' you're the man to do it, are you, in the state you're in?'

'I wouldn't ask Janet to do it.'

'I'm not Janet,' Betsy said, adding, under her breath, 'thank God.'

When, late last night, they had come upon Agnes Brodie shivering in the lee of the hedge they had assumed that Matthew had passed away. Tom and Henry had bundled their mother indoors. Betsy had unsaddled the mare and horse, had rubbed them down and given them oats and water. When she had entered the cottage, the curtain had been drawn over the old man's bed and Tom and Henry had been kneeling by their mother's chair. Henry, white as a sheet, had told her that Mr Brodie was still breathing but that he might not last the night. Then he had sent her to bed. But this morning the old man had been sitting up, supping porridge from a spoon, more alert than he had been in days.

Betsy rolled up her sleeves and plunged the fork into the mud. She hoisted debris from the base of the ditch and swept it on to the bank. Tom spread it with the back of a spade. She thrust forward against the drag of the mud and worked the fork again.

Ten hours ago she had been twirling on the floor of the Drennan hall, hot and happy, with never a care in the world. If she'd been at home she'd have been looking forward to Hallowe'en which was only a few days off. Hallowe'en, that night when girls scared themselves silly with mirrors and candles or stole out into the kailyard to pull up roots to divine what sort of a husband fate had in store for them. Apples would be roasted, nuts scattered on the hearth, and Mr Rankine would creep into the byre hooting like an owl and grab the dairymaids as they fled in mock terror. There would be no such goings-on at Hawkshill; Matthew Brodie disapproved of Hallowe'en, so Henry told her. Besides, the old man was very sick and the shadow that death threw over the farm was far more terrifying than any cast by imaginary witches or make-believe warlocks.

Betsy was just about to toss a second forkful on to the bank when Tom caught the fork with the tip of his spade and pinned it to the ground.

'You're soaked up to the arse, Betsy. Doesn't it bother you?'

'Aye, it bothers me,' she said, 'but I'm wet now an' I'll be wetter still if the rain comes on. Do you want this job finished, or do you not?'

'It's not your ground, Betsy, nor are we your kin,' Tom said. 'What matter to you if it isn't finished?'

'Don't you need to plant the seed Henry bought?'

'There is no seed, Betsy.'

'So your mother lied to Mr Hewitt?'

'Aye, she did,' Tom said, 'but there'll be no room for lies come Saturday, none to satisfy Hewitt at any rate.'

Although they were alone in the vast, empty landscape Betsy lowered her voice. 'Can she do nothin' for you? Rose Hewitt, I mean?'

'Rose?' He seemed surprised. 'What could she do?'

'Talk to her daddy?'

'She has no sway wi' her daddy.'

'Did you – did you take her?'

'That was never my intention.'

'Intention or not, did you?'

'Do you think I'd take a young girl out o' spite, Betsy, or for what lever it might give me with her father? No, I intend to marry her.'

'But the debt, Tom? What about the debt you owe to Hewitt?'

'The debt will be paid,' he said, then, as the first spots of rain began to fall, picked up his spade and went doggedly back to work.

He was lying on his side, face to the wall, not so much sick, Betsy thought, as sulking. Agnes Brodie closed the curtain with a snap. A big wooden tub had been brought in from the barn and filled with warm water from the mash-boiler in the stable. A few precious scraps of soap had been pressed into a piece of cheesecloth and two worn towels draped on the chair by the fire. Betsy knew she was being cosseted but could not fathom a reason for it. She had intended to wash at the pump as usual and was surprised to be summoned to the cottage, handed a beaker of tea spiced with a dash of whisky and told to take off her clothes.

The bleak October afternoon had bled early into dusk and around half past three Tom had chased her home. He was out there still, though, chopping channels in the ploughed ground while the rain fell soft as gossamer.

The tea trickled into her belly and the whisky warmed her. The water in the tub steamed, the logs in the hearth crackled. Too exhausted to care about modesty, she stripped off her shirt and bodice and unloosed her skirts.

'Henry? Is he . . .'

'Aye,' said Janet, smirking, 'he's peepin' through the crack. Go on, McBride, give him an eyeful o' your treasures. I'll wager he's never seen the like o' them before.'

'Pay her no heed,' Agnes Brodie said. 'Get in the tub.'

Betsy stepped into the big tub. Covering her breasts with her arms, she slipped into the warm water. Hitching her knees to her chest, she tried, vainly, to make herself small. She flinched when the soap-bag touched her shoulder blades. It crossed her mind that this was how maids were prepared for the bridal, the stink of the byre laved away to leave them clean and pink for their wedding night. Agnes squeezed suds on to her broad back then, leaning over, dropped the soap-bag into her lap.

Sighing, Betsy elevated a leg and began to scrub off the mud.

Clucking disapprovingly, three broody hens peered out of the straw and when Henry entered the barn one of the big black rats that fed off the middens scuttled past him and shot out into the darkness. A lantern on a hook by the door threw smoky shadows across the barn. Tom had stripped to bare muscle. Unlike most men in a state of nature, he managed to look arrogant even without his clothes. Not for the first time Henry felt a seedy little stab of envy at the size of his brother's parts which, in Henry's view at least, were prodigious.

Tom had filled two buckets and an iron pail from the pump and had plucked a handful of straw from the stack to serve as a wash-cloth. He stood now, straddle-legged, in a puddle of dirty water chafing his hairy thighs and blowing hard, for the barn was, at the best of times, draughty. Henry had spent the afternoon attending his flock and smelled strongly of sheep but not for all the tea in China would he bathe bare-buff in this weather.

'Sluice me down, Henry, an' be quick,' Tom said.

Henry lifted a pail, splashed water over his brother's chest and heard Tom gasp with the shock of it. He picked up Tom's shirt and tossed it to him in lieu of a towel. He watched Tom dry his legs and belly.

Henry said, 'Have you decided?'

Tom climbed into his breeks. 'It's not for me to decide.'

'No,' Henry said. 'It's Father's decision.'

'He doesn't know what he's askin' of us.'

'Oh, I think he does,' said Henry.

'Well, it'll not be me who does it.'

'Would you deny him his dyin' wish?'

Tom draped his coat across his shoulders. 'I'm many things, Henry, but I'm no murderer.'

'It wouldn't be murder,' Henry said. 'It would be mercy.'

'Do you want him dead?'

'He's dead already,' said Henry. 'He's well aware he'll never put a foot out o' that bed again. It's not a matter o' months or weeks but days an' hours.'

'It's a crime against nature, Henry. I want no part in it.'

'Don't you want a part o' Hawkshill?'

'Damned foul ground,' Tom cried. 'Would you have us pour our life's blood into this pit an' die broken, like Daddy?'

'The ground didn't kill him,' Henry said.

'What did then?'

'Parsimony,' Henry said.

'Parsimony?'

'Poverty, if you prefer it,' Henry said. 'One vice follows from the other, like the chicken from the egg.'

Drawing his coat about him, Tom advanced on his brother.

'Are you blamin' Daddy for fallin' into debt? If you are I'll thrash you to within an inch—'

'Be easy,' Henry said. 'I blame no one but Hewitt. When we quit Ballantrae for Hayes, he knew Daddy was desperate enough to sign on to a bad bargain.'

'Now you're blamin' me, are you?'

'Nah, nah,' said Henry soothingly. 'The past's past. It's the future we have to look to. Daddy knows that better than anyone. If he dies before tomorrow midnight we've a chance to make things right.'

'Some chance!'

'Better than no chance,' said Henry. 'Daddy was always a practical man. The canker might devour his flesh but his spirit's as stout as ever. He knows if he dies tomorrow there's hope for the rest o' us, but if he survives until Saturday there's none.'

'He told you this, did he?'

'He did.'

'When?'

'Last night after you'd gone to bed.'

'Liar!'

'Ask him then, ask him yourself.'

'I – I can't,' Tom said.

'An' I know why.' Henry tapped his brother's chest. 'You won't ask him lest he makes you bend to his will.'

'Mother . . .'

'Mother will do what's best for us.'

'An' Janet?'

'Need never know the truth.'

'Did you plan for this all along?'

'Not me,' said Henry. 'He's the one thought it out while he lay fightin' for every damned breath, listenin' to us squabble about the future.'

'An' you would do it?'

'No,' said Henry, 'but I would see it done.'

'By me?'

'By both o' us, hand on top o' hand.'

'Jesus! Jesus!'

'It's how Daddy wants to go, Tom, with his sons at his side.'

'Oh, God, Jesus!'

'Ask him,' said Henry again. 'Talk to him. He'll make you see sense.'

'It isn't sense,' Tom said. 'It's madness.'

'Why is it madness?'

'Because, damn it, we could swing for it.'

'If there was proof, aye, but there'll be no proof,' Henry said. 'The death o' a dyin' man will raise no eyebrows.'

'Oh, God, Henry, surely you don't mean to do it tonight?' Tom asked.

'No,' Henry answered. 'Tomorrow – in the early afternoon.'

Soon after supper Tom and Henry had gone behind the curtain to sit with the old man. Betsy had been unable to catch even a word or two of their conversation before she had joined Janet in bed. Something was in the wind, though, something that did not smack of desperation. Tonight the boys' mood was quiet and sombre. Only chattering Janet seemed oblivious to it. When the girl slipped an arm about her waist Betsy did not resist at first but when Janet blew lightly into her ear, she heaved round and snapped, 'What's wrong wi' you? Have you got fleas?'

'I wish I was more like you, Betsy,' Janet said wistfully.

'Huh, you're not wishin' for much.'

'If I had a figure like yours I'd have had a man by now,' Janet said. 'Your cousin's a fine big fellow, has he . . .?'

'No, he has not.'

'I wonder if it hurts.'

Betsy jabbed an elbow into the bolster. 'What's brought this on, Janet?'

'Daddy thinks you were Mr Rankine's whore.' Janet giggled. 'I heard him say it when you first came here.'

'Whore, is it? I'm nobody's whore, I'll have you know.'

'Mr Rankine put it in you, though, didn't he?'

'It's none o' your blessed business,' Betsy said. 'What right have you to discuss such things when your father's dyin' next door? Have you nothin' in your head but what men do to girls?'

'I know what Tom would do to you if he had the chance.'

'Tom's in love wi' someone else.'

'Aye, Rose Hewitt. She wouldn't be the first,' said Janet. 'But he'll take what he can get in passin' wi' never a quiver o' conscience. I think he brought you here 'cause Johnny told him you were easy.'

Betsy kept her temper, just. 'In two days' time, Mr Hewitt will grab hold o' this farm an' this cottage an' you'll all be headed for the workhouse. At least I'll have a home to go to an' a man who'll pay me a wage.'

'Once Daddy's gone,' said Janet smugly, 'Henry'll find us a better place an' I'll be off this damned hill an' out in the world. He doesn't love me, you know. He only loves his precious boys. No matter what wicked things they do, he always forgives them. He never forgives me *anythin'*.'

'God, but you're heartless,' said Betsy.

But she knew that her life was almost as mean as Janet's. Whatever shine she cared to put on it, she *had* been little more than Johnny Rankine's whore. She *had* come to Hawkshill in the hope of trapping Tom Brodie into marriage. And tomorrow or the day after she would be sent back to her father's house and John Rankine's byre and whatever she had learned of love would lie behind her, like leaves in the dust.

'What's that?' Janet sat bolt upright. The sound of sobbing came from the kitchen. 'Has he gone? Has my daddy gone?' Then, to Betsy's amazement, she scrambled from the bed and rushed into the kitchen, crying, 'Daddy, Daddy, don't go, don't go. Don't leave me.'

Tom did not go out to the long field that morning. Betsy was sent to help Janet clean out the byre. The old man was very still and calm. He put up with Agnes's attentions without protest and even allowed Tom to feed him a few sips of bread and milk. No mention was made of the fact that this was the last day of October and that early tomorrow morning Neville Hewitt would arrive with a Sheriff's officer brandishing an eviction notice.

It was close to noon when Agnes called Betsy and Janet from the byre. Tom and Henry were already supping broth at the kitchen table. The curtain was drawn over the bed. Betsy ate her broth in silence. As soon as the meal was over Tom rose and left the room.

Looking down at his feet, Henry said, 'Betsy, can you drive a cart?'

'Aye, I've drove the market cart for Mr Rankine once or twice.'

'Will you be good enough to take Janet to Drennan to fetch Dr Glendinning?'

Janet glanced up. 'Is it Daddy? Is he worse?'

'Take the small cart an' the mare,' Henry went on. 'Tom's makin' it ready right now. There's a nip in the air today so put on your shawl. Janet, make sure you give Daddy a kiss before you go.'

'Will the doctor require to be paid?' Betsy asked.

'He'll be paid when he gets here,' Henry answered.

'If it's urgent,' Janet said, 'why doesn't Tom ride to fetch him?'

'Tom's needed here.'

'But—'

'Don't argue, Janet, not today,' said Henry. 'Do what you have to do then be on your way.'

Betsy said, 'What if the doctor's not at home?'

'Wait at his house till five o'clock,' Henry told her. 'If Glendinning's not back by then, come home as fast as you can.'

Betsy fetched her shawl and draped it over her shoulders. Janet slipped behind the curtain and Betsy heard the old man's voice, soft and light, consoling her. She blew out her cheeks, tucked the ends of the shawl into her belt and went out into the grey daylight. Tom had hitched the smaller of the mares to the cart. He stood like a servant at the animal's head, holding the reins in one hand. He glanced at Betsy, and then away. She longed to take him in her arms but he was stiff and formal and she knew he would only rebuff her.

She climbed into the cart and took the reins.

'He's not goin' to last the night, is he?' she asked.

Tom answered, 'No,' then, without another word, went back into the cottage and closed the door.

Most folk believed that Tassie Landles was nothing but a charlatan whose predictions were too dependent on the credulity of daft young girls to be taken seriously. Even so, only a brave man or desperate woman would venture near Tassie's shop after dark on Hallowe'en and a superstitious few would not even look down as they crossed the Ramshead bridge in case the witch woman took offence and cast the evil eye on them.

Peter Frye's mother had more reason than most to fear Tassie's wrath but Peter and his brother subscribed to the belief that 'auntie' was little more than a confidence trickster with an expert knowledge of the healing properties of herbs, a skill closer to medicine than magic. If either of the boys had stumbled into the cottage below the bridge that pitch-black October night, however, they might have been less sceptical, for the ceremony upon which Tassie Landles was engaged was not one to be taken lightly.

The rumour that Tassie had inherited her gifts from a gaggle of Renfrewshire witches had no basis in truth. She had learned her craft from her foster-mother, Alice Landles, who had been handed, by chance, a receptive girl child to rear side by side with her talentless sons.

Hounded from the Isle of Man, Alice's ancestors had settled in Ayrshire where they had bred through the female line a number of soothsayers, divinators and healers while successfully concealing the darker aspects of their calling. Only one of the Landles' clan, 'Bloody' Jarvis Garvie, a rather effeminate warlock with a taste for blood, had ever been foolish enough to reveal himself and on the tenth day of December 1696 had met a sticky end on the gibbet at Ayr's old crossroads and even now, almost a century later, had a habit of making a nuisance of himself by popping up unbidden to relay bad news from the other side of the great divide.

Seasonal feasts and sabbats held no attraction for Drennan's apple-cheeked egg-seller. Tassie was far too level-headed to attach herself to the Ayrshire covens. She despised the droning, shrieking, half-crazed women who claimed congress with demons and she certainly did not care to subject her body to endless rounds of copulation with men attired in flea-bitten hides in the belief that such blasphemous acts would increase her powers.

The practice of necromancy was difficult and dangerous enough without pretending to flit about on broomsticks or any of the other preposterous tricks that owed more to fevered fantasy than to fact.

The rituals with which Tassie made ready for Hallowe'en had more affinity with Catholicism than the skirling orgies cooked up by Old Nick's acolytes. She rarely neglected to begin her day with a recitation of the White Paternoster and made use of candles, beads and a crucifix as well as the traditional elements of earth, fire and water to fix the boundary over which troubled souls dared not cross.

She had been fifteen before Alice had allowed her a glimpse of the world unseen. Quite naturally, Tassie had been terrified by the shapeless apparitions that had loomed up in the cramped kitchen and the tantrums they displayed. She had clung to her foster-mother's skirt, cowering behind bowls and candles while the entities came and went like rain on the wind, and when they were gone Alice, exhausted, had fallen into bed and had slept for half a day. Small wonder, Tassie thought, that most women who claimed to be witches preferred to prance about with Satan's all-too-human emissaries than square up to the tribulations of dealing with the restless spirits of the dead.

She had taken out the parchment on which Alice had written the four primary commands which were, in effect, old Latin prayers culled from long forgotten sources. She had poured white wax into copper moulds to fashion candles that would burn with long, clear yellow flames and would not flare or flicker however busy the air became. She had laundered her linen robe and dried it on a loop of red string. She had washed three bowls in well-water and filled each one separately with earth from her herb garden, water from the running river and gouts of dried moss that, when lighted, would smoulder for hours.

Clad in the linen robe, she was seated in her armchair by the fire sipping brandy and studying the old parchment on her lap when, around half past ten o'clock, the door flew open and a gust of wind swirled into the room. An ordinary man or woman might have supposed that a sudden squall had blown in from the sea and, starting up, have barred the door against the freakish weather.

Tassie was not deceived. She watched the cosy little fire in the hearth roar into a sheet of oily blue flame that just as quickly died away again. Fear closed her throat and squeezed her bowels. For a single awful moment, she imagined that death had come for her, that this was how it arrived, not with a gasp or sob but in a sudden suffocating rush. She had just enough presence of mind to keep hold of the precious parchment, however, to tug a string of beads from a pocket in her robe and, leaping to her feet, cry at the pitch of her voice, '*Cease and be still*,' and when the air had quietened a little, cry out again, '*Who is it comes?*'

There was little to see, only a faint wisp of light, like tattered lace, hanging in the shadows. She had not summoned the spirit, nor had she admitted it but she was curious to discover its identity and the purpose that brought it here.

On impulse, she said, 'Garvie? Bloody Jarvis Garvie, is that you?'

And a peevish, lisping little voice answered, 'Yeth.'

PART TWO

Smugglers' Coast

9

By half past eight on Saturday morning the corpse had been dressed and placed in a pine coffin. Tom and Henry were in the process of carrying it to the barn when Neville Hewitt galloped into the yard. He flung himself from the saddle, charged up to the boys, leaned over the coffin and peered into the face of the deceased whose expression of indifference only riled the landlord further.

'What the devil is this?' he shouted. 'What are you doin' with this man?'

'Layin' him out before burial,' said Henry.

'Why? But why?'

'Because he's dead,' said Tom.

Carpenter and undertaker had arrived to begin their work before the ink on Dr Glendinning's certificate of death had properly dried. During his trip to Hayes to summon them, Henry had ordered a cask of whisky, a half-pound of tobacco and five new pipes from Souter Gordon's. He had also notified Mr Turbot, the parish minister, though, strictly speaking, religion played no part in ceremonies of death and burial, which were regarded as civil matters.

He had not, however, deemed it necessary to inform Neville Hewitt.

Bad news travelled just as fast on country roads as it did in busy towns and shortly before eleven on Friday night, when Neville and his paramour were chortling over a glass of sherry before bundling into bed, the surgeon's assistant had arrived at the door to deliver word that the tenant of Hawkshill had finally shaken off the mortal coil.

'He doesn't look dead to me,' Neville Hewitt cried, tweaking the corpse's nose with a forefinger. 'I smell deception here.'

Tom lowered his end of the coffin and pulled Hewitt back before he could manhandle the dead man further. 'What you smell,' he said, rather too evenly, 'is vinegar. My father has been in part preserved.'

'Preserved for what?' said Neville Hewitt. 'Posterity?'

'Tomorrow's Sunday,' said Henry. 'My father can't be interred until Monday, not if we're to see him off in style.'

'Style? Style, is it?' Hewitt raged. 'How can you see him off in style when you don't have two halfpennies to rub together? Where's my money?'

Henry pointed at the corpse. 'There's your money, Mr Hewitt, laid down for burial wi' the best man who ever ploughed a furrow. He'll take his debt to heaven wi' him, an' let the good Lord arbitrate on just who owes what to whom.'

'How obligin'!' Neville Hewitt said. 'How very damned obligin' of him to give up the ghost mere hours before the debt fell due. Are you sure you didn't help him on his way?'

'My father died peacefully in the middle o' yesterday afternoon,' Henry said evenly. 'If you doubt me, I'll show you Glendinning's certificate.'

'Was Glendinning here when he died?'

'Alas, no,' Henry said. 'The doctor arrived a half-hour too late.'

'So Glendinning's in it too, is he?' Hewitt said. 'The Sheriff'll hear about this conspiracy, mark my words.'

'The Sheriff's already been informed,' Tom said. 'Mr Frye is at this moment postin' notice on our behalf. If you're thinkin' o' takin' us to court, Mr Hewitt, I ought to warn you the law's firmly on our side. Henry an' I are now tenants on a twelve-year lease, the breaker clause wiped out by death. We've half a year to find a half-year's rent. You can't throw us out before the first day o' May an' only then if we fail to pay what's due.'

'By God, Brodie, I rue the day I ever took pity on that connivin' farmer from Ballantrae,' Neville Hewitt said. 'I can wait, however. I can wait till May. You'll have heavy bills for this grand wake you're plannin' an' with neither crop nor cattle to sell you'll be deeper in debt than ever. The law will not protect you then and you'll have no one left to murder.'

'Watch your tongue, Mr Hewitt,' said Henry quietly. 'If you spread scurrilous rumours about the manner o' my father's passin' not only will you not be believed, you'll find yourself on the wrong end o' a suit for slander.'

'Unless there's proof,' Neville Hewitt said.

'Proof of what?' said Henry.

'That your father was helped on his way.'

'My father died at his appointed time,' said Henry.

'Appointed by whom, I'd like to know,' Neville Hewitt said.

'By God, of course,' said Henry. 'Now, if you've no more business here, I'll ask you to leave. We've much to do before my father's put to the ground.'

'Arrangin' a merry time, I suppose,' Neville Hewitt said, 'at my expense.'

Then, before Brodie's sons could turn ugly, he hurried off to find his horse and ride, fuming, back to Drennan.

Neville Hewitt had come and gone before the girls emerged from the byre. They toted the milk to the slope-roofed lean-to and poured it into flat pans. When the cows had been led back to the field and Janet had gone to feed the calves, Betsy returned to the yard. Henry was unloading a keg of whisky from Souter Gordon's cart. He conversed cheerfully with the delivery boy and even shared a joke when clay pipes were unearthed from a straw box and, together with a rope of black tobacco, carried into the cottage.

Betsy looked round for Tom. The flare of a taper caught her eye and she crossed the yard to the open door of the barn and, hesitantly, peeped in. He was kneeling on the dirt floor melting the end of a candle with a taper. The lantern, lid cocked, was beside him and one candle was already firmly fixed in the neck of an old wine bottle.

There had been much discussion as to whether the body should be displayed in the back room or on the bed in the kitchen; neither solution had seemed practical. The cottage would soon be crowded with mourners who would expect to be treated to food, drink and a pipe of tobacco and not be chased away if they were inclined to linger. It had been agreed that Matthew would be more comfortable laid out in the barn where members of the family would take turns watching over him and friends and acquaintances could pop in to pay their last respects.

Looking down at the old man's face, foreshortened and tranquil, Betsy found it hard to believe that Matthew Brodie was not simply asleep. The frown had vanished, the creases that had scored his cheeks were planed away. In that uncertain moment Betsy had a glimpse of what he must have looked like before work and worry took their toll, and realised that Matt Brodie had once been handsome too.

Tom glanced up. 'What do you want, Betsy? There's nothin' for you here. Away into the house an' help my mother.' He eased the candle into the neck of the bottle. 'What's wrong wi' you, girl? Have you never seen a corpse before?'

'Do they always look like that?' Betsy asked.

'Like what?'

'Peaceful.'

'He died peaceful – at the very end,' Tom said.

'Were you at the bedside?'

'Aye, the three o' us.'

'Did he say anythin'?'

'Nah, he just stopped breathin'.'

'It was his time, then?' Betsy asked.

Tom stared at her for a long moment. 'Aye, it was his time.'

'What'll you do now?' Betsy said.

'Give him a funeral fit for a lord.'

'An' after that?'

Tom pushed himself to his feet, came around the coffin and put a hand on her shoulder. 'We'll do the best we can.'

'Will you be wantin' me to stay?'

'Do you want to stay?'

She shrugged. 'Will Mr Rankine pay my fee?'

'Is it only your fee you're worried about, Betsy?'

'Three pounds the year an' keep. Am I worth that much?'

'That much, an' more,' Tom told her.

'Then I'll stay,' said Betsy.

Mr Ogilvy and Peter Frye met by chance a half-mile below the road end. Mr Ogilvy was driving a little pony-cart. Peter was mounted on one of his father's stallions. He had ridden hard from Copplestone as soon as the factor had brought him news of Matthew Brodie's death. The bond of friendship demanded that he stand by Tom in his hour of need and offer whatever assistance might be required, legal or otherwise.

Matthew Brodie's relatives were few and far between: a brother in the colonies, an older sister on a Hebridean island – Peter could not remember which – and a distant cousin in Kildare. Agnes Brodie's kin hailed from the Highlands. According to Tom, they had judged Matthew unworthy of inclusion in the clan and had cut themselves off from Agnes after her marriage. If the old man was to be accorded a grand-scale send-off it was up to Tom's friends to provide it.

'Ah, Peter, Peter,' Mr Ogilvy called out. 'A sad day, a sad day, indeed.'

Peter brought his horse into step with the pony. 'It's all that,' he said. 'My heart goes out to the family.'

'The loss of a father leaves a sore wound,' said Mr Ogilvy. 'I dread the day when my daddy's called to the bosom o' the Lord.'

'Your daddy?' said Peter. 'I wasn't aware you had a daddy.'

'I keep him in Kilmarnock.'

'You keep him, do you?'

'I see to his needs an' visit him once in a while,' said Mr Ogilvy. 'He has a wife, of course. He's had two o' those since my mammy died but this one seems determined to stay the course. Since she's young an' I've no wife o' my own, she'll probably inherit my paltry fortune.'

'That's a gloomy thought, Robert,' Peter said.

'One can't help but dwell on one's own mortality when another man's life has been cut short.'

'Cut short?' said Peter.

'Taken at the prime, I mean.'

'Ah yes, of course,' Peter said.

'There's no cloud without a silver linin', though,' Mr Ogilvy went on. 'If we're sad on Tom's behalf think how much sadder a certain flax manufacturer must be. In addition to losing twelve months' rent, old Hewitt's saddled with the Brodies for another half-year at least.'

'How that must stick in Hewitt's craw. He—' Peter cut off short at the sight of a woman seated by the roadside. 'Who the devil's that?' he said.

'It looks to me like Tassie Landles,' said Mr Ogilvy.

'Dear God, you're right!' Peter said and rode forward to greet his aunt.

★   ★   ★

Rose spread butter on a muffin and cut the muffin into small squares. She dropped a blob of jam on one and popped it into her mouth.

'Poor Tom,' she said. 'He must be stricken with grief.'

'Or dancing a jig,' said Eunice Prole.

'What, with his father dead?'

'It's not Tom Brodie's father you should be concerned about,' Eunice Prole said, 'it's your dear papa.'

'Oh, Papa will recover his temper soon enough.'

'I wouldn't be so sure o' that,' the woman said. 'He was counting on havin' Hawkshill to lease out again. I wouldn't voice sympathy for the Brodies when your father's within earshot if I were you.'

'I would, however, like to pay my respects.'

'No,' Eunice Prole cried, 'a spark to dry tinder that would be.'

Rose had remained in her room as long as possible that Saturday morning. Her father had stormed about downstairs, shouting and cursing horribly, then he had rushed out of the house. Mrs Prole had clumped upstairs to tell her that Tom's father had died.

'When will the burial take place?' Rose said.

'Monday, I expect,' said Eunice, 'in Hayes.'

'I assume Papa will not attend?'

'Hah!' Eunice said scathingly. 'Now listen to me, don't you even think about tryin' to slip away to comfort Tom Brodie. Anyway, women aren't allowed in the kirkyard.'

'I wonder why not?'

' 'Cause they spoil solemn occasions wi' tears.'

'Do men not cry, too?'

'I don't know what men do.' Eunice leaned across the breakfast table and covered the girl's hand with her own. 'This much I do know, Rose Hewitt: now is not the time to defy your father. He's very angry an' it'll be the worse for you if you cross him now.'

'What can he do to me that he has not done already?' Rose said airily.

'Marry you off to Lucas Fergusson, for one thing.'

'Never!' Rose said, a little less airily. 'He can't force me into a marriage against my will.'

'Can he not?' the housekeeper said. 'You've no idea what your daddy can do when he takes the bit between his teeth.' She leaned closer, crushing the girl's hand. 'He'll see you dead before he'll give you over to Brodie. Besides, now Tom Brodie has charge o' the farm he'll not be so eager to promise marriage.'

'He loves me.'

'Once he's satisfied his lust all those dandy promises will be forgotten. He'll go back to ploughin' his fields an' mowin' every maid who take his fancy. When he finally decides to take a wife,' Eunice went on, 'it'll not be some chit o' a girl with skin like alabaster and teeth like pearls who doesn't know one end of a cow from the other. Nah, nah: Tom Brodie will marry his own kind, an' you're not that kind, Rose Hewitt, an' never will be.'

'I will make myself that kind.'

Eunice released her grip on the girl's hand. 'You've no idea what "that kind" are like, let alone what's expected o' them. Much as I dislike you, I pray you never have to go to bed cold an' hungry, rise at cockcrow an' milk cows with hands so chafed you can hardly find the teats.'

In a small, timid voice, Rose said, 'At least Tom will not beat me.'

'Wait, just wait,' Eunice Prole said. 'When you're eight months gone, your belly so swole you can hardly breathe an' he throws you down and prods you just because he's too drunk to care, when that day comes you'll think your daddy's whippings were nothin' but love-bites and wish a rosy arse and a bruise or two was all you had to put up with.'

'Tom's not like that.'

'They're all like that,' Eunice Prole said.

'Is Papa like that?'

The housekeeper hesitated. 'No, your papa's a gentleman. Now, if you were to marry Lucas Fergusson an' drop him a son, you'll be treated like the Queen o' Sheba and want for nothin' ever again.'

'Lucas Fergusson's an idiot.'

'Better a devoted idiot than a ploughman wi' his brains in his breeks.'

'Tom has the tenancy of the farm, does he not?'

'Aye, if he can hold on to it,' Eunice said. 'Whatever profits come Tom Brodie's way will slip through his fingers like sand. If it wasn't for that brother o' his – an' the devil's own luck – he'd be begging on the streets by now. Is that what you want for yourself, Rose Hewitt, to share a stall in the poorhouse with a wastrel?'

'Tom is not a wastrel.'

'Then he must prove it.'

'How, how can he prove it?'

'By making Hawkshill profitable,' Eunice said, 'and there's not the faintest chance o' that happenin'. Come May, when the next rent falls due, your father will have his property back an' Tom Brodie will rue the day he ever tried to get you into his bed.'

'Did it ever occur to you, my dear Mrs Prole,' Rose said, 'that being bedded by Tom Brodie might be the lesser of two evils?'

'Two evils? What's the other?' the housekeeper said.

'Being married to Lucas Fergusson, of course,' said Rose.

In all the years that Peter had been acquainted with Tassie Landles he had seldom known her stray further from her cottage than the market square. It came as something of a shock to find her seated on damp grass at the track's end, four miles from Drennan.

She was wrapped in a patched greatcoat, half-laced boots, sticky with mud, protruding from under a frayed blue cotton skirt. She had no bag, no basket, not even a stick to lean upon. When he reined his horse and dismounted she looked up and, blowing out her cheeks, fashioned a strange, apologetic popping sound by way of greeting.

'Aunt Tassie,' Peter said, 'what are you doing so far from home?'

'Aye,' she said, 'it is a far piece an' a hard road for old legs. I came in the hope o' catchin' you afore you went up the hill.'

'So you've heard about Mr Brodie?'

Tassie nodded. 'From the horse's mouth.'

Peter hunkered by the woman's side. 'What do you mean by the horse's mouth, Aunt Tassie?'

'He came to me last night.'

'Who came to you?'

'He came to me through Bloody Jarvis.'

'Are you feeling quite well?' said Peter.

'Don't you recall what night it was?' she said.

'Hallowe'en,' Peter answered. 'Our servants had a high old time.'

'Jarvis comes sometimes on Hallowe'en,' said Tassie. 'He comes through the door wi' messages from souls in distress.'

'Ghosts, do you mean?' said Peter.

'They speak to me, you know.'

'What did this Jarvis – ah – person say that's brought you here to Hayes?'

'He's not at peace.'

'Jarvis?'

'The farmer, Matthew Brodie.'

Peter's mouth went dry. He glanced round but Mr Ogilvy had tipped down his hat brim so that nothing could be seen of his face. He took his aunt's hand. Her fingers were curled into her palm, her knuckles cold as ice. He had no notion if she was telling the truth or if her truth was simple self-delusion.

Last night the Copplestone servants had set up a great tub of water in the yard and, while he had watched from the door and his parents from the window, had ducked each other time and again in some mockery of a witchcraft trial. Then, with the youngest girls in the lead, they had set off for the kitchen garden to pull up roots to measure how potent their future husbands might be.

At first he had laughed at their antics but condescension had gradually been replaced by unease when the girls and boys – grown men and women too – had trailed across the parks to the ruin of the Auld Kirk o' Copplestone. An hour or so later, he had caught the skirl of a bagpipe and saw flames leap up and, drifting on the wind, had heard shrieks and cries that may or may not have signified merriment. This morning, the house servants had been dour and hang-dog, not only chastened but scratched and scraped, as if whatever game had engaged them had been rough enough to draw blood.

'This Jarvis fellow,' he said, 'is he alive or dead?'

'Dead, long dead.'

'But he comes back, does he, when you summon him?'

'I canna summon him. He comes an' goes as he pleases.'

'And it was this entity who told you Matthew Brodie had died?'

'Aye, Jarvis brought the word.'

The hair on the nape of Peter's neck prickled. 'When did the apparition appear to you?'

'Ten, or soon after.'

'Do you expect me to believe that you learned of Mr Brodie's death from a phantom?'

'I did,' said Tassie.

'I had no idea,' Peter said, 'you were possessed of such arcane gifts.'

'I wouldn't be talkin' about it if I hadn't received a message.'

'A message?' Peter shifted his weight nervously. 'For me?'

'For Tom Brodie.'

'Who is the message from?'

'From his father,' Tassie said. 'Matthew Brodie's not at peace. The manner o' his dyin' has left him searchin' for a restin' place. Tell Tom his daddy's still with him an' his promises must be kept.'

'What does it mean, Miss Landles?' Mr Ogilvy asked.

'Tom Brodie'll know what it means.'

'How can I possibly deliver a message from beyond the grave when the old fellow's corpse is still lying in the house?' Peter said. 'Tom will think I've gone mad.'

Tassie lifted herself with a hand on the young man's shoulder. 'He'll believe you. He knows what really happened an' how his daddy died.'

'Good God!' said Mr Ogilvy. 'Do you mean to say old Brodie was—'

'Hush, sir!' Tassie put a finger to her lips. 'There's more here than any o' us are required to know. Will you tell Tom what I've told you, Peter?'

'What?' he said. 'What must I tell him?'

'That all his promises must be kept before the spirit can rest.'

'If Peter won't tell him,' said Mr Ogilvy, 'I will.'

Peter swung round. 'Don't tell me you believe her, Robert?'

'I'm very much afraid I do,' Mr Ogilvy answered.

Then he helped Tassie into the trap to drive her home to Drennan and left Peter, thoroughly flummoxed, to square up to Tom Brodie on his own.

10

Mr Fergusson had been out of town for the best part of a week. He had travelled to Wigton to pick up a parcel of yearling calves and had ridden part of the way home with the drovers.

On his return, it did not take him long to arrange to meet his friend, Neville Hewitt, in Caddy Crawford's. He was quite unprepared for the violence of the flax manufacturer's entry into the public house, which almost knocked the door off its hinges, or the haste with which Neville downed not one but two glasses of brandy at the counter.

'Neville, what on earth's got into you?' Mr Fergusson asked.

'The bastard died on me,' Neville Hewitt snarled.

Mr Fergusson led his friend into the garden, pushed him on to a bench, and fed him another shot of brandy from the bottle.

'The wake, the funeral feast, whatever name you care to give it,' Neville Hewitt fumed, 'is taking place right now with, no doubt, the bloody Brodies dancin' round the damned coffin to celebrate the fact they've bested me.'

'The more they dance, the more they'll drink,' Mr Fergusson pointed out. 'The more they drink, the more they'll spend.'

'My money – every mouthful – my money.'

'Well, be that as it may, they're not good for it.'

'Good for it? Good for nothing!'

'If they buy drink on credit, they're not buyin' seed, are they?'

Mr Hewitt tossed back a fourth glass of brandy. The fiery liquid seemed to calm rather than inflame him. Clutching Mr

Fergusson's sleeve, he said, 'That's true, Walter, that's true. They might bury my money with the old bastard's body but they're burying their future too. Hah! Yes! You're right!'

'Of course I am,' said Mr Fergusson modestly. 'The Brodies represent a common breed of men who'd rather bleat about injustice than practise prudence. They'll blame you an' God an' the weather without a glance in the mirror at their own shortcomings. In a word, they're victims of their own base natures.'

'True, very true.'

'You an' I, Neville, we know better.'

'We do, we do.'

'It's just a matter of time until base nature catches up with them. The half-year's rent due in May comes to what?'

'Thirty-five pounds.'

'Not exactly a fortune to far-sighted gentlemen like us, Neville, but to shiftless spendthrifts like the Brodies it's a king's ransom.'

Neville Hewitt nodded. 'Hmm, I see what you're a-drivin' at, Walter.'

'Are you short?'

'Pardon?'

'Strapped for capital.'

'No, I – well, I'm – things have been better,' Mr Hewitt admitted.

'Can you ride the wave until May?'

'Aye.'

'Then do so,' Mr Fergusson said. 'Ride the wave until May, cut the Brodies loose – and we'll have ourselves a summertime wedding.'

'A wedding?'

'Your daughter an' my son,' Mr Fergusson said. 'Did you suppose I'd abandoned the project, Neville?'

'Why wait until May?'

'From what I gather, your daughter's still in thrall to Brodie. I don't want my boy encumbered with a resentful wife. Better for all of us – Rose, too – if she rejects Brodie an' accepts Lucas for what he's worth.'

'I doubt if she'll ever do that,' Neville Hewitt said.

'She will if she's made to see Brodie in his true light.'

'How can we make sure that happens? By ruining him?'

'No,' said Mr Fergusson, 'by letting him ruin himself.'

Johnny Rankine had been the first mourner to arrive at Hawkshill. He was installed in the kitchen sipping whisky, munching oatcakes and murmuring homespun platitudes when Peter Frye rode into the yard. From the window, Betsy watched the lawyer's son peer into the stable and byre and finally the barn, as if looking for someone to direct him.

She said, 'It's Mr Frye, Tom.'

'See to his horse, Betsy, will you?' Tom said.

Betsy was relieved to leave the cottage. She had already grown tired of Mr Rankine's sentimental commiserations. She went out into the yard. Peter Frye had nosed the horse half into the barn. When she came up on him from the flank, she saw that he was craned forward in the saddle, staring down, all agog, at the body in the coffin. When she cleared her throat, he jumped in the saddle and it took all his skill to prevent the horse kicking over the trestles. He backed the stallion out of the barn and dismounted. The animal remained fretful. He pranced away from the barn and, if Peter had given him free rein, would surely have galloped off.

'Easy, Cawdor.' Peter stroked the horse's neck. 'Be easy, boy.'

'What's wrong wi' him?' Betsy asked.

Peter ignored her question. 'Where's Tom?'

'Inside.'

'Who's with him?'

'His mother, Janet, Henry – an' Mr Rankine.'

'Oh, Johnny's here, is he?' Peter Frye clicked his tongue. 'Damn!'

'There's a rail behind the byre, Mr Frye. Hitch him there till he calms down. It might not be wise to put him in the stable.'

'You're right, Betsy,' Peter told her. 'He's got the devil in him this morning. Show me this post, please, then ask Tom to come out.'

'Are you not for goin' in, Mr Frye?'

'I require a private word with Tom first.'

She led the young man behind the byre and watched him hitch the stallion before she went into the cottage and, a moment later, followed Tom out into the yard. She watched the men embrace and then, arm-in-arm, enter the barn.

Janet appeared in the doorway.

'Is that Mr Frye?' she enquired excitedly. 'Is that Peter?'

'Aye.'

'Is he not for comin' in to see us?'

'He'll be . . .'

Tom came into view. He backed away from the barn, arms outstretched and fists raised. Peter followed, stooped like a wrestler seeking a hold. They moved across the yard, Tom retreating, Peter advancing until, as if in response to a hidden signal, they rushed together and embraced again.

'Janet,' Betsy said. 'Fetch Henry, fetch Henry out here. *Now*.'

Rose had never seen her father falling-down drunk. Even when he had tramped upstairs to beat her for some misdemeanour, real or contrived, he had always been in charge of his faculties. That Saturday afternoon, however, he was not in charge of anything, not his wits, his legs, or his bladder.

It was all the Fergussons, father and son, could do to drag him from the pony-trap, lug him up the front steps and lay him on the floor of the hallway where Mrs Prole, with a face like thunder, waited to take command. Seated on the stairs, quiet as a mouse, Rose watched with a mixture of incredulity and amusement.

'What,' Mrs Prole barked, 'have you done to my master?'

Mr Fergusson removed his hat. For a moment, Rose thought he was about to plant a foot on her father's chest like a hunter with a trophy but he used the hat merely to wipe off the trail of vomit that adhered to his coat. 'I've done nothin' to your master, madam,' he said, 'except rescue him from the gutter.'

'I've never seen him this drunk before,' Mrs Prole said.

'No more have I,' said Mr Fergusson. 'Indeed, instead of castin' blame, my dear lady, you might thank me for being on hand.'

'Where did the trap come from?'

'I sent a boy to my house to fetch it.'

'Well,' said Mrs Prole, 'for that I suppose you deserve our gratitude, but why did you get him into this sorry state in the first place?'

'I did nothing of the kind,' said Mr Fergusson. 'If we had been matching glass for glass would I be standing before you now, sober an' upright?'

The housekeeper peered down at the object on the floor. 'Neville has reason enough to forget himself, I suppose,' she said. 'Temper got the better o' temperance, for once.'

'Do you wish us to carry him through to his bed, Mrs Prole?'

'Certainly not,' Eunice Prole replied. 'I changed the sheets this mornin' an' I'm not havin' him spew all over them. Leave him where he is. I'll deal with him when he sobers up.'

'In that case' – Walter Fergusson put on his hat – 'we'll be on our way.'

'Will you not be takin' tea first?' Mrs Prole asked.

'No,' Mr Fergusson answered. 'We've—'

But Lucas had spotted the girl on the staircase. He gave his father a thump in the small of the back, and said, 'Aye, missus, thank you, we'll stay for a wee dish o' tea.' Then, stepping over the master of the house, he waited for Rose to come down to him.

'For God's sake, Tom, pull yourself together,' Henry said. 'Do you intend to let some old wife's tale play havoc with your reason?'

'He's here,' Tom said. 'I know he's here.'

'Aye, there he is,' said Henry, 'our daddy, dead as a doornail. Look at him, man, look at him. Do you think he's about to rise an' point the finger o' blame when all we did was what he told us to do?'

'The egg-wife knows, she knows, she talked wi' him.'

'She did *not* talk with him,' Henry declared. 'She contrived some tale to impress Peter, that's all. She probably wants to scrounge a free glass or two an' a dinner at our expense.'

'Bob Ogilvy heard her. What if he spreads the story?'

'There's no story to spread,' said Henry. 'Nobody knows what happened, only the three of us.'

'An' Daddy,' Tom reminded him.

'Well,' Henry conceded reluctantly, 'yes, an' Daddy.'

'Then,' Tom said, 'how did Tassie Landles find out?'

Henry held no strong conviction about the afterlife. Much of the preaching he heard in church seemed bent towards keeping the poor in their place. Even so, he was scornful of soothsayers, divinators and clairvoyants. In his opinion the future had more to do with good management than messages from beyond the grave.

'How did she know Daddy was dead,' Tom said, 'when she's four miles away in Drennan? Explain that if you can, Henry. Explain why Daddy sought her out to tell us he's not at rest?'

Henry lost his temper. 'God damn it, Tom,' he shouted. 'Father's dead, stone dead. He's nothin' now but putrifying flesh.' Wheeling, he thrust his hands into the coffin and hauled up his father's corpse. 'See. See. There's nothin' here.' He clasped his father's head in both hands and shook it violently. 'What have you to tell us, old man? Come on, out with it? Where's your voice now? Let's hear you speak.'

There was a little snap, like a twig breaking. Matthew Brodie's head toppled on to his breast and his mouth popped open. A thin trickle of preservative splashed over Henry's fingers and, before he could release his hold, flicked into his eyes. 'Jesus!' he cried and leapt back, clutching his face. 'It burns,' then he stumbled out of the barn in search of the pump while Tom heaved his father's remains back into the coffin and, murmuring apologies, did his best to soothe the battered corpse.

He watched her bosom rise and fall. He squinted covertly at the curve of her hip when she rose from the chair to pour tea. He wondered what lay between her thighs, veiled by skirts and petticoats. He was sure now that she would not break like a piece of china under his weight or giggle at the size of him when he towered proudly over her. He had Nancy Ames's word for it that he was normal, not just normal but as fine a figure of a man as she had ever joined with. He would never have dared tackle Nancy if she had not danced with him. She was big and buxom, with a laugh like a braying donkey, but she did not laugh at him – oh, no – and when any of the other girls laughed at him she gave them a clout or a rip with her claws and told them what a grand man he was and how he would make any of them squeal if they were fortunate enough to have him which, since she'd got there first, was as unlikely as a snowfall in July.

'Lucas, you're spillin' your tea.'

He wrenched his gaze away from Rose Hewitt. 'Uh?'

'Mind your manners, lad. You're not at home now,' his father whispered, then, winking at the gaunt housekeeper, said, 'I really do not know where his mind is half the time. He's in a wee world of his own.'

'They're all alike at that age,' the woman said. 'She's just the same.'

'I am not.' Rose Hewitt raised an eyebrow. 'I am preoccupied with higher matters, if you must know.'

'Higher matters?' his father said. 'What might they constitute?'

'Music, my music.'

'Ah, the harp.'

'The harp,' the woman said scornfully. 'The harp's not a proper instrument at all.'

'Is so,' Miss Hewitt said.

'Why not give us a tune or two?' his father said. 'Let us be the judges.'

'It would hardly be seemly, sir, to fill the house with melody when my father's lying supine in the hall.'

'He's fast asleep,' the woman said. 'Hear him snore.'

There was, indeed, a sound of snoring from the hall, snoring punctuated by intervals of breaking wind. Lucas was inclined to snigger but, sliding his gaze to Rose Hewitt once more, he suppressed the vulgar impulse.

'Go on, lass, give us a tune to cheer us up,' his father urged.

'I play only for my own pleasure, Mr Fergusson.'

'Lucas enjoys a good tune, don't you, son?'

'Uh-huh.'

'You should hear his lusty singing when he thinks no one's listenin'.' His father reached across the table to tweak his son's cheek. 'I've heard you, Lukie, warblin' away like a blackbird round behind the barn.'

If only his father knew what really went on behind the barn then his father wouldn't be so blasé about it, Lucas thought.

So far he had given no hint to his parents that he had finally uncovered the silky folds and swellings that God had bestowed on Eve. Nancy was all for keeping it to themselves, though every girl for miles around seemed to have heard what had happened on the night after the dance and how he had proved his manhood at last.

He could not get enough of Nancy now, nor she of him, but having discovered the joys of congress with one woman, it did not take him long to speculate on what it might be like with other members of the fair sex and how they might differ from sturdy Nancy Ames who, even Lucas realised, was a bit on the hairy side. He was not so daft as to imagine that mowing a lady would be the same as mowing a farm servant or that Rose would be carried off into transports of delight as soon as he dropped his breeks; yet her pretty face, dainty figure and creamy complexion roused him from his usual torpor and prompted him to make an effort.

'I'll sing, if you'll play, Miss Hewitt,' he heard himself say.

'No,' Miss Hewitt responded bluntly.

'Will you take a walk wi' me then?'

'A walk?' Rose said. 'I do not walk out with gentlemen.'

'A ride then,' Lucas persisted, 'in our cart.'

'Good God!' his father said. 'Lucas, what's got into you?'

'We could drive down tae – to the bridge,' Lucas blundered on.

'Thank you, Lucas,' Rose said. 'I have seen the bridge and, frankly, I have no desire to see it again.'

'Tomorrow?'

'Tomorrow's Sunday,' Rose reminded him.

'Oh, aye, so it is,' Lucas said. 'Monday then?'

She hesitated. 'I am, as it happens, free of engagements on Monday.'

'No,' the woman said. 'Oh, no, you don't.'

'Come now, Mrs Prole,' his father said, 'what harm—'

'Brodie's father's being buried on Monday.' Pushing back her chair, the woman scrambled to her feet. 'Don't you see, Mr Fergusson? It's another of her ruses to cadge a ride to Hayes to meet up with Tom Brodie.'

'Ah, yes.' His father nodded. 'Very clever, Rose, very clever indeed.'

'I'll take you to Hayes,' Lucas offered gallantly.

'No, you will not,' his father said and before Lucas quite knew what was happening, pulled him up by the arm. 'As for you, Rose Hewitt, if you think you can take advantage of my boy's trustin' nature when it suits you, I suggest you think again.'

'Advantage?' Lucas said. 'What advantage?'

'Never mind, son, never mind,' his father said and rather roughly, Lucas thought, dragged him, protesting, away.

Tom and Mr Turbot, the parish minister, had been at loggerheads for years. The reverend gentleman had grown used to insults in which his countenance, to say nothing of his bodily odour, was compared to that of a fish. He diligently avoided preaching from texts relating to the hapless mariner, Jonah, and cautiously monitored his remarks to the younger element in the congregation but, otherwise, resigned himself to being on the receiving end of a host of piscatorial jokes, few of which were either original or amusing.

The arrival of the young Brodies in Hayes had added an element of malice to the abuse, however, for Tom Brodie seemed to believe that the Church of Scotland existed solely to prevent him fornicating with any female who took his fancy and that he, Angus Turbot, was responsible for it.

It was with some trepidation, therefore, that Mr Turbot rode up to Hawkshill on Saturday afternoon to offer comfort to the widow. To his surprise there were no horses in the yard, no buzz of conversation from the cottage and when he led his pony by the rein towards the barn door, he was amazed at the sight that met his eyes.

The old man's coffin was propped on breast-high trestles draped with white sheets, a half-circle of candles in bottles arranged around it. In the course of forty years in the ministry Mr Turbot had seen corpses laid out in far less dignified surroundings but what really brought him up short was the sight of Tom Brodie on his knees, his hands clasped in an attitude of prayer. He could make no sense of the prayer, though, for the young man's voice was slurred as if, Mr Turbot thought, he was drunk – which, knowing Tom Brodie of old, might very well be the case.

Henry Brodie stood behind the coffin, arms folded.

Spotting the minister, he called out, 'Thank God, Mr Turbot. You've arrived in the nick o' time. Come in, sir, come in, an' see if you can talk some sense into my brother who is, I fear, tottering on the verge o' madness.'

'Grief has taken hold of him, I expect,' the minister said.

And Henry, shaking his head, said, 'Guilt.'

Betsy was not entirely surprised to find Mr Turbot in the barn. She was shocked to see Tom on his knees at Mr Turbot's feet, though, his face ravaged by some emotion she could not identify. The kindly old minister stroked Tom's hair as if he were a child, or a sheepdog. Henry drew her into the alley that separated the barn from the cottage gable and addressed her in a rasping tone that seemed to indicate anger rather than sorrow.

'Keep out o' it, Betsy,' he said. 'Keep Janet out, too. Tell her Tom's sick.'

'Is he sick?' said Betsy.

'I fear he might be losin' his reason.'

'Will I run to Drennan for Mr Glendinning?'

'He's better off with Mr Turbot,' Henry said. 'It's a disorder o' the mind, not the body. I hope to God we don't have too many brothers to entertain tonight. Tom's in no fit state to greet anyone.'

'What is it? Is his heart broken?'

'He blames himself for Father's death. It's not reasonable, I know, but his head is full o' dark forebodings.' Henry wrapped an arm about her waist and, sighing, rested his head on her shoulder. 'I fear for his sanity, Betsy, truly I do.'

'Perhaps he'll recover after the burial.'

'Perhaps,' Henry said. 'Meanwhile he insists on sittin' with the body throughout the night. I knew Tom would take it hard but I didn't think it would come to this.'

'Would you like me to stay with him?'

'No, I'll take the first watch,' said Henry, 'my mother the second. We'd best keep Janet out o' it. She'll only upset Tom with her prattle. My mother an' I will make sure he doesn't do anythin' rash.'

'Rash?'

'Harm himself,' said Henry.

A cold shiver ran down Betsy's spine. 'Why would he do that?'

'He's fixed in his mind he murdered Daddy, an' must make amends.'

'How can he make amends for somethin' he didn't do?'

'God knows!' said Henry, then taking Betsy by the arm, guided her out into the yard. 'Tom's not himself. Pay no heed to whatever he tells you. Do you understand, Betsy?'

'I do,' Betsy said, though she was not at all sure that she did.

II

If ever there was a sight to cheer her heart it was Connor McCaskie, her huge, tousled-haired cousin, coming up the track. He rode on a pony that seemed too small for his bulk, his long legs tucked up to keep his boots from trailing the ground, but the pony was sturdy enough to bear not only Conn's weight but also two big canvas-wrapped bundles strapped across the saddle.

'Hoh there, sweetheart!' Conn called out. 'Where's this solemn wake I've been hearin' about? Is there drink to be had, a warm fire to thaw out me bones an' perhaps a bite to eat as well?' He heaved himself out of the saddle. 'I'm famished.'

Betsy rushed from the cottage and hurled herself into Conn's arms with enough force to cause him to stagger. He wrapped his arms around her and lifted her from the ground and the greeting turned into a bear-dance whose unseemly jollity finally lured Tom from his vigil.

On Saturday night a half-dozen Freemasons had straggled up the hill accompanied by a few of Tom's cronies from the Bachelors' Club. There had been a celebration of sorts, a restrained affair. Tom had refused to leave the barn and had been barely civil to those brave souls who had toddled in to offer condolences. After the mourners had gone, Henry had persuaded Tom to eat a few mouthfuls of boiled ham washed down with whisky; then, with a little groan, he had toppled sideways and had fallen asleep on the dirt floor beside the coffin. He had slept the whole night through with a bolster under his head and a blanket tucked around him and when the family had gone off to church Betsy had remained behind to watch over him.

Conn offered his hand.

Tom shook it limply.

'It's my cousin from Ireland,' Betsy said. 'Surely you remember him?'

'Aye, he bought our cattle.'

Never one to stand on ceremony, Conn draped an arm over Tom's shoulder. 'Sure, an' it's a sad day for you, Mr Brodie, an' for your family. I never had the good fortune to meet with your dada but by all reports he was a fine man.'

'He was all that, Mr McCaskie.'

'Conn to my friends, of which, I trust, you're one.'

'If you'll excuse me, Conn,' Tom said, 'I've an urgent duty to perform,' then he headed for the outhouse that hid the latrine.

Betsy said, 'How did you learn that Mr Brodie was dead?'

'Your mother told me soon after I landed.'

'At Ayr?'

'Port Cedric. There are too many revenue officers hauntin' the quays for me to haul into Ayr these days. The Crown's offering bounty for information on contraband cargoes, so everyone who's not one o' us might well be one o' them.'

'Is that a cargo you have on the pony?'

Connor laughed. 'Nay, sweetheart, it's a case o' bottled wine an' a cask o' French brandy for the Brodies. I thought there'd be mourners pouring in from far an' wide. I missed my mark on that score, I reckon.'

'Tom's watchin' over his father's corpse an' won't be drawn from it,' Betsy said. 'He blames himself for what happened.'

'From what I hear, Tom should be relieved. Is the farm not his now?'

'Unfortunately, the farm's still Hewitt's,' Betsy said. 'There's still rent to pay, or will be come spring.'

Tom returned from the outhouse buttoning his breeks. He said, 'Betsy, where's my mother?'

'Gone to the kirk, all three o' them.'

'Oh, aye, it's Sunday,' Tom said. 'See to it that Mr McCaskie gets somethin' to eat. I must return to my prayers. Tomorrow my father will be put to the ground – an' I don't have much time.'

'Much time for what?' Conn said.

But Tom, head bowed, was already heading for the barn.

There were no collections of love letters in the handful of books her papa had accumulated over the years. Stuck for a model, she strummed a few chords on the harp for inspiration and tried to imagine the sort of letter Heloïse might have written to Abelard if his father had just passed away.

It was no easy task to convey condolence and undying love on a single page and she penned four drafts before she was satisfied that she had struck the right note. She burned the drafts in the candle-holder and floated the ashes from the window then sealed the letter and concealed it under the base of the harp where not even the vigilant Prole would be likely to find it.

Papa, not surprisingly, was not in the best of spirits.

Mrs Prole had left him lying on the floor of the hall until he had shown signs of recovery, at which point she had cajoled him to his knees and, with Rose's assistance, had helped him into the bedroom. Grumbling and cursing, she had undressed him, washed his face, wrapped him in a frayed sheet in lieu of a nightgown and had rolled him into bed. Rose had retired early to wrestle with her love note and did not see him again until he shambled into the parlour, dressed in a robe and slippers, shortly after nine on Sunday morning.

'Good morning, Papa,' she chirruped brightly. 'Did you sleep well?'

'He slept badly,' Eunice Prole shouted from the kitchen. 'He tossed an' turned an' snored like a grampus. Didn't you hear him?'

'I can't say that I did,' Rose called out.

Her father groped for a chair, seated himself at the table and covered his face with his hands. 'For God's sake, girl,' he groaned. 'Hold your noise.'

'Does your head hurt?'

'Aye.'

'Shall I pluck you a hair from the dog?'

'No, no! God, no!'

Mrs Prole appeared bearing a brandy glass filled with a glutinous liquid.

'I've just the thing to settle his stomach,' she said. 'Here, Neville, drink this down an' you'll soon be right as rain.'

'What is it?'

'Cream o' the milk, raw egg, lemon juice an' a dash o' vinegar.'

'Oh, pity! Oh, mercy!' her father mumbled and, rising, rushed from the parlour and across the hall to the closet where he remained, retching, while Rose finished her breakfast.

'I take it,' she said, at length, 'that Papa will not be attending church?'

'His stomach's in a worse state than his soul, by the sound o' it,' said Mrs Prole. 'No, he'll not be attendin' church. We'll go without him.'

'Would it not be better for you to attend him in his distress?'

'An' let you wander the streets on your own?' Eunice Prole said.

'What harm can befall me in the house of the Lord?'

'It's not the house o' the Lord that worries me,' Eunice Prole said. 'It's the mischief you might get up to afterwards. If we miss the forenoon preaching we'll attend the other church in the afternoon.'

'I do not care for the other church,' said Rose. 'I prefer to occupy our own pew, particularly as I've a great deal of praying to do.'

'For the soul o' a Hawkshill farmer you never even met?'

'For my peace of mind,' Rose said, 'and yours, dear Mrs Prole.'

'Leave my peace of mind out o' it. If you're hell-bent – I mean, determined to attend church this morning then you'll go with me or not at all.'

'And Papa, poor Papa?'

'Let him stew,' said Eunice.

The change in Lucas Fergusson was quite astounding. He'd had a haircut for one thing, not the usual shearing but a proper tonsorial touch-up from a touring barber who had arranged his straw mat into endearing waves and had brought out the colour with bear's grease and lashings of powder. Lucas had also acquired a tall hat with a snappy brim, a cravat, a pair of kidskin gloves, a silk handkerchief that spilled from his pocket like a Highland freshet, and, of all things, a Malacca cane with a silver knob on the end.

Rose had never been within four hundred miles of London's Haymarket but it seemed to her that Mr Fergusson's one-and-only had brought the Haymarket to Drennan and if the rig had been a shade less ostentatious she might have been more impressed and less amused by it.

Drennan's parish church was much grander than the kirk at Hayes. It had pillars for one thing, an imposing servants' gallery and a collection of rented pews that stretched like ribs from the side aisles and rubbed shoulders with the cushioned boxes of the gentry. The Fergussons were not gentry but they were, by most standards, well off and commanded a bench close to the base of the pulpit. The Hewitts, being less well off, had a pew much further back.

Rose and Mrs Prole were settled before the Fergussons made entry. No hang-dog shuffle down the crowded aisle for Lucas today; he loitered in the vestibule until his mater and pater were seated, then he strutted into view and, with more confidence than elegance, cruised down the aisle at a slow enough pace to give every man, woman and goggle-eyed child a good long look at him.

He should not, of course, have brought the cane into church, nor should he have wafted the handkerchief about like some dandified snuff-taker on a Brighton promenade, but, Rose thought, the poor lad knew no better and, having claimed attention, could not be blamed for enjoying his moment of glory.

She was less charitably disposed towards him, however, when he paused by her pew and with a sweeping bow that, thanks be to God, dislodged his hat at last, leaned over Mrs Prole's defences and, winking both eyes at once, wished Rose the very best of the day. He polished off the greeting with a flourish that announced his affinity with the fair maid of Thimble Row and, to shrewd observers, clearly defined his intentions.

'What,' Mrs Prole hissed, 'was that all about?'

'It seems our friend Lucas Fergusson has discovered himself.'

'Then he should un-discover himself before he becomes a laughing stock,' Mrs Prole said. 'What's wrong with the fellow?'

'It's an awakening, I think,' said Rose.

'An awakening?'

'I believe he has fallen in love.'

'With you?'

'Of course,' Rose said. 'Who else would he fall in love with?'

Four miles to the north-west, in Hayes' shabby little church, Mr Turbot was halfway through morning service. Though he was under no obligation to do so, he turned his announcement of Matthew Brodie's passing into a eulogy that had Agnes reaching for her handkerchief. He praised the man's endurance, his devotion to his family and the strength of his faith in God, a faith that had seen him bear a grievous illness without complaint, secure in the knowledge that he would soon be admitted to the company of heaven and enjoy rest eternal in the bosom of the Lord.

For some reason, that particular phrase caught Henry Brodie off guard. He burst into tears, and, with his sister's arm around him, crouched, shaking and sobbing, so that even those men and women who had no liking for the Brodies were moved to pity. Henry had not quite recovered his equilibrium when the service ended and the congregation filed out into the street. There was no flirting today, no smirking talk of matters amorous. The girls who would normally have hung about in the hope of catching Tom's eye turned quickly away from the sight of the implacable Henry with a tear-stained face and trembling lip. Agnes and Janet were surrounded by the ladies of the parish. It was left to Peter to rescue Henry from the throng.

He linked arms with his friend's brother and led him down a side street.

'Is it Tom?' he asked.

'Aye, it's Tom,' Henry admitted. 'It's always Tom, isn't it? Tom this, Tom that, an' is poor Tom sufferin'? Well, he was my father, too, Peter, an' inflexible though he could be at times, I loved him.'

'I'm sure you did.'

Henry wiped his eyes on his sleeve and sighed. 'Did Tom tell you about the promise?'

'No,' Peter said awkwardly. 'No, he did not.'

'There, at the very last, with almost his last livin' breath, my daddy said, "Look after Tom, son. Look after Tom," an' then we – then he died.'

'It proves your father trusted you, Henry.'

'Perhaps so, but, damn it, Peter, I wish his last words had been a blessin' not a curse, for lookin' after Tom is a curse,' said Henry. 'He'll hide himself away until some woman takes his fancy then he'll use Daddy's death as an excuse to demean himself again with drink an' fornication.'

'Don't judge him too harshly, Henry. We all like a tipple now and then and we're all much interested in the ladies. It's a natural thing at our age and not particularly demeaning.'

'It will be demeaning if we lose the farm,' Henry said. 'I wish you hadn't told my brother what the old woman told you. It's set him off on a half-mad course o' repentence at a time when I could have done with his help.'

'I take it you don't believe what my aunt told me?'

'Not a damned word,' said Henry. 'But Tom – oh, Tom's always been "sensitive" to things unseen, which means he's just as much in thrall to superstitious drivel as any dairymaid or thick-eared labourer. I'm more concerned about how we're going to pay for the funeral an' scratch thirty-five pounds from the ground before spring comes round than I am with ghostly voices hurling recriminations from beyond the grave.'

'You're lying, Henry,' Peter told him. 'You *are* concerned.'

Henry glanced over his shoulder at the passers-by in the main street. 'You'll just have to take my word on it that the old woman chose the worst possible moment to stick her nose into our business.'

'In fairness,' Peter said, 'I don't think Tassie chose the moment.'

'You think she was "chosen", do you?'

'I think she may have been.'

'Then,' Henry said angrily, 'you're as bad as he is an' I'll thank you not to come to Hawkshill again unless you promise to let the matter rest.'

'Tom won't let it rest.'

'No, he'll play it to the hilt,' Henry said, 'while it suits him. It provides him with an excuse for evadin' his responsibilities until something comes along to allow him to square his conscience an' go swaggerin' out to make more trouble for me to deal with.'

'I don't agree with you, Henry,' Peter Frye said. 'You're too much like your father for my taste.'

'Whether I am or whether I'm not, I now have to shoulder my father's burdens – includin' Tom,' Henry said. 'Will you come to the farm tomorrow about noon to accompany the coffin to the kirkyard?'

'Of course, I will,' Peter said. 'For Tom's sake.'

'That's good enough for me,' Henry told him and, turning on his heel, returned to the main street to find his mother and sister and hurry them home to Hawkshill before the drizzle thickened into downpour.

It hadn't occurred to Lucas that his father's employees had lives of their own. He was startled to realise that Nancy Ames was not as footloose as she pretended to be and had five stalwart brothers to defend her honour and one or two admirers who did not take kindly to being usurped by a perfumed whippersnapper.

'Looo-kuss.' Nancy minced towards him. 'Where did ye get the hat?'

Feathers and cheap flounces could not disguise the girl's lowly origins. Lucas – the new Lucas, with his cane, gloves and handkerchief – would have preferred to ignore her. He had intended to waylay Rose Hewitt and instigate a wooing but his way was blocked by the very woman who had awakened him to the joys of manhood in the first place, by Nancy and her five, broad-shouldered brothers. He regretted that he had sent his parents off in the pony-trap and had been tardy in linking his arm with that of Miss Hewitt as soon as she emerged from church. He looked around desperately for his true love, as if true love alone might rescue him, but Rose and the house-keeper had left the gathering and were heading up the slope towards Thimble Row.

Hooking an arm through his, Nancy spun him in the direction of Caddy Crawford's ale-house. 'Ye'll be takin' me for a wee bite o' dinner then,' she informed him, 'you an' your fancy hat.'

'Will I?' said Lucas.

'Ye promised ye would.'

'Promised?' Lucas said. 'When did I promise?'

She leaned against him, licked his ear and whispered, 'Last Tuesday, when ye were slippin' it intae me.'

'Aye,' growled one of the brothers who had crept up to Lucas's elbow. 'Surely you remember slippin' it intae her, Mr Fergusson?'

At the top of the slope, where Thimble Row began, Miss Hewitt and Mrs Prole paused to observe young Mr Fergusson being led away towards the ale-house by a not unattractive milkmaid and a small army of rough-looking males.

'It seems, my dear,' said Mrs Prole, 'that you've a rival for Mr Fergusson's affections?'

'It does, does it not?' Rose said. 'Oh, well, no matter.'

'How fickle you are, Rose Hewitt. Will you not fight for him?'

'Of course I will, dear Mrs Prole, of course I will,' Rose said, then, giggling like a five-year-old, took Eunice by the arm and trotted her off home.

Grief, or anger, had sharpened Henry's appetite. He attacked the broth Betsy ladled out for him as if he had not seen food for a week. Janet was by the hearth stuffing her face with the remains of a veal pie and Agnes, still in her bonnet and cape, knelt by the fire, sipping tea. There was a curious air of relief in the cottage, of heartiness almost, as if the body had already been taken away and the Brodies were ready to move on.

Conn sat at the table with a glass of whisky in his fist. Janet could not take her eyes off him. If Conn was aware of her scrutiny he was not embarrassed by it and, now and then, glanced in her direction and blessed her with a wink.

'Sure now,' he said, 'will you be havin' a piper to play him down the hill?'

'No,' Henry said, waving his spoon, 'no piper.'

'No piper?' said Conn. 'Why not?'

'My father wouldn't have wanted it,' said Janet.

'Well, well!' Conn said. 'It's a dour sort o' feller who wouldn't want a piper to play at his funeral.'

'My father,' Henry said, 'was a dour sort o' man.'

'When I set out on my journey westward, by heaven, I'll be sure to have a piper or two to let the good Lord know I'm coming,' Conn declared. 'An' you, Henry, will you have the music, or will you not?'

'Music won't matter to me if I'm dead,' Henry said.

'So,' said Conn, 'you'll not be sitting in ethereal form on the top o' the grave mound to observe the proceedings?'

'I do not believe I will,' said Henry stiffly.

'You'll be gone, fleeing up to heaven fast as your wings will carry you?'

The subject of an afterlife was a touchy one. Betsy had heard Tom and Henry go at it often enough in the late hour. She moved around the table and, as discreetly as possible, touched her cousin's shoulder in the hope that he would take the hint and skate away.

'Aye, or fallin' through the floor to fry in hell,' said Henry.

'No heaven without a hell,' Conn said. 'It's fair, I suppose, to balance one against the other. But if the Lord's as forgiving as we're taught to believe then there's worse than us to stoke Old Sootie's fires.'

'Do you belong to the Church o' Rome, Mr McCaskie?' Agnes asked.

'I belong to any church that'll have me,' Conn replied. 'But, no, I was baptised in the wee kirk at Ferryford, just ten mile down the road from here before my father's – ah – his business took him back to Ireland.'

'What was your father's business, Mr McCaskie?' Janet enquired.

'Trade,' Conn answered promptly. 'Free trade.'

'Free trade?' said Janet. 'What sort o' trade's that?'

Glancing up over his soup spoon, Henry grinned. 'The best kind o' trade there is for a man who has no scruples. Isn't that right, Conn?'

'Smack on the mark, Henry,' Connor McCaskie agreed. 'Smack on the mark.'

Then, to Janet's bewilderment, and Betsy's relief, both men burst out laughing.

It was well after dark before her cousin left Hawkshill. He said he would return to take his place among the mourners for the march to the kirkyard if no one objected, which no one did. He kissed Betsy, hugged Janet, shook Agnes's hand, murmured a few words to Henry then mounted the pony and, with a saddle lamp to guide him, rode off down the muddy track.

When Betsy entered the barn a few minutes later she found that Tom had straddled the wooden chair and had fallen asleep again. It was cold in the barn, dismally damp. She shook Tom gently. It took him all his time to swing his legs from the chair and when he tried to stand upright he staggered and might even have fallen if Betsy had not caught him. He was so cold that he sucked all the warmth from her body and, in seconds, she too was shivering.

She said, 'You can't keep this up, Tom. If you do, you'll join your father in the grave before long. Go an' eat your supper an' warm yourself indoors.'

'I can't,' Tom said. 'He might come back.'

'Nah, nah,' Betsy said. 'Conn's gone for the night.'

'Conn?' Tom said. 'No, not McCaskie; my daddy.'

'Is that what you're waitin' for, Tom, for your father to waken up?'

'He came to that woman, that witch woman in Drennan.'

'Came to her?' said Betsy.

'He spoke to her.'

'How did he speak to her?'

'Peter told me; he spoke to me through her.'

'An' you think he'll speak to you again?' said Betsy.

'I do. I do.'

In flickering candlelight, with the coffin casting a gigantic shadow on the straw and the barn alive with the stealthy rustling of rats and mice, Betsy was almost tempted to believe him. She glanced at the old man's bloodless features, soft and waxy now. For an instant, she almost expected him to open his eyes, part his thin lips and order Tom to go indoors and eat his supper like a good boy.

'He's not at rest, Betsy.'

'He looks at rest to me, Tom.'

'His spirit's not at rest.'

'Look,' she said, 'if he – if he speaks then I'll fetch you.'

Tom propped his elbows on the side of the coffin and peered into his father's face, so close, Betsy thought, that he might be attempting to breathe life back into the corpse.

'Tom,' said a stern voice. Betsy almost jumped out of her skin. 'Tom, do as Betsy tells you an' go in.'

She spun round and let out a cry.

'Sorry, lass, I didn't mean to alarm you.' Henry stepped out of the darkness into the candlelight and took her by the arm. 'What's this daft brother o' mine been sayin' to scare you?'

'I told her the truth,' said Tom.

'The truth?' said Henry. 'What truth would that be, Tom?'

'That Daddy's still with us.'

'Oh, aye.' Henry endeavoured to sound off-hand. 'He'll be with us until tomorrow, Tom, then he'll be with us no more. It's sad, but it's the way o' the world.' He placed a hand on his brother's shoulder and turned him away from the coffin. 'Mother has a fine, rich mutton broth on the fire. There's a piece o' veal pie left an' cheese in plenty. There's also the cask o' brandy Connor McCaskie brought us just beggin' to be tapped. I'll stand watch until midnight, then, as seems fittin', we'll keep Daddy company together, just the pair o' us, through until dawn. What do you say to that suggestion?'

Betsy watched Tom's shoulders sag and, slowly, he nodded.

'Brandy,' he said. 'McCaskie brought us brandy, did he?'

'Claret, too.' Henry eased Tom towards the door. 'He's a generous sort o' fellow is Mr McCaskie, though I've no doubt he'll quaff his fair share tomorrow.'

'Aye, tomorrow,' Tom said. 'Tomorrow.' Then, shaking off his brother's hand, headed out into the yard.

Betsy said, 'I'll go with him.'

Henry said, 'No, lass, stay an' keep me company. My mother would like Tom to herself for a while.'

He pulled out the chair, lifted the blanket from the floor and shook it. He offered the chair to Betsy and when she had seated herself, draped the blanket about her shoulders. He rested his hips against the base of the coffin, folded his arms and looked down at her.

'Exactly what *did* Tom tell you, Betsy?'

'Only that Tassie Landles had heard from your father.'

'Do you believe her?'

Betsy hesitated. 'No.'

'What else did Tom say?'

She looked up at him, frowning. 'Nothin', Henry. I swear that's all.'

He inched away from the trestle and, coming round behind her, stood for a moment with both hands on her shoulders.

'You're an honest girl, Betsy McBride,' he said. 'We're lucky to have you.' And then, like a benediction, he kissed the top of her head.

Four men and two women followed the cart from the heights of Hawkshill. The rain had eased but cloud still hung over the hills. The hedgerows were black and dripping and the cattle in the long pasture oddly silent as the cortège rolled past. The coffin was roped to the bed of the cart but when the slope steepened above the turnpike it tipped forward and might even have up-ended if Conn hadn't stepped up, slammed it down with his forearm and, matching his pace to that of the horse, held it firm and flat until the cart wheeled on to the level.

Agnes had said her farewells before the coffin had been screwed shut and, in keeping with tradition, had remained at home to nurse her grief. Janet and Betsy walked, arm-in-arm, four or five paces behind the men. They wore shawls over their heads, no bonnets, and long lengths of black cotton were tied in loose knots at their waists. The men wore Sabbath clothes, as sombre as their wardrobe could provide. Even the Irishman had borrowed a jet-black coat to cover his goatskin vest and looked, Betsy thought, more like a priest than a pirate with the garment buttoned up to his throat.

The men were bareheaded, their hats held down by their sides. When the cart turned into the lane that led to the graveyard, Betsy saw that the mourners gathered by the gate were bareheaded too and thought how unfamiliar they looked shorn of their hats and caps.

The gravedigger's son took the reins of the horse from Henry and guided the cart to a gravel patch that linked the church to the burial ground. The brothers, flanking the gate, let the mourners pass between them with no more acknowledgement than a dip of the head. Betsy and Janet took up position outside the dry-stone wall that separated the graveyard from the road. There were no other women present – Matthew Brodie had not been well liked by the fair sex – and only twenty or so men.

The grave, dug deep, looked raw and unnatural. The mound of earth and turf beside it, soaked with recent rain, stained the verges with pale brown mud. Wary of losing their footing, the gentlemen stood back until the coffin was brought from the cart by Tom, Henry, John Rankine and Peter Frye and, holding the base in one hand to steady it, the burly, black-clad stranger whose presence added a note of mystery to the occasion.

The coffin had no handles. It was borne on a cradle of ropes. The pallbearers shuffled awkwardly across the grass and on Mr Turbot's instruction eased the chest over the edge of the grave and lowered it into the depths. Kneeling, Tom fed the rope through his fingers inch by inch as if, Betsy thought, he could not bear to sever connection with the man who had fathered him. At length, he got to his feet and brought up the rope. Shaking it free of clay, he handed it to the gravedigger's son; then Mr Talbot committed Matthew Brodie's body to the ground and his spirit into the keeping of the Lord.

'Oh, Daddy, Daddy!' Janet murmured and, for the first time, wept.

A moment or two later a young man sporting the blue cross-bands and the brown leather satchel of a licensed carrier nudged Betsy in the small of the back. 'Pardon me, miss, is one o' them gentlemen Mr Brodie?' He fished a letter packet from the satchel and squinted at it. 'Mr Thomas Brodie?'

'Aye.' Betsy pointed. 'That's him.'

'Well,' the carrier said, 'I've got a letter for him.'

'A letter?' Janet sniffed up her tears. 'Who's writin' letters to our Tom?'

'Despatcher not recorded,' the young man said. 'I was told Mr Brodie'd be at the church in Hayes at two o' the clock.'

'Where did you pick up this letter?' said Betsy.

'In Drennan, miss, at the office.'

'Drennan, is it?' Janet held out her hand. 'You can't disturb Mr Brodie now. Give it here. I'll see he gets it.'

'An' who might you be, miss?' the carrier asked suspiciously.

'I'm his sister,' Janet told him and snatched the letter from his grasp.

With only a few cows in milk it did not take Betsy and Janet long to hurry through the evening chores. The candles in the barn had been extinguished but light flooded from the cottage window and the girls could hear the gabbling roar of Tom's cronies who had come up from Hayes to give old Matt Brodie the sort of rousing send-off of which he would have thoroughly disapproved.

'Did he tell you who sent it?' Janet asked.

'Not a hint,' Betsy answered.

'Whoever it was,' said Janet, 'he's well pleased wi' himself.'

'Oh,' said Betsy, 'I think we can guess who it's from.'

'Rose Hewitt.' Janet nodded. 'Aye, it would hardly be from her daddy, would it? At least he never had the gall for to turn up at the graveside, though I saw old Fergusson lurkin' at the back o' the crowd.'

Betsy had no doubt that the letter had been sent by Rose Hewitt. She had observed the care with which Tom had opened the packet, how he had stopped stock still on the walk out of the graveyard and had smiled, sleek and sly, and had quickly folded the letter and slipped it into his pocket when Peter Frye had ridden up to offer him a saddle for the journey back up the hill.

There was a sense of relief in the company now that the burial was over. Talk was not of the life that was gone but of the life that lay ahead, as if, Betsy thought, old Mr Brodie had left no mark worthy of record.

In a week or so Henry would take his mother to Hayes to admire the stone the mason would put up. Some token would be left by the widow, a spray of evergreen most like, then the book would close on the former tenant of the farm of Hawkshill and the next chapter in the Brodies' history would begin.

The girls moved across the yard to wash their hands at the pump.

'I'd give a guinea, if I had one, for a glimpse o' that letter,' Janet said. 'I'd fair like to know if he's bedded her yet.'

'He talks about marriage.'

'Aye,' said Janet. 'He'll talk about marriage till the moon falls out o' the sky but it's not a wife our Tom wants.'

'What about you, Janet?' Betsy put in. 'What do you want?'

'Huh!' said the girl. 'I'll take what I can get an' be thankful for it. I'd run off wi' yon cousin o' yours, though, if you hadn't put a collar on him first.'

'There's no collar – mine or anyone's – round Conn's neck,' Betsy said.

'Does he not like girls, then?'

'Oh, he likes girls well enough,' Betsy replied. 'I've heard he has a "wife" hid away on the Isle o' Man an' others, like as not, in Ireland.'

'None here in Scotland?'

'None I've heard of.' Chuckling, Betsy dug an elbow into young Miss Brodie's side. 'Now don't you go thinkin' you'll be the first. Our Conn's a rover, here then gone again.'

'Did you really stab a gypsy, Betsy?'

'Ask Conn.'

'Will he tell me the truth?'

'I doubt it,' Betsy said and, still chuckling, dried her hands on her skirts and headed back across the yard to snatch a bite of supper before the gentlemen consumed everything in sight.

In spite of appearances Conn was sufficiently sober to bend his mind to business. As soon as a suitable occasion presented itself he steered Henry away from the crowd in the kitchen and, pipe and glass in hand, persuaded him to step outside for a breath of air. Henry did not need much persuasion. He took no pleasure in watching his brother, emboldened by drink, flirting with Betsy McBride while Johnny Rankine bawled out verse after verse of the obscene ballad, 'Poor Peggy Rafferty', and the lads joined in the choruses.

'There'll be many a spill on the road home tonight,' Conn said.

'Serve them right,' said Henry. 'Ribald nonsense like that isn't suitable for ladies' ears. My father must be spinnin' in his grave.'

'He was not a man for jollification, then?'

'That he was not,' said Henry. 'He didn't care for socialising o' any kind, particularly if strong drink was involved.'

Conn sipped from his glass. 'Laughter isn't sinful, is it?'

'Nah, nah,' said Henry. 'I'm not the prude my father was, thank God, but I'm not like my brother either. I believe in modesty an' moderation.'

Conn puffed at his pipe. 'Modesty an' moderation won't dig you out o' the hole, though.'

'The hole?' said Henry. 'What hole?'

'The pitfall o' poverty.'

'Why are you so interested in our family? Come along, Mr McCaskie, out with it. What do you want with us?'

Conn put down his glass and pipe. The racket from the cottage had grown louder. He raised his voice to make himself heard. 'Has Betsy told you how I earn my bread?'

'She told me you're a trader. You said as much yourself,' Henry answered. 'There's no shame in that – provided you pay your taxes.'

'What if I don't pay my taxes?'

'Then you'd be an outlaw.'

'An outlaw,' said Conn, 'is a quaint way o' puttin' it. Come now, Henry Brodie, you're no fool. Sure an' you've already deduced what I am.'

Henry nodded. 'A smuggler.'

'Born an' bred into the principle o' free trade,' Conn admitted. 'My father – Betsy's uncle on her mammy's side – feathered our nest in the good old days when the Isle of Man belonged to the Duke o' Atholl who set his own tariffs. One million pounds a year was the estimated loss to His Majesty's exchequer which is why, some twenty years back, His Majesty purchased sovereign rights to the island for seventy thousand pounds.'

'I've heard o' the infamous Revestment Act,' Henry said. 'I just don't see what it has to do with us.'

'Back to Ireland my daddy went,' Conn pressed on. 'He took us all with him, all except Betsy's mother who had fallen in love with an Ayrshire weaver an' followed him to Scotland. My daddy didn't give up his boats nor lose touch with those merchants who were unwilling to pay taxes.'

'I still don't see—'

'My brothers went off to America, to Virginia, where they fought for the patriots an' got their reward in land. When my father died I inherited his boats an' the routes he'd laid down for the cargoes,' Conn said. 'What's more I've merchants in Glasgow slaverin' for any free-trade goods they can lay hands on. Unfortunately the Crown has more revenue officers ranked against us than ever before. The best landin' beaches from the Solway to Ullapool are heavily patrolled and even the west coast is close to bein' locked up.'

Henry opened his mouth to repeat his question.

Conn forestalled him. 'I can land cargoes at Port Cedric clean an' quick. There's the ruin o' a jetty an' a thumbnail o' beach there. What there's not is a scrap o' shelter to hide the goods, not a cave, coppice nor farmhouse . . .'

'Ah!' Henry exclaimed. 'Ah-hah!'

'A farmhouse like you have here on Hawkshill.'

'We're two miles at least from the sea.'

'A half-hour's trail for ponies, an hour at the most for carts.'

'Across the turnpike?' said Henry. 'Is that not dangerous?'

'There's no traffic on the road at night. A skilled man can have a pony train across in five minutes. Once over the pike' – he punched his fist into his palm – 'it's a clear run to Hawkshill.'

'An' then?'

'Then you store the cargo until the merchants send for it.'

'Store it where?'

'There.' Conn jerked a thumb in the direction of the barn.

'Behind the straw, you mean?'

'Perfect cover.'

'There are rats, though, a plague o' them.'

'Rats can be got rid of.'

'More easily than customs officers, I imagine,' said Henry. 'How will the cargoes be collected an' taken away?'

'Piecemeal.'

'Over the moor?'

'Over the moor, it is,' Conn replied. 'Now, Mr Brodie, what do you say?'

Henry stooped and found Conn's glass. He wiped the rim fastidiously with finger and thumb and downed the dregs of the whisky in a swift gulp. He picked up the tobacco pipe, sniffed the bowl, then, holding glass and pipe before him, hoisted himself upright again.

'What's in it for us, Mr McCaskie?'

'A fortune,' Conn said.

'Enough to pay off our debts?'

'Ten times over.'

'An' set this place to rights?' said Henry.

'An' *buy* this place, if that's your wish,' Conn told him.

'How soon do you need an answer?'

'Soon,' the Irishman said. 'There's a brig anchored off Lochranza on the far side o' Arran with some black cargo on board; my cargo.'

'How soon is soon?' said Henry.

'Tomorrow,' Connor McCaskie told him. 'Wednesday at the latest.'

And Henry, with a tuneless little whistle, said, 'Oh!'

Curled up like a cat, Tom lay asleep at the foot of the ladder. Someone – Henry most like – had thrown a blanket over him. Johnny Rankine, fully clothed, was sprawled across the spars of the old man's bed. He had torn down the curtain and wrapped it round him and if he had not been snoring Betsy might well have taken him for dead. Conn and the other revellers had gone, unless, Betsy thought, they were laid out like sacks of meal on the floor of the loft.

At half past midnight when Tom's attentions had become too much for her she had retreated to bed. Agnes and Janet had joined her and she had spent an uncomfortable night wedged between mother and daughter.

At six she got up and put on her clothes and, yawning, took herself into the yard to wash her face at the pump and pay her call at the outhouse. Shivering, she returned to the cottage where Henry was boiling water in a little pan over the remnants of the fire. The table was littered with bottles and glasses, the floor greasy with spillings. The only untainted thing in the room was Henry who, bathed, shaved and clad in a freshly laundered shirt, looked as if he had risen from a good night's sleep with a clear head and a clearer conscience.

'Thank God,' he said quietly, 'that's over.'

'Have they all gone?'

'All except Rankine.'

'Conn, too?'

'First away,' Henry told her, 'though that's not sayin' much.'

'Will I waken your mother an' Janet?'

'Let them sleep,' said Henry. 'I'll fetch in the beasts.'

He brought the pan to the table and poured boiling water into the teapot. Slices of oat bread and butter and some slivers of cheese were laid out on two clean plates. Betsy ate bread and cheese and drank the strong, hot tea. It felt strange to be standing among the debris with nothing tidy or organised, nothing save Henry.

'Tell me a bit about your cousin,' he said.

'Connor?' said Betsy, surprised. 'He's much as you see him. He hides nothin' away.'

'Nothing save his true profession.'

'Aye, he can be dark about that.'

'He's a smuggler, is he not?'

'He told you?'

'He did,' said Henry. 'Has he ever been jailed?'

'Not that I've heard.'

'Where does he live?'

Betsy shrugged. 'Wherever he lands. I think he has a cottage somewhere on the Isle o' Man. He took his mother, my Aunt Netta, there from Ireland some years back. His sister an' her husband live on the isle, too. If he has a home anywhere it'll be on the Isle o' Man.'

'Is he a man of honour?'

'Honour?' said Betsy. 'Well, I don't know about honour.'

'Is he honest?'

'The revenue officers don't think so.'

'Would he cheat a friend?' said Henry.

'No,' said Betsy. 'Never.'

'How can you be sure?'

'He's my cousin.'

'Of course he is,' said Henry. 'Drink up your tea, Betsy, an' we'll forge on with the business o' the day. I've much to do before nightfall.'

It had been years since Henry had tasted salt spray on his lips. In the distant days of his childhood he had been taken now and then to paddle in the surf that licked Ballantrae's sandy shore and once, in the wake of a huge storm, to see the wreck of a sailing vessel that had been smashed upon the rocks. But the Brodies' little patch had been high up in the hills – much like Hawkshill, in fact – and the sea had been no more than a feature of the horizon.

Odd, then, that when he cleared the dunes, saw waves curling up on Port Cedric's tiny beach and experienced the soft, sinking sensation of sand beneath his heels, he felt as if his father were walking behind him and he was still a little boy who, confronted by such a vast and restless entity as the sea, might require a reassuring hand to hold on to or a leg to hide behind.

There was nothing to Port Cedric. The stone-walled cottage that had once housed the laird of Copplestone's fisher folk was a roofless ruin and the jetty where, a generation ago, Copplestone's little fleet had landed the catch was hardly more than a stump gnawed down by winter gales and high neap tides. Copplestone House, where the Fryes lived, lay a half-mile to the north but its parklands stopped short of the port whose sparse acres were leased out in small parcels for the grazing of sheep and goats.

If Henry had expected to find a handsome brig anchored off shore or a brace of longboats beached on the sand he was disappointed. Only a little smack was moored to the butt of the jetty, its mast lowered, its oars roped over the stern; no jolly crew drinking rum and dancing hornpipes either, just Connor McCaskie, in a woollen cap and brown cloth greatcoat, hunkered over a driftwood fire.

'Sure, here you are at last,' Conn said. 'I've a tater or two buried in the ashes if you fancy a bite o' dinner.'

'No, thank you,' Henry said. 'I ate dinner an hour since. Is this where you spent the night?'

'I berthed in Hayes with Betsy's folks.' Conn hoisted himself up. 'Though I'm not averse to sleeping under the stars if I have to. Has your brother recovered his wits yet?'

'Barely,' Henry said.

'Did you broach him with my proposition?'

'No.'

'No?' said Conn, frowning. 'Haven't you brought me an answer?'

'I have questions to ask first,' said Henry.

'I reckoned that might be the case. Load your cannon an' fire away.'

'This vessel anchored behind Arran, how large is its cargo?'

'Tobacco, two boatloads, perhaps three. Brandy casks, ten in all. Holland gin, another eight.'

'That's not much of a cargo for a brig,' said Henry.

'Sure, that's only the black cargo,' Conn told him. 'The rest is listed on the manifest to keep the customs at Greenock happy.'

'I see,' said Henry. 'If a King's cutter hoves into view then the black cargo is jettisoned an' the Excise presented with the manifest to check against legitimate goods in the hold.'

'It's not as easy as you make it sound, Henry.'

'I'll wager it isn't. How great is the risk o' being caught red-handed?'

'Fair to middling,' Conn admitted, 'but there's a fat slice o' pudding waiting for all concerned.'

Henry looked around. 'Is that your boat?'

Conn nodded. 'One o' several.'

'It's very small.'

'It is,' Conn agreed.

'How many trips from the brig will it take to ferry the goods ashore?'

'The brig has boats too.'

'I see,' Henry said. 'What then? Three trips?'

'Three or four.'

'How many ponies will you need?'

'Half a dozen.'

'We have two, just two.'

'Aye, but you also have strong horses and a couple of carts.'

'Who furnishes the land crew?' said Henry.

'You do.'

'In that case,' said Henry, 'we'll need my brother on our side, an' my mother an' my sister as well.'

'An' Betsy,' Conn reminded him.

'Yes,' said Henry, 'that's another matter I'd like to raise. How long has Betsy been party to your plans?'

'She knows nothing o' my plans.'

'If Betsy isn't involved,' said Henry, 'what brought you to our door?'

'An eye for opportunity,' Conn said. 'I was on the lookout for a safe beach an' a dry store. When I heard where Betsy was employed, I explored the situation further.'

'Did you buy our cattle simply to put us in your debt?'

'I bought your cattle to shine a favourable light on what I hoped might be a profitable partnership.'

'That's fair,' said Henry. 'When do you intend to make the landing?'

'Tomorrow night. High tide's at one o' the clock.'

'Come to the farm tonight,' Henry said, 'about an hour after dark. I'll give you an answer then.'

'Why not now?' said Conn.

'Because,' said Henry, 'there are more necks on the block than mine.'

He had struggled all morning with a sour stomach and might have accepted Johnny Rankine's offer of a ride into Hayes to partake of a medicinal glass of ale at Souter Gordon's if the women had not ganged up and chased the old reprobate off home before he could do more damage to Tom's moral fibre, not to mention his intestines.

By mid-afternoon, Tom had recovered sufficiently to sneak out to the stable to reread Rose Hewitt's love letter. He was touched by her words of comfort and soothed by her promises of kisses to come. He had already begun to plan his courtship when Henry arrived home and gathered the family into the kitchen to tell them of Connor McCaskie's offer.

'Daddy's not cold in his grave,' Tom snapped, 'an' you're doin' deals with an Irish smuggler. God, Henry Brodie, what's come over you?'

'Common sense,' said Henry.

'Is it common sense to have us clapped in irons?'

'Would you have us go beggin' to Neville Hewitt for another six months' credit? There's not the devil's chance we can crop enough profit from Hawkshill to pay the half year, not the devil's chance Hewitt will do anything but evict us. Didn't Daddy prove to us that thrift an' dog labour aren't enough to raise a man out o' the dirt?'

'I have plans,' said Tom haughtily.

'Plans involvin' Hewitt's daughter?' said Henry. 'Those aren't plans, man, they're dreams. Even if you do talk her into marrying you, Hewitt will cut her off without a farthing. He never liked Daddy, but he *hates* you.'

'Tom's never had the stomach to do anything on his own,' Janet put in. 'We blamed Daddy for it but I'm thinkin' it was Tom's weakness all along.'

'Shut your mouth, girl,' Tom told her. 'This has nothin' to do with you.'

'Oh, but it does,' said Henry. 'If we take up McCaskie's offer then we're all in it together, an' if we're caught we'll all swing.'

'What about Betsy?' said Janet.

'I could be doin' with a bit o' excitement,' said Betsy. 'I'll stay.'

'Black goods hid in our barn,' said Tom. 'City folk comin' an' goin' at all hours o' the day an' night: do you suppose such activity won't be noticed?'

'By who?' said Henry. 'There's nobody on this hillside but us an' none o' us are going to clipe to the revenue officers.' He moved closer to his brother. 'Think on this, Tom: if we assist in enough landings, not only will we have spring rent but we'll have enough left over to drain, dress an' seed every miserable acre. Hewitt may hate you but, by God, that won't stand in his way o' taking our money. An' if all goes well, who knows, one day we might buy Hawkshill.'

'If you buy Hawkshill you'll be a landowner, Tom,' said Janet, 'an' you'll have your pick o' the lassies then, all right.'

Tom wrapped his hand over his brow. 'My father was an honest, God-fearin' man—' he began.

'An' look where it got him,' Agnes Brodie put in. 'Do it, Henry. Tell the Irishman we're on his side. Tell him we're in.'

13

Agnes leaned on the board as bold as a warrior queen and let out an excited 'hoh' when the horse dragged the cart across the turnpike on to the long scoop that led to the beach. Betsy guided the horse cautiously down the track until a faint radiance in the sky outlined the mounds that backed the beach.

'There,' Agnes Brodie hissed. 'See.'

Betsy reined the horse and stared anxiously at a man crouched in the lee of the dunes. For an instant she thought the game might be up before it had even begun. She wondered how she would react if torches flared and muskets cracked, if she would meekly surrender or, abandoning the widow Brodie, throw herself from the cart and wriggle off into the darkness like a weasel.

Henry spoke up. 'Stay with the cart, Mammy. The sand's too soft to bear its weight. Betsy, come with me.'

Betsy handed the reins to Agnes, climbed over the cartwheel and followed Henry and the ponies through the dunes. She felt less exposed now that she was on foot. The ponies, startled by the sight of the sea, stamped and snorted as Janet brought them round the prow of the dune and led them to the jetty.

Tom, Conn and several other men were strapping panniers to the horses and unloading casks from a small boat. Betsy sensed that there was a ship out in the darkness but all she could see were the pale tops of the waves gathering and cresting not far from shore. Cargo was already piled at the head of the jetty, not great bales and hogsheads but miniature kegs and small oilskin-wrapped parcels just large enough for a man to carry.

Conn, a cask on each shoulder, murmured, 'Good evenin', ladies, a fine night for our venture, sure an' it is.' He eased past the ponies and went on up the beach, followed by two strangers, similarly burdened.

Betsy was amazed at the smugglers' efficiency and the speed with which the loading was accomplished without the flicker of a lantern and no more than a muttered word or two. When the ponies were packed, Janet led them off through the dunes. Betsy was instructed to return to the cart and follow the ponies back to Hawkshill. She climbed into the cart, retrieved the reins from Agnes and, with difficulty, brought the horse round in a narrow circle. The wheels sank into the sand and the cart tilted. For a moment it seemed that it might topple but the rack of casks had been topped by small kegs, expertly battened. The cargo remained snug and secure as the cart jerked and levelled and ploughed forward on to firm ground.

The slope was more severe than Betsy had realised. It took the best part of a half-hour to reach the turnpike. Janet and the ponies had already gone across. Betsy reined the horse and fixed the brake and would have clambered down to check that the way was clear if Agnes had not stopped her.

'I'll do it,' Agnes said.

With the agility of a woman half her years, she hopped from the cart and stole out from the shelter of the thorn hedge that lined the scoop.

Betsy could barely make her out as she stood in the centre of the road and, looking first one way and then the other, waved her shawl in a signal that all was clear. Betsy urged the horse forward, felt the wheels lift and clatter and then, with a sigh of relief, ran the cart into the mouth of the Hawkshill track.

The widow Brodie scrambled up beside her, panting.

'Are we safe now, Betsy?' she asked.

'Safe as we'll ever be,' Betsy answered. 'We'll be home in half an hour.'

'Thank God for that,' said Agnes Brodie. 'I'm dyin' for a cup o' tea.'

Conn and his crew did not accompany the cargo to Hawkshill. They would sweep hoof and wheel marks from the track with clumps of broom, then, so Henry said, return to the smack to catch the breeze that came with the turn of the tide and by daylight would be safe in harbour, miles from Port Cedric.

For Betsy and the Brodies the hard work had just begun. Horses and ponies were unloaded and stabled, then, fortified by a dram of whisky and a dish of tea, the young folk set out to hide the contraband while Agnes, well wrapped against the chill, stood watch at the head of the track.

The size of the black cargo caught everyone off guard. As the night wore on Tom and Henry bickered and snarled at each other and, if they had been less exhausted, might even have come to blows. Digging out straw to form a hiding place released a legion of rats. Janet – not squeamish about such things – speared as many as she could with a pitchfork and tossed the corpses on to the dung-heap. Barred up in the kennels, the dogs were wide awake and, smelling blood, set up a great hullabaloo, while the farm's feral cats crept from behind the outhouses and pounced, squealing, on the vermin.

It was dirty, noisy, back-breaking work. Only fear of being caught red-handed when daylight came kept the Brodies at it. As it was, the sky to the east was streaked with butter-coloured cloud before the last cask was rolled into place and the last matt of tobacco lugged up to the loft above the kitchen safe from the predations of rats and mice. By then it was close to seven o'clock. Betsy and Janet went off to fetch the cows while Henry and Tom swept the barn and made it tidy. There was no reason to suppose that anyone would come tramping up the hill from the village or that customs officers would get wind of the shipment and descend on the farm. Even so, when the family gathered at the table for breakfast they shared a sense of foreboding magnified by exhaustion and the knowledge that, weary as they were, there was still a day's labour on the farm to endure before they could rest.

'How long does the Irishman expect us to sit on the stuff before he comes to take it away?' Tom asked.

'I've no idea,' Henry answered.

'I thought you knew everythin'.' Tom grumbled. 'I thought you were an expert on our new life o' crime.'

'Stop it, Tom,' Agnes told him. 'It'll go easier next time.'

'Damn it, Mammy, there'll be no next time. I've had enough.'

'Did you suppose Mr McCaskie would hand us a fistful o' money for sittin' on our arses?' Janet piped up.

'We've seen not one penny o' McCaskie's money yet,' Tom retorted. 'Here we are with enough untaxed alcohol in our barn to float a frigate an' enough tobacco to smoke half the herring in the Irish Sea, none o' it hidden well enough to deceive a five-year-old let alone a revenue officer, an' you don't even know when the stuff will be collected or how much our rake will be.'

'Fifteen per cent,' said Henry.

Tom scowled. 'Fifteen per cent o' what?'

'What we're given.'

'Given by whom?'

'I have the price list,' Henry said. 'Conn gave me the price list.'

'I thought you knew nothin' about it,' said Tom.

'Nah, nah,' said Henry. 'I just don't know how long we'll have the goods in store or how they'll be collected but I know roughly what they'll fetch. The half ankers will bring one pound an' eight shillings each. The casks contain over-proof

French brandy, crystal-clear an' potent enough to kill a man with a mouthful. The dealers will tint them wi' caramel and water them down.'

'An how much are the casks worth?' Janet asked.

'Eight pounds an' fifteen shillings,' Henry replied.

'Each?' said Betsy.

'Aye, each. That's twenty-six shillin's per cask for us.'

'How many casks?' said Janet eagerly.

'Twelve,' said Henry. 'When we add in our cut on the half ankers o' gin an' the tobacco . . .'

'It's a half-year's rent,' said Janet.

Henry nodded. 'Near enough.'

'Huh!' said Janet, sitting back. 'Half the year's rent for one night's hard work an' you've the gall to complain, Tom Brodie.'

'I could've earned that sum honestly,' Tom muttered.

'How?' said Janet. 'Tell us how?'

'By the sweat o' my brow.'

'Well, if it's sweat you're hankerin' after,' Janet said, 'you'll have plenty o' that when you start sowin' the winter wheat.'

'The field's not ready for seed yet,' Tom said.

'Then make it ready,' his mother told him. 'The ground's dry enough to accept the harrow, is it not?'

'The horses are too tired to work today,' Tom said.

'Is it the horses, or is it you?' Janet said. 'Lazy beggar.'

He lifted his hand to slap her then thought better of it. He heaved himself to his feet and stretched his weary arms above his head. 'No,' he said. 'I'll not punish the horses for our profit, Henry. Are you fetchin' sheep down to the shelters today?'

'Probably.'

'Then I'll give you a hand wi' that.'

'We'll need to pull the last of the turnips before the frost sets in,' Henry said. 'If the girls are up to it, they might . . .'

Betsy lifted her head.

'Listen,' she said. 'There's a cart come into the yard.'
And the Brodies were suddenly still.

It was not so much a cart as a wagon, a long, four-wheeled
English-style dray of the sort used to haul hay harvests on large
farms on the southern ranges. Betsy had never seen one like it,
certainly not one with a garishly painted hood and a high prow
ornamented with pots and pans. It was drawn not by feather-
footed draught horses but dainty creatures with silky manes
and sharp little hooves that would not, she thought, have been
out of place in a circus ring. Neat the horses might be but they
were muddy, plastered with mud, in fact, as if they had been
driven at speed through a bog. The cart's broad wheels were
also caked with mud and even the driver, a small, spry man in
a green frock coat, top boots and a tall, tall hat, appeared to
have been sprayed with the stuff. He reined the horses and
applied the brake to the wagon.

Pots and pans, dangling from hooks around the driver's
station, rattled and jingled. Reaching back, he touched each of
them with the tip of his whip to silence it, then, tipping his hat,
cried out in a jovial, jingly sort of voice, 'It's the road's end at
last, an' not a moment too soon.' Then, casting aside his whip,
he sprang to the ground and shot off around the barn where he
made water noisily for several minutes while Betsy and the
Brodies gawped at the circus horses and the circus horses, not
at all nonplussed, gawped back.

Wiping his hands on a handkerchief, the little man reappeared.

In spite of his wrinkles and knobbly cheekbones Betsy
reckoned he was still on the cheerful side of sixty. He ignored
Tom and Henry and made straight for Agnes Brodie. Plucking
off his hat and bowing, he said, 'You must be the widder what
all the talk's about.'

'Talk?' said Agnes. 'What talk?'

188 Jessica Stirling

The little man tapped his nose with his forefinger. 'Can't be but one widder as pretty as you this side o' the Falls o' Clyde so' – he popped on his hat and tapped it down – 'I reckon I've sprinkled my scent on the weeds o' Hawkshill, leastwise I hope so. Mrs Brodie, is it?'

'It is, an' you?'

'Dingle,' he said. 'Rufus Dingle o' that ilk.'

'What ilk?' said Agnes.

'I am, by adoption, a Paisley buddy.'

'I might have guessed it,' said Agnes. 'They're all daft in Paisley.'

'I'm no weaver, ma'am. I'm a carrier to the gentry.'

'Well,' Agnes said, 'we're the only gentry this side o' the moor so if you've brought the money you may have the goods. That is what you're here for, Mr Dingle, is it not – the goods?'

'It is – an' I have,' Mr Dingle said.

'Didn't waste much time, did you?' Tom said.

'Not I, sir,' Mr Dingle said. 'When there's a dearth o' French brandy in the city o' Glasgow then a man must strike while the iron's hot.'

'A scarcity o' spirits in Glasgow?' Tom said. 'That's hard to believe.'

'Cheap spirits, sir, brandy in partic'lar,' Rufus Dingle informed him. 'Brandy's the tipple favoured by gentlemen these days. My employer's waitin' with tongue hangin' out for Mr McCaskie's shipment to be delivered.'

Henry laughed. 'Well, Mr Dingle, it occurs to me you've been on the road most o' the night an' must be famished. Come into the house an' partake o' a bite o' breakfast while we roll out the casks.'

'Thank ye most kindly, sir,' said Mr Dingle, 'but we camped last night in the shelter o' the Lang Rocks so the horses are fresh an' the family fed.'

'The family?' said Agnes.

'Girls,' Mr Dingle called out, 'it's safe to show yourselves.'

From the rear of the wagon four young girls appeared. Whether they were Mr Dingle's children or grandchildren Betsy had no notion. They ranged in age from twelve to eighteen, all sallow-skinned, dark-haired and as cheerful in disposition as the old man himself.

It occurred to Betsy that they might be tinkers – the painted wagon and display of tin-ware suggested as much – but she was too polite to enquire. Conn, it seemed, was as much a man of business as a seaman, the Brodies' farm but a link in a chain that stretched from the quays of Europe to the inns and ale-houses of Glasgow. She followed the carrier into the barn and heard Henry ask, 'Will your wagon bear the whole load, Mr Dingle, or only the brandy casks?'

'Casks only,' Rufus Dingle answered. 'A local carrier is pitched for the gin an' tobacco, I believe. I can only hide so much in my wagon. Though we steer wide from the coast, there's always a chance we might bump into a King's officer who'll not be distracted by my girls or taken in by our disguise. All bein' well, we'll reach the Lang Rocks before two an' wait there for dusk to fall. Our destination is Paisley. We'll travel easy through the night an' ride into town with the market traders tomorrow mornin'.'

Mr Dingle's girls had torn away the straw and were trundling the casks into the yard where Tom and Janet waited to assist with the loading. In a moment or two Betsy would join them; meanwhile, intrigued by the conversation, she lingered on Henry's heels.

'How long have you known Conn McCaskie?' Henry asked.

'Never met the man,' Mr Dingle replied. 'He sends word to my employer by messenger, settin' a time an' a place then I'm brought in to fetch. How long have I been ferryin' black goods? Five years, close to.'

'No trouble in that time?'

'Aye, sir, trouble enough when we undertook long hauls to an' from the caves near Ballantrae; worse when we used the ruin on the far side o' Ayr. Two o' my boys, God bless 'em, were careless at the tipple an' were near laid by the heels an' had to be whisked off by boat to lie low for a while.'

'Where are they now?'

'Dublin, last I heard. Quite happy there.'

'Tell me,' said Henry, 'is Hawkshill safer than Ayr?'

'Much so,' said Mr Dingle. 'It'll serve well for a time if Mr McCaskie can keep the landin's secret an' you have no enemies.'

'Enemies?' said Henry.

'Did Mr McCaskie not tell you?' Rufus Dingle pursed his lips. 'The Crown's agents have put a bounty on every smuggler's head, a reward for information that leads to a charge an' a conviction.'

'How much?' Betsy asked.

Mr Dingle glanced up. 'A chestful o' silver, so I've heard.'

'*What?*'

The carrier laughed. 'Pay no heed to my blathers, lassie. Thirty guineas is more like the thing. Still, there are folk enough who'd sell their souls for thirty guineas. If you've enemies in the parish, I'd be cautious, if I were you, an' not let your silver flash nor the drink loosen your tongue. Otherwise, this is a good, safe spot to store McCaskie's goods an', with luck, we'll accrue some profits for a minimum o' risk.'

Henry stepped to one side as two young girls rolled the last cask out of the barn. 'Speaking o' profit, Mr Dingle . . .'

The carrier laughed once more and, dipping a hand into a pocket of the green frock coat, produced a heavy leather purse. He held it up by the ties and let it pendulum to and fro. 'One hundred an' five pounds in coin o' the realm, sir,' he said. 'If you've a desire for to count it, I can spare you ten minutes.'

'No, Mr Dingle,' Henry said. 'That will not be necessary. We may be new to this game but I've already learned that trust is the rule, not the exception.'

'Trust it is then,' Mr Dingle said and, nodding to Henry to hold out both hands, dropped the purse into them.

They were gone in no time. Betsy barely had a chance to peep into the wagon to see how the casks had been hidden – in cupboards beneath the bunks – before the girls were bundled into the back and Mr Dingle cracked his whip, brought the dray around and, with a wave and whoop, headed off up the sheep track that led on to the moor.

It was a long haul to Paisley by her lights, for she had never travelled further than Ayr. It occurred to her that His Majesty, King George, had only himself to blame for turning honest citizens into thieves by burdening them with iniquitous taxes to finance his foreign wars and pleasure palaces.

'*Look!*' Janet shrieked. 'Have you ever *seen* so much money?'

Henry rolled up his shirt sleeves and, grinning, seated himself at the table and began to arrange the coins into little columns.

'Guineas,' Tom said. 'All guineas. My God!'

'One hundred of them by the look of it,' said Henry. 'Our friend McCaskie doesn't trust banknotes, it seems.'

Janet picked up one of the coins and weighed it in her palm. 'I just pray they're real,' she said.

'Of course they're real,' said Henry. 'If you were an importer o' cheap liquor would you be stupid enough to cheat your supplier?' He looked over his shoulder at his mother. 'I'm just sorry Daddy never lived to see this day.'

'He would not have been pleased,' said Agnes.

'What about you, Mammy,' said Janet, 'are you pleased?'

'I don't like havin' this much money in the house,' Agnes admitted.

'It won't be here for long,' Henry told her. 'I've to deliver the cash to Conn McCaskie on Friday afternoon.'

'Where will you meet?' Tom asked.

'Caddy Crawford's yard,' Henry answered. 'Someone will uplift the gin an' tobacco before then, I imagine.'

'Think how much money we'll have then,' Janet crowed.

'Aye,' said Henry, 'a king's ransom.'

And everyone, including Tom, laughed.

The weather had turned cold at last, not quite cold enough to sketch frost patterns on her window but cold enough to drive her downstairs to while away a dreary afternoon with her feet planted in the kitchen grate.

Dorothy, red-nosed and sniffling, was peeling potatoes, while Mrs Prole gave the silver its weekly polish and grumped at the girl to use her handkerchief not her sleeve. She was a sad sight, was Dorothy, all bleary-eyed and hang-dog, but she received no sympathy from the housekeeper who claimed never to have experienced a day's illness in her life and saw no reason why she should be inconvenienced by the ailments of others.

'You're not dyin', girl,' she said. 'You've no fever.'

'Ah'm sair, but, awfy sair. Can ah dot go home, Mrs Prold?'

'Do you suppose you'll be better cared for in the orphanage than you will be here? No, child, it's far better to work through a head cold than lounge in bed feelin' sorry for yourself.'

'Aye, Mrs Prold,' said Dorothy meekly.

Rose was thinking of other things, specifically of Tom Brodie and his failure to respond to her letter. Logically, she realised that Tom would still be mourning his father and have a lot more on his mind than love. Even so, she was irked by his silence and inclined to blame Dorothy for not bringing her a letter from the carrier's office, as if the day-maid were responsible for the farmer's indifference. Dorothy coughed; a rasping bark.

'It might be the sweating sickness, you know,' Rose remarked.

'Nothin' of the kind,' said Mrs Prole. 'I've seen the sweating sickness in all its glory an', believe me, it bears no resemblance to a simple cold.'

Dorothy shivered, a wee bit ostentatiously perhaps, and mopped her brow with the back of her hand. 'Ah am hod,' she said. 'Ah can feel id comin' on.'

'Then,' said Mrs Prole, 'when you're finished here, take yourself to the doctor an' he'll put the leeches on your belly.'

'Leeches?' Dorothy shivered with somewhat more conviction. 'Naw!'

'Tassie Landles will give you a remedy, I'm sure,' said Rose.

'Ah don't have any money, but,' said Dorothy pathetically.

'I'll lend you sixpence,' Rose said.

'Where did you get sixpence?' Mrs Prole enquired.

Rose shrugged. 'From Lucas.'

'Lucas Fergusson gave you money? For what, I'd like to know?'

'No, my dear Mrs Prole, I have not been selling kisses to Lucas,' said Rose. 'I took a few pence from Papa's box, if you must know.'

Eunice buffed a fork in silence, satisfied that embezzlement was a lesser sin than lechery. Besides, Rose was not the only member of the household who, now and then, removed a little extra change from the master's cashbox. 'Be that as it may,' Eunice said, at length, 'I'll not have you throwin' good money into the hands o' that witch. She's in league with the devil, you know. Her cures are nothin' but Satan's charms, to lure you into his evil clutches.'

'They work, but,' said Dorothy and before the housekeeper could chastise her fell into a spasm of coughing so violent that it threatened to overturn the water bucket.

Mrs Prole threw down the fork and raised her hands to heaven. 'Oh, very well,' she snapped. 'If you intend to spend the rest o' the afternoon splutterin' into our dinner, I suppose you'd better go home.'

'Dank you, Mrs Prold, dank you.'

Dorothy pushed back the stool and, tottering slightly, put on her shawl and made for the hall. Rose accompanied her to the door, slipped a silver sixpence into her hand and whispered, 'If you have time to drop in at the carrier's office first thing tomorrow, I'd be obliged.'

'Aye, Miss Rose, ah will,' the orphan promised and with a wobbly little bob of gratitude set off through the chill evening air for the cottage by the bridge to buy herself a remedy.

Walter Fergusson was well aware that his son had discovered the joys of copulation. On the one hand he was relieved that Lucas might now be counted upon to produce grandchildren; on the other, he was leery of Lucas's choice of a mate, or, rather, of the mate who had chosen him.

Nancy Ames came from a clan of rough-hewn, rough-tongued day-labourers, notoriously addicted to drink and fist-fighting. While her lineage suggested that she would be fertile – her mother had borne ten healthy babies in almost as many years – she was, none the less, uncouth and uneducated.

Walter was sufficiently versed in the ways of the world to realise that it would only be a matter of time before the ardent Miss Ames declared herself pregnant. A bit – quite a bit – of skirt lifting and squealing in the hayloft was one thing, squiring Nancy Ames to Caddy Crawford's after church was quite another. Such public displays of 'affection' when brought to the attention of the Sheriff or the board of the Kirk Session would surely constitute a promise of marriage that would be difficult to disprove.

'Let him marry the girl,' Walter's wife declared. 'Let him get his leg o'er her as often as he likes when she has a ring on her finger.'

'And have the Ames family spongin' off us for the rest of our lives?' Walter retorted. 'No, Flora, my love. Lucas can do better than Nancy Ames.'

'Some milk an' water lady with a dowry, I suppose.'

'The dowry is not the issue,' Walter said. 'The issue is – well – the issue.'

'What are you jabberin' about, Walter?'

'Breeding, my dear, breeding.'

'Haw!' Flora snorted. 'You're a dab hand at pickin' cows, Walter, but when it comes to pickin' women your judgement didn't prove very sound.'

'How was I to know you . . .' Prudently, he bit his lip.

'If you *had* known I had but one calf in me,' said Flora, 'would you have gone in search o' another bride?'

Walter cleared his throat. 'Certainly not.'

'Och, what a liar you are, Mr Fergusson.' Flora caught him by the ear and kissed him. 'There's no point in tellin' Lucas to keep his breeks buttoned. You can hardly expect Lucas to swear a vow o' chastity when Nancy Ames has her legs spread for him.'

'Quite!' said Walter. 'We must be more subtle about it.'

'Subtle? How?'

'By replacin' Nancy Ames with another.'

'Another what?' said Flora Fergusson.

'Another object upon which Lucas can lavish his – ah – affection.'

'It took us long enough to get Lukie to lavish his affection on an eager dairymaid,' Flora pointed out.

'Lucas isn't besotted by Nancy Ames,' Walter said. 'Now he's found the way, as it were, his eye's beginning to rove in other directions.'

'In the direction o' Thimble Row, you mean?'

'He was certainly attentive enough to Rose Hewitt when we took tea there,' Walter said. 'Indeed, I caught him lookin' at her as if he wanted to smear her with jam an' eat her all up.'

'She's a girl, not a tea-cake,' said Flora. 'She has a mind o' her own.'

'Yes – an' a lover waiting in the wings.'

'Brodie?'

'Brodie,' said Walter. 'I'd hoped Brodie would bring himself down – in fact, I'm convinced he will – but I can't wait for it to happen of its own accord, not with Lucas dandlin' Nancy Ames every chance he gets.'

'Put them together,' Flora suggested. 'Put them together, our Lukie an' Hewitt's daughter. Let him show her what he's made of.'

'That's the problem, Flora: what is he made of?'

'Well,' said the grazier's wife, 'there's only one way to find out.'

14

Fattening cattle in the stall had never been Matthew Brodie's way. He had declared it as a policy, not a necessity, but by the time they were half grown the boys had known better. Many an argument had raged when the weather had pinched towards winter, arguments that the old man had invariably won since the livestock, like everything else, was in his name and under his thumb.

Even when the hayloft was crammed and the oat bins spilling over, he had kept the cattle in the field, sustained only by watery grasses and scant picks of hay draped on the hedges. The method was not efficient enough for Tom or humane enough for Henry who detected an element of near cruelty in his father's indifference to the welfare of the cattle, as if he resented the fact that the beasts had to be fed at all.

On that day in early November it struck both boys that their father's passing, however grievous, was not without compensations. One hundred guineas stowed safe under Henry's bed undoubtedly skewed their perspectives and fatigue, added to guilt, blunted their inclination to work. What remained of the morning after Mr Dingle's departure was spent plotting how best to spend their profits and, egged on by Janet, in calculating how many landings it would take to earn enough to buy Hawkshill's seventy sour acres outright.

Betsy did not grudge the Brodies their fancies but, as an outsider, she realised how precarious their castles in the air might turn out to be. She was disappointed in Henry, who was usually more down-to-earth than his brother, but in the course of that idle forenoon even he seemed to be swept away by a conviction that money would bring happiness and that, come the month of May, all their troubles would be over.

Breakfast drifted eventually into dinner. Agnes used the remains of Monday's funeral feast to prepare roasted cheese and a fruit cake pudding. Tom poured cups of wine to wash it down. The afternoon might well have deteriorated into a tipsy spree if, shortly before one o'clock, two dour gentlemen in caped greatcoats had not ridden into the yard leading a string of three sturdy ponies. They retrieved and paid for the tubs of gin and packets of tobacco and with hardly a word spoken headed off up the moor road, leaving Hawkshill clean and uncontaminated once more.

At Janet's urging, Henry fetched the purse from the loft. He spilled guineas on to the table, added the sum that the merchants had paid for the gin and tobacco and, counting aloud, conducted a final gleeful tally.

Clutching a wine cup in both hands, Janet bounced up and down, crying, 'Twenty-three pounds, twenty-three pounds for us.'

'An' eighteen shillings,' said Henry.

He got up from his chair and clasping Betsy by the waist danced her round and round while the furniture shook and the coins shivered and spread like a puddle across the table.

'Tomorrow,' he said, 'I'll ride into Drennan an' pay Conn.'

'I'll ride in with you,' Tom said.

'Don't you trust me to conduct the business properly?' Henry said.

'He's goin' to Drennan for to see his sweetheart,' Janet crowed.

'What if I am?' said Tom. 'What harm is there in that?'

Henry shrugged. 'None, I suppose.'

'Not if he keeps his mouth shut,' said Agnes.

★   ★   ★

Grief, guilt and love had not entirely robbed Tom of common sense. It had never been his intention to stride up to Neville Hewitt's door and demand an interview with the flax manufacturer's daughter. In fact, he had a much more pressing reason for accompanying Henry to Drennan.

He could hardly believe that only a week had elapsed since he had crouched on the old man's bed and watched – or, rather, heard – his father pass from life into death, unable to lift his hands from the bolster. It had taken all Henry's strength to tear him away and he still felt as if a part of him had been torn away too, like a bee's sting. Rose's tender letter had, in part, restored him, but he longed to be back behind the plough, black earth spitting from the blade, the wind clean and cutting in his face; longed to have things as they had been a year ago with nothing more than debts to trouble him.

'Here,' he said. 'Let me down here.'

'What,' said Henry, 'aren't you comin' in?'

'Nah,' Tom said. 'McCaskie's your man, not mine. You can tote up pounds an' pence well enough without my aid.'

'One drink to show your gratitude,' Henry suggested.

'Gratitude?'

'What's wrong wi' you, man?' said Henry. 'Aren't you pleased to have money in hand?'

'Money that can get us hanged.'

'Moralisin' doesn't become you,' Henry said. 'Besides, it's hypocritical.'

'I'm not the hypocrite; you are.'

'Well, the way I look at it is, what's past is past,' Henry said. 'If we keep our heads an' stick together we've a shiny future ahead o' us.'

'Robbin' the taxman, you mean?'

'Oh, damn you, Tom,' said Henry mildly. 'Go off an' do what you have to do. Give her a kiss from me if the opportunity arises. But remember, not a blessed word about the business that's brought us to town.'

'Aye, aye,' Tom said wearily, and jumping down from the cart strode off along the market street.

'Where is Dorothy?' Eunice Prole plucked pathetically at Rose's sleeve. 'Tell me the truth; is she dead?'

'She's unwell, of course,' Rose said, 'but to the best of my knowledge she has not given up the ghost.'

Mrs Prole fluttered open one eye. 'Who told you?'

'Loon Leach, the rat-catcher's boy, called about an hour ago. He's very concerned.'

Mrs Prole frowned. 'Why would the rat-catcher's boy be concerned?'

'He hopes to marry Dorothy some day.'

Mrs Prole struggled to sit up in bed but, totally devoid of strength, fell back against the pillows. She groped for Rose's hand which Rose, rather magnanimously, gave her. 'It's the sweatin' sickness, isn't it?'

'No, my dear Mrs Prole, it's not the sweating sickness. There is, I gather, an outbreak of intermitting fever presently sweeping through the town. Loon tells me that in the early hours of the morning the sound of coughing is quite deafening.'

'Send for Dr Glendinning.'

'I think,' said Rose, 'it would be wiser to send for Papa.'

'Neville mustn't see me like this. Fetch Glendinning.'

'Are you ordering me to take to the streets without a chaperone?'

Eunice Prole was too sunk in self-pity to recognise sarcasm. Every bone in her body ached and she felt as if a pint of caustic soda had been poured down her throat. The fever had come upon her suddenly in mid-morning. By noon she had been so ill that she had all but swooned. Rose had helped her out of her clothes and into a flannel nightgown and had put her to bed in the master's room.

Rose dipped a cloth in a bowl of cold water and applied it to Eunice's brow. The woman groaned and closed her eyes.

'Go,' she croaked, 'go an' fetch Glendinning.'

'I'm reluctant to leave you,' Rose fibbed. 'Besides, Dr Glendinning may not be at home.'

'Find him, find him,' said Eunice Prole desperately. 'I've no wish to be called to the bar of heaven just yet.'

'Very well.' Rose left the cloth on Mrs Prole's forehead. 'Do you want anything before I leave?'

'My – my Testament.'

Rose retrieved the well-thumbed book from the table in the housekeeper's room and put it on the blanket by Mrs Prole's limp hand. Then, with a little yelp of pleasure, she snatched her winter cloak from a hook in the hall and skipped nimbly out into Thimble Row.

'It's you, is it?' said Tassie Landles. 'Well, I canna say I'm surprised.'

'Did the teacups warn you to expect me,' Tom said, 'or is it bones you scatter on the floor, like the tinky wives do?'

'Neither teacups nor knuckle-bones, Mr Brodie,' Tassie Landles answered. 'Where did you tether your horse?'

'I came on foot.'

'From Hayes?'

'Market Street. My brother has business in town. I rode in with him.'

'Does your brother know you're here with me?'

Tom shook his head. 'No.'

'I see,' Tassie said. 'What is it you want, Tom Brodie?'

She had been crouched by the hearth feeding small nuggets of coal into the fire when he had pushed open the door. She rose now, stiffly, wiped her dusty fingers on her apron and faced him. She had clapped eyes on the family from Hawkshill only two or three times but Peter had kept her abreast of its failing fortunes and she knew more about Tom Brodie than Tom Brodie might consider proper. She was not at ease with him, however, for she could not explain the nature of the limping, lisping spirit, Jarvis Garvie, or the message he had carried from the far side of the grave.

Tom darted a nervous glance about the room as if he expected a host of malicious entities to leap out from behind the furniture.

He said, 'Is my father present?'

'There's no one here but us, Mr Brodie.'

'Has he not come to you again?'

'He did not come to me at all.'

'So the message you sent with Peter . . .'

'I didn't make it up, Mr Brodie.'

'How did you know my father was dead?'

'It was All Hallows' Eve; the door was open.'

'Door?' Tom Brodie said. 'What door?'

'The door between this world an' the next.'

'Do you expect me to believe that?'

'Believe what you like, Mr Brodie,' Tassie said. 'I'm not obliged to explain myself to you.'

'Unless I cross your palm wi' silver, is that it?'

'I don't want your blood money.'

'Blood money?'

'What else would you call it?'

'It had nothin' to do with money. My father died a natural death. The canker took him away. If you think otherwise . . .'

'What I think has nothin' to do wi' it.' Tassie found the chair and seated herself without turning her back on the farmer. 'I didn't ask for the visitation.'

Tom moved closer. 'Neville Hewitt put you up to it, didn't he?'

'Neville Hewitt?' Tassie said. 'I've never exchanged so much as a word wi' Neville Hewitt. I do not know the man.'

'But you do know his daughter.' Tom bent forward until his face was no more than an inch from hers. 'You intend to tell her, don't you? Aye, I see it now. You intend to spread poisonous allegations about me an' my family, disguised as messages from the other world – unless I pay you to keep quiet.'

She pushed him away with her forearm and said, 'Blackmail, aye, blackmail's a grand excuse, Mr Brodie. Blackmail an' connivance are things you understand an' it would soothe you to have it so. But it's not so, Mr Brodie, an' theatenin' me willna' make it so. I heard what I heard an' passed on what I was told to pass on.'

'Told – by whom?'

'That's no matter.'

'It is, indeed it is.'

'The man, the messenger is dead, long dead.'

'One o' Satan's legions, I suppose.'

'The devil doesn't work through me,' Tassie said, 'nor I through him.'

'You came runnin' fast enough to Peter Frye with the story.'

'I handed on the message,' Tassie said, 'as I was charged to do.'

'To keep your bargain wi' the devil?'

She got to her feet, placed a hand flat on his chest and, to her satisfaction, felt him flinch. 'There's more o' the devil in you, Tom Brodie, than there is in me,' she told him. 'It's the torment o' the devil that brought you here today.'

He said nothing for a moment then, drawing himself up, confessed, 'Aye, that's as close to the truth as makes no matter.'

Stepping past him, Tassie took glasses and a bottle from a cupboard. She poured from the bottle and offered him a glass.

'What is this stuff?' he asked suspiciously.

'Brandy,' Tassie answered. 'Peter brings it me. Do you want it watered?'

Tom sniffed and sipped, shook his head and drank. He gave a little shiver and put the empty glass down upon the table.

Nursing her glass, Tassie seated herself again.

She drew in a deep breath. 'He told you to do it, did he not?'

'He did,' Tom admitted.

'An' you obeyed him, as a son always obeys his father?'

'We did.'

'All o' you?'

'All save Janet,' Tom said. 'We – we smothered him.'

'Did he resist?'

'No.'

'It wasn't his time, though, was it?'

'No, it wasn't quite his time,' Tom told her. 'Is that why he's not at rest?'

'What did you promise him?'

'To hang on to Hawkshill.'

'Can you do that?'

'Aye, we can,' said Tom. 'Thank God, we can.'

'Was that your only promise?'

Tom paused. 'No.'

'What were the others?'

Stubbornly, Tom shook his head.

'Was it to marry Betsy McBride?' Tassie asked.

'Did Daddy tell you?'

'Your daddy has no voice in the invisible world.'

'In heaven, you mean?' said Tom.

'In a world that lies just short o' heaven.'

'Is he lingerin' there because we murdered him?'

'He's there because his spirit can't rest. That's as much as I can tell you.'

'How can I help him?' Tom said. 'What can I do?'

Tassie lifted her shoulders. 'I don't know.'

'Can you communicate with this spirit who speaks on his behalf?'

'I thought you didn't believe in spirits?'

'Damn it,' Tom growled. 'Can you summon him, or can't you?'

'I can't,' said Tassie, shrugging again. 'What do you want from him?'

'I want to see him at peace.'

'It's you wants peace, Tom Brodie,' said Tassie. 'Whether it's a restless spirit or remorse that haunts you there's no worse promise than a promise made to a dyin' man.'

'Because,' Tom said, 'it can never be absolved?'

'Because it can be easily broken,' said Tassie.

'An' no one will know, you mean,' said Tom, 'no one will ever know.'

'Just you,' said Tassie and then, again, 'just you.'

It was too cold to sit out of doors. Several old men were gathered round the fireplace, puffing on pipes and eking out their half-pints while keeping a weather eye on the passing show. Precious little show there was to entertain the ancients, for the ale-house was quiet at that hour of the afternoon. They had already discussed the fever that had leaked into the town and agreed that alcohol and tobacco were ideal remedies to keep the plague at bay.

Conn set down two drams of whisky and squeezed himself into a corner seat. His greatcoat was unbuttoned, his goatskin vest thrown open.

'Do you have the money?' he asked.

'I do,' Henry answered. 'It's in a purse in my pocket.'

'Keep it hidden for the present,' Conn said. 'Is it all there?'

'To the last penny,' said Henry.

'Did it go well?'

'It went quick,' said Henry. 'In an' out again in the blink of an eye. I take it you've done business with Dingle before?'

'Many times,' Conn said. 'Him an' his darlin' daughters.'

'They are his daughters then?'

'Sure an' they are. What did you think they were?'

'His wives, perhaps,' said Henry.

Conn laughed softly. 'He's a carrier from Paisley, man, not an Eastern potentate.'

'Who were the others?' Henry enquired. 'The ones with the ponies?'

'They're from Kilmarnock. That's all you need to know.'

'It's all I want to know,' said Henry. 'Will transfers always be completed so smoothly?'

'Maybe,' said Conn, 'maybe not.'

'If not,' said Henry, 'we'll have to arrange better storage.'

'No bad notion,' said Conn. 'How are the rats?'

'We'll deal with the rats,' said Henry. 'Meanwhile, we'll keep the tobacco packets well out o' their reach.'

'And the tea,' said Conn.

'Tea?'

'The duty on tea runs at a hundred an' twenty-nine per cent, though there's talk o' the government climbing down since hardly a cup is brewed in England that hasn't come out o' a smuggler's hold.'

'Will it be tea next time?'

'Maybe,' said Conn, 'maybe not.'

'You're not very forthcomin', are you?' said Henry. 'Can't say I blame you. We're novices at this game an' the less we know the better.'

Conn drank his whisky and got to his feet. 'You did well enough for novices, Henry. The dealers are pleased with the new arrangement. If we keep the landing place secret an' have the luck then we'll empty the warehouse in Nantes before summer's out.'

'Nantes?' said Henry. 'I thought—'

'Hush now,' said Conn. 'Hush.'

Signalling Henry to follow him, he ducked through the rear door into the empty garden where, in a matter of minutes, the purse changed hands and Henry was paid his share.

'How soon will you need us again?' Henry asked.

'Soon,' the Irishman answered, 'very soon.'

'Before the end o' the month?'

'Before the end o' next week more like,' Conn said and, buttoning his greatcoat tightly over the purse, slipped out through the gate and swiftly disappeared.

Chance it was, pure chance that brought the would-be lovers together. Tom had just turned from the head of the bridge road into the tail of Market Street when a figure in a hooded, blue wool cloak all but bumped into him. She was so fixed on her purpose that she did not glance up even when he called her name. He caught the cloak, found her arm and brought her round to face him.

'Rose,' he said. 'Ah, Rose, it's you.'

'Tom?'

When he kissed her, her lips were cold. When she sighed her breath formed a pale cloud between them. He snuggled inside the folds of the cloak and pressed himself against her. Buttons, buckles, fabrics were all cold, everything cold until he found the pocket of warmth between her waist and shoulders and sliding his hands across her back tightened his grip.

'Tom,' she whispered, 'what are *you* doing here?'

'I came with my brother.'

'Where is he?'

'Caddy Crawford's, I think. He has business there.'

'And you?' Rose said. 'Did you come to find me?'

'No,' Tom said; then, instantly, 'Yes.'

Traffic in the street was frozen in the grainy November light, as if the world had stopped to let the farmer and the flax manufacturer's daughter embrace.

'Where's the woman, your keeper?'

'At home in bed. She has a fever,' Rose told him. 'I'm on my way to purchase a remedy from Tassie Landles.'

'Would it not be more sensible to consult a doctor?'

'Sensible?' said Rose. 'Who are you to talk of being sensible?'

'True,' Tom said, 'I've no sense at all when I'm with you.'

He took her hand and steered her away from the bridge road. 'Come, dearest, I'll walk with you as far as Glendinning's house. He'll provide better medicine than your old witch woman.'

'I – I cannot walk with you, Tom.'

'Why not?' He led her across the pavement that bordered the market square. 'Are you afraid your father will see us?'

Her father, in fact, had gone to Glasson, eight miles south, to negotiate with a flax grower for a crop that had not yet been planted. It was unlikely that he would return before nightfall. The Fergussons might be in from the country, however, and she did not know what would happen if Tom and Lucas came face to face. She had heard tales of Tom Brodie's temper and had no wish to be involved in a scene.

'Did you receive my letter?' she said.

'Aye, an' I thank you for it.'

'It cost a shilling for a special delivery.'

'The comfort it brought me was worth far more.'

'Why did you not answer?' Rose said.

'I didn't know how.'

'Have you no pen, no paper?'

'I meant how to get it safely into your hands.'

'I had that arranged,' Rose said.

'Did you?' said Tom. 'Then you have my apology.'

'Dorothy, our day-maid, is instructed to collect my letters

from the carrier's office. Dorothy, unfortunately, is also sick with the fever. Is there a letter awaiting me at the carrier's office, by any chance?'

'A letter?'

'From you.'

'No,' said Tom, puzzled. 'Why do you need a letter when you have me in the flesh?'

She disentangled her hand but, not being entirely graceless, took his arm instead. The square was quiet. The fish-sellers had packed up hours ago and the three or four stalls that remained open had no customers. With the coming of evening the cold had become more intense, a dry cold that promised the first real frost of winter.

'Don't you care enough for my feelings to write?'

'Of course I care for your feelin's,' said Tom. 'Did it escape your notice that I was engaged in buryin' my father?'

'Yes,' she said curtly. 'Your father!'

He stopped and drew her to him again. He put his hands on her shoulders and brushed aside her hood. Her cheeks were red, her nose too. He sensed that if he tried to kiss her she would twist her head away.

The chance meeting in the nub end of a cold November afternoon had thrown him off kilter. Mention of his father sparked doubt, a fear that Tassie Landles had told the truth and his daddy would not rest until the deathbed promise had been fulfilled. Holding Rose Hewitt in his arms did not relieve his guilt. When he looked beyond her into the still grey haze he imagined that he could see his father lurking by the corner, half hidden, watching him.

'My father,' he said, 'was a fine man an' deserved better.'

'Better?' she said. 'Better than what?'

'Me,' Tom said.

'Well,' said Rose, regretting it even as she spoke, 'he certainly did not teach you much by way of manners.'

'What do you mean?'

'You say you love me . . .'

'Well, I do.'

'But not enough to write and tell me so.'

'Rose, for God's sake!' Tom said. 'It's been barely a week since we put him to the ground. I've been busy with family matters.'

'Oh, yes, family matters,' Rose went on, loathing herself for doing so. 'It's always family matters with you, Mr Brodie. I fear it will always be so. If you have no time to spare for me, no thought or care for my feelings, I would be greatly obliged if you would tell me, for there are other young men who care for me more than you seem to do.'

'What young men?'

'That is none of your concern.'

'Of course it is.'

'Mr Fergusson's son, if you must know.'

'Luke?' Tom grunted wryly. 'Lucas Fergusson is no threat to me.'

'Are you so confident that your charm will sweep every young woman off her feet that no man is a threat to you? If that's the case, Mr Brodie, then I beg you to think again.'

'Rose, please don't bicker. I'm in no mood—'

'Oh, and all that counts is your mood, is it? Day in, day out, I waited for word from you. I didn't expect a sheaf of verse or reams of elegant prose; a word would suffice, a word of polite acknowledgement.'

He removed his hands from her shoulders, folded his arms and looked down at her with more pity than pride. 'My family's interests are your interests too, Rose. When I said I intended to marry you, I meant it. But I won't come cap in hand without land o' my own.'

'Hawkshill?' Rose said. 'You will never be the owner of Hawkshill.'

'I wouldn't be so sure o' that.'

'My father will never sell.'

'He will if the offer's high enough.'

'You cannot pay the rent, let alone—'

'Aye, but I *can* pay the rent. I've money now,' Tom said. 'Whatever Lucas Fergusson has to offer I'll soon be able to match.'

'Have you been drinking?'

'Not a drop.'

'It strikes me you have been drinking, for this is not sober talk,' Rose said. 'I may seem like a simpleton to you, Mr Brodie, but I have sharp ears. I've heard how close to the ground you mow your crop; how, only a week since, you were in peril of being thrown out of Hawkshill without a farthing to your name.'

'By your father,' Tom reminded her.

'Yes, by my father, who, by the by, is not well pleased at being cheated.'

'Cheated?'

'How did you come by this sudden windfall? Tell me that, if you will. Who have you tricked this time?'

'So' – Tom blew out his cheeks – 'you take me for a trickster, do you? Well, dear, I'm nothin' of the kind. I thought you loved me enough to be patient, a wee, tiny bit patient. Dear God, if you can't wait a week for a letter from a man in mournin' perhaps you'd better marry your Mr Fergusson an' let him shower you with everythin' your intolerant heart desires.'

Her lip trembled. She said, 'If that's what you think of me, Mr Tom Brodie, I will bid you good day.'

She turned on her heel and walked away, not towards the bridge road but diagonally across the market square towards Thimble Row.

'Wait.' Tom saw her hesitate. 'Rose, please wait.'

She looked so small – not dainty now but childlike – that even without desire he longed to take her in his arms and tell her that he loved her. But he was not at all sure that he did love her or that he had ever loved her, that what he felt far down in his belly was not regret but relief. And when she paused and looked round, he swept off his cap and bowed, a withering, arrogant, sardonic bow that, had he but known it, almost broke her heart.

15

'Chink,' said Henry, patting his pockets. 'The first thing we must do is pay Betsy. She's received not a penny from us since the day she arrived an' we can't depend on John Rankine's charity for ever. Hold out your hand, Miss McBride.' He counted three pounds and ten shillings. 'It's little enough, lass, but we've seed to buy an' rent to pay.'

'It's more than enough,' said Betsy.

'Enough to keep you with us?' Agnes Brodie asked.

'Aye,' Betsy answered. 'I'd rather stay here if Mr Rankine will let me.'

Tom stood behind her, sullen and silent. She looked round at him. He gave her a nod, no smile or wink, just a nod.

'When can we expect another cargo, Henry?' Janet asked.

'Next week, so Conn informs me,' Henry answered. 'However, we're farmers not smugglers an' mustn't neglect the fields an' the livestock.'

' 'Specially since we'll be the owners soon,' said Janet.

'That day may never come,' Henry told her. 'I doubt if Hewitt'll let Hawkshill go at less than seven pounds the acre an', however careful we are, it can only be a matter o' time before the revenue officers start sniffin' round Port Cedric – or somebody sells us out for the bounty.'

'Now who would do that to us?' said Janet.

'Any one o' a hundred folk,' Tom said. 'Greed is a great leveller.'

'Tom's right,' said Henry. 'We'll deal wi' one shipment at a time, make sure we've a year's rent put away an' sink the balance in improvements. Or, if we do earn enough money' – he paused – 'we could look for another place at a more reasonable price.'

'No,' Tom said sharply.

'Is it not worth considerin'?' said Henry.

'No,' said Tom again. 'We promised Daddy.'

'Daddy would be the first to absolve us from that promise if he thought we could do better for ourselves,' said Henry.

'We can do no better than what we have here,' Tom said.

'You've changed your tune,' said Janet.

'Only to suit changed circumstances,' Tom told her.

'What if the circumstances change again, son?' his mother asked.

'We'll shift with the wind,' Tom answered, 'as we've always done.'

'An' look where that got us,' said Janet.

'To the brink o' starvation,' Agnes said.

The boys and Janet stared at their mother who, Betsy guessed, had rarely voiced a complaint when her husband was alive.

'Do you blame *me* for that, Mammy?' Tom said.

'I blame nobody,' Agnes Brodie said.

'You can hardly blame Daddy,' said Tom.

'Can I not?' said Agnes.

'What more would you have had him do?' said Henry. 'He worked harder than any man in Ayrshire to keep us from sinkin' below the waves.'

'An' he still died in debt,' said Agnes.

'He wouldn't have died in debt if Hewitt had kept to his side o' the bargain,' Tom said, 'an' if he hadn't got sick.'

'Blame Mr Hewitt, blame the sickness,' Agnes Brodie said. 'Blame foul ground an' bad weather. Blame poor seed an' high prices, an' anythin' else you care to name. The fact is your father forged a bad bargain an' like the stubborn fool he was, stuck by it rather than admit he was wrong. It wasn't sickness brought my Matthew down nor was it Tom's mischief. It was your daddy's pride, his obstinate pride. He thought his way was God's way an' somehow God would reward him for it.'

'Oh, Mammy,' said Janet. 'How can you say such things? I thought you loved him?'

'I did,' Agnes said. 'I loved him in spite o' his faults. He had virtues too, virtues in plenty. But I'd have loved him more if he had once, just once, admitted he might be wrong. I did every blessed thing he asked o' me when he was alive but what use is loyalty now, or love for that matter?'

'Callous,' Tom said. 'God, but you're callous.'

Agnes scraped her chair forward and, stretching out a hand, stirred the guineas that Henry had left upon the table. 'Look at all this coin. We're better off now than ever we were when Matthew was with us.'

'Aye, it's sad Daddy didn't live to see it,' Janet said.

'Sadder still to realise he even failed at failure,' Agnes said. 'Take what you need for seed, Henry, put the rest in the cashbox an' give it to me.'

'To you?' said Tom. 'What do you want with it?'

'I'll keep it safe,' Agnes promised.

'From robbers?' Janet asked.

'From you lot,' Agnes Brodie said.

Her father arrived home shortly after eight, cold, footsore and in a thoroughly bad temper. Frost had stiffened the ruts on the Glasson road and licked the turnpike with a film of ice and his mare had stumbled and slithered so badly that he had been obliged to dismount and walk her the last few miles to the stable.

Rose opened the door and helped him off with his coat.

'Supper,' he called out. 'Eunice, where's my supper?' He scowled at his daughter as she knelt to remove his boots. 'Where's Eunice?'

'Unwell,' Rose told him. 'According to Dr Glendinning it's a touch of the fever and will pass in a day or two.'

'What?' her papa cried. 'Eunice is sick?'

He pushed Rose away and clumped to the housekeeper's cubby.

'Eunice, Eunice, my dear, where are you?'

'In the big bed,' Rose told him, 'in your room.'

He raced across the hall, threw himself into the bedroom and pitched on to the bed with such force that the fire in the grate released a startled puff of smoke and all the glassware chattered.

Eunice was propped up by a bolster which, Rose thought, was just as well or Papa might otherwise have smothered her. He stuck out his legs to keep his boots from soiling the bedclothes and, balanced on his belly, wrapped his arms about the patient.

'My dearest, dearest darlin',' he moaned. 'Do not abandon me. Please, I beg you, do not desert me.'

'*Kek*,' said Mrs Prole, eyes popping. '*Kek, kek.*'

Twisting round, the flax manufacturer addressed his daughter who had followed him into the bedroom. 'What? What did she say, Rose?'

'She's coughing.'

'*Kek, kek, kek.*'

He pushed Mrs Prole back against the bolster and spanning her head with both hands inspected her closely. 'Blood, is that blood on her mouth?'

'Squills, I think,' said Rose.

Eunice coughed again and, fending Neville off, stuck out her tongue. 'Liquorice, you fool,' she said. 'I'm suckin' a Pontefract cake.'

'Thank God!' Neville said and, liquorice notwithstanding, planted a kiss on her lips. 'I thought I'd lost you too.'

To Rose's consternation, Mrs Prole drew her father to her breast and hugged him fondly. It had not occurred to her that her papa and the gaunt housekeeper might be in love. She was not naïve enough to ignore the evidence that they shared a bed and, try as she might, could not put from her mind the grisly thought that Papa and Mrs Prole engaged in certain acts more suited to a married couple than a housekeeper and her employer.

She cleared her throat loudly.

Chin resting on Neville's shoulder, Eunice said, 'You'll need to make your father's supper. There's broth in the black pot an' potted meat in the larder.' Then, burying her nose in Neville's neck, she surrendered to another fit of coughing.

Rose went into the kitchen. She had already stoked the fire, added water to the mutton broth and put the pot on the grid to simmer. All evening she had kept herself busy, running to drag Dr Glendinning from his house across the row, running to attend Mrs Prole and administer the medicine the doctor had left, running, in effect, from Tom Brodie's rejection.

She opened the door of the larder and stepped inside.

It smelled, as it always did, of cheese, a pleasant, muffled odour. The shelves were lined with jars and bottles, butter urns and egg-boxes. Mouse-proof wire domes covered platters of bacon and strips of smoked fish from which Mrs Prole whipped up breakfast kedgerees to a recipe that she claimed to have learned from a Hindu on the quays at Ayr.

Eunice Prole might beat her, might snap and snarl, but Eunice Prole also saw to it that she was well fed, that her dresses were properly stitched and her petticoats laundered. Was it fear of losing her place that made Mrs Prole so vile and vicious at times, Rose wondered, or the scars of a childless marriage?

Perhaps, she thought, there's a lesson here for me. She was not, after all, Heloïse and Tom Brodie was no Abelard. She had invented a romance where no romance existed. He had danced with her, kissed her, promised to elope with her, but the fact remained that he was nothing but a coarse hill farmer with a wicked reputation and an unhealthy conceit of himself.

It dawned on her then that she had envisaged Tom Brodie not as a husband but as a lover and that Tassie Landles' prophecy of a grand house and umpteen children might be less a promise than a threat.

The door of the larder, weighted with lead, closed softly upon her and she was enveloped in warm, muffled darkness tinted with the smell of cheese. Unsure what she wanted now or why Tom's contemptuous gesture had caused her so much pain, she crouched down, making herself small, pressed the heels of her hands into her lap and, rocking back and forth, whimpered softly.

'Rose?' her Papa said, not harshly. 'Where are you, Rose?'

She got to her feet, wiped her eyes and opened the larder door.

'I'm here, Papa,' she said. 'I'm here,' and, carrying the plate of potted meat, went out to serve his supper.

Janet lay flat on her back, the blanket pulled up to her throat.

'He met her,' she said. 'I'm certain he met her. You could tell by how smug he was.'

'I didn't think he was smug,' said Betsy.

'He was gone for more than an hour, Henry said. Wouldn't say where he'd been. You know what that means.'

'I don't know what that means.'

Janet dug an elbow into Betsy's ribs. 'There's only one thing on his mind these days. Did he meet her, do you think? An' why has he gone out again?'

'He's gone to a meetin' o' the Bachelors' Club.'

'He could be slippin' it into her at this very minute for all we know.'

'Janet!'

'If we're patient for a nine-month then we'll find out.' Janet giggled. 'If our Tom sticks a bairn in her belly, Hewitt'll have to agree to a weddin' whether he likes it or not. Mind you, it'll help Tom's cause if he can slap down a bag o' chink for to buy this place.'

'Half this place,' said Betsy. 'Henry will want his share.'

'Aye,' Janet conceded, 'I suppose he will.'

'Five hundred pounds,' said Betsy, 'is an awful lot o' money.'

'Henry says we can expect another cargo next week.'

'It was easy last time,' Betsy said, 'but winter's at our heels an' even Conn can't control the weather.'

'Well,' Janet sighed, 'winter won't last for ever. When Mr Arbuthnot comes to Drennan again I'll have a new dress an' new ribbons an' Tom says he'll teach me the steps for the dances.'

'Is that all this means to you?' said Betsy.

'What else would it mean to me?' Janet said. 'Money draws money, you know. If word gets out the Brodies are doin' well then the lads will prick up their ears at the promise o' a dower chest an' come flockin' to my door.'

'If the wrong word gets out,' said Betsy, 'we all wind up in jail.'

'Nah.' Janet dug her in the ribs again. 'Conn'll see us right.'

'Conn will see himself right. He'll disappear.'

'He might be your cousin,' said Janet, 'but I think he has a fancy for you. If he goes, he'll take you wi' him.'

'I don't want to go with him,' said Betsy.

'Then you're daft,' said Janet. 'God, I tell you, if Conn McCaskie wagged his wee finger in my direction, sailor or no sailor, I'd be off like a hare. Don't you want a man to take care o' you, Betsy?'

'I'd rather take care o' myself, thanks.'

'More fool you, then,' said Janet and, punching the pillow, rolled on her side to sleep.

However reticent the bachelors had been at the graveside and however rowdy at the wake, when the club convened for the November meeting their expressions of sympathy were profuse and sincere. Some gentlemen – those who knew him least well – were surprised to see Tom in the chair. He had been absent from the last two meetings of the Masonic lodge and was, after all, still in mourning. Those who knew him better – or thought they did – were also surprised, for the last time they had seen him he'd been bowed down and bedraggled and as close to crazy as made no matter.

Now, just a few days later, he seemed to have recovered his *joie de vivre*, to be almost his old self again. He ordered, and paid for, three extra bottles of claret with which to offer a toast to his dear, departed father and express his gratitude to all the brother bachelors who had given him comfort in his distress. No one, of course, was crass enough to enquire if he had received comfort from the virgin of Thimble Row or if his vow to marry Hewitt's daughter had been modified by circumstances and veered more towards the bed than the altar.

Before formal proceedings got under way, Peter rested a hand on Tom's shoulder and tactfully enquired if all was well, while Mr Ogilvy, standing close by, bent an ear to catch the young farmer's reply.

'Never better, Peter, never better.'

'That – that thing with my Aunt Tassie . . .?'

'Put behind me, well behind me.'

'I'm glad to hear it,' Peter said. 'I don't know what came over her.'

'Well, it's all over, Peter.' Tom looked up, grinning. 'I bought her off.'

'Bought her off?' Mr Ogilvy chipped in. 'How?'

'Cash in her hand.'

'Did you visit her at her shop?' said Peter.

'Of course. It was obvious to me that the old hag was only after a handful o' silver to keep her mouth shut.' Tom, still smiling, glanced from one to the other. 'We'll hear no more from Tassie Landles, I reckon.'

'Well,' said Peter, at a loss for words. 'Well, that's – that's grand.'

'Has he gone away?' Mr Ogilvy murmured. 'Your father, I mean.'

'Sent packing,' Tom answered and, laughing a little too heartily, thumped the table with his fist to bring his fellow bachelors to order.

Whether it was an unexpected effect of remitting fever or the spontaneous demonstration of mutual affection that she had witnessed on the previous evening Rose could not decide, but all pretence of discretion was abandoned. To her surprise, Papa did not even leap out of bed, harrumphing, when she, in Dorothy's stead, brought in the morning tea. Mrs Prole, still weak and bleary-eyed, merely raised her head an inch or two from under her employer's arm and uttered something un-intelligible that may have been a greeting or was, more probably, an instruction regarding breakfast.

Papa ate toast and bacon at a card table in the master's bedroom and plied Eunice Prole with titbits from his plate. She was better, it seemed, but not much so. After Neville had departed for the manufactory and Rose had administered her medicines, she turned over and fell fast asleep.

Rose washed the breakfast dishes in a tub of warm water, scoured the pans with a handful of sand, scalded the teapot, and added more water to the mutton broth which, though it stood hard as mortar in the pot, would certainly do one more day. That done, she checked the contents of the larder and, feeling rather pleased with herself, made note of comestibles that were running low.

She had no desire to hide in the attic or to slip out into the streets. Indeed, the thought of venturing into the market square and perhaps encountering Tom Brodie again filled her with dread. She did not know how she would react if she met him again; hoity-toity, she supposed, brushing aside his apologies with a flounce and flick of her wrist, as if he meant nothing to her.

She drank tea and munched an oatcake in lieu of dinner and, thinking of Tom, stared out of the narrow kitchen window into grey November mists. Then, before melancholy could take too firm a hold, she leapt up, tied on an apron, grabbed the iron pail, a short-handled brush and shovel and headed for the parlour to clean out the grate.

She had gone no further than the hall when a tentative knock upon the front door drew her up short.

She hesitated, then, thinking that it might be Loon bringing news of Dorothy, propped the pail against the stairs and, still clutching the brush and shovel, opened the door.

The only evidence of Lucas Fergusson's less-than-sober Sabbath outfit was the tall hat with the snappy brim which he did not – or could not – remove. Balanced on one hand was a great lump of beef, bleeding into a gauze wrapper, and on the other a leek and oatmeal flan.

'Miss Hewitt,' Lucas said, with a wriggle. 'Good afternoon.'

'Good afternoon to you, Mr Fergusson,' Rose answered, trying vainly to hide the brush and shovel behind her back. 'What brings you to our door?'

Lucas thrust out both arms as if he were about to embrace her. 'These.'

The lump of beef wobbled and might have toppled to the ground if Rose, with great presence of mind, hadn't dropped the brush and shovel and caught it.

'What,' she said, 'are they?'

'Gifties,' said Lucas.

'Gifties?' said Rose. 'Oh!'

'I'm supposed tae say they're tokens o' my affection,' Lucas informed her, 'but you can't hand a lassie a bit o' beef an' expect to be taken seriously.'

'Well, Lucas,' said Rose, 'I'm presently acting day-maid and on my way to brush soot from the flues so I'm in no position to take anyone seriously. Please, do step inside.'

'Are you sure?'

'I'm sure.'

She led him through the hallway into the kitchen where she relieved him of the flan and put it, and the beef, safely away in the larder. When she popped her head around the larder door she saw that Lucas had hunkered down to warm his hands at the fire.

'Tea?' she said. 'I've no beer to give you, alas, and no cake.'

'Tea'll do me fine.'

She closed the larder door, stepped close to him and reached for the caddy that rested on the high shelf to the right of the fireplace. He stood up and placed both hands lightly about her waist.

'Mr Fergusson! Really!'

'Just givin' you a lift,' he said, alarmed at her indignation. 'My mother's a small person too an' when she needs somethin' from the high shelves . . .' He backed away, hands raised. 'I didn't mean tae . . .'

'Of course not,' Rose said. 'I was caught unaware, that's all. Indeed, it's I who should be apologising to you, Lucas, for entertaining you in the kitchen. The parlour fire has not been lighted, however, and the room is very cold.'

'Aye, it's cold all right,' Lucas agreed uncertainly. 'Maybe I should be on my way since I've done what I was sent here tae – to do.'

'Nonsense!' Rose told him. 'Sit, sit there. Tea will be delivered shortly.'

Lucas removed his hat and greatcoat and placed them neatly on a vacant chair, then, flipping up his coat-tails, warmed his backside at the fire while Rose tackled the business of tea-making.

'What *were* you sent here to do, Lucas?' she asked.

'Deliver the beef an' stuff,' Lucas replied.

'And who was it sent you?'

'My mother,' Lucas said. 'My father met your father in the street this mornin' an' heard that your wifie – your house-keeper – was sick an' you were nursin' her on your own.'

Rose raised an eyebrow. 'Beef *and* a flan?'

'For supper,' Lucas explained, adding, 'my mother says.'

'Well, that's very kind of her,' said Rose. 'And very kind of you, Lucas, to take time off from your work to ride into—'

'I walked.'

'To walk into Drennan to deliver her gifts.'

'I wanted tae come.'

'May I ask the reason?'

'Tae – to see you, Rose.'

'Oh!' she said. 'Well, I'm flattered.' He flapped his coat-tails and wriggled, though whether it was shyness or over-heating that caused him to do so Rose did not care to speculate. 'However,' she went on, 'I'm not entirely convinced that it's proper for us to be alone in the house.'

'Where's the wumman?'

'Ah, yes, the wumma – woman is here, albeit incapacitated.'

'She's what?'

'Laid low,' said Rose without a hint of patronage. 'She has the fever.'

'Nancy has the fever.' Lucas clapped a hand to his mouth. 'I shouldn't have said that!'

'Why ever not?'

'Mam said I wasn't tae – to talk about Nancy.'

'Is she your sweetheart?' Rose said.

'I'm not at liberty for tae – to say.'

'Oh, go on, Lucas.' Rose nudged him as she carried the teapot to the table. 'You may confide in me.'

'She's not my sweetheart, nah.'

'I saw you with her after church, Lucas. She gave every appearance of having some claim upon you. If she's not your sweetheart perhaps she's your lover.'

'I thought the two things were the same.'

'Well, they're not.'

'Is Tom Brodie *your* lover?' Lucas asked.

'Certainly not.'

'Your sweetheart, then?'

'Tom Brodie is not the issue,' Rose said. 'Tell me how you stand with the dairymaid, with Nancy.'

Lucas pulled away from the fireplace and took a seat at the table. He hooked his ankles round the spar of the chair and tucked his elbows into his ribs. He was knotted with embarrassment but he was also eager to expose his manly credentials to this polished young girl.

'I've took her,' he said, at length.

'I'm not quite sure what you mean by "took",' Rose said.

'Had her.'

'Cojoined with her, you mean?'

'Mowed her,' said Lucas, flushing. 'Aye.'

Rose put down the flower-patterned saucer and cup and seated herself across the table from her guest. He was wriggling again, squirming almost, but she could tell by his daring, darting little glances that he was more proud than ashamed of his congress with the dairymaid and the fact that she, a lady, had given him an opportunity to brag about it.

'Why are you telling me this, Lucas?'

'You asked me, but.'

'I did, did I not?' Rose admitted. 'Well, now that you have – em – got it off your chest, perhaps you would be good enough to elucidate.'

'Eh?'

'Expand,' said Rose.

'Nancy says I'm better'n any man she's ever had.'

Rose experienced a sudden burning in her cheeks and a tingling sensation in the pit of her stomach. She sniffed, cleared her throat and pressed on. 'How many men has Nancy had?'

'Eh?' Lucas repeated.

Rose felt sure that the grazier's son was not as stupid as he pretended to be and was enjoying the risqué game of question and answer just as much as she was. 'What is Nancy's criterion?'

Lucas swallowed hard. 'Same as yours, I suppose.'

'I mean, on what is Nancy's judgement based?'

'She's done it before,' said Lucas.

'Have – I mean, had you?'

'What?'

'Done it before.'

She had never been alone with a young man, except for a few brief minutes with Tom Brodie in the institution library. Although she did not equate Lucas with Tom, Lucas was here and Tom was not. The novelty of the situation, and its intimacy, excited her.

'I've done it now, but,' Lucas said.

He had sneaked a hand between his thighs and made no attempt to hide it. Even as she watched, he seemed to grow in confidence. She realised, too late, that he had mistaken her interest in his association with the dairymaid as an invitation to be forward.

'Have you done it yet, Rosie?' he asked.

Speechless and burning, she shook her head.

'Not even wi' Tom Brodie?'

'Not with Tom Brodie, not with – with anyone.'

'It's good,' he said. 'Aye, I tell you, it's good with Nancy Ames.' He looked up and met her eye. 'It'd be even better with you.'

'Why do you say that?'

' 'Cause you're lovely.'

'But I don't – I haven't . . .'

'I'll show you,' Lucas said.

She scrambled to free herself from the chair but her limbs felt as if they did not belong to her and her legs would not function properly. She was no more than halfway out of her chair when Lucas caught her. His chin was smooth and he smelled of soap. His lips were not rough, his tongue not thrusting. For an instant it seemed as if tenderness would overcome desire, then he clasped her hips, bent his knees, swept up her skirts and cupped her most intimate part.

'Lucas, no,' she gasped. 'No, Lucas.'

'See,' he said. 'See.'

She felt the hand move, tugging a little – then it was gone. She was shaken by the ease with which he had caught her out, the speed with which he had released her. She waited for him to reach for the ties of his breeches and go on, go forward, but he did not. Twice now she had been brought to the brink and abandoned, but Tom's reluctance had been calculated and Lucas's, she sensed, was instinctive.

'Is – is that what you do to Nancy Ames?' she heard herself say.

'Nah, I do more, a lot more.'

'Why did you stop, Lucas?'

''Cause you're a lady.'

He was not cold or self-righteous. He did not flaunt his self-control. He was as distressed as she was, red-cheeked, breathing like a broken bellows and obviously uncomfortable. He crabbed around the table and sat down once more, both hands pressed into his lap.

'I shouldn't have done that,' he said, half to himself. 'You're only a wee lassie. It wasn't right.'

'Why wasn't it right, Lucas?'

''Cause I'm *the* man,' he said. 'Damn it, I'm the man.'

'Must the man always take responsibility?'

''Course he must,' Lucas said. ''Course he bloody must.'

'Have I no say in the matter?'

'Aye, you can always say no.'

'Does Nancy Ames ever say no?'

'You're not Nancy Ames,' Lucas murmured.

She smoothed down her skirts, squared her apron and composed herself.

'Thank you, Lucas,' she said.

'For what, but?' He sighed. 'I touched you.'

'You did,' said Rose softly. 'You touched me.'

'You won't tell your daddy, will you?'

'No, I won't tell a soul. It's our secret, Lukie.' Leaning over the table, she kissed his cheek. 'Our secret.'

'Who's that you've got there?' said a voice from the hall.

Draped in one of Papa's old robes which was too short to hide her skinny ankles, Eunice Prole shuffled a few steps towards the kitchen.

'Is that Tom Brodie?'

'It's Lucas,' Rose said, going forward. 'Lucas Fergusson. He brought a piece of beef and a flan, gifts from his mother.'

'Thank her kindly,' the housekeeper said. 'An' give the boy some tea.'

Then, with Rose at her elbow, she tottered back to bed.

And Lucas, heart pounding, made good his escape.

16

The cold spell lasted no more than a day or two then rain returned, a mild, soft misty rain that soaked through everything and made the sheep miserable. Conn's calves, great sturdy beasts, were brought to the byre. Labouring by the scant light from the cottage window, Henry constructed pens in a sheltered corner of the yard to accommodate them. Evening and morning milking was done by lantern-light, and the days grew shorter.

Seed was purchased from a merchant in Drennan, good, dry, runny seed. The sacks were stored in the stable. It was late in the year for planting Siberian wheat but Tom and Henry agreed that three fair days would be enough to strew the long field and Tom went out with the harrow before dawn. The girls broke down the dung-heap that had grown almost as tall as the cottage roof and Henry carted the loads out to the field.

The seasonal chores were undertaken with enthusiasm. The gloom of the past weeks seemed to have been left behind. Betsy wondered if it was the old man's absence, not seed in the stable and money in the cashbox, that inspired the Brodies to work so hard. Agnes in particular seemed anxious to put the past behind her. She washed sheets and blankets, repaired clothes and cooked substantial meals. She returned to sleeping in the big bed in the kitchen alcove and lay propped up on the bolster issuing orders that her sons very largely ignored.

Agnes was making ready for bed. Tom dozed in a chair by the hearth. Janet knelt on the floor at his feet staring dreamily into the fire. Henry worked on his ledger at the table. Chin on hand, Betsy sat opposite him, nodding, almost asleep. There was no warning from the dogs, no clash of hooves on the straw-strewn ground outside. The first indication the Brodies had of a late evening caller was a sudden thud upon the door and, a moment later, the creak of hinges as the door swung open.

Tom leapt to his feet and grabbed a three-legged stool to use as a weapon. Henry flung himself from the chair, spread his legs and raised his fists.

Janet cried, 'Are we caught?'

'Be calm, be calm.' Conn held up a placating hand. 'Sure an' did you not hear me announce myself?'

'Nah, we did not, sir,' Janet angrily informed him. 'What sort o' an hour is this to be droppin' by?'

'Sure an' I didn't think it was so late.'

Tom put down the stool. Henry, a little shamefaced, dismantled his pugilistic pose while Betsy, wide awake now, ran to her cousin and kissed him.

'You took us by surprise,' she said, 'that's all. Have you had supper?'

'An' where's your horse?' said Agnes.

'I've had my supper, an' I've no horse. I came on foot,' Conn said. 'I'll accept a sip o' whisky if there's one on offer then I must be on my way again. The boat's moored at Port Cedric an' I don't wish to leave it there o'er long.'

'At Port Cedric,' Tom said, 'with a cargo?'

'No cargo,' Conn answered, 'not tonight.'

'When then?' said Janet.

'Thursday mornin',' Conn told her. 'Brandy's the cargo, just brandy.'

'What hour?' Henry enquired.

'Two o'clock. We'll unload on the half tide. There's a ten-gun cutter patrollin' the waters o' the Kilbrannan Sound an' the longer our Dutchman lies at anchor off Port Cedric the more chance she'll be challenged.'

'Is the cutter huntin' you, Conn?' Tom asked.

'Nay,' Conn assured him. 'It'll be ill luck if we're spotted, but I'm not the sort o' feller who leaves anything to chance when I've invested my own money on a shipment.'

'How long will we be expected to hold the stuff?' said Tom.

'A day, at most.'

Conn was clad in a short black oilskin jacket and was hatless. The rain had made his hair curl even more than usual. It hung over his forehead in ringlets that on any other man would seem girlish. He drank the whisky but when Betsy offered the bottle, shook his head.

He seemed, she thought, less ebullient than usual.

'What's wrong, Conn?' she asked him. 'Is it dangerous?'

'A mite,' Conn admitted. 'I took my chance on the offer o' a cargo o' raw brandy an' I paid for it, cash down, without partners. I'm shoulderin' the risk by myself an' the sum involved makes even an old salt like me tremble.'

'Only brandy, then?' said Janet.

Conn nodded. 'No kegs or packets, just brandy.'

'How many casks?' said Henry.

'Thirty-two.'

'Thirty-two!' Tom exclaimed. 'How can we handle thirty-two casks, man? It'll take every horse an' pony we've got, an' only four hours or so to ferry the stuff from the beach to the farm before daybreak.'

Conn shrugged. 'I never said it would be easy.'

'Will you be there to help?' said Betsy.

'Can't be done, my honey,' Conn told her. 'It'll take my lads all their time to smother the tracks an' push before daylight.'

Tom said, 'Why are you askin' us to run this extra risk?'

'For extra profit?' Henry suggested.

The Irishman gave a wry grunt. 'Well, Henry Brodie, years o' cattle tradin' have sharpened your skill at spottin' a bargain, I see.'

'Twenty percentage,' Henry said, 'or you find another store.'

Conn hesitated then offered Henry his hand. 'Twenty it is then, Mr Brodie – but only on this cargo.'

'It had better be worth it,' Tom said.

'Aye, but it will be, son,' said Agnes cheerfully. 'Believe me, it will.'

Tom did not care much for harrowing. Unlike ploughing, the pace did not encourage contemplation. The wooden frame skipped and skittered over the furrows and the work was constantly interrupted by a need to stop the horses and pick up stones. He was not happy, not content. He could put neither the girl nor his promise to his father out of his mind. His agitation was not helped by his mother's enthusiasm for what was after all a crime against the interests of the Crown. He resented her zeal. It did not become a widow woman and spoke of hidden depths, facets of character that he had never noticed when his daddy had been alive. When chatting with Betsy or Janet she would chuckle and flap her hands like a flighty young thing. When she brought out the cashbox and counted the haul he was reminded of a miser in a French play he had once read. Her satisfaction seemed gloating, as if she respected the guineas in the box more than his father's memory.

The gravestone was up in the kirkyard. Henry and he had gone to inspect it but Mammy had brushed aside his invitation to accompany them. She had hung off until Sunday when she and Mr Turbot had strolled among the headstones and, almost in passing, had glanced at the stone that marked Matthew Brodie's last resting place. It had felt like a stab in the heart when he had heard his mother say to the minister, 'I should have brought flowers but there are no flowers. I'll bring some snowdrops in the spring. He'll wait patient till then, I'm sure.' And she had shed not one single tear to bless the stone that marked the spot where the man who had died to save Hawkshill had laid down his bones.

The dung smelled sweet in the drifting rain. There was no time for another ploughing, no time to be 'modern'. Henry and Betsy forked the ripe manure in great sweeping swathes across the field while Janet steered the cart, crisp and brisk in spite of the dreary, wetting weather. Gulls and rooks had gathered again and jeered him for the mess he had made of his life. He watched Betsy from the corner of his eye. Her hair, thick as a corn sheaf, was bound with a bandana and her skirts tucked into her belt, showing flesh up to her thighs. He saw her dip and lift on those fine, strong legs, saw how her breasts swayed when she flung the dung, sliding it from the fork at the top of the arc, then stood braced in the cart for a second or two with her arms aloft and her face raised to the falling rain as if she were drinking it.

If he hadn't climbed to the window ledge in Thimble Row, if he hadn't kissed Rose Hewitt's soft lips, if he had been less impulsive, less romantic by nature, he might have taken Betsy McBride and blunted the edge of his hunger between her legs. It was winter, though, and wet. There were no bowers to lie in, no blossoms dripping from the boughs to shelter him while he fondled and cajoled and made up pretty compliments to justify that thrust, that cry when he leaned down and into her and saw her eyes close and her mouth open and felt her legs kick and the pulse of her female parts grab and squeeze him.

'Tom?'

'Uh?'

'Look to the west,' Henry called out.

His brother, smeared and tousled, stood by the wheel of the cart, grinning and pointing. He tightened his grip on the rein but did not halt the progress of the rattling harrow. He glanced behind him.

'What?' he shouted.

'See, the sky's clearin'. We'll have a fine night for it after all.'

'A fine night for what?'

'The run,' Betsy told him. 'The brandy run.'

She was lathered with bits of straw and horse manure, her shins streaked with greenish-brown cattle dung. She waved the short-handled fork in the air as if, like a witch, she had triumphed over the weather.

Henry, looking up at her, let out a whoop.

'An' the promise o' a fair day tomorrow, lass,' he cried, 'a fair day or two to see this damned field seeded.'

'Damned field it is, too,' Tom murmured and when Henry had clambered into the cart once more, drove the horses on even faster than before.

Eunice Prole was up but not much about when, around two o'clock, she was summoned to the door by a tentative knocking. Dorothy had not yet returned to work. The rat-catcher's lad had informed them that the girl was still very weak and Mr McFee, superintendent of the orphanage, would not let her rise from her bed and had even summoned Dr Glendinning, at parish expense, to attend her for a second time. Rose expressed concern for the day-maid but Eunice, still sore and shaky, grumbled that a snot-nosed orphan was having more attention lavished on her – at parish expense – than she deserved.

The housekeeper was on her feet and dressed, though even simple tasks took an age to perform and left her so exhausted that she was compelled to sit down and rest. Rose was only too willing to assume the burden of housekeeping and was, surprisingly, rather good at it. In less charitable moments Eunice was inclined to believe that beating the child blue-black had turned her into a polite, efficient and reasonably biddable young woman for, at that time, she was too dependent upon her master's daughter to detect an element of cunning in her obedience.

After some shaky fumbling, Eunice managed to open the door.

She peered through tired eyes into the daylight.

'Yes?'

'Is Mr Hewitt at home?'

'No, he's at the manufactory.'

'Miss Hewitt, Miss Rose Hewitt?'

'Gone out for provisions,' Eunice said. 'Who, may I ask, are you?'

The woman was not entirely unfamiliar. Eunice had a notion that she had seen her several times before but had not, to her recall, been introduced. She struggled to put a name to the small, weather-browned face.

'Mrs Fergusson, Mrs Walter Fergusson,' the woman prompted.

'Ah! Oh! Aye, of course,' Eunice said. 'I'm sorry.'

'You're the housekeeper, are you not?'

'I – I am.'

'You'll do,' said Lucas's mother, and shoved her way inside.

The cape was waterproof and the hood capacious enough to keep out rain but the garment was thick and clinging and made her perspire as she hurried into the heart of the town. She went first to the orphanage to call upon Dorothy who, as it happened, was not quite so close to death as Loon had led them to believe.

The girl was seated in a low-backed nursing chair by the stove that dominated the long room. There were three or four other folk present but when Rose was shown in by Mr McFee, a fierce-looking but kindly old fellow, they sidled off and left Rose alone with her wan little servant.

Poor Dorothy was pale and shrivelled, as if the fever had thrust her from childhood into premature old age. She was dressed in a patched nightgown, a pair of man's stockings and a blanket, clean but threadbare, was draped over her shoulders. She was pleased to see Rose and accepted her mistress's gift of a sugar cake and two apples gratefully but did not have the strength to sustain a conversation for long. Rose soon took her leave, for she had much to do that afternoon and not much time to do it in.

She hurried along the lane behind the market square and down the alley to the bridge. The river was high and noisy but in her haste she was hardly aware of it. As she turned on to the path that led to Tassie Landles' shop, she encountered Tom Brodie's friend, Peter Frye, carefully guiding his horse by the fore-rein up the slippery slope from the shop.

'Why,' he said, 'if it isn't Miss Hewitt. This is a pleasant surprise.'

He was certainly handsome, Rose thought, but he was only a year or two older than she was and, compared to Tom, or even Lucas, seemed like a half-grown boy. She would have preferred to hurry on but the horse, a sleek chestnut stallion, blocked her way. She drew up, threw back her hood and offered the young man a cold little greeting.

'Are you here to seek a fresh fortune, Miss Hewitt?' Mr Frye enquired.

'I'm here to purchase a remedy for our housekeeper, who is ill.'

'The fever, is it?'

'It is, Mr Frye, the fever.' She paused. 'Is Tom – is Mr Brodie in town with you, by any chance?'

'Alas, not today,' Peter Frye said. 'I believe he's dressing one of his fields or, should I say, one of your father's fields.'

'Dressing?'

'Spreading muck,' Peter said. 'Manure.'

'I see,' said Rose. 'My father will be pleased to hear it.'

'Will he,' Peter Frye said, 'or will he simply be curious as to how you came by the information?'

'Indeed, sir, your point is well made,' Rose conceded. 'Have you been to seek your fortune from Miss Landles?'

'Hardly,' Peter said. 'She is, in fact, my aunt. I've been delivering a few small luxuries to brighten her life. She is not at all well off, you know.'

The horse stamped and tossed his head impatiently but Mr Frye did not seem to be in a hurry. Rose moved a half step closer.

'Do you believe your aunt has mysterious powers?' she said.

'I do not doubt that she believes she has.'

'That's not what I asked you,' said Rose.

For a long moment he stared at the snouts of foam that nosed against the bridge piles. He opened his mouth, closed it, then, with a sigh, said, 'Yes, I do – but I do not take her pronouncements too seriously.'

'Why is that?'

'Because they are open to many interpretations.' He glanced at the river once more. 'Did Tom tell you?'

'Tell me what?'

He shook his head. 'Nothing.'

Rose had lost all sense of urgency. 'What is this secret that you share with Mr Brodie that I do not? Does it concern me?'

'You?' Peter said. 'No, no.'

'Have you spoken with Tom recently?'

'I met with him at the Bachelors' Club a night ago.'

'Did he mention me?'

'Only in the most general way,' Peter said.

'Are you not his friend? Are you not in his confidence?'

'Well, I like to think that I am.'

'Tell me then,' said Rose, 'am I more to him than a diversion?'

'I really could not say. I mean . . .'

'What do you mean, Mr Frye?' Rose persisted. 'After all, you were with him when he made his first approach to me. Were you not the horseman who carried him off that night in October when he climbed to my window and made such a nuisance of himself?'

'I confess – yes, it was me.'

'Then you must know what's in his mind.'

'No one knows what's in Tom Brodie's mind,' Peter told her. 'Indeed, I'm not sure Tom knows himself. Look, Miss Hewitt, I'm beginning to find this conversation tiresome. It's not my place to discuss your friendship with Tom Brodie.'

'Does Mr Brodie think I'm tiresome?'

'Really, Miss Hewitt, I must be on—'

'You are all the same, you bachelors,' Rose said. 'You care for nothing but yourselves. When next you meet your friend, I would be grateful if you would inform him that I no longer care to receive his attentions. I have received a proposal from another gentleman.'

'What other gentleman?'

'A gentleman of considerably more standing than Tom Brodie.'

'Who is this paragon? What's his name?'

'His name is my secret, sir, until we announce our betrothal,' Rose said. 'Now, if you would be good enough to move your horse, you are not the only person who has business to attend to.'

Peter nudged the horse aside to let the haughty young woman pass and, frowning, watched Tom's light-o-love trip down the slippery pathway and vanish into the shop.

'Do you know,' said Flora Fergusson, 'I'm thinkin' it's no bad thing for us to have an opportunity for a wee quiet talk.'

'Why is that, pray?' said Eunice.

'Unless I miss my guess you're Neville's tower o' strength.'

'Well' – Eunice was not too exhausted to preen a little – 'well, it's kind o' you to say so, Mrs Fergusson.'

'Walter tells me you have more than Neville's ear in your pocket; you have his confidence as well.'

'It's true that Nev – Mr Hewitt does lean upon my opinion in matters of a domestic nature,' Eunice said.

'Is *she* domestic? The girl, the daughter?'

'Rose? Oh, yes,' said Mrs Prole. 'Rose is very domestic.'

'How did she come by way o' the facts?'

'Facts?'

'The facts o' nature all young women must have at their fingertips.'

'I explained the cycles of the moon to her, of course.'

'An' the other?'

'What other would that be, Mrs Fergusson?'

'Babies.'

Hand shaking slightly, Eunice did her bit with the silver teapot and poured a thimbleful of tea into her cup. She looked up, smiled wanly and shook the pot in Mrs Fergusson's direction. 'A drop more?'

'No, thank you.'

Eunice gripped the teapot in both hands and lowered it to the stand. 'By the by, your leek flan was delicious. I must have the recipe for—'

'Does she know about men?' Flora Fergusson put in.

'She's been warned against them, if that's what you mean.'

'I mean, is she fit for to be a wife?'

'Well, she's sound in wind an' limb an' comes from good stock.'

'Aye, stock's important. How did her mammy die?'

It dawned on Eunice that Rose was being evaluated by the same criteria by which Walter Fergusson might judge a heifer.

She said, 'Consumption.'

'Inherited?'

'I really couldn't say.'

'Is her granny still alive?' Mrs Fergusson asked.

'Dead long since.'

The grazier's wife frowned and, holding her cup in both hands, dipped her mouth to it and sipped. She was uncommonly small, almost dwarf-like. It occurred to Eunice that Walter had not picked his bride by weight or, for that matter, appearance. 'Be that as it may,' Mrs Fergusson said, 'my Lucas has set his heart on marriage.'

'To Mr Hewitt's daughter, to Rose?'

'At the minute he's not fussy but, aye, he seems to favour your lass.'

'She's not "my lass", Mrs Fergusson.'

'You reared her, though.'

'I helped,' Eunice admitted.

'An' you have influence over her.'

'Yes, I suppose I do,' Eunice said. 'However, if you've come here today to discuss a marriage settlement, it's not my place to—'

'Too early for that sort o' talk,' Flora Fergusson put in. 'She'll have to be won round first.'

'Won round?' said Eunice. 'You mean wooed?'

'Aye, that, but more than that,' said Mrs Fergusson. 'You see, our Lucas is a sensitive lad. He may not look it, not on the outside, but he's a gentle soul an' as shy as a bloody buttercup in spite o' all we've done to correct him.'

'He doesn't appear shy,' Eunice suggested mildly.

'He is, take it from me, he is,' Mrs Fergusson growled. 'He's . . .' She sought for the word: '. . . impressionable.'

Eunice nodded. 'Easily led.'

'He needs a woman to keep him straight, a wife with a bit o' spunk who'll steer him through life an' not take advantage o' his tender nature in or out o' the bed-chamber.'

'The bedchamber?'

'He's frightened o' women.'

'I thought he was havin' it—' Eunice bit her tongue.

'Because he's so easy led we'll need to rein him in before he lands in the sort o' trouble that'll cost money.' Mrs Fergusson put down her cup, bent forward until her chin almost rested on the tablecloth and glowered up at the housekeeper. 'There are o'er many temptations for a young man these days, far too many uncouth lassies who'll take him by the – by the nose an' stake a claim to him an' a share o' the fortune my Walter's built up.'

'Yes,' said Eunice. 'I do understand your predicament, Mrs Fergusson, but what can I do about it? I mean, I can't order Rose to marry your son. Rose Hewitt's a very determined young lady with a mind o' her own. If she thinks for a second she's bein' pushed into marriage by me or her papa she'll dig in her heels an' resist.'

'Exactly the sort o' young lady who'd suit us – I mean, Lucas – to a tee.'

'I'm sure Mr Hewitt would regard it in a similar light,' Eunice said. 'It would be a great relief for us – him to have Rose off his hands. I mean, of course, to see her settled with a fine young man like your Lucas.'

Flora Fergusson pulled herself upright, though the increase in height was hardly noticeable. She tapped her hands on the table. 'Good!' she said. 'Now all we have to do between us is get the pair o' them to see sense.'

'How do you propose we do that?' said Eunice.

'Clap them together, leave them alone together . . .'

'An' let nature take its course, you mean?'

'Precisely,' Flora Fergusson said and held out her cup, *sans* saucer, to partake of a drop more tea.

Tassie was in the garden feeding hens when Rose Hewitt found her. She was not well pleased to see the flax manufacturer's daughter, even less pleased that the girl had come upon her unannounced, since she did not care for strangers parading through her little house. She had just got rid of her nephew, Peter, who had been kind enough to bring her a fresh bottle of brandy but who had quizzed her rather too forcefully about the form in which 'the ghosts' appeared and the manner of their address. If there was one thing Tassie disliked more than a sceptic it was a convert who required the mysteries of death and the life hereafter to be pinned down and classified like tables in a textbook.

'Rose Hewitt,' Tassie said. 'To what do I owe the pleasure o' a visit?'

'I have a question,' the girl said.

Oh, aye, here it comes, Tassie thought, another one who's been made privy to Tom Brodie's guilty secret and who's here to plague me with questions I can't answer.

The girl's demeanour had changed, though. She was no longer the scared wee creature who had called for a fortune a few weeks ago. She had swagger now that was both imperious and insolent, as if she had finally learned her superior place in the scheme of things and felt obligated to exploit it.

Tassie scattered another handful of corn and shouldered the basket in which the feed was kept. 'What's your question, then?' She sighed.

'The fortune you gave me, the prediction, can it be changed?'

'It canna *be* changed,' Tassie said, 'but it might change o' its own accord.'

'Do you talk in riddles because you cannot give me a straight answer?'

Tassie did not take kindly to being challenged by a young girl, even if she was a flax manufacturer's daughter. 'I talk in riddles, lass,' she said, 'because the future *is* a riddle. Only when the future becomes the past an' you look back on it will you know if you found the answer you sought, if each small choice you made durin' the search was the right or the wrong one.'

'So,' the girl said, 'the grand house, the children, the tears – all just made up to appease me?'

'I didn't make it up.'

'Then where did it come from?' the girl said scornfully. 'The cat?'

If only you could be with me when the door opens, Tassie thought, you'd not be so free with your mockery. If you had a half grain of sense you might realise that the world and the world beyond are full of shadows that obscure our destinies, that nothing is ever clear from one minute to the next and the future will always take us by surprise. 'I saw what I saw,' Tassie told her. 'What you make o' it is up to you.'

'Did you really "see" me in a veil, weeping?'

'Are you unsure o' Brodie, is that what's brought you here?'

At that a little of the pith went out of her; she nodded meekly.

'So you should be, lass,' Tassie said. 'There might be love there, a heart as hot as a furnace flame, but Tom Brodie will never bring you peace. Is it peace you want, peace an' contentment, or the drama that goes with uncertainty? Your future's wrote in the plural, Rose Hewitt, and it's up to you to find the answer.'

'Only one answer,' the girl said, 'one correct answer?'

'If it's not to be Brodie it'll be another,' Tassie said. 'If not him, still another, but you'll never be sure if you're makin' the right choice, for love's a puzzle in itself, as mysterious as any bit o' magic.'

'There's no magic here,' Rose Hewitt said, 'only mystery.'

'Aye, lassie, but when the mystery goes the magic goes too an' you'll be left with a dry heart an' naught but regrets.'

'A bleak prospect,' the girl said. 'Is that my future?'

'In time, in time perhaps,' Tassie said, 'but not for many years yet. Now, come into the house an' let me mix you a remedy to ease poor Eunice Prole's distress.'

'How did you know that Mrs Prole is distressed?'

'The cat told me,' Tassie Landles said, and laughed.

17

Betsy's feet and hands throbbed, a noose of pain gripped her forehead and the scar under her hairline burned. There was no frost at the beach but the wind that snaked across the dunes had teeth and the waves sliding up the slope of the shore clasped her calves in an icy vice. There was only one man with Conn. The boat in which the casks had been ferried from the Dutch vessel was too small for the load and, pitching violently, catapulted several casks into the surf. Conn yelled to Betsy and the Brodies to rescue his precious cargo and, brandishing an oar, plunged up to his chest in the water. The only light was a ghostly haze against which the black shapes of Conn, the boat and the bobbing casks were outlined. Betsy waded into the surf, with Henry and Tom thrashing beside her, to collar the floating casks. Conn's man, precariously balanced in the rocking boat, tipped the rest of the cargo into the shallows. Conn, drenched, crawled from the sea, screaming, 'How many, how many have we lost? Do we have them all?' for the prospect of several casks of raw French brandy floating loose in the firth was frightening. They rolled the casks on to the sand above the tideline and Conn counted them; none, as it happened, was missing. Even so, as soon as the casks were counted Conn climbed back into the boat and he and the man rowed off into the darkness, leaving Betsy and the Brodies to pack and transport the black cargo.

It was a half-hour after milking time before they reached the farm. Cows were lowing in the field, stalled calves bellowing.

The dogs added their voices to the hullabaloo. Frost was thick, everything bristled with it. The cottage and outbuildings were printed calico-white against the fall of the hillside. Agnes steered the cart to the barn where Janet, who had gone on ahead, had lighted a lantern to guide them. Betsy barely had strength enough to unrope the casks and lower them to the ground. There was no sense of relief, no triumph, at being home. It took close to an hour to trundle the casks into the barn and hide them, by which time the sun had appeared over the rim of the moor and the cows were bawling louder than ever. The boys were in no better shape than Betsy. They had borne the brunt of the stacking. Even the horses and ponies tottered with fatigue as Tom led them to the stable to feed and rest.

Betsy slumped on the remains of the dung-heap, too exhausted to crawl to the house. Henry gripped her wrist and fitted a whisky bottle into her fingers.

'Drink,' he said.

Shaking, she spilled a quantity of the stinging liquid down her chin before, with Henry's help, she got the bottle to her lips. She tipped her head and gulped. The whisky travelled like fire down into her chest and belly. She let out a groan, and leaned her brow on Henry's hip.

He was wet too, the cloth of his breeks plastered to his legs. 'If I fetch in the cows, will you see to them? Can you manage that for me?'

'Aye,' she answered dully.

'Good girl,' he said. 'Good girl,' and helped her, gently, to her feet.

Gathering her robe – his robe – about her shrunken breast, Eunice kissed Neville's freshly shaven cheek and slid a plate of hashed beef, topped with a runny egg, on to the breakfast table.

'Ah!' Neville said. 'Ah! Delicious, Eunice, quite delicious. I hadn't expected to taste your cooking for another week or so. Are you up to it?'

'I am, my dear. I am – though only just.'

'Where's Rose?'

'Still asleep.'

'I'll rouse her then, for she has work to do.'

'Leave her be, Neville. I need to speak with you on a serious matter.'

'A matter regarding your health?' Neville said anxiously.

'No, concernin' Rose. I had a visit from Flora Fergusson yesterday when Rose was out. I said nothin' of it last night for I confess I was too tired to raise the matter when you came to bed.'

Neville lifted his spoon and shovelled hash into his mouth without taking his eyes from his housekeeper. 'Go on, tell me; what did Mrs Fergusson want?'

'She wants Rose for her lad, for Lucas.'

'That doesn't surprise me.'

'Have you an' Mr Fergusson discussed the possibility o' such a match?'

'In a circular sort o' way, aye, we have.'

'Is he after her dowry, Neville?'

'Dowry? Hoh! What dowry? No, my dear, between you an' me, it'll benefit us more than it'll benefit Fergusson to match Rose with his son.'

'Flora Fergusson thinks Rose'll make a good wife.'

'I'm sure she will,' Neville said, 'which is one reason I don't want her to throw herself away on some rat-faced farmer.'

'Brodie?'

'Brodie, of course Brodie. Is he still sniffin' around her?'

'Rose says not.'

'Do you believe her?'

'Rose says Brodie's too busy seedin' his fields to bother with her.'

Neville sat up. 'How did she come by that information?'

Eunice frowned. 'I really couldn't say.'

'Didn't you think to ask her?'

'I wasn't payin' much attention,' Eunice said. 'She just – just let it trip into the conversation.'

'Are you sure she hasn't been meetin' Brodie on the sly?'

'She's had precious little opportunity to meet anyone,' Eunice pointed out, 'apart from Lucas Fergusson who, as you know, favoured us with a visit. Besides, if Brodie *is* busy seedin' . . .' She shrugged.

Neville let out a little clucking sound. 'Is it true, I wonder?' he said, half to himself. 'An' if it is true, where the devil did Brodie find money to buy seed?'

'Well, there's only one way to find out,' Eunice told him.

'Ask Rose?'

'Ask Brodie,' said Eunice.

By noon the sun had gathered sufficient strength to melt the frost and the sky was blue and cloudless; in all respects, an ideal day for sowing Siberian wheat. With Tom on the drill, himself on the harrow and the girls with the dip-bags walking between, Henry reckoned that two days would see it through, though he was still not convinced that planting before Christmas would result in a good crop, or any crop at all. Under the circumstance, he thought, the point is moot, for he was the only person awake on Hawkshill and even the horses were too worn out to work that day.

Dried off, warmed and fed, the women and his brother were in bed, dead to the world and snoring. If he had been less conscientious, he would have joined them in the land of Nod, because his back ached, his legs trembled and he could hardly keep his eyes open. He had rounded up his sheep and driven them down from the moor to the steep-sloping pasture behind the barn where three giant oak trees provided a degree of shelter. He had put out a rack of hay and chopped up a few turnips since, in his book, a ewe well nourished in the first few weeks of pregnancy would carry to term whatever the winter threw at her.

As a rule he enjoyed shepherding but today he was too tired to take pleasure in anything. When the mutton was safely folded, he clambered over the wall, padded past the barn and headed across the yard to snatch forty winks before evening milking. He squinted into the sun, scanning the line of the hill for a sight of Mr Dingle's caravan but, to his relief, saw no sign of it. With a passing glance into the barn to make sure the casks were safely hidden, he shuffled wearily to the cottage and had just reached out a hand to open the door when something caused him to look around.

The horse was tethered to a branch of the rowan tree that leaned over the thorn hedge at the head of the track. For a moment he thought it was Tom's mare and wondered what Tom was doing up and about. Then, peering, he realised that the animal was too well shod and saddled to be Tom's and that Hawkshill had a visitor.

He was instantly awake, instantly alert.

He raised his hand to knock on the door to rouse his brother then, recalling Tom's sorry state, pushed himself away and ran to the end of the yard that gave the best view of the policies.

He reached the gate that led to the infield just as Neville Hewitt, coming over the old pasture, arrived there too. The men glared at each other as if each suspected the other of being an intruder. Hewitt put a hand on the gate and Henry, after the merest pause, opened it and let him step into the yard.

Coldly, but politely, he enquired why Mr Hewitt was wandering over the Hawkshill acres, and if he might be of assistance.

'I heard you were plantin' seed,' Neville Hewitt said.

'Well, as you can see, we're not,' said Henry.

'Aye, but the long field's been turned for it.'

'The long field has long needed turned.'

'Turned an' dressed in November?' said Neville Hewitt. 'What else can that be for but to take Siberian wheat? Are you hopin' to sell an early crop to make up the rent? If that's your intention, Brodie, I can tell you the draw will be too light to fetch ten pounds let alone thirty at the mill.'

'I didn't know you were versed in modern methods o' farmin', Mr Hewitt,' Henry said. 'Perhaps you had better stick to flax an' leave the choice o' crop an' the method o' plantin' to us.'

'Where is he?'

'Who?'

'Your brother.'

'Tom? I believe he's gone into town – Hayes, I mean, not Drennan.'

'To buy more seed, maybe?'

'More seed?' Henry arched his brows. 'Now where would we get money to buy a single bushel o' seed, let alone more o' the stuff?'

Neville Hewitt looked around. 'Where are your women-folk?'

'Indoors, havin' their dinner.'

'Is it not late for to be havin' dinner?'

'We don't keep town hours here, Mr Hewitt.'

Hewitt snorted. 'Where is it, Brodie? Where have you hidden it?'

Stone-faced, Henry said, 'Hidden what, Mr Hewitt?'

'Is it in the barn?'

'There's nothin' in the barn but hay and straw.'

'As your landlord I'm entitled to inspect your buildings.'

'I'm not sure you are, sir,' said Henry. 'May I ask what you expect to find in our barn that you wouldn't find in every barn in the shire?'

'Wheat seed.'

'Oh!'

'Do you take me for a fool, Brodie? I know you bought ten bags from Mr Fletcher's seed store not three days since.'

'How do you know that, Mr Hewitt?'

'Your town's too small to harbour secrets, Brodie. Fletcher told me. He also told me you paid cash.' Neville Hewitt smirked. 'Now, where's the seed an' where did you find the cash to pay for it?'

'The seed, sir, is stored in the stable.'

'An' the cash?'

Henry thought quickly. 'My father had some money put away.'

'Did he, indeed?' said Hewitt. 'Money put away – yet he couldn't pay my rent. That situation might interest the Sheriff, don't you think? Deception comes close to bein' a crime.'

'No crime,' said Henry. 'The money was put away years since in the form o' a small annuity from my grandfather's will. My daddy converted it into a burial fund that couldn't be touched till he died.'

'Very glib,' Neville Hewitt said. 'Where did this convenient sum lie in repose, may I ask?'

'The Farmer's Bank in Dundee.'

'Dundee?'

'Where my father came from, an' his father before him.'

'An' the Farmer's Bank paid you – how?'

Henry realised that he had dug a pitfall for himself. If he claimed the sum had been paid by draft then Hewitt might track it down and expose the lie; yet no bank, let alone one in far-off Dundee, would despatch a courier with cash in his pouch unless the sum involved was very large indeed.

He had been deprived of sleep for too long; his capacity for fabrication had dried up completely. For one impulsive moment he was tempted to drag Hewitt to the barn, tear away the straw, show him the brandy casks and cry, 'There, damn you! There's where our money came from, money to buy the seed you failed to provide.'

He opened his mouth, faltered, and heard his brother call out, 'Twenty pounds, Hewitt. Twenty pounds wouldn't satisfy you. Twenty miserable pounds grown like a weed out o' the four pounds Scots my grandfather earned for fightin' for the King against Charlie near forty-five years ago. Some good came out o' that Jacobite debacle, you see, though it took its own sweet time to flower.'

Neither Henry nor Hewitt had noticed Tom emerge from the cottage. He was clad in his nightshirt, a pair of filthy old breeks hauled over it, his feet bare. He carried a piss-pot in one hand – a full pot by the look of it – which slopped and splashed as he strode across the yard towards the field gate.

'Would you have not just the skin off our backs, Hewitt, but the last bloody halfpence we have in the world, my granddaddy's legacy,' Tom went on, 'his payment for being loyal to the Crown – twenty bloody pounds accumulated over forty years for you to snatch away? Nah, nah, nah!'

Hewitt took a pace backward. He might badger and bully the younger Brodie but he was mortally afraid of the elder who, in his eyes, was half roads to being a lunatic. He reached for the bar of the gate and might have shinned over it if Henry had not stuck out an arm to keep his brother at bay.

'Easy, Tom, be easy,' Henry said.

'What the devil does he want wi' us now?' Tom shouted.

'He heard we had seed. He wants to see it.'

'Then show him the damned seed an' let him be on his way.'

'No,' said Neville Hewitt. 'No, no. Now you've explained . . .'

He closed his eyes and covered his face with his hands as Tom Brodie hopped on one leg and, wheeling, flung the contents of the pot in a wide arc that, for a bizarre moment, formed a little rainbow against the sun's rays before it splashed across the cobbles of the yard.

'Get out o' here an' leave us alone,' Tom Brodie snarled.

'I – I will,' Neville said abjectly. 'I mean, I only came to see if you needed – anything.'

'From you? Hah!' Tom Brodie cried. 'It's too damned late for that, Hewitt, too damned late.' Then, shaking the pot at arm's length, he turned and headed for the barn where the weaver McBride's daughter stood in the open doorway, her arms folded across her breast, her rumpled cotton nightgown, thin as Bible paper, clinging to her belly and thighs and looking, Neville Hewitt thought, as if she too had just tumbled out of bed.

'I think you'd better leave, Mr Hewitt,' Henry said.

'I think you may be right,' Neville Hewitt agreed.

Cutting round behind the dung-heap, well out of Tom Brodie's reach, he found his horse and mounted up. He paused only long enough to glance back at the farmer and the big-breasted servant girl hugging and laughing in the mouth of the barn and then, with a rumble of understanding, rode swiftly away.

PART THREE

Candles at Noon

18

It was late in the year before the first snow fell. It came from the south-west, billowing in over the firth from Ireland and beyond that, Betsy supposed, America, though her knowledge of geography was so hazy that it might have been Holland or France or that mysterious place called Nantes where her cousin purchased his goods.

Wherever Conn secured his cargoes, within a month he had brought enough of them to fill Mrs Brodie's cashbox.

One foul landing did not deter him. Ten days after the near disaster in the surf of Port Cedric he had returned with a larger boat, more hands and a shipment of wine, tobacco and tea. Then, in the first week of the Christmas month, with the tide so high it almost reached the dunes, he had delivered twenty casks of brandy and condemned the Brodies to another night of grinding labour.

Finally, with the first flakes of snow dithering out of the darkness, he had brought in a boatload of tea, boxed, wrapped in oilskin and so tightly roped that there seemed to be nothing but hemp to protect the valuable leaves.

The boxes were small but very heavy. The horses slithered on the hill above the turnpike until, for safety's sake, Henry jettisoned some of the load and, risky though it was, left it by the trackside until daylight when Tom and he, skating over a dusting of snow, collected it in the cart.

Tea was Mr Dingle's favourite cargo. Taxed to the hilt, it fetched more than brandy on the underground market. In a display of gratitude and, he claimed, affection, he presented the widow Brodie with a New Year gift, a small but very ornate clock, and Janet and Betsy each with a muslin scarf printed in a peacock pattern which, he said, was what all the fine ladies in Paisley were wearing to keep the wind from clawing at their throats.

Caught unprepared by the carrier's generosity, Agnes gave him ten fresh eggs in a little basket and a cannikin of milk from which the cream had not been skimmed. Then, dashing to the cashbox, she withdrew four shillings which she presented to the Dingle girls, though one of the girls, giggling, said she would rather have a kiss from Mr Brodie, which request Tom charitably fulfilled by way of a dividend, not just to the bold young hussy who had asked for it but to her sisters, too.

'What about me?' Henry cried. 'What do I get?'

No one seemed inclined to give Henry anything, no one except Betsy who, chuckling, clasped him in a bear-hug, lifted him off his feet and planted a kiss on his brow, while Mr Dingle's girls cheered.

That night the Brodies gathered round the table and tallied their profit for the year. Betsy's share came to twice her wage. The following forenoon she ploughed down to Hayes through knee-deep drifts to give part of the windfall to her father.

'Aye,' Jock McBride said. 'How, may I ask, did you earn it since the Brodies haven't two brown halfpence to rub together?'

Primed in advance, Betsy answered, 'Old Mr Brodie had a burial fund.'

'An' they shared it with you?' said her father sceptically.

She sat at the oval table in the kitchen supping soup. The snow had stopped but the sky was still leaden. Her mother had already lighted two candles to brighten the gloom. 'Tom spoke to Mr Rankine at the lodge last week,' she said. 'Old Johnny's agreed to release me. I'm to be the Brodies' live-in from now on, waged by them. That's why I have this money now.'

'Don't lie to us, Betsy,' her mother said. 'We know what Conn's up to an' why he's so often in Hayes.'

Betsy hesitated. 'Did Conn tell you?'

'Conn didn't have to tell us,' her mother said. 'We've known for a long time what Conn McCaskie is an' what he does. If he's spendin' time on this part o' the coast it can only mean one thing.'

'Tell me the truth, lass,' her father said, 'are you runnin' smuggled goods for your cousin?'

'I'm not sayin' I am, Daddy, an' I'm not sayin' I'm not.'

'It's wrong, you know,' her father told her.

'It's wrong if she gets caught,' her mother said. 'Now, Jock, we'll say no more about it. The less we know the better, 'specially as there's a bounty on Conn's head.'

'His head?' Betsy said, alarmed. 'They wouldn't hang him, would they?'

'Transportation, most like,' her mother said. 'Him an' his crew an' his runners – anybody the revenue officers catch wi' untaxed goods.'

'Who talked you into it?' said her father. 'Conn or Tom Brodie?'

'Nobody talked me into it,' Betsy said. 'I decided it was better to shift wi' the wind than serve Johnny Rankine for the rest o' my days. I've no wish to bear John Rankine's bastard an' be shut out o' the market for a husband. Aye, Daddy, you an' Mam are well practised in turnin' a blind eye to some things, so I'm not askin' you to do anythin' you haven't done already.'

'I knew nothin' o' this,' her father protested. 'If I had known what that rogue Rankine was doin' to you . . .'

'Well, you know now,' said Betsy. 'I'd rather take my chances with the Brodies than with dirty old Johnny Rankine. Where's Effie, by the by?'

'Deliverin' cloth,' her mother said. 'She'll be back soon.'

'Deliverin' cloth on a day like this,' said Betsy. 'She'll be frozen.'

'She's used to it,' Jock McBride muttered.

'Aye, we're all used to it, aren't we?' said Betsy. 'Well, it might be time to get used to better things. Do you want my money – Connor's money – or do you want to continue ridin' your high horse?'

'How much is in the purse?' the weaver asked.

'Six pounds.'

'How many hours sweatin' at the loom would it take you to earn six pounds, Jock?' her mother said. 'Thank the lass an' let her finish her dinner.'

He paused for a moment then leaned forward and kissed Betsy on top of the head. 'I always thought you were a good girl,' he said, with a sigh. 'Well, I suppose you are – despite.'

'Despite what, Daddy?'

But her father had gone off, with a tear in his eye, to finish the work that lay on his loom.

Driven by a strengthening wind, snow began to fall again as Betsy climbed the track to Hawkshill. Fortunately, she was close enough to home to pick out the lights in the cottage window. There was something comforting in the sight of the farm battened down against the weather, the cattle penned in the byre and, thanks to Henry's foresight, the sheep snuggled under the big trees in the fold behind the barn. She plodded across the yard, her shawl cowled over her head, the pretty scarf that Mr Dingle had given her tucked into her collar.

Henry, lantern in hand, was waiting for her. 'Here you are at last,' he said. 'I was just about to come lookin'.' He put an arm about her. 'Did it go well with your father?'

'Well enough. I told him Mr Rankine had let me go.'

'So you're ours now, Betsy McBride?'

'I am, Mr Brodie, all yours,' Betsy answered, and followed him indoors to the fire.

Drennan under snow was a pretty sight, its angular rooftops softened, its awkward corners rounded out. Even late after-noon carousers, old men all, debouching from Caddy Craw-ford's ale-house, experienced a little of the magic of winter, a magic that would soon vanish in a welter of chilblains and chapped hands. Rose could not recall the last time she had been out in snow. In winter her mother had kept her wrapped up like a precious egg. Later, her father had imposed a curfew, not to protect her from wet feet and swollen fingers but from the corruption that lurked in Drennan's alleyways and the villainous seducers who, apparently, prowled the streets what-ever the state of the weather.

Lucas Fergusson was no seducer, though. Lucas did not know how to flirt, let alone seduce. While he had once manoeuvred himself into a position to touch her intimately and had kissed her once or twice since then, Rose did not feel threatened by the grazier's son. Being easy in his company – and in control – she allowed herself to enjoy a few of the childish pleasures that her coddled upbringing had denied her.

Lucas and she were not alone in hurling snowballs at the monument in Market Street. Every small boy in town, and a number of girls too, were peppering the old market cross and when that activity palled, fell to snow-fighting, while honest folk, more amused than annoyed, crept past before they could be spotted and marked as targets. Dorothy, now recovered from her brush with death, romped and squealed and rolled in the fresh snow and, pausing, tipped her face to the fluttering sky to taste the sweet, cold flakes upon her tongue. It mattered not a jot to anyone that Rose was a flax merchant's daughter and Lucas a grazier's son when they stood back-to-back, like Highland warriors, and took on all comers. Orphans and servants, ditch-diggers and cowherds, day-school boys and girls too small to do much more than scrub a stoup or wrestle with a water-bucket were united in battle until the snow became too thick and the cold too intense to endure and everyone slithered off home.

'Look at you,' said Mrs Prole, 'like two polar bears. Shake off your coats before you . . . No, come in, come in an' let me close the door before the carpet's ruined. Lucas Fergusson, what are you thinkin' of?'

If the housekeeper had known what was in Lucas's mind her welcome would have been less enthusiastic. Lucas was thinking that he had never seen anyone or anything quite so beautiful as Miss Rose Hewitt with her cheeks flushed and eyes shining and one small snowflake clinging to her nether lip.

'Lucas?' Eunice Prole snapped. 'Do you hear me?'

'Uh?' He blinked and brushed snow from his lashes. 'Aye, Mrs Prole.'

'Rose, where are the herrin' I sent you for?'

'No herrings,' said Rose. 'None to be had anywhere.'

The housekeeper, hands on hips, did not reprimand her. She held out her hand, took the girl's cloak and hung it on the hook. 'Well,' she said, 'I can't say I'm surprised. The boats'll have scuttled for shelter in Ayr harbour an' what fish there was at our market will have been sold long since. Lucas?'

'Aye, Mrs Prole.'

'Does your mother know where you are?'

'She knows I came to visit Rose.'

'Did your father bring you into town?'

'Nah, I walkit – I mean, walked.'

'Well, you won't be able to walk home again, that's for certain.' Mrs Prole sighed. 'Provided your mother won't think you're lyin' frozen in a ditch, you'd better lodge here tonight.'

'She'll know where I am,' said Lucas. 'She'll know I'm safe.'

'Of course, she will,' said Rose and, taking him by the hand, led him into the parlour where a bright fire burned and the table was set for supper.

Neville Hewitt had returned early from the manufactory. Hearing his daughter in the hall, he hastily leaned an elbow on the mantelshelf, planted a foot on the fender and prepared to peer down his nose at the grazier's son.

'Lucas,' he said gravely, 'you are welcome in my house.'

'Thankee, Mr Hewitt.'

'You will always be welcome in my house.'

'Thankee again, Mr Hewitt.'

'Now, young man, will you partake of refreshment?'

Lucas.nodded. He was rumpled and damp and his boots leaked on to the rug, but if either Papa or Mrs Prole noticed the damage he was causing they were too polite to mention it.

At that particular moment Lucas was as close to handsome as he would ever be. Cold air and vigorous exercise had added a healthy glow to his pale cheeks, his fair hair had arranged itself into dense little curls, his long eyelashes fluttered almost coquettishly and awkwardness imparted an endearing quality that seemed more like innocence than weakness.

Rose watched her father pour sherry from a decanter into four fluted glasses. He placed the stem of one glass neatly between Lucas's trembling fingers, gave the second glass to Mrs Prole and handed her the third.

'On such a night as this,' her papa declared, 'a toast is undoubtedly called for. What do you say, Lucas? Shall we announce a toast to the arrival o' winter or raise a glass to my lovely daughter?'

Lucas answered without hesitation. 'Lovely daughter, sir.'

'To Rose, then,' Papa declared. 'To Rose an' her future happiness.'

Stepping forward, he touched the rim of his glass to each glass in turn, then, with a gesture, urged his daughter and the grazier's son to do the same.

Outside the long window the blizzard raged. The fire in the grate hissed as snow trickled down the width of the chimney. The candles in the stand on the table fluttered. It was warm in the room, wonderfully warm, wonderfully bright. Rose looked over her glass into the young man's pale blue eyes and heard Mrs Prole murmur, 'Oh, Neville, don't they make a perfect couple?'

'They do,' her papa whispered. 'Indeed, my dear, they do.'

And just at that moment little Rose Hewitt was almost inclined to agree.

By dawn the blizzard had blown itself out and, as the morning advanced, a glint of sunshine showed through the scudding clouds. The land was downed with snow and dimpled with blue shadow as far as the eye could see. Tom grumbled and Janet complained but Henry said they had the aesthetic sense of toads and he for one was prepared to put up with a bit of discomfort for the novelty of seeing everything smooth and clean.

Great ramps of snow had built up against the stable and byre. Tom and Henry plied their broad wooden spades for the best part of an hour before Agnes, who had appointed herself the family arbiter, declared the job done and despatched her boys to lug hay and fetch cabbages and turnips from the barn.

There was no possibility of reaching Hayes. Drifts were hedge-high on the track and routes through the fields no easier. There was food enough on the shelves and a sufficiency of vegetables to keep the Brodies nourished and, if the worst came to the worst, a couple of hens that might be sacrificed.

The short hours of daylight were spent feeding stock. Conn's huge shaggy-coated calves, stoutly penned, had escaped the worst of the blast but, glowering over the poles, displayed their displeasure at being imprisoned by bawling and thumping their heads on the wall of the byre until a rack of hay spiced with cabbage stalks and a dribble of molasses gave them something else to think about.

Tom was not so easily appeased. The snowfall kept him from the fields and from taking his pleasures, such as they were, in town. One lodge meeting would certainly go by the board. It was also unlikely that the family would be able to attend service on Sunday and poor Mr Turbot would be left to deliver his Christmas sermon to an empty church. All morning long Tom remained restless. Henry and he conducted heated debates on the nutritive value of cattle fodder and traded insults that became more and more pointed until Agnes, sensing trouble, called a halt and barred contentious topics from the dinner table.

'He's pinin', that's all,' Janet chirped up. 'His heart's broke 'cause he can't get down to Drennan to cuddle his lady-love.' She sniggered. 'He can't even write her a letter since there's no carriers on the roads.'

'Thank God we're not expectin' a cargo from Conn,' Betsy said. 'Think how it would be strugglin' up from Port Cedric in this weather.'

Tom scowled.

'Aye,' Henry said, 'an' we got the seed into the ground in the nick o' time, did we not? It'll be fine an' warm in the drills beneath the snow.'

Tom continued to scowl.

'We've feed enough for the beasts, an' food enough for ourselves,' said Agnes, 'so we can sit out a week or two o' bad weather without sufferin'.'

'Tom's sufferin', but,' said Janet. 'Look at his sour face.'

'Leave him alone,' said Agnes. 'He has a lot on his mind.'

Closing her fist and stiffening her elbow, Janet raised her arm just enough to illustrate her meaning. 'Aye, an' we all know what it is.'

'For God's sake!' Tom leapt to his feet. 'What's wrong wi' you?' He slapped a hand flat on the table, making the plates and cups jump. 'Daddy dead not these two months an' you sit round smug an' smilin'. How many winters did he go hungry just to see us fed? Eh? Have you forgotten what it was like when there was naught but a handful o' oats in the bin an' we were sharin' cabbage stalks wi' the cattle?'

'It's because we haven't forgotten, son,' Agnes said, 'that we take such pleasure in our improved condition now.'

'Hah!' Tom said. 'Do you think the money we have is real? It's no more real than – than a fairytale. Do you think we'll never go hungry again? If you do, then I pity you. Do you hear me, I pity you.' Then he stumped off to the ladder and, hauling himself up by the arms, vanished into the loft.

Janet glanced at her mother and pulled a long face. 'What's bitin' him?'

'Guilt,' said Henry.

'Guilt?' said Janet. 'What's he got to be guilty about?'

'He promised Daddy he'd take care o' us,' Henry said.

'We're doin' better than we ever done before, aren't we?' said Janet.

'Aye, but no thanks to him,' Henry told her.

'He feels cheated,' Agnes added.

'I see.' Janet blew out her cheeks. 'He needs to be the big man, does he? He needs for to be our saviour?'

'Along those lines, yes,' Henry said.

Then, before his sister could become too inquisitive, he tapped Betsy's arm and asked her if she would help him feed the sheep, an invitation that Betsy was only too pleased to accept.

The oaks had broken the force of the wind and the sheep, being not entirely devoid of intelligence, had found sheltered lies in the lee of the big trees. They were hungry, though, and hunger had driven them to nose about in the snow. They had trampled a yellowish ring around the fold and accumulated great sticky balls of snow on their fleeces. When Henry and Betsy appeared, they bleated desperately, threw themselves into the breast of the drift that sloped from the little wall and struggled to reach the shepherd or, rather, the sack of hay and chopped turnips on his back.

There was heather still on the hill and deer had come down from the heights of the Lang Rocks to feed upon it. Betsy could just make them out as they roved along the crest. As soon as the snow melted Henry would take the tups up to the moor again, for heather provided a good nibble, though he would continue to feed the lambing ewes until the drop. Betsy had seen evidence of how neglect could ruin a flock and had often heard farmers cursing their ill luck at a poor lambing when luck had nothing to do with it. Henry was a good shepherd, though, and treated all his sheep, even those being fattened for the knife, with something bordering affection.

She watched him straddle one hapless ewe that had thrust herself into the arch of the drift. Taking the animal by the shoulders, Henry hauled her, struggling and braying, out of her predicament. Betsy hadn't realised how strong Henry was – he seemed quite slight and not at all muscular – until he lifted the sheep from the tail of the drift. She noticed too that when he spread a trail of fodder around the trodden ring the sheep bumped and nuzzled at his legs without any fear at all.

He shook chaff from the sack and slung the sack over his shoulder.

'That'll keep them happy till the morn,' he said.

He looked up at the deer on the hill, then, turning, shaded his eyes and peered at the sun slipping down behind the islands far out to sea.

'God!' he said. 'Do you not just love it here, Betsy?'

'I do,' she said, 'some o' the time, anyroads.'

Taking her arm, he helped her over the wall. The snow was cold on her legs, but not numbing. Under her smock she was warm, as warm as the seed in the drills in the long field, perhaps. He put his hands about her waist and held her, his breath mingling with hers in the cold air.

'Will you stay with us, Betsy?'

'I'll stay as long as you've need o' me.'

'For Tom's sake,' Henry said, 'or mine?'

'It's good work an' I'm happy with it.'

'That's not the answer I'm lookin' for.'

'It's the only answer I've got to give, Mr Brodie.'

'So,' he said, still holding her, 'it's Tom, is it? Still Tom?'

'I don't know what you mean.'

'Aye, but I think you do, Betsy,' Henry said. 'Did my mother not warn you that Tom wasn't for you?'

'I think that's somethin' for Tom to decide.'

'He's not right for you, Betsy. He's my brother an' I'll stand by him but not at the cost o' your happiness. Do you love him?'

'What sort o' question's that?'

'An important question – important to me, anyhow.'

'Tom's not in love with me. He's in love with the Hewitt girl.'

'Tom blows like a weathercock with every change in the wind.'

'I'm nothin' compared to the Hewitt girl.'

'She's only a passin' fancy. He believes he's in love with her because she's out o' his reach. That's our Tom for you, Betsy,' Henry informed her. 'Bein' in love with Rose Hewitt won't stop him marryin' someone else.'

'Who else?' Betsy said. 'Is there another lassie on his list?'

'Aye,' Henry said. 'You.'

'Me?'

'He promised our daddy – a deathbed promise – he'd marry a suitable woman,' Henry said. 'You're the most suitable woman he's ever like to meet.'

'Is that all I am to him?' Betsy said. 'Suitable?'

'There are worse things to be, believe me,' said Henry.

'Aye, five years with Johnny Rankine taught me that much.'

'I know all about Johnny Rankine's nasty habits.'

'Does Tom?'

'I'm sure he does.'

'Is that why he hired me?'

'He didn't hire you,' Henry said. 'He only made the arrangement.'

'First I'm suitable an' now I'm an arrangement.'

'When you're as poor as we are,' Henry said, 'a suitable arrangement is sometimes the best you can get.'

'Does bein' poor mean you can't fall in love?'

'No, but it means you have to be careful who you fall in love with.'

'Well,' said Betsy, a little haughtily, 'I might be poor an' I might be ugly, but, by God, I'm fast learnin' how to be careful.'

She had never been so close to him for so long before but it seemed that Henry had no desire to pull back. 'Aye, Betsy,' he said, 'the thing is, we're not poor now. That might make a difference.'

'A difference?' she said. 'To Tom, do you mean?'

'He's saddled wi' a promise he can't keep,' Henry told her.

'How does he know till he tries?'

'Oh,' Henry said, pursing his lips. 'Is that how the land lies?'

'The land,' said Betsy, 'has nothin' to do with it.'

'Oh, no, lass,' said Henry. 'The land has everythin' to do with it.'

'I was speakin' – you know what I mean?'

'I do,' said Henry. 'Unfortunately, I do. Look, the sun's just fired the peaks o' Arran. It'll be dark in a half-hour.'

She followed his gaze in spite of herself.

'Aye,' she said. 'We'd better be gettin' back.'

'We'd better,' Henry agreed and, taking her arm, helped her over the snow bank and down into the slush of the yard.

It was bitterly cold in the attic room but neither Lucas nor Rose seemed to notice. Seated cross-legged on the bed, Rose had draped a blanket over her shoulders and Lucas, squatting on the bare floorboards, had pulled up his coat collar to cover his ears. We must look, Rose thought, like a pair of orphans huddled on the steps of the poorhouse or like tinkers waiting for some kind soul to light the cooking fire.

'Are you sure you don't want to go down to the kitchen, Lukie?'

'Nah,' he said. 'I want for you tae – to play some more tunes.'

'These aren't real tunes, you know.'

'They sound real enough to me.'

'You are very gallant.'

'Am I?' Lucas said. 'Nobody ever ca'ed me that before.'

'What does Nancy call you?'

'She never says much o' anythin'.'

'Really? I heard she was quite a chatterbox.'

'She doesnae – doesn't talk like you, but.'

'No,' said Rose. 'Few people do.'

'Sing me another song, eh?'

'What song would you like?'

'Anythin' – the one about marmalade.'

'Marmalade?' Rose chuckled. 'Oh, you mean Abelard?'

'Aye, him.'

The light in the room was very strange. Cold blue reflections from the snow on the window ledge divided the planes of Lucas's face like an ill-printed pattern. She struck a chord from the strings of the harp. 'Do you know, Lucas,' she said, 'you're the first young man ever to climb the staircase and be alone with me in my bedroom?'

'Is that a fact?'

'It is, indeed, a fact,' Rose said, 'a curious fact.'

'How, curious?'

'Curious in respect that we could if we wished close the door and lie together on the bed and neither Papa nor Mrs Prole would be any the wiser.'

'Aye, they would.'

'Why do you say that?'

''Cause they'd hear you weren't singin'.'

'I'm not singing now, am I?'

Lucas pondered. 'That's true.'

'Would you like to lie with me, Lucas?'

'I would.'

'Did it not occur to you, last night, that you might steal upstairs from the housekeeper's cubby an' slip into my nice warm bed?'

'You'd only scream.'

'Are you sure?'

'Would you not, but?'

'Well, Lukie' – Rose stroked another plaintive chord from the strings – 'the fact of the matter is that I was ready for you.'

'Were you, Rosie?'

'I would not have been entirely surprised if my papa had dragged you out of your bed in the cubby and escorted you upstairs.'

'I don't understand.'

'Of course you don't,' Rose told him. 'Your recent – ah – experiences with Nancy Ames notwithstanding, you are an innocent soul, Lucas. I fear you've been made a tool in a plot to bring me to the altar.'

'The altar?' Lucas shuffled closer to the bed. 'Like in marriage, like?'

Rose nodded. 'Like in marriage, like.' She pressed the harp to her breast and went on, 'I've no objection to marrying, Lucas, but I will not be trapped into it. I prefer to choose my husband in my own good time.'

'Choose me,' Lucas timidly suggested. 'Please, choose me.'

'If I hadn't flirted with Farmer Brodie,' Rose explained, 'my papa would have let you drown in a snowdrift before he'd have allowed you to spend one night under his roof. No, Lucas, you're a tool, an unsuspecting tool, in a conspiracy to marry me off.'

'I don't mind bein' a tool.'

'No, but I do,' said Rose. 'Your papa and mine have, I fear, reached an agreement and will stop at nothing to bring it to fruition.'

'What sort o' agreement?'

'Financial, most probably,' Rose said. 'The terms of the agreement do not concern us, merely the signature; by which I mean that part of my papa's scheme which will ensure I'm put well beyond Tom Brodie's reach.'

'Have you – done it wi' Tam Brodie yet?'

'I told you before, Lucas – no.'

'Will you – will you do it with me?'

Rose paused before answering. 'I believe the experience might not be unpleasant, Lucas, but I'm afraid I must decline. The intention of our elders is not only to throw us together to encourage a friendship but to put me in a position where I have no other choice but to marry you.'

'Would that be such a bad choice, Rosie?'

'Not such a bad choice at all. But, you see, it would not be *my* choice. If you had given in to temptation last night, rest assured my father or Mrs Prole, or both together, would have burst in upon us, crying havoc and insisting that you marry me post haste to make of me an honest woman.'

'You are an honest woman, but.'

'Thank you, Lukie,' said Rose sincerely, 'but I'm not honest at all. If I were I wouldn't be telling you all this.'

Lucas sighed. 'You want Brodie for a husband, not me, is that it?'

'No, that's not it,' Rose assured him. 'Indeed, I'm not sure I do want Tom Brodie for a husband; nor am I sure that Tom Brodie wants me for a wife. What I do want, however, is to be free to make my choice when I'm ready to do so and not be browbeaten into marriage just to suit my father.'

Lucas sat back on his haunches and laughed. 'Me too,' he said. 'Me too.'

'Are you not in love with Nancy Ames?'

'Naw.'

'Then it's a double trap,' Rose said, 'a trap to keep you from having to marry your dairymaid and to prevent me being free to marry Mr Brodie.'

'I'd never've thought o' that,' said Lucas.

'Of course not,' Rose told him. 'You're far too – romantic.'

'Never been ca'ed that either,' Lucas confessed.

'Well, now we understand each other perhaps we might agree on a compromise,' Rose said. 'We'll pretend to play the game our parents have devised for us while being careful to avoid the pitfalls.'

'What does that mean?'

'It means you keep to your bed and I keep to mine.'

'I thought that might be it,' said Lucas.

'Are we agreed?'

'Aye, Rosie, we're agreed.'

'Shall I sing you the marmalade song now?'

'Aye, but . . .'

'But what, Lukie?'

'I'd like tae – to give you a kiss first.'

Rose glanced towards the door then, still holding the harp to her breast, tilted her chin and pursed her lips. Lucas rolled forward on his knees and, keeping his hands tucked into his lap, kissed her.

'God, Rosie,' he said, 'you're frozen.'

'Yes,' Rose admitted, 'I suppose, actually, I am.'

19

It was Christmas Eve before Lucas returned to the bosom of his family who, without much tact, promptly enquired what he had been up to for four days and three nights down in Mr Hewitt's house with only Miss Hewitt for company.

Trading kisses and cuddles was the obvious answer and the Lucas of old might well have blurted out the truth, but Rosie's tutoring had added an element of subtlety to the young man's character. He swanned about the calf shed and dairy parlour with a superior smile and, whenever the question was put to him, repeated the phrase that Rosie had dinned into him, 'Ah-hah! That 'ud be tellin'.' The answer satisfied no one, least of all Nancy Ames whose offer of an act of intimacy in the hay barn was rejected with an airy wave of the hand; a response that roused in her first a murderous fury then the melancholy recognition that her charms were no match for those of the bitch of Thimble Row and that her chances of becoming mistress of the Fergusson estate had vanished in a shower of snow.

Mild winds and a spit of rain thawed the surface of the turnpike. Frantic digging tunnelled a corridor through the Hawkshill drifts and, soon after dinner, Tom set out for Souter Gordon's in search of cheerful company and the latest news from Drennan.

Christmas meant little to the good folk of Hayes. There was nothing festive about Hayes' dank little ale-house. If Tom had hoped for a rousing time with a gaggle of fellow bachelors he was doomed to disappointment. As for fresh news from Drennan, there was none. Mail coaches were stuck on the roads to the north and no one in Souter's parlour that afternoon had a sound enough reason for wading four miles to town through mud and slush.

Tom hung about for half an hour, growing more depressed by the minute. He had, he supposed, no reason to be depressed. He was young, healthy and handsome, the family coffers were bulging and Hawkshill had been saved. He could give Hewitt the stink-finger, hold his head high in any company and, if he were patient, seek out a wife to suit his taste and status. Even so, he was weighed down by the promise he'd made his father. God knows, he had broken so many promises to the old man when the old man had been alive that breaking one to him now he was dead would be all too easy.

'Hoh, Tam, I hear you've a crop in the ground.'

'Aye, that we have.'

'Wheat?'

'Wheat it is.'

The elder motioned Tom to join him in the ingle by the fire, but it wasn't much of a fire and the old fellow was a notorious bore. Tom shook his tankard and gestured towards the door to indicate that he was just about to leave.

The ale-house was cramped and stank of beer. The ancients huddled by the fireplace. Souter, leaning on a barrel, was half asleep. The shaggy sheepdog, old too, that sprawled in the gangway, broke wind. Tom's depression deepened. Where were the lassies, where were the lads? Where was song and jest, a fiddler's tune to stir the blood? Where were all the things that justified dreary hours alone in the fields, early mornings, bleeding blisters and hacked heels? Where, he thought, was life itself? In Drennan, perhaps, but not here in this miserable hovel in this miserable wee town.

'Damn!' he said, under his breath and, thumping down the empty tankard, grabbed his cap and headed for the door.

For a moment or two he was tempted to set his compass for Drennan, convinced, against reason, that Caddy Crawford's would be buzzing like a hive and he would be welcomed with open arms; convinced, against reason, that he would bump into Rose and she would simper and forgive him for his churlishness and in one of the snow-drenched lanes they would kiss and his love, his passion would burn brightly once more.

No living soul was visible in Hayes' stunted main street. Rain leaked from the cloud lid and pitted the snow mounds piled in the gutters. The only sound was of water trickling in the runnels beneath the snow.

Tom hesitated.

Four miles there and four miles back again?

For nothing, like as not.

He wandered along the road in the direction of the Hawks-hill track. He passed the butcher's shop, all shut up, the baker's too, the seeds-man's store with naught but a single candle in the window; the saddler's – closed – and the room above it, site of so much jollity, dark as the pit.

He arrived at the corner and looked up at the church. Its slate roof was patched with snow, its blunt steeple capped like wax dried on a candlestick. The cemetery was dun-coloured and sullen, its stones protruding from shrunken hummocks of snow. He leaned on the wall and peered across the graves, seeking the stone that marked the place where his father lay.

'Daddy?' he said, not loudly. 'Daddy, are you still here?'

No answer came – which seemed to indicate that his father had gone on or, more likely, was too sulky to reply. Suddenly losing patience with his fantasy, Tom turned and headed for home.

★   ★   ★

Papa lay asleep in the chair in the parlour. In Rose's opinion it was not a very comfortable chair but then her father was not a very comfortable person. None the less, he had managed to adjust his limbs to the furniture and with head tipped back, mouth open and the soles of his shoes beginning to steam in the heat from the fire, he was clearly dead to the world.

Lucas had left soon after breakfast. Christmas Eve or not, it had been a loose-endish sort of day. In England lovely things were happening. The humblest houses were decorated with evergreens, masters and servants exchanged greetings, gifts were traded and tomorrow there would be feasting, dancing and merriment, bells would ring in all the steeples and everyone would go to church, eat enormous dinners and, in general, be very happy – which is more than could be said for the residents of Drennan to whom cracking a smile was chore enough.

It crossed Rose's mind that the English Christmas portrayed in books might not match the true state of affairs, but she preferred to believe the fiction. Anything was better than a Scots New Year which, to Rose's way of thinking, was naught but an excuse for hard drinking, false bonhomie and rants about the race's inherent superiority.

All afternoon she trundled about the house and not until dusk did she begin to appreciate what ailed her and why she felt so out of sorts. Dorothy was back in harness, Mrs Prole restored to fighting fettle and, with Lucas gone, she had fallen to brooding about the state of the nation, about which she knew very little, and the state of her heart, about which she knew even less.

With markets closed and fishing boats confined to harbour, Mrs Prole had been thrown back on the contents of the larder. She had unearthed a tub of pickled tripe and had steeped the disgusting stuff overnight and boiled it for half a day. She was now in the process of transforming the cow's stomach into a dish fit for a king by adding quantities of chopped onion, a bit of withered celery and, of all things, half a pint of sour milk while Dorothy 'excited' – Mrs Prole's expression – the heaving mass in the pan with a wooden spoon.

Handkerchief to her nose, Rose wandered into the kitchen.

'What's wrong with you?' said Mrs Prole, glancing round. 'Don't tell me you're showin' signs o' the fever?'

'No,' Rose answered. 'Is that what we're having for supper?'

Dorothy, grinning, dipped her spoon into the pan and lifted a dripping hank of cow's innards, which reminded Rose of nothing so much as old flannel.

'Nothin' wrong with a nice plate o' tripe an' onions,' said Mrs Prole. 'Your father's very fond of it an', indeed, so am I.'

'Well, I'm not,' Rose said. 'I'll make do with an omelette, thank you, and a little piece of the boiled ham.'

'Boiled ham's gone,' Eunice Prole told her. 'An' if you want an omelette you can make one yourself.'

'I'm not sure I know how to make an omelette.'

'Then it's high time you learned,' Eunice Prole said. 'How are you ever goin' to manage a kitchen if you can't even break eggs?'

'Manage a kitchen?' said Rose. 'Why would I want to manage a kitchen?'

'When you're marrit,' Dorothy put in. 'I can make a om'lette.'

'See,' said Mrs Prole, 'Dorothy understands.'

'Understands what?'

'That a wife must know her way about a kitchen if she hopes to command the respect of her servants. Trouble with young men these days,' Eunice Prole went on, 'is that they're far too pampered by their mammas. Take my word on it, a man might be willin' to make allowances in the bedroom but he'll accept no excuses at the supper table.'

'Loon says ah'll be a grand cook an' he'll see me right in the—'

'Dorothy, be quiet,' Rose snapped. To Eunice, she said, 'Am I to take it that you're grooming me to be someone's wife?'

Eunice Prole said, 'Come now, child, we've all got eyes in our heads. It'll only be a matter o' time till Mr Lucas Fergusson has his feet under your table.'

'If you think I've the slightest interest in marrying Lucas Fergusson you are sadly mistaken,' Rose said.

'Then,' Eunice said, 'why are you pinin' for him?'

'Pining? Am I pining? Of course I'm not pining for Lucas Fergusson.'

'Then,' Eunice said, 'who *are* you pinin' for?'

'No one.'

'Nonsense! I know pinin' when I see it.'

'Oh, you are impossible,' Rose spluttered. 'Quite impossible.'

Waving the handkerchief over her head, she strutted off through the hall and upstairs to the attic where snow still blanketed the window ledge and the temperature was barely above freezing.

When she levered up the frame the snow slumped inward in a moist little rush. She pulled down her sleeve, swept away the slush, leaned into the damp evening air and surveyed the length of Thimble Row and the slice of Market Street, where Lucas and she had had so much fun.

She had been too clever for her own good. Her ruse had worked too well. She had entertained Lucas and been entertained by him and – yes – had rewarded him with a kiss or two, tentative little kisses that did not bruise her lips as Tom Brodie's kisses had done. She had been curiously comforted by his awkwardness, flattered to the point of embarrassment when he had called her his Snowdrop, his Cauliflower, his Daffodil and, blowing into her ear, his Wee Brown Wren. She had never thought of herself as any of these things, particularly a cauliflower, but being compared to a snowdrop and a little brown wren had pleased her.

In the evenings, after supper, Papa had insisted that they play whist and she had found Lucas to be an able partner. When Papa, desperate to keep his guest amused, had invited her to fetch her harp and sing for them, she had done so without persuasion. She had sung the whole of the 'marmalade' song while, to her astonishment, Lukie had softly joined in, word for word, remembered.

Christmas Eve, Christmas Eve! She stretched over the sill, half hoping that Lucas would come loping into view, then she looked to the corner around which on that stormy autumn night not so long ago Tom Brodie and his friend had galloped off into the teeming rain.

'Oh, Rose,' she said aloud. 'Oh, Rose, you fool!' And, slamming shut the window, trotted downstairs to ask Eunice to show her how to break eggs.

Tom had not been drunk when he had returned from Hayes. He had shouted to Janet to fetch him a towel and had gone straight up to the loft where Henry was already changing into dry breeches and a patched old shirt. Betsy had heard the brothers growling and had expected another quarrel over supper.

Janet told her that every Christmas Eve Matthew Brodie had insisted on reading from his Testament and, as close to midnight as habit allowed, had them all kneeling on the floor while he'd offered up a prayer to God for having sent His Son to earth to take on the burden of man's sins and guarantee, at least for the righteous, a billet in heaven.

'I wonder if my daddy's in heaven now,' Janet said. 'If he's prowlin' round the Lord's many mansions in search o' a cheap bit o' land to plough.'

'What about eternal rest?' Betsy asked.

'Not for my daddy,' Janet answered. 'Not for him, never.'

Henry came down into the kitchen. He found one of the clay pipes that had survived the wake and filled it from a pouch of tobacco. When his mother asked him if he knew what Tom had been up to in Hayes, he shrugged. 'Dead as old mutton down there, so Tom says.'

'He didn't meet up with the love o' his life then?' Janet said.

'I think he's lost interest in Miss Hewitt,' said Henry.

'He wouldn't turn her down, though, would he?'

Henry released a mouthful of smoke. 'No, dearest, I doubt if he'd turn her down. I doubt if he'd turn down any lassie the mood he's in right now.'

'One o' those moods, is it?' Janet said.

'One o' those moods,' Henry agreed and, dawdling to the fireplace, projected a stream of tobacco juice neatly between the pots.

In due course Tom appeared, a bottle of claret under his arm and a half-full bottle of brandy in his hand. 'Here, lassie,' he said to Betsy, 'wet your throat wi' a mouthful o' this.'

Betsy shook her head. 'No brandy for me, Tom, not before supper.'

'Oh, she's affectin' the manners o' a lady, is she? Is it not amazin' what transformations a wee bit o' chink in the pocket can render?' He placed the brandy on the table and, making a fork with his fingers, expertly drew the cork on the wine. 'Still, even if you'll not share a glass with me, Betsy, it's incumbent upon me in the spirit o' the season to say how ravishin' you look wi' your hair combed an' that ribbon round your throat.'

'Ravishin'?' Betsy said. 'I've never been called ravishin' in my life.'

'An' never been ravished either, eh?' Tom's jocularity was brittle, his eyes hard. 'Well, my dearest, if you won't accept ravishin' as a compliment from a gentleman, will you blush if I call you sonsy?'

'Sonsy?' Henry shook his head. 'It's your supper you're needin', Thomas, if only to nourish your vocabulary.'

'Don't you think she's sonsy, Henry? See how she tosses her head an' how hot she blushes.' He caught Betsy by the waist before she could escape and, drawing her close, pinched her cheek with forefinger and thumb. 'Little roses, little roses there, see,' and might have said more if his mother had not clouted him on the back of the head with a spoon.

'If you start rampagin' round the house with a skinful o' drink,' Agnes said, 'I'll smash every one o' those bottles you've hidden upstairs.'

'Ooow,' said Henry. 'She's found your hoard, Tom.'

'Aye, an' the ones in the stable, too,' said Agnes. 'Just how many have you stole from Mr McCaskie?'

'Ah, nah, nah,' said Tom, without contrition. 'I'm a thief, Mam, like the rest o' you, but I only steal from the Crown, not from the hand that feeds us. The brandy's what's left from Daddy's wake an' the claret I brought up from the Bachelors' Club, bought an' paid for.'

The table was already set with bowls, spoons and forks. Agnes knelt by the fire to stir a pot of rich beef stew which, at this lean time of the year, was a treat beyond imagining. Propped on a chair with a thread-basket at her feet and a needle in and out of her mouth, Janet picked out a frayed seam on a threadbare petticoat and carefully re-stitched it.

'What about the whisky?' Janet said. 'Where'd you get the whisky?'

'So you've been snoopin', too, have you?' said Tom.

'The whisky's mine,' Henry butted in. 'It's only one small jug, lest you think I'm goin' to the dogs too.'

'Too?' Tom said.

'Also goin' to the dogs,' said Henry.

Tom pulled out a chair and straddled it, front to back. He rocked it forward like a hobby horse and brought it close to

Henry who took a puff of his pipe and deliberately blew a plume of smoke over his brother's head. 'Sound in grammar if not in sense,' Tom said. 'But tell me, man, do you really have me marked for a drunkard who'll come to a bad end now we've riches behind our dreams o' avarice?'

'Beyond,' said Henry, 'beyond our dreams o' avarice; a nicely turned phrase invented by Dr Johnson, I think.'

'I stand on my error,' Tom said. 'Since it's hair-splittin' we're into, however, how would you define the word *prig*?'

'Surely I don't require to define the word when I typify so many of its meanings. In your opinion, Tom, ain't I the embodiment o' priggishness?'

'Aye, man, you are.'

'Sober, chaste an' industrious?'

'Supercilious, conceited an' self-righteous,' said Tom.

'Betsy,' Agnes said sharply. 'Help me carry the pot to the table.'

'Wait, Betsy,' Tom said. 'Let my priggish brother look you over.'

'Don't be daft, Tom,' said Henry. 'Let the girl serve supper. I'm starved.'

'Nah, nah,' said Tom. 'Give us your assessment o' our Betsy here, tell me what a prig like you really thinks o' her.'

'For God's sake, Tom!' Henry exclaimed.

'Leave Betsy be,' said Agnes, but did not insist on it.

'Answer me, Henry,' Tom said. 'Answer me, if you dare.'

'Betsy's the best worker—'

'Hah!' Tom slapped his knee. 'I guessed you'd say that.'

'The best worker an' the most congenial company,' said Henry.

'Congenial company,' Tom said. 'Ah, now we come to it. See, Betsy, see how he steals up on the truth. You're in love wi' the lassie, Henry, are you not? Come along, be man enough to admit it.'

'Stop it. Please stop it,' Betsy pleaded.

'I've great respect for Betsy,' said Henry. 'Great respect.'

'Prig!'

'An' – an' affection.'

'She's a servant, man, a common servant,' Tom said. 'By God, sir, a fellow in your position should not be fallin' for a farm servant.'

Henry carefully knocked the dottle from his pipe and placed the pipe on the shelf above the fireplace. His expression was bland, his movements graceful. He stepped around his sister's chair while Tom watched him warily. He brushed against Betsy, lightly touched her arm as he made his way to the table. He drew out a chair, facing his brother, reached for the brandy bottle and a glass and poured a generous helping of the fiery spirit.

'That's better, laddie,' Tom said. 'A dash o' Dutch courage'll do you the world o' good.'

With his forefinger Henry pushed the glass across the table.

'Here,' he said quietly. 'Drink it, Tom. Drink it down an' show us what a grand fellow you are, for *you'll* need all the courage you can muster if you ever, ever once, slander Miss Betsy McBride again.'

'Oh, I see,' Tom said cautiously. 'An' what if – by accident, say – I do?'

'I'll thrash you,' Henry informed him. 'I'll thrash you, drunk or sober, until you can't stand up.'

For a moment it seemed that the devil in Tom would propel him across the table to grab his brother by the throat, then, like a cloud passing, his mood changed. He sat back, and laughed. 'Ah, Henry,' he said. 'Don't you see? I've as much respect – aye, an' as much affection – for our Miss McBride as you do. Still, still . . .' He reached out and picked up the glass. 'Far be it from me to let good brandy go to waste. Will you not join me, Betsy? There's more than enough for the pair o' us, since my brother's determined to remain sober.'

He lifted the glass and looked at her, the malicious, calcu-lating hardness gone from his eyes. 'Join me, my love, an' let's make merry together, as merry as folk in our station in life ever can.'

She realised then what he intended to do and wondered how he would go about it, how he would separate her from the herd.

'Betsy?' he said, holding out the glass.

'No,' she said, at length. 'No,' and watched, shivering a little, as he drank the glass dry.

Stuffed full of meat and awash with claret, Janet fell asleep in her sewing chair soon after supper. She slept elegantly, knees together, hands folded in her lap, fair hair spilling across her brow. She did not snore but did let out uncertain little whimpering sounds from time to time as if she were dreaming of being pursued and could not decide whether or not she wished to be caught.

Conn's cash had provided a fine Christmas feast and when Henry raised a toast to their Irish benefactor even Tom joined in without cavil. Betsy suspected that Tom's intention was to get drunk in as short a time as possible or, perhaps, to feign a condition where anything he did might be put down to the demon drink. It was not the demon in the bottle that frightened her but the demon in the man. He did not ogle her, did not stare at her bosom and made no attempt to touch her, yet she knew he wanted her.

At ten o'clock Agnes took herself to bed behind the curtain. At five after the hour Janet wakened and, keen to recapture her dream, perhaps, stumbled into the back room and closed the door. A few minutes later Henry put away his pipe, yawned and headed outside to relieve himself while Tom, chair tilted back and legs stretched out, eyed her openly.

'So, Betsy,' he said, 'is it bed for you too, or will you sit a while an' keep me company?'

'Aren't you tired?'

'Not me.'

'Are you goin' to finish the bottle?'

'No, the bottle's been put to rest. I'll not disturb it.'

'What are you sittin' up for, Tom? Is it to welcome Christmas?'

'Christmas deserves no welcome from me,' he answered. 'New Year's the time for celebration, when you put all your sins behind you an' start anew.'

'What do you hope for in the year ahead?' Betsy asked.

'Better weather an' a heavy harvest,' Tom answered. 'Aye, I know Henry thinks I'll pour my share o' Conn's profits over my gullet but I've a bigger stake in Hawkshill than you might imagine.'

Henry returned to the kitchen. 'Takin' my name in vain, Thomas?'

'We're talkin' o' the year to come,' said Tom. 'Our plans for the future.'

'Plans?' said Henry, frowning. 'What plans?'

'When it's best to lime the meadow an' if we can hire some extra labour to help drain the marsh round the lochan,' said Tom. 'Whether we should buy young cattle in the spring or increase the size of the sheep flock is a matter for discussion, too. What do you think, Henry?'

Henry shook his head. He was cross-eyed with the need for sleep. He closed the door, dropped the latch, and squeezed Betsy's shoulder by way of bidding her goodnight. She looked up at him and smiled.

'Goodnight, Henry,' she said. 'Sleep well.'

'Aye, lass, you too.'

She watched him approach the ladder to the loft, waited for him to pause, hand on the spar, to turn and look at her, at

Tom, then change his mind and come back into the kitchen to sit with them. But he did not. He toiled up the ladder and closed the hatch without looking back.

She had lost her protector, not lost him so much as brushed him aside.

Now she was alone with Tom – but which Tom: the arrogant, brooding, unfathomable Tom or the other, coarse and cocky, who would take her without conscience? It was not that she did not care – she cared very much – for a longing to win Tom Brodie's attention had first brought her to Hawsks-hill and the hope that he might fall in love with her had kept her here.

When he beckoned she went to him. She stood before him while he clasped her bottom and drew her between his knees. She was neither eager nor reluctant; a little part of her stood aside, like a shadow, as if her body were not her own. He untied the ribbon around her throat, unfastened the high-top button of her shirt and the tapes beneath. He cupped her breasts and brought them to his mouth. He did not hurt her, did not bite her as old Johnny had done. He circled her nipples with the tip of his tongue and looked up at her as if to gauge the moment when she would yield up everything.

In the stable a horse coughed and snickered. Behind the sailcloth curtain, Agnes Brodie groaned and turned over. Henry's footsteps creaked on the floor of the loft. The bed-board thumped as he swung himself into bed.

Tom slipped a hand beneath her skirts. When he lifted her skirts, she felt the hardness of him against her stomach. He kissed her, stroked her and found her with his fingers. She was swollen and wet. His hand was hidden, his wrist trapped in her petticoat. She tilted her hips and slid on to his fingers.

'Not here, Betsy,' he said. 'Not here.'

For an instant she thought that she had not been enough for him, that she had disappointed him. She lowered her feet to the floor and let Tom lift her upright. He was crouched over, breathing in short, stiff, urgent gasps. He crept across the kitchen and fumbled a candle and a battered tin lantern from the shelf. He lit the candle with a taper, fitted it into the lantern, then, grabbing her hand, pulled her to the door. He paused to snatch his greatcoat from the hook then with the lantern in one hand and the coat thrown over his shoulder, he tapped the latch, pulled open the door and dragged her out into the yard.

The air was cold on her cheeks and breasts. They scurried across the yard just as they had done that autumn day when she had first arrived. She ran ahead of him into the barn. Stealthy sounds came from the hay as mice, rats and cats, disturbed in their nocturnal foraging, slipped out of sight. The great, bristling wall of straw, loosened by too much handling, loomed out of the darkness, shiny in the lantern light.

Tom put the lantern on the floor. He reached into the wall of straw and hauled down an armful. He strewed the straw across the floor and flung the greatcoat on top of it. He did not take her in his arms, did not kiss her. He pushed her down on to the greatcoat. She lay there, watching, as he broke the button on his breeches and snapped the ties. He was gaunt and hairy and grim-looking in the upward cast of light. She caught her skirts and lifted them. She spread her legs as wide as they would go. She saw him close his fist and touch himself, once, twice, and, with a nod, once more.

Then, like a wolf, he fell upon her, and she closed her eyes.

20

Three days before New Year's Eve, the Hewitts and the Fergussons met in the vestibule of the parish church. There was a deal of nodding across the pews before the service and, during the long, exacting sermon on resolution and redemption, glances were exchanged between the Fergusson boy and the Hewitt girl, glances that were, in the minister's lofty view, quite unsuited to the occasion.

Rose had spent much time fussing over her hair. Lucas, too, had devoted considerable attention to his coiffure but had finally discarded the cravat, the silk handkerchief and the Malacca cane and had replaced the kidskin gloves with a pair of woollen mittens that made him look less like a schoolboy than a pensioner. He still sported the tall hat, though, and when he stepped from the door of the church and confronted Rose, he bowed and dropped the hat to the flagstones. There would always be an element of the clown in Lukie, Rose decided, but she could not ignore the light that shone in his eyes, a light that spoke of love, fairly pure and fairly simple.

'Lucas? Are you well?'

'Aye, Rosie. An' are you – well?'

'Very well, thank you.'

'None o' the fever?'

'No, none of the fever.'

'Me neither.'

'Oh, that's good, very good.'

'Can you walk?' he said.

'I *can* walk,' Rose said, 'and I *will* walk if that's your wish?'

'Aye, will you walk wi' me then?'

'How far will we walk, Lukie?'

He hesitated, trying, she thought, to summon up an answer that he had almost certainly rehearsed. 'Tae – to the ends o' the earth.'

She offered him her arm. 'To the end of Thimble Row will do for now,' she said. 'I believe you've been invited to take tea with us.'

'Tea?'

'And cake,' said Rosie.

'Ow, cake!' Lucas said. 'Yum-yum!'

It took her a moment to appreciate that he was making fun of himself, which is something that Tom Brodie would never do.

They walked through the gathering by the gate and along the broken pavement in the direction of Market Street. Rose was aware that Nancy Ames was somewhere in the crowd – gnashing her ugly teeth, no doubt – and that Papa and Mrs Prole were squeezing into Mr Fergusson's trap and would quite soon trot past them, waving. But Lucas and she were too caught up in each other to pay much attention to the passing throng or to notice that, leaning on the wall of Caddy Crawford's tavern, the old witch woman, Tassie Landles, had her beady eye on them.

He had taken her twice, once quickly, then for a second time with slow, jerking thrusts of his backside that had lifted her from the greatcoat and pushed her into the wall of loose straw. He had spoken not a word while he had mowed her and, hurtfully, had hardly spoken to her since. Even in the glowering light of the morning after – Christmas Day – he could barely bring himself to wish her a seasonal greeting, and since then had avoided or ignored her altogether.

She had been shaken by the ferocity of his love-making – a far cry from old John Rankine's fumbling – and had been too carried away by her response to judge him at the time. When she thought about it afterward – and she thought of little else – she found in his taking of her no trace of warmth. For all it mattered to Tom Brodie, she might have been any girl.

Bottled up in the cottage, it was impossible to hide Tom's animosity from the family. It took all Betsy's strength of will not to weep on Henry's shoulder or blurt out the truth when Agnes asked her, 'What's he been up to, dear? Why is he so offended?' By way of answer, Betsy raised her hands, widened her eyes and shook her head as if the origin of Tom's foul mood was as much a mystery to her as it was to everyone else.

On Sunday Tom went off early, and alone, to church.

Although the head-high drifts had shrivelled they were still stout enough to block the track to cart traffic. Agnes was supported by Henry and Betsy to prevent her slipping and breaking bones and Janet went on a few steps ahead to call out warnings of icy patches. It was not until they reached the old toll road that Agnes felt secure enough to walk arm-in-arm with her daughter and Henry and Betsy, falling a few steps behind, had time alone.

'Come now, Betsy,' Henry said quietly. 'Tell me what ails you?'

'Nothin'. I'm fine.'

'Aye, but you're not fine,' said Henry. 'What went on between you and Tom on Christmas Eve?'

'Nothin', I swear.'

'Don't lie to me, Betsy. Did he force himself on you?'

'No,' said Betsy, for that was the truth.

'Tom says all sorts o' things when he's boozin',' Henry told her. 'Things he doesn't really mean.'

'God!' said Betsy. 'Is Tom all we ever talk about?'

'Daddy's death hit him very hard.'

'He was your daddy, too.'

'Yes,' Henry said. 'But it's different with Tom.'

'Why must you make excuses for him?'

''Cause he's – I don't know – easily broken.'

'Easily broken!' Betsy exclaimed, loudly enough to cause Agnes to look round. She lowered her voice. 'If he is easy broken, like you say, why does he always get his own way? An' why, when he doesn't get his own way, does he fall into a black mood, as if the whole world was against him?'

'I don't know,' Henry admitted. 'That's the mystery.'

'If you ask me,' Betsy said, 'he's selfish an' spoiled.'

'Too much was asked of him, too much expected.'

'Is that what broke his daddy's heart?'

'Oh, that's harsh, Betsy, very harsh.'

She quickened her pace and gained a few steps but Henry soon caught up. He linked her arm in his and she did not have the gall to resist. Besides, the church was visible now and there were other folk on the road. In a few minutes they would be caught up in the Sunday gathering and she would be safe for a time from Henry's probing.

'Betsy,' he said, 'will you give me one straight answer, please, then I'll bother you no more with my questions?'

'One answer, Henry, that's all.'

'Did Tom ask you to marry him?'

The question caught her off guard.

'Marry *me*?' she said. 'Tom has no thought o' marryin' me.'

'Did you turn him down?'

'I didn't turn him down,' said Betsy.

'Tom did *not* ask you to marry him?'

'No.'

'Well, well.' Henry patted her arm. 'Well, well, if it isn't that . . .'

'It must be something else,' said Betsy, and called out a greeting to her daddy who was waiting by the kirkyard gate to give her, in advance, a pretty little trinket by way of a New Year gift.

The Fryes and all their servants had trotted out to enjoy Mr Turbot's gloomy farewell to the Auld Year and, in spite of the weather, the little church in Hayes was close to overflowing. Peter's brother, David, had returned from Edinburgh and his sisters, their husbands and children filled the magisterial pews while sundry visiting maids and footmen, decidedly put out at having to rub shoulders with rustics, occupied the gallery.

Tom had anticipated the crush. He had arrived in plenty of time to secure a seat directly behind the landowner's box. He had a need to converse with Peter and could not bring himself to wait for the next meeting of the Bachelors' Club. Fortunately Peter spotted him and inveigled himself into an end seat in his father's box. With a nephew and two small wriggling nieces beside him, he managed to snatch a word or two with his farmer friend in the course of the service and, at its conclusion, evaded the clutches of his family long enough to meet Tom on the gravel that linked church and graveyard.

On that Sunday afternoon the differences between the men had never been more apparent. Peter was clad like a gentleman and Tom like an impoverished farmer. There was no ribbon in his hair, no shine to his boots, no swagger to his gait. When Peter appeared at the corner he took off his hat and held it in both fists in the manner of a supplicant.

'Good God, Tom! You look awful. Have you been too much at the bottle?'

'Not enough at the bottle,' Tom said grimly. 'I've troubles enough without compoundin' them with drink.'

'Money again?' said Peter.

'No, not money; not just money.'

'Then it must be a woman,' said Peter. 'Is it Miss Hewitt, by any chance?'

'Have you seen her of late?' said Tom.

'Not so much as a glimpse.'

'Nor me,' said Tom.

'Do you want me to provide you with an escort for another window-climbing escapade?' Peter said. 'A New Year surprise for the lady, perhaps?'

'We're far past that nonsense,' Tom said. 'She's taken umbrage at me, for some petty reason. Frankly, Peter, I'm inclined to look elsewhere for a wife.'

'A wife?'

'It's time I settled down,' said Tom. 'With my father gone, I've inherited responsibilities I can't ignore an' quite soon I'll need a steadfast an' reliable wife to stand by me in the shoals o' life.'

'The shoals of life?' said Peter. 'Really?'

'Do you think I should marry?'

'Well, I – honestly, Tom, I don't know how to answer you. Do you have a particular candidate in mind?'

'Betsy McBride.'

'Your dairymaid?'

'Our farm servant,' Tom said.

Peter hesitated. 'Well, you wouldn't be the first farmer to marry a servant – far from it – and the young lady in question is certainly handsome. Tell me, Tom, have you tested the waters in that direction?'

'Aye,' Tom admitted grudgingly. 'I have.'

'And was she – satisfactory?'

'She was.'

'Is she with child?' said Peter.

'God, no! At least, I've not heard if she is.'

'Have you given the girl any indication of your intentions?' Peter said. 'Apart, that is, from mowing her?'

'None.'

'Is she in love with you, do you suppose?'

'Oh, aye,' said Tom. 'She's in love with me. Why would she not be?'

'Why, indeed?' said Peter. 'Look, Tom, I'll have to leave you. My father will be sending out scouts at any moment and I do have certain family obligations that I must, in conscience, fulfil.'

'Family first, eh? Always family first?'

'Let's arrange to meet soon after New Year,' said Peter, 'when we'll have time to discuss the matter in all its ramifications at greater length.'

'Aye,' Tom said. 'After New Year.'

Peter administered a short, soft punch to his friend's shoulder. 'Meanwhile,' he said, 'be cautious, Tom, I beg you. Don't do anything rash.'

'As if I would,' said Tom.

A huge sea was running on the last morning of the year. It took Conn all his time to beach the boat at Port Cedric and all his strength to drag it above the tideline. Desperation, not bravado, had driven him to attempt the crossing from the Isle of Man in so small a boat. If the wind had not been behind him he would surely have been swamped by the cross-currents around the Mull of Galloway. As it was, he had steered by starlight and the compass and, just as dawn opened the sky to the east, had picked up the flood tide that ran fast into the firth.

It had been a day and a night to put behind him; a day and night when the fabric of his 'business' had been stretched to breaking point and only quick thinking and a fast horse had saved him from falling into the clutches of the revenue officers.

An isolated fisher cottage six miles north of Ramsey had been his refuge for the best part of five years. He had brought his mother from Ireland and installed her there. His sister and her husband lived not three miles away. And there he had stowed his cash in an old sea-chest that, according to his mother, had once belonged to Black Dog Donaldson, the infamous pirate, though Conn questioned the truth of that tale. It was not just cash he had sacrificed to make good his escape but also six hogsheads of unfiltered brandy that the skipper of the Dutch trader, *Reindeer,* had offloaded a week before Christmas.

The Isle of Man, not Nantes, was Conn's warehouse. It was rare for him to make the long voyage to the town on the Loire or to any European port these days. His father had originally set up the chain of purchase. Conn had secured it by enlisting the services of the sons and grandsons of the former slave-traders with whom his father had done business thirty-five or forty years ago. He had opened a lucrative market in Scotland where dislike of King George and his 'English' taxes was rife. Whatever daft stories his cousin Betsy and her friends chose to believe, he had no wife, no children, no pillow upon which to rest his head, only Black Dog Donaldson's ancient sea-chest and the silver it contained; and the chest, as far as he knew, was now in the hands of the captain of the revenue cutter, *Vigilant,* together with six hogsheads of undiluted spirit.

It was dinner time when Conn staggered into the cottage at Hawkshill.

'Conn! My God, man, what brings you here?' Tom cried.

The Irishman seemed smaller, somehow. Breeks, boots and goatskin vest were stained with salt water, his hair matted with sand. It was all he could do to find the chair that Janet pulled out for him then, throwing dignity to the winds, he slumped across the table and clutched his head in hands.

'Finished,' Conn groaned. 'I'm finished.'

'What is it, Conn?' Betsy put an arm about him. 'Tell us, please, what's happened?'

'Everythin'.' Conn groaned. 'They've took everythin'.'

'Who?' said Henry. 'The revenue?'

'Aye, the revenue. Some blackguard sold me out.'

'Good God, man!' said Henry. 'Have the officers followed you here? Are we all about to be arrested?'

'We've nothin' to hide,' said Betsy. 'Have we?'

'Only him,' Tom told her. 'We'd best get him out o' here.'

Conn pushed himself up on an elbow. 'Sure there's nothin' to fear,' he said. 'It happened on Man. I was pounced on comin' home from the inn in Ramsey. They were lyin' in wait for me not far from my cottage, six on foot armed with muskets led by an officer on horseback. I dragged the officer from his horse, mounted, an' rode off as if to make back into town. Instead I doubled on to the long track above the cliffs and down to a sand beach where I keep the smallest of my boats.'

'Don't tell me you sailed across from Man in darkness?' said Henry.

Conn nodded. 'It was no pleasure cruise, believe me.'

Henry poured whisky and handed a glass to the Irishman. They watched in silence as he swallowed the stuff and, with a heavy sigh, sat back. 'I came here,' he said, 'because I knew I'd be safe among friends.'

'You are, Conn,' Betsy told him. 'You're safe here.'

'Lie up for a day or two,' Tom told him. 'Rest an' recover.'

'I – I can't pay you,' Conn said.

'What does that matter?' said Henry. 'You've done enough for us an' it's our pleasure – I mean, our privilege to return the favour.'

'Sure and you're kind, so kind.' Conn squeezed Betsy's hand and for an embarrassing moment appeared as if he were about to weep. 'I thought I was safe on Man. Safe I was, too, until the Crown offered that damned bounty. I should have smelled trouble in the wind.'

'Who betrayed you, Conn?' Betsy asked.

'Martin, my damned blackguard of a brother-in-law, damn his soul to the fires o' hell,' Conn growled. 'He knew I'd black goods on the premises and had no option but to hold them till the next spell o' fair weather. He wheedled and nagged at my sister, Kathleen, and at my old mother, too. My old mother who never did anyone a bit o' harm and had no notion what the scoundrel was up to.'

'Aunt Netta?' Betsy said. 'Surely they haven't arrested her?'

'Nay, nay,' Conn said. 'Martin sent Kathleen down yesterday mornin' to take Mam away to Martin's farm to bring in the New Year. I was supposed to collect her again today, by which I mean, I suppose, tomorrow.' He cupped a hand to his brow. 'I've lost all count o' the days.'

'Why would your brother-in-law, this Martin fellow, sell you to the revenue officers?' said Janet. 'Did you not give him his share?'

'His share?' said Conn, showing temper. 'Martin's no smuggler. Sure an' he doesn't have the tripes for it. He crouches on his thirty acres with his thumb in his mouth an' makes his boys do all the work. His boys! His slaves! Ten an' twelve years old an' already broken by hard labour. Oh, I slipped Kathleen a shillin' or two now an' then for to put food in their bellies, an' I bought two pigs from him when he was threatened with eviction – two pigs so starved you could count their ribs – but it was never enough for Martin.'

'This,' said Janet cautiously, 'is not how we thought you lived, Conn.'

'Well, it's the truth o' it.' Conn massaged his brow. 'I knew the knell would sound one day. The King's officers are tightenin' the noose all round the coast. When I found a safe landin' place at Port Cedric an' a family willin' to shift for me, I became greedy, I suppose. Greed was my downfall. Too many sailings, too many black goods, too many risks to fill the chest with silver while the way was still open. At least bloody Martin made no profit from his treachery. The price – thirty English pounds – is on my head an' my head's still on my shoulders.

But I've lost my money, all the money I need to make purchases an' pay my crews. Sure an' as if that wasn't bad enough, six hogsheads o' brandy, bought and paid for, have gone down too.'

Henry placed another glass of whisky before him. Conn, with a nod of gratitude, downed it. His eyes had lost their fire and his lids were heavy. His voice, when he spoke again, wavered. 'I am as you see me, like Adam cast out, without a penny to me name.'

'Not so,' said Henry. 'You've two prime bullocks ready for the block.'

'Oh!' Conn said, brightening a little. 'So I have now, so I have.'

'An'' – Agnes set the cashbox upon the table – 'you also have this.'

'This?' Conn frowned. 'What's this?'

'Close to one hundred pounds,' Agnes said.

'No, Mrs Brodie, I can't be takin' your money.'

'Well,' the woman said, 'it's there if you ever need it to help you start up again. Meanwhile, you're welcome to stay with us for as long as you wish.'

'What I need most of all,' said Conn, 'is a place to sleep.'

'Take my bed, then,' said Janet and, before anyone could stop her, ushered the big Irishman into the little back room.

The snow had melted on the off-side of the long field and rooks, crows and a host of small, starving birds had fallen on the earth to dig up the wheat seeds. Half a crop could be lost to the feathery scavengers before the seeds had a chance to take root and it would now be part of Betsy's duty to scare them away. On that gloomy afternoon, the last of the old year, however, Henry and Tom had put their differences aside and had gone out together with the whirligigs to chase the birds off and, with a hoe between them, cover the seeds as best they could.

The whirligigs were frivolous-looking things made up of lengths of old rope and bits of string decorated with paper bows, each fastened to a handle that the men swung over their heads as they advanced across the drills. There were dogs too, two skulking collies that dashed and snapped hither and thither, zigzagging across the field in pursuit of any rook, crow or starling foolish enough to set food before safety.

'Do you believe the Irishman's story?' Tom said.

'I've no reason to doubt him, have you?' said Henry.

'None, save that it doesn't chime with what we know of him.'

'We know nothin' of him,' Henry said. 'Even Betsy's been kept in the dark. No more than you might expect from a man who makes his livin' outside the law.'

Tom swung the whirligig around his head and watched a skein of starlings rise reluctantly from the furrows ahead of him. 'Anyroads, it was all too damned good to last. Did I not tell you it was a dream, Henry? A man gets only what he pays for in honest toil.'

Henry tamped down earth with the blade of the hoe. 'Transportin' those cargoes might not have been honest but, by God, it was toil enough.'

Tom laughed. 'Aye, it was all that.'

'We still have close to one hundred pounds, English, in Mammy's cashbox,' Henry said. 'Rent for a year an' a fair piece left to scrape this place into shape an' make it yield.'

'Not enough,' Tom said.

'More, much more, than we've ever had in our lives before.'

'Still not enough,' Tom said. 'In eighteen months we'll be stuck wi' foul ground an' unpredictable weather again an' no better off than we were before Daddy died; not much, anyway.'

'What *will* it take to make you happy?'

'More than money,' Tom replied.

'Are you still frettin' about Hewitt's daughter?'

'No, she was a passin' fancy.'

'You liar.' Henry smiled. 'Here, give the gig another whirl before the crows have our eyes out.'

Tom flicked the knots at one recalcitrant crow that refused to tear itself from the furrow. The bird hopped, rose, fell, and hopped on, keeping itself just out of range. Tom said, 'I'm inclined to think I might be better lookin' for a wife near home.'

'MacCreadie's daughter's already turned you down.'

'Not MacCreadie's daughter, no.'

Henry leaned on the hoe, the whirligig draped over his shoulder. 'Who then?' he asked.

'Betsy, our Betsy,' Tom answered.

Henry said nothing for a half-minute, then, 'There are all kinds o' practical difficulties to consider before either one o' us can take a wife.'

'Like what?'

'Where we would sleep?'

'Thought o' that,' Tom said. 'Mammy goes in with Janet, you take the big bed an' Betsy – my wife an' I have the loft to ourselves.'

'What,' said Henry, 'if I decide to take a wife too?'

'You'd have the big bed in the kitchen.'

'Hardly private, is it?'

By the edge of the field one of the dogs put up a hare. The men watched the chase in silence. The hare hugged the rim of the snowline, darting this way and that until the collie, for all its experience, became confused and, barking loudly, swung back towards its masters.

'It's a daft argument,' Tom said, 'since you've no mind to marry.'

'Oh,' said Henry, 'but I do have a mind to marry. I just haven't found the right lassie yet.'

'So you've no fancy for our Miss McBride?'

'Betsy wouldn't have me,' Henry said.

'She'll have me, though, won't she?'

'Oh, aye,' said Henry thinly. 'No doubt she'll be yours for the askin'.'

Then, sticking the hoe in the ground and swinging the gig savagely about his head, he broke from his brother and strode off towards the lochan, intent, it seemed, on nothing more profound than scaring crows from the furrows and protecting the seed in the ground.

On the stroke of midnight, Agnes wound the house's three clocks, Tom poured whisky from the jug and Janet, nothing ventured, threw herself into Mr McCaskie's arms and plastered his face with kisses. There were kisses and hugs all round, though, Henry noted, Betsy did no more than buss his brother on the cheek, and even that was done without fervour. He gave the girl a kiss himself and held on to her for a moment or two, enjoying her warmth, her softness, as she snuggled into the crook of his arm.

There were tears for the year that was gone, the year that had taken Matt Brodie with it, and a certain amount of joy, too, for the change in fortune that Mr McCaskie had brought them.

At Janet's urging the dark-haired 'stranger' was given a lump of coal and a bowl of oatmeal and sent out into the darkness while the door was closed and bolted. There was an odd air of expectancy in the kitchen while a minute ticked by and then another before rapping on the door broke the tension and Henry, laughing, said, 'Now I wonder who that could be? Who's come to be our first foot, an' will he bring prosperity?' Then, with some ceremony, he shot the bolt, tipped the latch, flung open the door and invited Conn to step across the threshold and shake his hand.

It was not a happy start to the New Year for the Irishman, homeless, penniless and on the run, but he played his part well and ate and drank and put up with the fuss that was made of him, as if he had steered across the choppy waters from the Isle of Man for no other purpose than to celebrate New Year with the Brodies.

It was also the first New Year in quite a while that Tom had not stuck on his hat, buttoned his greatcoat and ridden out to meet his cronies to 'first foot' Johnny Rankine, make hay with half-tipsy lassies and trail home a day later, half drunk and quite uncontrite, to square up to his father's wrath.

There were toasts and speeches, memories shared and hopes aired. Janet, who had no head for strong waters, fell asleep on Conn's knee and was carried across his shoulder like a sack of meal and put down on the bed in the back room which Conn had vacated for a blanket and pillow on the floor of the loft.

At a little after two o'clock Agnes took herself to bed. Tom, too sober for his own good, casually enquired if Betsy would care to take a turn about the yard to bid a good New Year to the horses. And Henry, sharing a last glass with Conn, cocked his head and waited, hardly daring to breathe, for Betsy to answer.

'I'll see enough o' the horses in the mornin', thank you, Tom,' Betsy said and, just a little flustered, hurried off to join Janet in bed.

The men chatted for another half-hour while Conn laid out his plans, such as they were, for reviving his fortunes. Then, deflated and a little depressed, they relieved themselves in the yard and, one by one, climbed the ladder and put themselves to bed.

The boys had long enjoyed the luxury of a bed each; hardly beds at all but, rather, low, narrow cots assembled from old timber that Matthew Brodie had planed and pegged together under the steeply sloping roof. Henry lay with his head to the north, Tom with his feet pointing east, the candle on the floor between them, a guddle of clothes and boots all round. One shaky-legged table and one spavined chair were pushed hard against the gable to provide space for Conn to stretch out which, with a yawn and murmured goodnight, he soon did, humped under the grey blanket like a porpoise or a whale.

Tom rested on his back, hands folded on his chest, and stared up at the beams and slates just above his head. He knew every crack, every cranny, every knot and splinter as well as he knew his own body, for many and many a night he had lain thus, tormented by lascivious thoughts or, worse, nursing a raging sense of injustice against his father and the world at large.

At what hour, precisely, he fell asleep, Tom had no notion.

If he slept and if he dreamed he was not aware of it, only that at some point in the course of the night his father came to him, as real and solid as he had ever been in life. He stood hard by the bedside, clad in his work clothes, and passed a hand to and fro a few inches from Tom's nose. All the doubts of daytime and the doubts that came with the night, those violent little flecks and flashes that troubled Tom perpetually, were suddenly soothed away, and he knew with absolute certainly that the only way to be rid of the ghost was to give the ghost what it wanted, whatever that might be.

There was an unusual bustle in the streets of Drennan, for New Year's Day was a general holiday when families gathered and gifts were exchanged and men strolled out to partake of a dram or two in Caddy Crawford's and shake the hand of anyone who chose to call himself a neighbour or a friend.

No one, least of all Rose, was surprised to find Lucas Fergusson hopping about on the doorstep just a few minutes after noon. He had donned his gaudy clothes for the occasion and looked, Rose thought, charmingly eccentric as he lurched across the threshold. He juggled three packages, two quite large and one quite small, and might have scattered them across the floor in his eagerness to kiss Rose's ruby lips if she hadn't relieved him of his burden.

'Who is that?' Mrs Prole cried, peeping from the kitchen. 'Is that Lucas?'

'It is, of course it is,' said Papa Hewitt from the parlour. 'Welcome, my boy, welcome, an' a good New Year to you an' yours.'

'Thankee, sir,' Lucas mumbled. He hastily kissed Rose before the housekeeper or Mr Hewitt could rush out to prevent it. 'I've brought you somethin', dearest, somethin' nice. I bought it wi' my own money, too. The cheese's for your father an' the mittens are for the wumman, Mrs Pro—'

'Hush, Lukie.' Rose placed a finger on his lips. 'Don't spoil the surprise.'

She helped him off with his long coat and removed his tall hat and placed it carefully, square on the stand. She picked a fleck of lint from the wing of his waistcoat and adjusted his cravat, smiling up at him all the while. Then, the moment over, she turned him to face Eunice Prole who, drying her hands on a towel, hastened out of the kitchen and embraced him possessively. A split second later Neville emerged from the parlour and, shaking the young man by both hands, led him off to drink a glass of wine before dinner.

The cheese was duly unwrapped, a fine ripe round of Ayrshire's best. The mittens were neat-knitted in pale blue wool and came with a matching scarf that Eunice declared delightful. The little package, smaller than a tinderbox, was reverently placed on Rose's hand and, with Lucas rocking nervously by her side, carefully unwrapped.

Rose looked up, eyes shining. 'Lucas,' she said, 'it's beautiful.'

'Picked it myself, I did.'

The silver heart, pure and plain, lay on a cushion of red velvet, the filigree chain whorled about it, the hook-clasp so tiny that it was almost invisible.

Rose lifted the pendant carefully between forefinger and thumb.

'Picked it myself from Duke's in Ayr,' said Lucas.

'Put it on, put it on,' Mrs Prole urged.

'No,' Neville Hewitt said. 'Let Lucas do it.'

She trickled the chain into his palm and turned her back to him. For once he was not clumsy, not all fingers and thumbs. She felt his hands brush her neck and saw the silver heart slide down upon her bosom.

Mammy had told him he must go down on one knee, take her hand and speak out as if he meant it. Daddy had told him he must first have words with Mr Hewitt to ensure there was no impediment. But all that sage advice flew out of Lucas Fergusson's head as he stood behind Rosie and smelled her fragrance and saw the graceful curve of her neck and the slope of her breast.

He put a hand to her waist and another on her shoulder and, leaning into her, whispered hoarsely, 'Rosie, will you marry me?'

And Rosie, swinging sharply round, said, 'Yes.'

21

Mr Ogilvy could not imagine why, on a cold grey afternoon with the new year only three days old, the egg-seller of Drennan had appeared in his yard. The buying and selling of coal was not a particularly lucrative business, mainly because Mr Ogilvy was not a particularly enterprising fellow and had made no attempt to open new markets. He 'ticked over' on four or five hundred pounds a year which was sufficient to support his aged father and his aged father's new wife, and to keep himself in beefsteak and claret.

He lived in an apartment above the office, three small, rather dusty rooms, but spent most of his time at a desk on the ground floor where his customers could find him. He employed a clerk, stable hands and drivers. He purchased coal from Lord Craigiehall or, rather, his lordship's factor, and distributed it by the creel to homes and farms in Hayes and Drennan. He kept immaculate records and his logs and ledgers were his pride and joy.

He was, in fact, engaged with complicated three-column arithmetic when his clerk, peering from the window, growled a warning and Mr Ogilvy, looking up, saw the woman, framed by two small mountains of coal, hobbling through the gate of the yard.

'Good Lord!' he exclaimed.

Hopping from his high stool, he grabbed his coat and a cap, and hurried out to greet Tassie Landles before she could lay a curse on his mineral stock and reduce his hillocks to dross.

'Madam,' he said heartily, 'to what do I owe the pleasure? Are you after a creel or two of coal to heat your wee housie?'

'I have coal,' Tassie Landles told him. 'I've come tae bring you news, Mr Ogilvy, since you're Tom Brodie's friend.'

'Oh!' said Mr Ogilvy, recoiling slightly. 'Is it his father again? I mean, have you – ah – heard from – ah – Brodie deceased?'

'No,' said Tassie Landles, 'not lately.'

'Please, step inside,' said Mr Ogilvy. 'If you've a message to impart we'll be more comfortable indoors.'

'Here'll do,' said Tassie Landles. 'I won't take up much o' your time.'

'Well,' said Mr Ogilvy, 'impart away.'

'He's lost her.'

'Lost her?'

'Rose Hewitt. She's become attached tae Walter Fergusson's lad.'

'I think Tom knows that young Fergusson is, shall we say, in the running.'

'It's more than the runnin' now,' Tassie Landles told him.

'An engagement, do you mean, a betrothal?'

'Aye, so it would seem.'

'Did this information come to you in a trance, ma'am?'

'It came tae me from the Hewitt's day-maid, Dorothy.'

'I see,' said Mr Ogilvy. 'Is the child reliable?'

'She doesn't have the sense tae lie tae me.'

'She's afraid of you, in other words.'

'Without reason,' said Tassie. 'However, I've given you the news an' I'll leave it tae you tae see it gets up the hill to Tom Brodie.' She made to turn away.

'Wait,' Mr Ogilvy said. 'I'm curious as to why you're concerned about Tom Brodie an' his relations with Hewitt's daughter. Why does it matter to you who the girl marries?'

'It's not who *she* marries,' Tassie Landles said, 'it's who Tom Brodie will marry. He made a promise to his daddy an'—'

'Yes, yes, yes.' Mr Ogilvy had no wish to be reminded of it. 'I think we may take that as read.'

'He's a haunted man, is Tom Brodie, a haunted man.'

'He'll be a lot more haunted when he learns he's lost Rose Hewitt.'

'That may be,' the old woman said, 'but at least he'll be free.'

'Free of whom?'

'Just tell him what I've told you,' Tassie Landles said.

'Shall I drive you home?' Mr Ogilvy offered.

'I walked here, I'll walk back,' the old woman said and, turning, crabbed off towards the toll road that would take her back to town.

'Betrothed?' Tom shouted. 'Who brought you this piece o' news?'

'It – it's all round town, I believe,' Mr Ogilvy said.

'All round town, is it?' Tom said. 'Did she put it all round town? I wonder she didn't ride naked through the streets yelling her bloody news.'

'Tassie Landles told me, if you must know. She had it from Hewitt's day-maid, it seems. She came straight to me,' said Mr Ogilvy, 'though I can't for the life of me think why.'

'To taunt me,' Tom said.

'She – the old woman – says you're a haunted man.'

'Well, by God, she's right.'

They were standing by the door of the barn. There was nobody else in sight which, Mr Ogilvy thought, was perhaps as well. Something about the farm – and the farmer – frightened him now and talk of hauntings did nothing to calm his nerves.

'Are you – I mean – seein' ghosts?'

'It's not ghosts,' Tom told him. 'It's women I'm haunted by.'

'Well' – Mr Ogilvy edged towards his horse – 'I've told you what the old woman told me, Tom. I'm sorry Miss Hewitt didn't come up to the mark.'

'Oh, she came up to the mark, Robert, believe me,' Tom said. 'It's a ruse, don't you see? Rose has no intention o' marryin' Lucas Fergusson. She's takin' revenge on me for ignorin' her. She's employed the Landles woman to spread a rumour that she's engaged to that idiot Fergusson. You've been made a part o' it to give it credibility.'

'I hope you don't think—'

'What does she take me for?' Tom fumed. 'How gullible does she suppose me to be, eh? She's tryin' to make me jealous, that's all. Well, by God, if that's the game she wants to play she'll rue the day she took me on.'

Mr Ogilvy retreated a few more steps towards the rail.

Tom had not done with him yet. 'I had it in mind to put Rose Hewitt behind me,' he blurted out, 'to settle for another sort o' wife. But, as God's my witness, I'll not be made a fool of. Lucas Fergusson's no match for me, Robert. Now I'll prove it to him, aye, an' to her. If Fergusson wants her, he may have her, but only after I've finished with her.'

'I thought you wanted to marry her?'

'Marry her? I wouldn't marry Rose Hewitt if she came crawlin' through the dung-heap on her hands an' knees. It's not a weddin' band she'll have from me, Robert, but a lesson, a lesson like no other.'

'Tom, please, don't be hasty.'

'What was my promise to the bachelors, Robert: that I'd have the cutty off Rose Hewitt's back before the barley showed green?'

'You said you intended to marry her,' Mr Ogilvy reminded him.

'A guinea – no, make it five – says I'll have her naked before January's out. Then we'll see if the engagement holds an' if Lucas Fergusson is enough for her after she's sampled the real thing.'

Mr Ogilvy was not such a coward as all that; he drew himself up and faced the ranting young farmer squarely. 'Tom,' he said, 'I'll have no part of such a dishonourable wager. We might be bachelors an' keen on the ladies but what you propose is nothin' short of scandalous, nothin' short of—'

'Rape?' Tom said. 'Are you frighted by the word, man, struck dumb by the idea that a sweet, sheltered girl like Rose Hewitt might be beggin' for it?'

'In your opinion, only in your opinion.'

'I can read the signs, Robert, even if you can't.'

'Be careful, Tom. It might not be a game at all, you know.'

'Love's just a game, whatever rules it's played by.'

'Aye, an' love misplaced can get you hanged.'

'Awa' ye go.' Slapping the horse on the crupper, Tom brought it round for Mr Ogilvy to mount. 'Awa' ye go, old man, an' leave love an' love-makin' to those o' us who still have the spunk for it.'

And Mr Ogilvy, deeply troubled, climbed up into the saddle and rode off down the Hawkshill track without another word.

Dorothy came sidling from the kitchen as soon as Rose appeared for breakfast.

'*Psst*,' the day-maid said, out of the side of her mouth. '*Psst*.'

'Pissed?' said Rose, much taken aback. 'Who's pissed?'

'Nah, nah,' Dorothy whispered. 'See. Here. A letter.' Covered by the folds of her apron, she pressed the little packet into her mistress's fist. 'It was there this mornin' at the carrier's office, waitin' for to be collected.'

'A letter?' Rose's heart beat a little faster. 'For me?'

'Aye.'

'What were you doing at the carrier's office?'

'Lookin' for your letters. You never telt me to stop.'

'No, true, I didn't,' Rose said.

'What's goin' on out there?' Mrs Prole called out.

'Nothing, nothing,' Rose replied.

Giving Dorothy a push, she sent her trotting back into the kitchen, then, heart beating faster still, hid herself in a corner of the hall and furtively examined the writing on the packet; a quick, slashing, upright script that could only have been penned by one man.

'Tom,' she murmured, 'Tom.'

Hiding the packet in a pocket of her petticoat, she hurried into the parlour to stuff down a muffin and a boiled egg and, as soon as decency allowed, make good her escape upstairs.

When Janet asked him where he was going, Conn didn't have the heart to lie. He was well aware that the Brodie girl had a fancy for him – the fact that she kept climbing on to his knee was hint enough – but experience had taught him that it was wise to let starry-eyed lassies down without hurting their feelings or, more importantly, making enemies who might be tempted to betray him. There was, he realised, a bit of an irony in that way of thinking now, given that it was not a love-struck female who had turned him in but his bloody brother-in-law and – at least by proxy – his sister, Kathleen.

He had never been in such a position before, cut off from the place he had learned to call home, cut off from the funds he needed to conduct his business, cut off from the business that had been the core of his existence for longer than he could remember. He gave the girl a grin and a wink and told her he was going to look at the sea.

'Can I come with you?' Janet said eagerly.

'Sure an' have you no chores to do today?'

'How long will you be gone?'

'Oh, an hour or two, at most.'

'I'll not be missed for an hour or two,' said Janet, then added, 'Come to think o' it, I doubt if I'd be missed if I disappeared for a week.'

Conn laughed. 'Fetch your shawl an' we'll take a stroll down to Port Cedric an' make sure nobody's stolen my boat.'

She was twenty and he was thirty-four. She was the daughter of a dour tenant farmer and had travelled no further than Ballantrae. Since birth, almost, he had been a rover and an outlaw, at ease in rough company and a bringer of joy to many ladies in many ports. He had been loved by some and had loved a few in turn. One in particular, Helene van Zelyn, the wife of a Dutch skipper, would have thrown up everything, including three children, to run off with him if he, with an aching heart, had not called a halt to the affair.

Something about Janet Brodie reminded him a little of Helene. Janet was younger, though, not so plump, and had not one scrap of the sophistication that had first drawn him to van Zelyn's wife, a sophistication that, when he thought back on it, had proved to be less cosmopolitan than corrupt.

Janet took his arm and then his hand.

Conn did not object.

The wind was directly off the sea and you could taste the heaving mass of bladder wrack that the winter storms had torn from the tideline. A keen wind whipped the breakers into great green scoops that drenched the stump of the jetty and groped up towards the dunes.

Janet dropped the shawl from her head and tipped her chin and the wind caught her hair and drew it away from her face, skinning her with the force of it. She looked, Conn thought, new-washed, new-minted, and, really, not at all like Helene van Zelyn.

They walked down the path through the dunes and turned towards the clump of reeds behind which he had hidden the boat.

He put his arm about her and held her tightly.

'Hoh, sir,' said a voice from nowhere. 'An' what might you be doin'?'

There was no sign of a cutter out to sea, no luggers or sloops, no craft but a handful of fishing smacks beating towards Ayr harbour; no evidence of a longboat or horses on the beach; nothing and no one at first but the tall young man who rose from among the dunes. He wore the braided hat of an Officer of Station and brandished a sword in one hand and a pistol in the other.

'We're takin' a breath o' fresh air, sir,' Janet piped up before Conn could open his mouth. 'Is there a law against that now?'

'Is this your boat?' the officer demanded, tapping his sword on the prow.

'My boat?' said Janet. 'Now what would I be wantin' wi' a boat?'

'Is it yours, sir? Speak up.'

Janet hugged Conn and, playfully, tugged at his collar. 'You villain, you,' she chirped, 'you've gone an' bought a boat for to take to the sea an' leave me in the lurch.'

'Chance would be a fine thing,' Conn said. 'Sure an' you'd grow wings like an albatross an' chase me down through wind an' waves.'

'Aye,' said Janet cheerfully, 'now I've got you, there's no escape.'

The officer was not amused by the badinage and not quite taken in by it. He sheathed the sword but kept the pistol, cocked, in his hand.

Janet turned on him. 'Since we've told you who we are,' she said, 'you might be decent enough to return the courtesy, eh, an' tell us why you're wavin' a weapon in our direction because this is public land an' we're doin' no harm.'

'Nay, but you haven't told me who you are,' the officer said.

'I'm Matthew Brodie's daughter,' Janet spoke up again. 'An' this handsome chap is my intended come over for to marry me.'

'Come over from where?'

'Cork,' said Janet without hesitation.

'Tell the girl to hold her tongue,' the officer said. 'You, your name?'

'Dermot O'Donnell.' Conn pulled the name from the air or, rather, from the depths of his memory; poor Dermot, dead of a fever all of twenty years ago. 'What matter to you what I'm called? Is it an offence these days to be Irish?' Boldly, he separated himself from Janet and stepped forward to look at the boat. 'It's a bit of a wreck, is it not? Are you for sellin' it, sir?'

'Is it his at all?' Janet called out. 'I wouldn't buy a hen from him, Dermot. He has the look o' a ruffian. Come away, dearest, come away.' Then she swung round as three other armed men appeared behind her.

They were clad in the loose smocks and canvas trousers that marked them as members of the water-guard, and each had a brace of pistols in his belt. They were less suspicious and surly than the tall young officer and, wandering down from the dune, gave Janet the eye.

'It's a cold day for courtin', sweetheart,' one of them said.

'It's never too cold for courtin',' Janet retorted, though she was suddenly less sure of herself, 'not when you've a fine strong man tae hang on to.'

'How long have you been in the shire?' the officer asked.

'Seven weeks,' Conn answered.

'How did you come here?'

'By boat from Dublin.'

'Dublin? And the name o' the boat you came on?'

'The *Swan*.'

'A coastal trader?'

'I paid my passage, fair an' square.'

'What trade do you follow, Mr – ah . . .'

'O'Donnell: I'm a sailmaker.'

'Do you have employment here in Scotland?'

'I hope to find employment in Ayr or perhaps in Greenock.'

'If he doesn't, we'll go back to Cork as soon as we're married,' said Janet. 'I've never been to Ireland an' I'm told it's a fine place for to raise a family.'

'You, girl,' said the officer, 'where do you live?'

'Up on the hill: Hawkshill.'

'How far is that, Jockie?' the officer asked.

The water-guard, Jockie, answered, 'Two miles, or three.'

'Then we'll ride up an' talk to her father.'

'My father's dead. He died three month since,' Janet said. 'It was then Dermot got sent for; he's my father's cousin's lad. Why are you askin' all these questions? Tell us what you want an' let us be on our way.'

'We want nothin' from you, sweetheart,' one of the water-guard said. 'We're in search o' a man named McCaskie who did dreadful injury to a King's officer over on the Isle o' Man.'

'That's enough,' the officer said.

'Let them go, sir. They're not smugglers.'

'Smugglers?' said Janet. 'Is it smugglers you think we are?'

The officer tucked the pistol into his belt. 'If this is not your boat, O'Donnell, you'll have no objection if we burn it.'

'Sure an' it's no barnacles off my bottom what you do with it.' Conn shrugged and took Janet's arm again. 'Burn away, an' be damned if it turns out to belong to a fisherman.'

'Wait,' Janet said. 'This man, McCloskie, is there a price on his head?'

'Thirty pounds, English,' Jockie said. 'Why? Do you know where he is?'

'If only we did,' said Janet. 'What a fine dowry that would make, dearest, would it not?' Then, bestowing a smile on the water-guards and with a little bow to the officer, wrapped an arm round Conn's waist and led him away.

They were halfway up the slope before Conn said, 'By God, Brodie, you've a quicker wit an' a steadier nerve than I gave you credit for.'

'It's not so steady now, Conn.' Holding out her hand, she displayed her shaking fingers. 'I'm just glad you dreamed up a name an' a suitable employment.'

'Sailmaker?' said Conn. 'Well, I was one, once. Soon after my father died my mother insisted on puttin' me out to learn an honest trade.'

'But you preferred smugglin'?'

'Better money; better fun, too.'

They paused and looked down on the beach. A thin coil of smoke rose from behind the dunes and blew away like breath on the wind. It was followed a moment later by a darker, thicker pall that billowed across the sand before it too vanished into the fading daylight.

'Ah, me poor old boat,' said Conn. 'God rest her, she done well by me.'

'Now you're stuck with us,' said Janet, 'an' no way out of it.'

'Well, there are worse places to be stuck, I suppose,' said Conn, and gave her a wink and a kiss on the cheek to thank her for not selling him out.

I have at last, my Fair Friend, determined to write to you and to set down in words the song that is in my heart, a song like that of which no thrush or blackbird, nor even the celestial skylark, has ever pour'd out with such sincerity. I love you, Miss Hewitt, I love you. I would have had you know it e'er now if it had not been for the devilish interventions of bereavement and the demands put upon me as the new head of my household, a duty one must, alas, place above love.

Rose knelt by the attic window, forearms braced on the sill, the letter, page after page of it, resting in her lap where, if she happened to be disturbed, she might hide it quickly in the folds of her dress.

> Among the profusion of hollow compliments which insidious or unmeaning Folly might dictate, I eschew them all save one. That one, my darling Rose, is no less apology for being the declaration of a passionate spirit and a loving heart that has languish'd in a damnable melange of Fretfulness and Remorse since our last chance meet upon the Drennan pave. Since then my soul has flutter'd round her tenement like a wild Finch caught amid the wintry snows and thrust into a cage.

'My goodness me!' Rose murmured, and struck into the second page.

> I am persuaded that what was told of me by the Prophetess of the Bridge was too much a prophecy of tears and not enough of love. If my neglect has awaken'd resentment in your breast, may God forgive me! Impossibility presents an impenetrable barrier to the proudest daring of Presumption but be assured that I would sooner gaze into the fiery focus of Hell than never meet again the eye of the goddess of my soul.

Come along, Tom, Rose thought, just tell me where and when.

Shuffling the foolscap impatiently, she found the final page and, plastering it against the window glass, peered at it: '. . . truly, from this cause, *ma chère*, I beseech you to meet with me at the hour of three o'clock on Thursday inst., within Crawford's ale-house where I might relieve my heartache and make amends.' Then a dashing signature block in which the word 'love' or, rather, 'Love', occurred five times.

Well, well, Rose thought, three o'clock at Caddy Crawford's on Thursday afternoon: I wonder how a man like Tom Brodie intends to relieve his heartache and just how he will make amends.

Folding the sheaf as small as it would go, she hid the wad with her other trinkets in the base of the harp and, with sharpened appetite, trotted downstairs again to devour another muffin and an egg or two before Eunice cleared away the breakfast things.

Her bleeding came as a great relief. She took herself to attend the condition in the back room. She was fortunate that the monthly visitation did not much affect her. She suffered none of the debilitating cramps that sent her sister Effie crawling to her bed; a slight headache and a certain sluggishness in focusing her thoughts were, as a rule, the worst of it. Betsy washed herself, fished out the flannels, put on her tight woollen drawers and was back in the yard before anyone realised that she had gone.

Conn had gone with Henry to scare birds from the long field and to keep a weather eye on the track in case the water-guards arrived unheralded. He had already sent notes, unsigned, to Mr Dingle's employer in Paisley and the tobacco-buyers in Kilmarnock and, on a borrowed horse, had risked riding into Ayr to deliver a warning to a sea captain who had a boat in harbour and friends in continental ports. Her cousin had no farming skills to exchange for keep but he was more than willing to shovel manure, tote feed and tend the mash-boiler and, with Janet as his guide, roam about the wintry pastures.

Conn was not the sort who would settle for a life on the land, though. Betsy feared that Janet, who had clearly lost her heart to the Irishman, would wake one morning to find him gone.

Meanwhile, she watched Janet bill and coo and Conn, in his cautious way, respond and felt a pang of envy that she had no one upon whom to lavish love now that Tom had taken and rejected her.

'Betsy, my love,' he called out, 'how handsome you look today.'

He had brought out the biggest of the plough-horses to groom in the yard. The horse dwarfed him and he crouched beneath it, like a little boy, peeping up at her archly, and eager to claim her attention. But she could not look at him now, though, whatever mood was on him, without recalling the cold, starved manner in which he had mounted her as if she were no more to him than a brood mare is to a stallion, or a sow to a hog.

She knew then, in the grey light of that Thursday morning, that she would never lie with him again, no matter how he doled out charm or how many casual compliments he tossed her. There was no love in him, no tenderness. She was no longer willing to pander to his wayward needs.

She went over to the horse and stroked its ears while Tom worked the bristle over the animal's shoulder to draw off dirt and stable scurf.

He was buoyant today, it seemed, and filled with vigour.

'Are you not rovin' out with your cousin, then?' he asked.

'Not me,' said Betsy. 'He's gone with Henry.'

'An' is Janet not trailin' at his heels?'

'She's sweepin' out the loft, I think.'

Tom leaned on the horse's shoulder. 'How long will McCaskie lodge with us, do you think?'

'Why don't you ask him?'

'He's not my special friend, nor my cousin either.'

'He'll stay until he considers it safe to leave, I suppose.'

'Safe?' Tom said. 'What does that word mean, I wonder?' He came around the flank and, with the horse's gigantic head dipping passively between them, grinned. 'How bonnie you are, Betsy McBride, how fair an' bonnie. Are you well in all your parts?'

She sensed the purpose behind his affability. He was fishing to find out if she had taken pleasure in mowing or if, perhaps, something had come out of it. She was tempted to tell him he was not so potent as he imagined himself to be and that there would be no anxious counting of days, no shamefaced announcement, no 'arrangements' to be entered into and that, fool though she might be, she was not foolish enough to run the risk again, not for any pleasure it might bring.

'Well, Betsy,' he said softly. 'Are you?'

'Aye,' she told him. 'I'm well, Tom, very well – in all my parts.'

'Good,' he said, 'that's good.'

He moved off round the side of the mountainous horse, effectively dismissing her. And Betsy, nothing loath, set off for the long field in search of more honest company, namely Henry and her cousin, Conn.

22

Caddy Crawford's was by no means the most disreputable drinking den in the shire of Ayr. There were taverns out by Galston, on the old toll road to the east, where women were not made welcome unless they arrived with their skirts over their heads and their stockings round their ankles. There were other inns and ale-houses, too numerous to count, tucked away in the backs of small towns and smaller villages where tinkers took their ease and even drovers, as rough a lot as ever downed a dram, thought twice before they ducked beneath the lintel for fear of being knifed or cudgelled.

In port towns, too, in fish-stinking alleys and sewer-like vennels, mean little hovels served potted liquor and pandered to a man's need to copulate and a woman's need to earn a crust by providing a room and a cot or, more likely, a leaky straw mattress, where the transaction could be conducted with a degree – a very small degree – of privacy.

Even in Souter Gordon's pitiful wee place in Hayes, there was a room – a cupboard, really – where a fellow might, for a small fee, abide in close proximity to one of the scullions from Copplestone House or test the matrimonial suitability of a farm servant or, if his need were dire enough, seek relief with one of the two local 'ladies' who plied a furtive trade for pennies and a glass of rum.

In Drennan, genteel Drennan, hypocrisy was rife. While Caddy Crawford openly served both males and females with drink and Sunday dinners, the two rooms that the tavern-keeper let out, by the hour or by the night, were discreetly entered by a corridor that also led into the yard. Consequently, one could never be quite sure who was seeking privacy, who the privy or who, as happened, might merely be a traveller in search of a good night's sleep.

Tom Brodie was not the only bachelor who had availed himself of Caddy's spartan rooms when winter rendered wooing amid the broom and bracken hazardous to the health of one's member. He had lured a girl from Pendicle in there once, and had bragged about it afterwards. And once, when he and Mr Ogilvy had befriended two spinster sisters who were stopping off en route to Dumfries, he had so charmed the younger that she had given him her all, very willingly, while Mr Ogilvy had endured umpteen hands of cribbage with the elder to keep her mind off what was going on next door.

It was here in one of Caddy Crawford's cubicles at three o'clock on a dreary Thursday afternoon that Mr Tom Brodie planned to join with Miss Rose Hewitt in a union that, if not exactly blessed, would surely stamp itself upon the girl's memory and, at least in Tom's opinion, spoil her for ever more.

In spite of his boast, it was not his intention to take Rose by force; there were still laws about that sort of thing. Besides, he was far too gallant ever to impose himself on a woman – Betsy McBride, perhaps, excepted – who had not been tuned like a fiddle beforehand.

Demure though she might be, Tom had no doubt that Rose Hewitt was ready for the sacrifice, that the falling-out between them would prove no impediment to seduction but might, in fact, add to it a dash of relish.

He had not forgotten Rose's eagerness to give her all on the night of Arbuthnot's dance. Indeed, he cursed himself for being so damned noble as to invite the poor bitch to wait for satisfaction until he speared her to the bridal bed. He was still blistered at her haughty attitude to the circumstances that had kept him from her, her failure to understand that female obsession with snaring a husband did not chime with reality and that death and taxes, rent and the finding thereof were matters of more import to a responsible man than puffing up a young girl's self-esteem.

Did she honestly believe that the announcement of an engagement to marry Lucas Fergusson, a weak-kneed, mealy-mouthed idiot, would disguise her longing for him, and the promise of a life of luxury in Walter Fergusson's lush pastures would compensate for turning her back on a nature so forceful and passionate that it would be worth any hardship?

He rode into Drennan in a state of heat and ranklement.

He had dreamed the dream again last night. He had seen his father standing by his bed, had felt the touch of the old man's knuckles on his brow and had heard, like the whisper of ripe barley blown by the wind, the old man's voice reminding him of his promises.

He knew now how to be rid of it, how by taking her he would be shot of it once and for all. He would have his revenge on Neville Hewitt for bullying his daddy unto death. He would have his revenge on the childish Rose, aye, and on the old woman too, the self-anointed prophetess who had dared dabble with his fate and might, at a pinch, be blamed for what he was about to do. Then, when it was over, when he had pierced and pleasured her, he would leave her begging for more, for he had already decided that he would take the woman, Betsy, for a wife and not the girl, not Rose.

He hitched the horse to the rail and gave it a nose-bag then, at no more than a minute to three o'clock, cocked his bonnet over his eye, tweaked his little pigtail, and entered Caddy Crawford's by the front door.

The old men, four or five of them, were huddled by the fire. Unusually, they offered no greeting but turned away, raised their shoulders, and were suddenly very interested in the condition of their boots. Caddy and his pot-boy were no more welcoming. They were crouched behind the counter, whispering together, and hastily looked away when Tom came in.

There were no bachelors in the room, no strangers save the pretty little female, Hewitt's daughter, who had settled at a corner table and had paid for a bottle of Caddy's best claret. When Brodie strode into the house, she lifted a glass in her dainty paw and called out, 'Tom, I'm here. See, here I am,' as if he could possibly miss her.

She was clad in white and black, a bit like a nun. Her black wool cape was open at the throat, the hood bunched about her shoulders. Tom was treated to the sight of her pleated bodice and, riding on the slope of her breast, a little silver heart rising and falling on a fine gilt chain.

'Tom, my dear,' she said. 'I am glad to see you.'

'Why?' he said, smiling. 'Did you suppose I wouldn't come?'

'Your letter . . .' She blushed. 'I thought you might be teasing me again.'

Tom took off his bonnet and seated himself on the bench, facing her. Caddy, the pot-boy and the elders at the hearth were watching him but, now that his father had passed on, he cared not a fig what tales might filter back to Hawkshill. In fact, it would be useful to have witnesses to confirm his account at the next meeting of the Bachelors' Club.

'I wouldn't tease you, my darlin' Rose, not for all the tea in—'

'Wine, a glass of wine?'

He checked the level of claret in the bottle and saw that it had not much diminished. Of course, it would hasten matters along if she were loosened a bit, though not, emphatically not, oiled to the point were she might feasibly deny that she had gone with him willingly.

He took the wine glass, twined his arm around hers, sipped from the glass and, tipping up his chin, brushed her moist lips with his.

'Every word,' he murmured. 'I meant every word, every syllable, that flowed from my pen. I'd have dewed the pages with tears of contrition an' sprinkled them with tokens o' love if it had been within my power. Did you like my letter, then?'

'Yes. Oh, yes, Tom. I've never had such a letter before.'

And never will again, Tom thought, though he kept the sentiment to himself. He kissed her once more.

She closed her eyes in ecstasy.

He peeped down at the pendant that rose and fell on her breast and saw that the little silver heart was already beating hard.

He sat back. She opened her eyes.

'What's wrong? What is it?'

'Nay, lass,' he told her thickly, 'I can't do this to you.'

'Do what to me?' said Rose anxiously. 'Kiss me, do you mean? What is there to stop you? I came for your kisses, Tom, for your—'

He put a finger to her lips. 'Hush, now, or I'll forget you're a lady.' He paused, then added, 'An' engaged to another.'

'Oh, that!' Rose said.

'That!' Tom said. 'That news was a dagger to my heart.'

'Phooh! A bagatelle,' the girl told him, 'a mere device, a machination, a ruse to throw my father off the scent. Do you suppose I'd be foolish enough to marry Lucas Fergusson when I might have you?'

'Well,' Tom said, 'no.'

She reached out for his hand and jerked him across the table. 'Did you not promise to run off with me? Did you not say you would be my husband first and my lover second?'

'Aye, I did.'

She ravelled his sleeve in her fist and said, 'My father will never agree to let you marry me, Tom, unless . . .'

'Unless?'

'If you were to become my lover first, and give me a child, what choice would my papa have but to agree to a marriage between us?'

'Rose, are you suggestin' . . .'

She glanced round, then back again. 'I've heard there's a room here that may be hired by the hour? Is that not so?'

'It – it is,' Tom admitted.

'Take me there. Take me there and do it to me now.'

'Do what?'

'Give me a child.'

'Well, actually, it may not be . . .'

'Do you not want me, Tom? Is that it?'

'No – yes, I mean, I want you. Of course I want you but . . .'

'Do you not want me for your wife?'

It was Tom's turn to glance round, not towards the corridor but at the elders by the fire and at Caddy Crawford who, with ears pricked, had hidden himself behind the barrels.

'Tell me the truth, Tom Brodie.'

'Aye, I want you for my wife.'

'Is this not the way to do it?'

'It's one way, certainly.'

'Then take me,' Rose said, quite loudly. 'Take me,' and scrambled out of the corner and held out her hand.

The old men were staring quite openly now, fascinated by the sight of Tom Brodie, the Hawkshill ram, being seduced before their eyes. And when Tom rose from the bench, tugged down his vest and threw back his shoulders, a tactless little whoop went up from the region of the hearth.

Without turning, Tom said, 'A room, Caddy. It seems I require a room.'

'Take the first door,' Caddy Crawford told him gruffly. 'Aye, the first door,' and, with his mouth hanging open, watched Matt Brodie's roaring boy being led away like a lamb.

'Here's the thing,' said Henry. 'I'd hoped we might buy Hewitt out one day an' have Hawkshill for ourselves.'

'It's every man's dream to have somethin' to call his own,' said Conn. 'I'm sorry I couldn't make it come to pass, my friend, but circumstances fell out o' my control rather briskly.'

'Are you sure the revenue officers took your money-box?' said Betsy.

'If they didn't, my brother-in-law would. He has no scruples nor honour.'

'Will he take care o' your mother?' Henry said.

'He'll do that all right. My sister would murder him if he didn't.'

'Can't you go back to Ramsey?' Betsy enquired.

'Not with every tink an' tidewalker lookin' out for me,' Conn answered.

'To Ireland then?' said Henry.

'Ireland?' Conn nodded. 'Aye, there's hope o' that. But how would I get there since I've not a brown penny to me name?'

'I'll buy your cattle back from you,' Henry informed him. 'I'll pay the price you paid us. Would that be enough to purchase your fare to Dublin town?'

'Enough, an' more.'

They were strolling side by side down the length of the wheat field. The little birds were still excitable but the rooks and gulls no longer feared the appearance of men, with or without the whirligigs. There were no signs yet of green shoots but with the earth warming and the days growing imperceptibly longer, nature would soon take her course.

'In Dublin, can you start up again?' said Henry.

'Start small,' said Conn. 'I can, but I'm not sure I've a wish to.'

'What would you do, how would you live?' Betsy asked.

'Trade,' Conn said. 'Trading is the one thing I know how to do. Sure an' not all my contacts are on the black side o' the law. If I'd a drop o' capital, just a drop, I'd scratch up credit from the shipmasters to help me along an' deal as a chandler from me own wee shop.'

'How much capital is in a drop?' said Henry.

Conn shrugged. 'Forty pounds, or fifty.'

'It would be a struggle, would it not?' said Henry.

'Sure an' it would at that,' Conn said. 'But have I not struggled all me life long an' have precious little to show for it?'

'Not even a wife,' Henry suggested.

'No,' Conn admitted, after a pause, 'not even a wife.'

She paused in the corridor, out of sight of the landlord, and let Tom kiss her throat and neck and lick her earlobe as if it were a sugar lump. He put his hand to her waist and then slid it upward to her breast. The cape, thrown back, was bundled behind her, pinning her against the wall. He ran his hands over her breasts and kissed her with an angry passion that, in spite of her distaste, roused a spark of doubt in her. When he thrust his thigh between her legs, crushing her skirts and petticoats, she let out a little gasp and, groping behind her, found the iron latch and flicked it up with her fingertips to let the door swing open.

'God Jesus, Rose,' he growled, 'I'm ready for you now.'

There behind her was the bed, a narrow wooden cot, stout enough in construction to bear the weight of two, one on top of the other. A clean sheet, a plaid blanket and two firm bolsters were visible in the faint light from the whorled-glass window. A fat beeswax candle was stuck in a metal holder on a spindle table, a tinderbox beside it, a jug and basin too, and even a pair of linen towels, neatly folded. And a chair, one chair, rush-bottomed.

And on the chair, a man, a young man, coiled as tightly as a spring.

Riding on Tom Brodie's thigh, she was driven backward into the room. His hands clasped her buttocks beneath the rumpled cloth. His nose and mouth were buried, nuzzling, in her neck. She let her legs go slack, as if she were about to swoon, and, throwing herself to one side, cried out, 'Lucas.'

There was no gentlemanly squaring off and no ruffian scuffle.

Tom Brodie did not know quite what hit him, only that the gloomy cubbyhole was suddenly illuminated by a dazzling white light. Blood gushed from his nose, flooded the back of his throat and turned his '*aaauuugh*' of astonishment into a strangled cry. Buckling, he fell forward, blood spouting in all directions, and lacked the sense to protect himself when Lucas struck again.

They were fair punches, bare-knuckled, fingers and thumbs curled into the palm, but there was weight behind them, weight and temper. The second blow caught Tom on the point of the chin. He heard his teeth crack, felt a strange jarring ripple shoot into the bones of his skull, then, rocking backward, slid into a pool of darkness that tasted, just for a moment, of treacle.

'Is he dead, Rosie? Have I kilt him?'

'No, no, Lukie, have no fear on that score.'

'What'll we dae – do with him now?'

'Put a bolster behind his head so that he doesn't choke on his own blood.'

'Blood?' Lucas said. 'Aye, there's a lot o' it, isn't there?'

'I do believe you've broken his nose.'

'He won't have the law on me, will he, Rosie?'

'Do not,' Rose said, 'be silly. You did no more than any man would do to protect the honour of his intended. Fetch down that bolster.'

Obediently, Lucas dragged the bolster to the floor and with Rose's help shoved it under Tom Brodie's skull, bending the stubby little pigtail to one side. There were bubbles of blood at Brodie's nostrils but he seemed to be breathing freely, if noisily, through his mouth.

'There,' Rose said. 'That will do nicely.'

'Now what?' said Lucas.

'We let him sleep,' said Rose and, taking her lover by the hand, stepped over the puddle of blood into the corridor and out via the garden gate into the streets of the town.

23

The good citizens of Hayes were all agog to see what sort of damage had been done to their rambunctious son. Mr Turbot's congregation was swelled that Sunday forenoon not by a sudden surge in piety but by simple curiosity. It was a great disappointment to all that Tom Brodie did not see fit to make an appearance and offer up his wounds to the judgement of the multitude.

The rumours that percolated down from Drennan were, to say the best of it, vague. They ran from an altercation with the hoof of a horse while heavily under the influence of alcohol – Brodie, that is, not the horse – to a murderous brawl with the denizens of Caddy Crawford's ale-house. Questioning of said denizens by young Mr Frye, aided by the crown that Mr Ogilvy slipped into the hand of Caddy Crawford, elicited a quite different story, one that had such a ring of truth that Messrs Ogilvy and Frye, in the name of friendship, decided to keep it to themselves.

When Johnny Rankine trotted up to Hawkshill to see what was what he found Tom incapable of uttering a word. His jaw was swollen, his eyes blackened, and his nose – well, the less said about his nose, the better. He slumped in a chair by the fire, clad in a nightshirt and an old greatcoat and glowered out of purple eye-slits and, now and then, licked his cracked lips with a bright red tongue, an action that appeared to engender more pain than relief. And when Johnny, rashly, touched him on the arm, he let out such a groan that the dairy farmer almost fell off his chair and soon thereafter beat a hasty retreat.

Peter Frye and Mr Ogilvy elected to call, in tandem, upon their bachelor brother on Sunday afternoon.

Henry met them in the yard and, in hushed tones, explained that pain had undermined the more sociable aspects of Tom's character and they would be advised to pay their respects and take their leave as quickly as possible.

'Good God, man!' Peter exclaimed. 'What did she do to you?'

Tom squinted round his swollen nose and answered with a snarl. Standing a foot or two behind Tom's chair, the Irishman, McCaskie, raised his fist to his mouth and coughed theatrically. Tom's sister Janet served tea.

Mr Ogilvy put his cup and saucer untouched on the table and addressed himself to Agnes. 'Has Glendinning attended him?'

'First thing,' Agnes answered. 'The doctor brought him home.'

'Is the nose broken?'

'The bone, aye, but the doctor tapped it back in place.'

'Will it heal properly?'

Agnes shrugged and, glancing at Tom, shook her head.

'Can he cope with food?'

'Gruel, a spoonful o' strained soup,' said Mrs Brodie. 'He can't even manage a taste o' spirits for it stings his mouth.'

'Any other injury?' Mr Ogilvy said.

'To his pride, only his pride,' Agnes murmured. 'He refuses to tell us what happened.'

'If you ask me,' Janet piped up, 'yon girl had a lot to do wi' it.'

Tom clutched the greatcoat to his throat and gave a murderous glare.

'No girl did that to him,' said Conn McCaskie. 'He fell off his horse.'

'He fell off somethin', that's for sure,' said Janet who, Mr Ogilvy gathered, was not entirely sympathetic to her brother's suffering. 'Whether it was a horse or a lassie is a matter o' speculation.'

Peter crouched by his friend's side. 'Is there anything you need, Tom, anything we can bring you?'

'Nuh.'

'Any message we can deliver on your behalf?'

'Plessage?' Tom managed.

'To the brothers at the club, say?'

'Nuh!'

'Very well,' Peter said, 'then we'll leave you to rest and, if we may, call again when you are more yourself.'

Tom nodded, winced, and closed his eyes.

In the yard, Henry said, 'Come now, Peter, I suspect you have information that's so far eluded us. I'd be grateful if you'd tell me what you've learned.'

Peter glanced at Mr Ogilvy who said, 'He took the girl Hewitt into Caddy's back room . . .'

'Did she go willingly?' said Henry.

'Apparently so,' said Peter. 'Indeed, from what Robert and I have gathered, she seemed eager for Tom's company.'

'Devil take it!' Henry muttered. 'There would have to be a woman involved. And Hewitt's daughter! God, there are times when I think my brother's completely mad. What did she hit him with – a chair?'

'We don't know,' said Peter. 'Caddy Crawford heard a bit of commotion but chose not to interfere. Tom staggered out of the room some ten minutes later and collapsed. Caddy sent for Glendinning who brought Tom home.'

'An' the girl?'

'Gone, vanished,' said Mr Ogilvy. 'There's more to it than Crawford's willin' to reveal. If you ask me, he was bribed to let someone into the room in advance.'

'But who?' said Henry.

'That we do not know.'

'Neville Hewitt?' said Henry.

'Possible but hardly likely.'

'In all probability only three people know the whole story,' said Mr Ogilvy. 'The girl, the assailant, and Tom.'

'An' Tom's too humiliated to tell anyone,' said Henry. 'Well, it seems my dear brother may have asked for what he got an' that, with luck, he may have learned a lesson from it.'

'I wouldn't count upon it, Henry,' said Peter Frye.

The harp no longer offered solace or perhaps she was no longer in need of solace. She fingered the strings reflectively and did her best not to gloat. She knew, however, that if she lived to be a hundred she would never forget how gawky Lucas Fergusson, without qualm or question, had defended her honour. He was a gentle soul at heart and only true love, bolstered by indignation, had guided his fist and he had been, at that instant, her tiger. The fact that she had put him into a position to be so did not detract from his bravery. She had been right to contrive a conclusive ending to the affair that never was, to make Lucas the instrument of her fate and prove once and for all to cocky Tom Brodie that there was more to a man than swagger and a flowery way with words.

The coarse Hawkshill farmer might have kissed her while perched on a window ledge and swept her off her feet on the dancing floor but such gestures were, by their very nature, open to deceit. And, she thought, with a little shake of the shoulders, I have enough deceit for two. What I need is an honest man who will love me without ever quite seeing through me.

She had stood by Tom Brodie's side or, rather, over him as he lay unconscious on the floor of Caddy Crawford's back room, though on one point the old witch woman had been wrong: she, Rose, had shed no tears. Now there was the matter of the house, the grand house that Mr Fergusson had promised to build for Lucas and her at the head of one of the grazing parks, a house with many windows and a view of the firth, and 'the chest of silver' that would be exchanged as a dower, though who would pay what to whom and what form it would take was Papa's business.

She touched the strings of the harp once more, then, with an impatient little sigh, pushed it away and went downstairs to inform Papa that it was time to post the wedding banns.

By midweek, spring seemed far away. Betsy and the Brodies were hard pressed by the onset of bitter weather and feeding the stock took up most of their time. Tom, playing the invalid, sprawled in his bed in the loft or lolled in the chair by the fire. He still had difficulty chewing but coped with liquids well enough to drain all the bottles on the shelves, so that not a drop of alcohol remained to warm Henry and Conn when they trailed in from work.

There were no visitors that week – Tom, it seemed, had scared them off – nor was there news from Hayes. It was far too cold to venture into town without good reason and Agnes had enough butcher meat stored in the larder to flavour soups and give body to her stews. It was, Henry said, almost like old times, except, of course, for the money in the box under his mother's bed.

It was cold everywhere, even in the house, but at least the cutting wind kept the snow at bay. Outdoor chores were done at the double, trips to the privy undertaken only out of sheer necessity. With Tom in command of the fireplace, there was precious little opportunity for intimate conversation and the evenings were whittled away in desultory chat.

'I know what Conn could do now he has no money,' said Janet.

'What's that?' said Henry.

'He could marry me,' said Janet lightly, though not quite lightly enough to deceive anyone into thinking that she did not mean it. 'You could marry me, McCaskie, an' carry me off to Ireland to cook your dinners, wash your shirts an' be your slave. What do you think of that?'

'Sure an' I think you could do better than a penniless sailor, Janet,' Conn said, though he did not dissuade her from insinuating herself on to his lap which, she claimed, was the warmest spot in Hawkshill. 'Besides, I don't need a slave. I've girls in every port from here to Madagascar leapin' o'er themselves to wash me shirts.'

'Aye, you old devil.' Janet curled a lock of his hair around her finger and gave it a tug. 'I believe you have, too, but not a one o' them a match for a good, hard-workin', God-fearin', country girl like me, innocent o' blemish an' sweet as an ear o' green corn.'

'Hoh, hoh, hoh!' Conn blew in her ear and made her giggle. 'More like a sack o' old 'taters.'

Betsy noticed how Tom's lips pursed in disapproval. This was flirting of a different order to any he had ever mastered, for Janet might be enraptured by the Irish lodger but Conn was too cautious to take advantage of her infatuation. Soon, Betsy knew, Conn would be on his way again with nothing but his mouldy goatskin vest to keep him warm at night.

She felt sorry for Janet, sorry for Conn too, but had not one drop of pity to spare for Mr Thomas Brodie who was incapable of loving anyone half so much as he loved himself.

Only God, and possibly Tassie Landles, knew what motivated Tom Brodie to leave Hawkshill before his nose had set or his bruises faded and to ride down to Hayes to chair the New Year meeting of the Bachelors' Club.

Muffled to the eyeballs, he arrived in the room above the saddler's shop to find Peter Frye on the point of calling the meeting to order. Arctic winds had not deterred the bored, hot-blooded bachelors from turning out and every chair was taken, every glass filled before Tom strode in.

'What's this?' he snapped.

'Pardon?'

Tom tossed his hat on to the table, hooked a finger into the scarf that covered his nose and mouth and tugged it down by an inch.

'I said, "What's this?"'

'Who's askin' the question?' piped up one young wag. 'Who's behind the mask? Is it Dick Turpin come back tae haunt us?'

'He's after the claret, boys. Stand an' deliver.'

'Not till he shows us his pistol.'

'If he flaunts his pistol in this weather, by God, his flint-locks'll drop off.'

Laughter and more laughter, a rolling wave of it: Peter put a hand on Tom's arm and said quietly, 'I didn't think you would show tonight.'

'Why not?'

'Because of – because the . . .' Peter stammered. 'Look, I'm sorry. I'd no intention of usurping your position as chairman. Now you're here, of course I'll stand down but, with permission, I'd like to make an announcement first.'

'An announcement?'

'I'm resigning as secretary, Tom.'

'Really? For why?'

'I am soon to go up to Edinburgh to join my brother and begin my studies in the law,' Peter said. 'In a word, I'm leaving Hayes.'

'I see,' Tom said. 'You're desertin' me too, are you?'

'Tom, I've a career to think of – family expectations – a life to lead.'

'Make your statement,' Tom said, 'an' damn you.'

He held Peter back with the flat of his hand and, standing at the head of the table, prepared to announce that the secretary had a few words to say prior to the commencement of business. He had barely opened his mouth, however, before the wags from Drennan resumed their onslaught.

'Show's your face, Mr Chairman.'

'Aye, strip aff the scarf, Tam, an' show us what she done tae you.'

It had not occurred to Tom that Rose Hewitt would be merciless enough to broadcast her account of the affair. He had prepared himself to lie, dissimulate, stand up to a ribbing, mock his misfortune and present his scars triumphantly by implying that he had taken Rose Hewitt, as promised, and had mowed her before, in the throes of ecstasy, she had reared up and stuck him on the nose. Now, in an instant, he realised that no amount of lewd detail would convince his brother bachelors that he was telling the truth.

'With the chair's permission, I – I have an announcement to make.' Peter stepped forward to rescue his friend from embarrassment. 'If you will . . .'

'Stuff an' snuff, Frye, let the man speak.'

'Aye, let's hear your excuse, Brodie, for bein' beat by a lassie.'

'Show us your smeller, Tam, give us a flash o' your neb.'

Slowly, Tom unwound the scarf from his jaw and cheeks, letting it drape across the table, then, with a flourish, tugged off the final fold, exposed his battered features and squashy blue and black nose and cried, 'There!'

The peals of laughter were as merciless as Rose Hewitt's betrayal. A strange buzzing filled his ears. If Peter had not been behind him he might have staggered from the table and fled downstairs.

The questions came thick and fast.

'*She* done that? Hewitt's daughter?'

'Nah, nah, not her but her lover.'

'I thought Tam was her lover. Who's her lover, then?'

'Fergusson's lad.'

'Lucas Fergusson? *He* done that?'

It was out, all of it, the squalid truth, the whole damnable truth, witnessed, attested and unimpeachable.

'Aye,' the wag from Drennan crowed. 'My old granddad saw it. He was there in Caddy's when it happened.'

'Lucas Fergusson? Lucas Fergusson broke Tom's nose?'

'Caught him in the act, did he?'

'Never got near the act, did you, Tom? Well, did you?'

He looked down the table at the jolly young reprobates whom he had brought together in the first place and over whom he had ruled for three happy years. He knew that he would rule over them no more. Whatever he said, whatever he did, whatever amorous conquests he added to his score, he would never again be their senator, their hero.

'No,' he said nobly. 'No, I did not get Miss Hewitt's cutty off, nor even her gloves. I elected to follow the path of decency an' preserve my moral integrity for my bride-to-be.'

'Liar, liar! She's not goin' to marry you, Tom Brodie.'

'She's goin' to marry Fergusson.'

'What?' Tom shouted. 'When?'

'The banns were posted in Drennan kirk last Sunday.'

'In four weeks she'll be at the altar by Lucas Fergusson's side.'

'In four weeks she'll be the virgin o' Thimble Row no more.'

The laughter throbbed in his ears and made the bones of his face ache. His eyes began to water and a thin trickle of mucus dripped from his nostrils. He wiped it from his upper lip with his sleeve. Then, before he broke into pieces, he put his hat on his head, wrapped the scarf about his neck and bowed, bowed low and deep, and, clinging to the last vestige of his pride, brushed past Peter and left his brother bachelors to their mockery, knowing full well that he would never run with their like again.

24

'Jamaica?' Conn said. 'Nay, Tom, I've never visited the West Indies.'

'What prompted that question?' said Henry.

'A fellow I encountered at a Mason meeting some months ago put the idea into my head. His life's become such a miserable muddle that he's seekin' passage to Kingston to start afresh.'

'Doin' what?' Betsy asked.

'Book-keeper on a sugar plantation,' Tom answered. 'There are employments aplenty in the Indies for educated men.'

'You're no book-keeper,' Henry said. 'You're a farmer bred in the bone.'

'I can read, write an' count as well as any man,' Tom said. 'What's to keep me here? Hawkshill isn't large enough to support us all.'

'Then why not look for a place of your own?'

'Without a wife?' Tom said. 'No sense in that.'

'So it's lack of a wife that's skewed your thoughts to strikin' out for the Indies,' Conn said. 'Hardly a sound reason, to my way o' thinkin'.'

'That girl, Rose Hewitt,' Janet put in, 'broke more than Tom's nose when she turned him down. She's marryin' Lucas Fergusson instead.'

Walter Fergusson and Neville Hewitt had pooled their resources and were planning a great wedding feast, news of which had swiftly drifted down to Hayes. It was rumoured that

Mr Arbuthnot had been summoned to put together an assembly in Fergusson's largest barn which had already been cleared and floored. Every dealer and drover with whom Fergusson had ever done business would be invited and a dozen hand-picked dairymaids – Nancy Ames was not one of them – would be Rose's bridal attendants and provide an arch of evergreens for the couple to walk through after the service.

Whenever Janet returned from Hayes with more gossip, Tom stalked off, sulking, to walk the fields alone. At home, in the evenings, he was curt with Henry and contemptuous of Janet's wagging tongue. He spoke civilly only to his mother and, rather more civilly, to Betsy. He made no further attempt to lure her out to the barn after dark, though, and demonstrated a measure of respect that did not, in Betsy's book, pass muster as affection and was pitched so low that she had no idea that she was being wooed.

It surprised her when Tom suggested that he might quit Scotland. He had gone so far as to write to an agent in Greenock who was employed by plantation owners to find suitable 'honest, hard-working young men' willing to travel to Jamaica now that the war with America was over and trade terms settled.

'What will your passage cost?' Agnes asked.

'Not a penny,' Tom answered. 'My employer pays for the passage.'

'How long's the term of employment?' said Conn.

'Five years.'

'An' then,' said Janet, 'I suppose you'll come sailin' back to Hayes wi' money spillin' from every pocket to flaunt yourself in front o' Rose Hewitt an' show her what she missed in choosin' Lucas Fergusson o'er you?'

'I may not come back at all,' said Tom.

'Aye,' said Conn quietly, 'you might die over there o' the swamp fever.'

'Is your mind made up on this venture, son?' Agnes asked.

'No, but I'm givin' it careful thought.'

'What of your friends?' said Henry.

'I have no friends.'

'Balderdash!' said Henry. 'There's Frye, for a start.'

'He's off to Edinburgh next month to study law.'

'Mr Ogilvy then?'

'Ogilvy treats me coldly,' Tom said. 'I'm not inclined to fan the flames o' a friendship extinguished through no fault o' mine.'

'No fault o' yours?' said Janet. 'Whose fault is it then?'

'If you don't hold your scoldin' tongue . . .' Tom threatened, then thought better of it. 'I've nothin' an' nobody to keep me here.'

Losing patience, Henry snapped, 'This is preposterous. You've no intention o' sailin' off to Jamaica an' leavin' us short-handed when we've a crop in the ground.'

'Hire day-labourers,' Tom told him. 'I'm easily replaced.'

'What about Conn?' said Janet. 'He'll help out with the harvest.'

'Now, lass, now,' Conn said warily. 'Sure an' I'm not for stayin' much longer. I've imposed on you long enough.'

'Will you just up an' leave me, Conn?' said Janet.

'Ireland's just across the water. I'll not be far away.'

'You will,' Janet said tearfully. 'You will, you will. Nobody wants me, not even you.' Then, to no one's surprise, she rushed off into the back room and slammed the door.

For a moment no one spoke, then, rising from her seat by the fire, Agnes went into the alcove and, kneeling, dragged the cashbox from beneath the bed. She carried it in both hands to the table and put it down, drew out a chair, pushed up her sleeves, then seated herself, and opened it.

'What are you doin', Mother?' Henry enquired.

'Lookin' for an answer,' Agnes told him.

'It's a cashbox, Mammy,' Tom said gruffly, 'not a crystal ball.'

She spilled the coins on to the table and spread them with her palms. She picked out crowns, guineas and shillings with nimble fingers and, with everyone gathered round the table, watching, quickly separated the contents of the box into three neat piles.

'Now,' she said, 'here's an answer; one answer for each of you.'

'Is this a trick, Mother?' said Henry.

'Are you goin' to make it disappear before our very eyes?' said Tom.

'That's exactly what I'm goin' to do,' Agnes said. 'Your daddy would have called our windfall the root of evil. For him there was no gain that didn't involve sufferin'. I've never let on about this before but he had his opportunities, aye, more o' them than you might imagine, but pride meant more to him than advancement. A good, God-fearin' man, that's what folk thought o' him. He was nothin' o' the sort. He'd no stomach for change. When change was forced upon him' – she glanced at Tom – 'then it was always change for the worse. It had to be, to justify his fears.'

'Fears?' Tom said. 'My daddy was the bravest—'

'Your daddy was a coward,' said Agnes. 'All his life long he hid behind prejudice an' injustice an' told himself he was the better for it, that bowin' down to fate made him superior. Well, there was nothin' superior about him, I'm sorry to say. If he hadn't died – aye, he did die bravely, I'll admit – then we'd be condemned to do as he did an' suffer for his principles.' She tapped the table lightly. 'So, here's money, here's cash, here are gains ill-gotten enough to bring the law down on us an' cause your father to turn in his grave. But here's chance too, here's change, here's opportunity, the hand fate dealt us through Mr McCaskie. Is it enough to test your mettle an' shine a light, like a noon-day candle, on what you really want from life?'

'Freedom,' Betsy blurted out, before she could help herself.

'Freedom it is.' Agnes Brodie looked up at Betsy and smiled. 'Freedom – within reason – to choose your future. Does that make you uncomfortable?'

'Not me, Mammy,' said Henry. 'I know what I want.'

'Fair spring weather an' an early crop? Those things aren't in the box, son, but a half-year's rent is.'

'I'll settle for that,' said Henry. 'Thirty-five pounds will do me fine.'

'An' you, Mr McCaskie?'

'You owe me nothin', Mrs Brodie. What I lost, I lost through my own stupidity. It'll be up to me to redeem it as best I can. Sure an' the money isn't mine to share, it's yours.'

'No, it's Janet's.'

'Janet's?' said Tom.

'Thirty pounds is Janet's dowry,' Agnes said. 'Isn't that a sum worth havin' for a man in your straitened circumstances, Mr McCaskie?'

'She loves you, Conn,' Betsy reminded him.

'I know she does,' Conn said, 'but if I take Janet to Ireland with me, it'll not be for the sake o' thirty pounds. I'll take her because I know she'll make me a good wife.'

'An' will you take her?'

'Do you know,' Conn said, 'I really think I will.'

'Hoh!' Tom said. 'You call that freedom, do you?'

His mother turned in the chair and, before he could retreat, caught his arm. 'What about you, Thomas? What do you want? How will you change your life for ever? There's thirty pounds here for you, an' a few shillin's left over, an' then the box is empty.'

'Aye, an' we're back just where we started,' Tom said.

'Oh, no, we're not,' Agnes told him. 'We're changed, all changed.'

'I think my daddy was right,' Tom said, squirming. 'That damned money *is* the root o' all evil.'

'Because it forces you to make a choice?' said Henry. 'Ah, Tom, when did opportunity become a curse? There, see what Mother's offerin' you. Put your thirty pounds in a purse an' catch the coach to Greenock, book passage on the next ship to Jamaica, become a book-keeper, or an overseer, or whatever occupation takes your fancy or, if that's all too much for you, pour the damned lot over your throat an' whore it all away.'

'Or find a wife,' said Agnes, 'an' stay.'

She released his arm and allowed him to step away from the table. He folded his arms and with his head cocked and a curious little smile on the corner of his lips, said, 'An' where, pray tell me, will I find a wife who'll take on a man like me?'

'Findin' women has never been your problem, Tom,' said Henry. 'Keepin' one is another matter.'

'Look at my face,' said Tom. 'Who'll want me now?'

'There's nothin' much wrong with your face,' said Henry. 'Oh, I see, you've found another excuse for bein' choosy.'

'Choosy?' Tom said. 'Nah, nah. I'm not choosy.' He straightened his shoulders and threw out his chest. 'What about you, Miss Betsy McBride? Will you marry me?'

From the corner of her eye Betsy saw Henry stiffen. She caught, too, the smug little smile that crossed Agnes Brodie's lips and knew that she was being used once more.

'Oh, no, Tom,' she said, quite evenly, 'not in a thousand years.'

Henry was no ploughman, at least not in his brother's view. Preparing the small field for barley on cold dry February days taxed his patience. He had set the coulter wide but, even so, the blade clogged and the horses baulked if he did not hold them tightly to the furrows while he scraped away the clay.

He had no reason to tackle the small field yet. The Scottish winter was by no means spent. Snow might arrive as late as March or April and thaw and rain combined wash out his hard labour. His one consolation was that Betsy came out to help him; Betsy had a way with the big horses, half cajoling, half commanding. She was good with sheep too and after Tom had gone to Greenock to register his name for passage to Kingston, she took charge of the lambing ewes and freed Henry to improve his skill with the plough.

Conn had left for Dublin but his promise to come back soon had been so heartfelt and sincere that Janet had wept on Betsy's shoulder for only half the night and, putting on a brave face, had pitched herself into the extra chores that Tom's absence had thrown up.

Henry had no doubt that Tom would return from Greenock. He had taken only five pounds from his share of the kitty and while he might be tempted to abandon his horses, his dogs and his family, he would not, Henry felt sure, leave twenty-five pounds lying on the table. There was also the question of whether or not Tom would expunge his anger at Betsy as well as Rose Hewitt in the stews of the port town and return chastened, if not apologetic, to Hawkshill as if he had never heard of Jamaica.

Henry's relief at Betsy's outright refusal to leap into Tom's arms was marred by anxiety. He was not at all sure six months' breathing space in the matter of rent would be enough to bring the farm to profit. If Tom did quit Hawkshill, he would have to hire hands for the harvest and wage a man to help with the horses and cattle, and if, as seemed likely, Janet went off to Ireland with Connor McCaskie, his mother would need help in the house.

The small field was so close to the home pasture that Henry could make out the cottage and the tail of the track as he ploughed. It was a level field and, though it had not been touched by a blade in five years, he was well aware that Tom would have ripped through it in not much more than a day.

He had been at it for almost three when, an hour after dinner time, he saw his brother clambering over the gate at the tail of the yard. He jigged the rein and let out a bark that he hoped would make the horses pull more willingly but Tom was upon him before he had carved out more than another foot or two of the unyielding soil.

'Do you call this ploughin'?' Tom's tone was critical, not teasing. 'I've seen moles dig a straighter line.'

'You're back then?'

'Aye, I'm back.'

'All booked to sail the seven seas, are you?'

'That I am.'

'When?'

'As soon as the agent assembles a cargo.'

'Next week, next month, next year?'

'By the month's end,' said Tom.

'Oh!' said Henry. 'Your mind's made up then, is it?'

'It is,' Tom told him. 'I'll be employed by a sugar merchant on a plantation near Kingston.'

Henry's shoulders slumped. He rested his forearms on the handle of the plough and stared at the ground. 'I never thought you'd go through with it, Tom,' he said. 'I thought your heart was here.'

'I have no heart,' said Tom. 'Daddy told you that often enough.'

'So,' Henry said, 'we helped him away for nothin'.'

'You still have the farm. I'll assign my share to you in writin', sealed an' delivered. It'll be up to you to square up to that graspin' bugger Hewitt from now on; up to you to care for Mammy an' . . .'

'Why are you doin' this, Tom?'

'Because there's nothin' left for me here.'

'Did that girl mean so much to you?'

'Rose? Nah, not Rose.'

'Do you mean to say Betsy . . .'

'Betsy?' Tom gathered saliva in his mouth and dropped a frothy white globule on to the earth. 'She was Daddy's choice, not mine. When she turned me down, my promise to Daddy lost all meanin'. Now, thank God, I can be rid o' him once and for all. Besides, Betsy McBride comes with nothin' to recommend her but a good pair o' shoulders an' strong thighs.'

'That's enough, Tom. I won't stand by an' hear you slander her.'

'Aye, I thought you'd a fancy for to bed her.'

'To marry her, Tom, if she'll have me.'

'She'll never have *you*, Henry, nor will you ever have her, as a bride or a lover. Once I'm gone she'll leave you. Mark my words, the only reason Rankine's whore put up with us was to get her hands on me. Well, I gave her what she wanted an' I'd have given her more o' it too if she'd been worth the bother – which, by the way, she was not.'

'Why are you tellin' me this?'

'Confession, Henry, is very good for the soul, so they say.' Tom laughed. 'I just don't want you to be disappointed if ever you do happen to get between her legs, unlikely as that may be. Our Miss McBride's after more than you can give her, even with a share o' McCaskie's money an' Mammy's blessing to help you along. It was me Betsy wanted an' me she's had. She'll not settle now for second best.'

Henry's face was as white as bog-cotton, his lips very red. He turned away and studied the smoke from the cottage chimney. 'Didn't it occur to you, Thomas,' he said, at length, 'that Betsy turned you down because she was disappointed in *you*, that as far as Miss McBride's concerned *you* turned out to be second best?'

'What can you offer her that I can't?'

'Love,' said Henry.

'Love?' Tom said scornfully. 'Pish an' piddle; that's love for you.'

'Is that what you told Rose Hewitt?' Henry said. 'Aye, it's small wonder Lukie Fergusson poked you on the snout.'

'He caught me by surprise, that's all.'

'He caught Rose Hewitt by surprise, too, it seems,' said Henry. 'Well, perhaps you'll fare better with the ladies in the Indies, Tom. Perhaps you'll learn . . . Ah, never mind. Go on your way with your stupid pride intact, an' let me get on with my ploughin'.'

'Here,' Tom said, reaching, 'give me the reins.'

'Damned if I will,' said Henry and, shaking off his brother's hand, urged on the horses through the clay.

As a child Agnes had heard tales of witches and warlocks and been warned against consorting with the devil or any of his wily henchmen. After she had married Matthew Brodie, she had learned about the nature of good and evil from her husband's daily readings from the Old Testament. She had also listened attentively to Mr Turbot who preached a gospel of forgiveness and redemption. But, not being much of a reader, she had never heard of the Greek gods and goddesses and how, to punish mankind, they had created the first woman, Pandora, to whom Tom had compared her with a shade too much venom to mean it as a compliment.

She cared about Tom, loved him as only a mother could love such an errant son, but she was not blind to his failings or the wayward beast that lurked within him, his selfishness. The only man who had ever had control over her first-born was his father for he, in his way, had been equally stubborn and selfish.

She had not forgotten the October afternoon when they had gathered about Matthew's sickbed and how shockingly tender the moment had been, how Tom had wept when his father had whispered in his ear and how, minutes later, had pressed his fists into the bolster and how in that final act of martyrdom her husband had restored his governance over them; nor could she explain the strange mixture of emotions that had tumbled through her when the bolster was peeled away and she had peered into Matt's sightless eyes and at his mouth, weirdly twisted in a last little farewell grimace, so tight that it was almost a smirk.

'What,' Janet said, 'if he doesn't come back?'

'Then you're better off without him,' Agnes told her.

'But I love him, Mammy.'

'Aye, you've made that plain enough.'

They were scrubbing shirts in the big wooden tub in the stable. Drawn from the drum of the mash-boiler, the water smelled of oats and, when Agnes added a lump of soft brown soap, foamed into slimy suds.

'Don't you think he's a good man?'

'I think he's a very good man,' said Agnes. 'If I didn't, would I have given him thirty pounds to take you off my hands? If you're convinced Conn McCaskie's the man for you, then it doesn't matter what I think of him.'

'What if he's caught and sent to prison?'

'Then you'll stand by him.'

'I will, I will,' said Janet. 'What if he's killed, though?'

'It'll take more than a stray ball from a revenue musket to kill McCaskie,' said Agnes. 'But if he is killed, if he drowns, say, you'll have him to cherish in your memory. You'll have him by you for always.'

'I've never heard you talk like this,' Janet said. 'I never knew you were so clever.'

'Nothin' clever about me,' Agnes told her. 'If I was clever, dearest, I'd find a way to keep you here but' – she shrugged – 'I'm not clever enough for that. If Conn McCaskie's your man an' you've no fear o' goin' off with him to see where life will lead, then you must do it.' She sat back on her heels and poked the bulging bubble of a shirt-tail with the beater. 'Who'd have thought half a year ago that there would be such grand choices for us to make. Your brother, Tom, might tell you the smuggler's money has ruined us but that's his fancy, not mine – an' not yours either, I hope.'

'What'll you do without us, Mammy? What'll happen to you?'

Agnes laughed. 'Who knows? One day, perhaps Mr Dingle will come ridin' down the hill in his jingly wagon with his girls all about him an' give me another clock.'

'Another clock?' said Janet. 'Is one clock not enough for you?'

'Not when you're my age, dear,' Agnes told her, and, pushing up her sleeves, attacked the dirty washing with her stick.

It had taken Rose an age to persuade her father to let her accompany him on his visit to Hawkshill. She had no reasonable excuse with which to bolster her request and, in the end, had been forced to resort to childish wheedling which, to her surprise, had eventually won her father round.

Eunice Prole might have had something to do with it, too. Rose had overheard her father and the housekeeper discussing the matter, which made a change from endless arguments about bridal gowns and bouquets and whether or not it would be fitting for Mrs Prole to be seen in public on Neville's arm.

'Why, though, why? Tell me that, Eunice. Why does she wish to go up to that dismal farm with me? Is it to throw herself into Brodie's arms or flaunt her pending marriage in his ugly face? Or, God save us, is she havin' second thoughts about marryin' young Fergusson?'

'No, Neville, certainly not that.'

'How can you be sure?'

'Because I'm a woman.'

'Oh, that old excuse.'

'Neville, take my word on it, she's in love with Lucas Fergusson. If there is a wistful element in her desire to look upon Brodie one last time I see no harm in it. Indeed, when she surveys the squalor in which the Brodies reside, she will, I imagine, heave a sigh of relief at her narrow escape an' go skippin' all the more eagerly to the altar.'

'Hmm! You have a point there, Eunice.'

'You're not goin' to fight with Brodie, are you?'

'No, I merely wish to see for myself what improvements he has planned an' to find out, if I can, where the cash came from. It is, after all, still my property an' I'm entitled to inspect it from time to time.'

'Hire a trap then, an' take Rose with you.'

Crouching in the hall, ears pricked, Rose murmured under her breath, 'Please, Papa, please.' And when she heard her father say, 'Oh, very well, Eunice. On your head be it,' she felt her heart skip a beat – though why this should be when she was betrothed to Lucas she could not properly explain, not even to herself.

Her engagement to marry Lucas and tie the Hewitts' fortunes to the Fergussons' had mellowed her father. He was almost, if not quite, reconciled to putting up with the Brodies for another half-dozen years and, with Eunice's warning not to lose his temper ringing in his ears, drove the hired trap at a gentle trot from Drennan to Hayes and up the steep track to Hawkshill.

She had put on her best dress, topped with the warm blue cape and a small mushroom-shaped hat with a modest feather that would not bob distractingly in her eyes or hide her ringlets. With Eunice's collusion she had touched her cheeks with rouge and dabbed a little on her lips, just enough to suggest that she was a girl no more.

The trap trundled into the yard. Her father loudly ordered the pony to 'whoa'. She sat perfectly still and composed on the board, hands in her lap, and peeped around the fold of the hood as Henry Brodie came out of the cottage and, at precisely the same moment, Tom emerged from the barn.

He looked quite different in a grubby coat and patched breeches, so different that for a second she failed to recognise him and wondered if there was a third male Brodie, a brother she hadn't heard of, some skinny half-wit whom the family had hidden away.

He stepped up to the trap and snapped, 'It's you, is it, Hewitt? What the devil do you want with us now?'

'A wee bit courtesy would do for a start,' her father retorted and clambered down from the board. 'I hear you've made improvements an' have a crop of Siberian wheat already in the ground. It's my right—'

'Your right?' Tom barked. 'What right have you—'

Henry caught Tom by the arm and pulled him back. 'As you well know, Mr Hewitt, we do have wheat in the ground an' every sign of an early crop. I'll walk you out there if you wish to see for yourself.'

Papa glanced round at her and shook his head. There were three women in the yard now, two by the door of an out-building and another, Tom's mother, on the step by the cottage door.

They made no move towards her and Rose guessed there would be no offer of refreshment, not even tea. They watched her with the same dumbstruck lack of comprehension that she had noticed in cattle. She felt her nervousness ebb and, twisting on the board, gave them her scrutiny. She was, she realised, superior to all of them, even the tall, broad-shouldered, fair-haired young woman who had come to the dance with Henry and who, with hands on hips, stared back at her now, unblinking.

'He's not interested in wheat, Henry,' Tom said. 'He's caught some rumour about my departure an' he's come to see if it's true.'

'Your departure?' Papa said. 'What's this?'

'Look at him, Henry, did you ever see such a miserable show o' innocence,' Tom said. 'That's why he brought her along, to soften me up an' loosen my tongue. Well, Mr Hewitt, you've no need for such duplicity.'

She looked round in spite of herself and, raising herself up, met Tom's eye. He was not Tom Brodie, not the Tom Brodie who had danced her feet off the floor, not the Tom Brodie who had kissed her, who had promised to love her until his dying day. He was another man, another fellow altogether. She felt a tiny, needle-like dart of pity for the damage she had done to him, though the disjointed nose did not detract one jot from his arrogant aura of masculinity which, even now, made her catch her breath.

'*Are* you leaving us, Mr Brodie?' she heard herself say.

'I am, Miss Hewitt. I'm bound for the West Indies in a week or so.'

'I – I do not think that we had heard that, no.'

'Then why are you here?'

Once more Henry intervened. 'Mr Hewitt's entitled to know what's happenin' in respect o' the lease, Tom.'

'What?' her papa said shrilly. 'Are you relinquishin' the lease?'

'No,' Henry said. 'I'm takin' it over.'

'I'll need a document, proof o' sole tenancy,' her father said.

'You'll have it, never fear,' Tom said. 'You can't stop me leavin'.'

'I've no intention of stopping you,' Papa said. 'On the contrary.'

'What do you mean by that?' Tom said. 'What concern is it o' yours what I do with myself now you've got her married to Fergusson's money?'

'Tom!' Henry said firmly. 'Leave this to me, please.' Then, talking all the while, he led her papa across the yard to a gate that looked out over the fields.

She folded her hands into her lap again and sat stock still, waiting.

He came to her, as she knew he would.

He put a hand on the rail and a foot on the step. For a moment, she thought that he was about to leap up, snatch at the reins and drive off with her.

She turned her head and looked down on him.

'Why didn't you wait for me?' he said quietly.

'I might have waited for you all my life.'

'Did you set no store by my promise?'

'Promises are too easy to make, too easy to break.'

'Huh!' he said. 'I didn't give you enough attention, I suppose. I didn't fawn over you like young Fergusson.'

'Think that if you will,' she said. 'It's far from the truth.'

'It wasn't a fair fight, you know.'

'Oh, yes,' she said. 'I'm well aware of that.'

'I'd have beaten him soundly in a fair fight.'

'I don't doubt it,' Rose said. 'Are you about to tell me I have broken your heart, driven you out of your home and sent you chasing off to the Indies to forget me?'

He laughed dryly. 'If I did, would you believe me?'

'Certainly not.'

'Ah, you're no fool, Miss Hewitt.'

'Are you really leaving us, Tom?'

'As soon as I have passage, aye.'

'The old woman, Tassie Landles – do you know who I mean?'

He nodded. 'I know her.'

'I sought my fortune from her not so long ago. I begged her for answers but she would not give me answers. She told me that all the answers were within me and that I must write my own future.'

'Well, you've done that, it seems,' Tom said.

'Yes,' Rose said. 'I have.'

'Without me?'

'Without you.'

He blew out his cheeks and stepped down from the side of the trap. He looked towards the gate and, following his gaze, Rose saw that her father and Henry Brodie were returning.

'Goodbye, Rose,' he said.

'Goodbye, Tom,' she answered and watched him turn away, knowing or, rather, hoping that they would never meet again.

25

There was, said Conn, a bit of urgency in the matter of departure, for at two o'clock that afternoon the vessel would be loaded and ready to sail from the coal company's wharf to the north of the harbour. He timed their arrival in Ayr almost to the minute, since the town was alive with revenue officers brought in by tender from a cutter in the roads. He was not conceited enough to suppose that King George had ordered the crew out to hunt for him, as he was a small fish in the smuggling pond, but he was cautious, very cautious now he had a bride in tow and a clean slate awaiting him in Dublin.

It had all been arranged in such a hurry that Agnes was still calling instructions to the Irishman while Henry and Betsy tossed the blushing bride-to-be's baggage into the cart and Tom hitched up the horse.

Conn had arrived at Hawkshill, breathless and footsore, soon after breakfast. He had ridden from Ayr on the early morning coach and had raced up the hill from the toll road as fast as his sea-legs would carry him.

His mouldy goatskin waistcoat and salt-stained trews had been replaced by a sober, second-hand coat and dark brown breeches. A tall hat was perched precariously on his curly locks which, to Betsy's dismay, had been trimmed so close to his scalp that he looked almost bald. Her piratical hero had been transformed into a respectable, slightly down-at-heel merchant who, if he crouched a little, might pass unnoticed in any town in Europe.

Crouch he did, too, not only crouch but kneel in the muck of the yard. Taking Janet's hand, he asked if she would be willing to put the cart before the horse, as it were, and accompany him that very afternoon across the Irish Sea to Dublin town where, on his solemn oath as a smuggler re-formed, he would marry her before a magistrate, or in a Protestant church, if that was her wish.

'Marry you?' said Janet, scowling. 'Marry *you*?'

'Sure an' there's nobody else kneelin' at your feet, is there?'

'That's true,' Janet replied. 'Let me think about it.'

'Well, think about it quick, sweetheart, for there's a ketch moored at the coal wharf in Ayr an' while it might not be a barge o' burnished gold, it's headed towards Ireland an' has passage booked for the pair o' us.'

'If I turn you down, McCaskie, will you get your fare back?'

'Nay, I will not.'

'Then I'll say *yes*,' Janet told him. '*Yes, yes, yes*,' and with a shriek loud enough to set the dogs barking, leapt into his arms and knocked him, sprawling, on to his broad backside.

It had been many years since Betsy had been in Ayr. Her brothers had taken her there once as a treat but she could remember little about the outing, as it had rained for most of the day and she had been miserable. There was no rain that afternoon, no sunshine either. The town looked anything but gay as the cart clattered over an old bridge into an avenue of warehouses and on to a wooden wharf surrounded by jibs and masts and great heaps of coal.

Betsy glimpsed the sea and, across the mouth of a river, saw-pits and a line of houses, rather grand, and above them some form of fortification. She had no opportunity to sightsee, though, for Conn yelled, 'There, there, man, over there,' and, a moment later, Henry reined the horse to a halt.

'Is that it?' Henry said. 'Is that your boat?'

'Aye, be quick.' Conn helped Janet down. 'See, they're ready to cast off.' He slung the bags under his arms and, ushering Janet before him, bounced across the gangplank before Henry or Betsy could leave the cart.

'Good God!' said Henry. 'She's nothin' but a floatin' coal hole.'

'Aye,' said Betsy, 'but look at the name on her bow.'

Henry grunted. 'The *Delight*: how appropriate.'

The plank was pulled in, ropes splashed into the sludgy water. On the deck below the mizzen mast Conn shook hands with a small man in a pea-jacket and woollen cap. There were crew all about, six or eight men. They leapt to their stations and the ketch dipped sluggishly and inclined her bow away from the quay. The big sails swelled, the small canvases above the bow filled and the *Delight*, catching the wind, swung out and headed for the open sea.

With Conn's arm safe about her, Janet leaned on the gunwale and waved until the ketch slipped behind the headland and sea and sky swallowed her up.

'Oh, my!' said Henry. 'My, my my!' and, slumping over the reins, covered his face with his hands.

He found her in the garden behind the cottage. She was feeding hens and had upon her shoulder a plump white dove that nibbled corn meal from her hand and, when she neglected it, nipped at her ear like a parrot.

There was little enough wind to stir the trees. Even the rumble of the river was muted that calm, cold, February afternoon. The garden was already green, far greener than the season justified, and, not for the first time, Peter wondered just what sort of magic his aunt practised.

His appearance in the garden caused Tassie no surprise.

She gave the dove a little tap to send it winging back to the cote.

'Where did you put the bottle?' she said.

'On the table indoors.'

'Brandy?'

'Yes.'

'French?'

'Sold as such, yes.'

'How is your mother?'

'She's well. I came to tell you—'

'That Tom Brodie's headed for the Indies.'

'How did you know that?' Peter asked. 'Did some spirit tell you?'

'Aye, a great black demon rode up tae my door on a stallion snortin' fire just for to tell me Tam Brodie's off to the sugar plantin's.' Shaking her head at her nephew's credulity, she scattered the last of the meal on to the grass and laid aside the feeding bowl. 'Just what do you take me for, Peter?'

'I really don't know what you are, Auntie.'

'I'm a poor old woman, shunned by her family, who sells eggs for to keep body an' soul together, that's what I am.' She came forward and pinched his cheek. 'Rose Hewitt's maid told me about Brodie. Is that spirit enough for you?'

'And the – the other thing?'

'What other thing would that be?'

'Oh, no, Aunt Tassie,' Peter said. 'Don't feign ignorance, if you please. You know perfectly well what "other thing" I'm talking about. Whatever frightened you enough to walk to Hayes at All Hallows' was something much darker in its origins than Rose Hewitt's day-maid.'

'Aye, there are precious few flies on you, Peter Frye,' the old woman conceded. 'Some day you'll make a fine advocate. When do you leave?'

'No,' Peter said. 'I'll not allow you to distract me. I'll answer your question only after you've answered mine. The ghost, the spirit, that – that thing from beyond, has it visited you again?'

'Now why would it come tae me again?'

'Aunt Tassie, has he gone?'

'Brodie? Not yet. Soon.'

'I don't mean Tom. I mean—'

'Are you askin' if Tom Brodie's quittin' Scotland in the hope o' leavin' his daddy behind?'

'That,' Peter said, 'is more or less the substance of it.'

'Though he sails tae the ends o' the earth,' Tassie said, 'he'll never leave his daddy behind. It's not his reason for quittin' Scotland, though. He's not bein' driven out by a ghost.'

'Then it must be the girl, Rose Hewitt. God, how I wish we'd never connived to bring them together. She brought him nothing but misery.'

'Aye,' Tassie said, 'but Tom Brodie showed *her* the way to happiness, did he not? Besides, if it hadn't been the flax man's daughter some other lassie would have brought Brodie down.'

Peter nodded. 'I fear you may be right, Aunt Tassie.'

'There will be another lassie, too, more than one, in fact.'

'Is that the cat talking, or have you heard from your friend Jervis again?'

'Jarvis,' Tassie corrected him. 'Nah, nah. There's no door wide enough to admit that rogue at this season o' the year. But anyone with half an eye can see Rose Hewitt's better off with her daft boy than she'd ever be with Brodie. He's the sort o' man a woman might enjoy as a plaything but only a woman as selfish as he is would ever mistake him for a husband. For all I've seen an' heard o' your friend Brodie, the Indies may be the best place for him.' She latched her arm though her nephew's and guided him towards the cottage. 'Now, Peter, tell me, when do you set out for Leiden to begin your study o' the law?'

'Edinburgh, Aunt Tassie,' Peter said. 'It's Edinburgh, not Leiden.'

'Is it now?' the old woman said. 'Is it really?' And, hiding a knowing little smile, led her nephew indoors for a drink.

⋆　　⋆　　⋆

They ate fried fish and drank ale at a tavern near the quay before, with daylight fading, they set off along the old toll road to Drennan, Hayes, and home.

Henry was very quiet. Betsy sensed that his sister's abrupt departure for an uncertain life in Dublin had caught him off guard. Tom, too, would be gone soon and Henry left to tend the farm with only two women to help him.

She preferred not to dwell on Henry's need to hire hands or on the disasters that might mar the months ahead. She thought, rather, of the ewes in the fold under the oaks, how in eight weeks' time there would be lambs to look after; how the bull would be brought up from Braystock's farm and how, in due course, there would be calves to nurse. Then she thought of the barn, empty of Tom's presence, and the loft above the kitchen, and how, after the rent had been paid there would be nothing to look forward to but more hard work and worry.

It was dark before they reached Drennan. Henry stopped to light a lantern which he hung from the pole above the horse's crupper. When he climbed into the cart again, Betsy draped an arm about his shoulder.

'What's that for?' he said.

'In case you think I'm leavin' too.'

'I wouldn't blame you if you did.'

'You won't get rid o' me that easily, Mr Brodie.'

'Is that a threat, Miss McBride?'

'More o' a promise,' Betsy said, and wrapped her other arm about his waist to steady him as the cart rattled over the Ramshead bridge.

Tom said, 'I've received a letter from the agent. I'll be off the day after tomorrow an' sail from Greenock on the mornin' tide on Friday.'

'When did this letter arrive?' his mother asked.

'I collected it from the carrier at the foot o' the hill an hour ago.'

'Show it to me.'

'Nah, nah,' Tom said. 'It'll only cause you to cry.'

'Do I look as if I'm ready to cry? Show it to me.'

'There's nothin' in it, Mam,' Tom told her. 'Besides, I've already packed it in my wallet in the big valise.'

'Packin' already?' Henry said. 'Can't you wait to be on your way?'

'Now the decision's been made,' Tom said, 'there's no point in loiterin'. Have you finished the small field?'

'It's done,' said Henry, 'for now.'

'When'll you plant?'

'March, if possible.'

'Daddy always ploughed three times before he sowed barley.'

'I'm well aware o' that.'

'Four bushels the acre will do it. Have you money to buy more seed?'

'What if I say no, Tom? Will you leave me some o' your share?'

'Not me,' said Tom. 'I lugged those casks up from the shore too, if you recall, an' earned every penny. Talkin' of which, Mammy, I'd like it now.'

'Show me the letter first.'

'Twenty-five pounds is the balance due to me,' Tom said. 'God knows, it's a cheap enough price to be shot o' me. If Betsy won't have me, Henry, maybe she'll have you now the field's clear.'

'But you wouldn't put a wager on it?' said Henry.

'Nah, nah, that I wouldn't do. Mammy, my money, please.'

'After you show me—'

'Now,' Tom snapped. 'Count it out now, you miserable old bitch, or I'll fetch it from the box myself.'

'There's no letter, is there?' Agnes Brodie said.

'Of course there's a bloody letter. If I wasn't sailin' for the Indies why would I need that money?'

With a glance at Henry and a shake of the head, Agnes went to the alcove, brought out the cashbox and counted out twenty-five pounds. Tom scooped the coins from the table and transferred them to the pocket of his coat.

'McCaskie's two bullocks,' he said, 'are as fat as they'll ever be after the feed you've stuffed into them. They'll fetch three times what you paid him an' more if you treat them to one more summer's grazin'.'

'Yes,' said Henry. 'I know.'

'Don't sell them to Fergusson, though.'

'I'll sell to whoever pays me the best price.'

'Not Fergusson, damn it, not Fergusson.'

'Perhaps old Braystock'll take them.'

'Aye,' Tom said, 'anyone but Fergusson. I'm not helpin' him pay for her damned weddin'.'

At that moment Betsy arrived home for dinner and Tom, without so much as a nod, turned on his heel and clambered up the ladder to the loft.

'What's bitin' him now?' said Betsy.

'He sails on Friday for Kingston,' Henry told her. 'He received a letter with boardin' instructions from the agent just an hour ago.'

'Or so he says,' said Agnes.

Supper was taken early. Conversation around the table was very subdued and, soon after the plates were cleared away, Betsy went to bed.

The bed seemed vast and quite uncomfortable with Janet no longer beside her. Betsy tossed and turned for an hour or more, going over in her mind how she really felt about Tom's departure. He had made it clear that he would not put up with weeping and wailing and had no intention of visiting any of his friends to make sentimental farewells; nor, he said emphatically, did he wish his mother or Henry to show up in Greenock to wave him off. He would depart with dignity, as befitted a man who had been betrayed by everyone he trusted; a remark that caused Henry to snort and Agnes to *tut* and shake her head.

There was more to Tom's flight than wounded pride, Betsy told herself, though she could not help but wonder if her rejection had been the final straw. If a penniless farm servant turned him down what hope was left for him in Hayes? She felt no guilt, however; no pity for handsome Tom Brodie who had treated her so callously. If he had not assumed she would be flattered by his sexual attentions she might have given in to the faded, far-off longing to be the wife of the tenant of Hawkshill. And if he, the great Tom Brodie, had been half as smart as he believed himself to be, he might have noticed that while he was busy suffering, she was busy falling in love with his brother.

She fell asleep at last, thinking not of Tom but of Henry.

It was still pitch dark and very cold when she wakened. She would not have wakened at all if he hadn't put a hand across her mouth and, leaning over her, whispered her name.

She opened her eyes. For a moment she thought he was about to take her again, then he said softly, 'I'm leavin' now, Betsy. I trust you not to rouse them. I prefer to steal away without fuss or flurry.'

She nodded and, when he took his hand away, said nothing.

'It's you I'll miss,' he said. 'When I think o' home, when I think o' Hawkshill bathed in summer sunlight, it's you I'll picture, Betsy McBride, you I'll miss most of all.' He brushed her hair with the palm of his hand. 'Remember now, not a word till mornin'.'

Then he kissed her, brusquely, and was gone.

★   ★   ★

'Is he up there?' Agnes Brodie called. 'Is he still in bed?'

'Nah,' Henry said. 'His bed hasn't been slept in.'

'In the barn, is he not in the barn? He'll be in the barn, surely.'

'No, Mammy, he's gone, bag an' baggage – gone.'

Henry, half dressed, climbed down the ladder from the loft.

With a shawl over her nightgown and her cap askew, his mother let out a shriek that conveyed more anger than grief. 'The wee bugger,' she said. 'He didn't even have the stomach to say goodbye to me.' She planted her feet on the floor and hoisted herself upright. 'Didn't you hear him leave, Henry?'

'Not a sound,' Henry said. 'He just – just stole away.'

'Stole away?'

Agnes dropped to her knees, fished below the bed, hauled out the cashbox, flung open the lid, then, blowing out her cheeks, sat back on her heels.

'It's here, the rent's still here, thank God.'

'At least he left us that,' said Henry.

'An' damn all else,' said Agnes.

She closed the box and pushed it back under the bed.

Betsy cautiously opened the bedroom door and peeped into the kitchen. 'What's wrong?'

'Tom's left us.' Henry shrugged. 'Up an' left us without a word.'

'Did you hear any noises in the night, Betsy?' Agnes asked her.

Betsy tugged the blanket over her breasts. 'No, nothin' at all.'

Agnes stamped her foot on the floor. 'Damn it, I've a good mind for to go after him an' shame him wi' my tears.'

'Go where?' said Henry. 'We don't even know what ship he's sailin' on. He wouldn't show us the agent's letter, re-member.'

'If there ever was a letter,' his mother said.

'What?' said Henry. 'Do you think he's not goin' to the Indies?'

'If you ask me, son,' Agnes said, 'he's just run off.'

'With Rose Hewitt, perhaps?' Betsy put in.

'Good God!' Henry cried. 'I never thought o'that.'

It was just after six when the coach appeared in Market Street. In the raw half-light of a winter morning Drennan was almost deserted. The rat-catcher and his boy were out and about and one or two dairymaids, wrapped in shawls, trudged past him without a second glance. Mist hid the houses in Thimble Row and there were no lights to be seen in any of the windows.

He had not slept at all and had tramped in from Hayes with the valise strapped to his shoulders, yet he felt strangely fresh and not in the least tired. There was just enough sentiment in him to nurture a hope that Rose might sense his presence in her town and, with tears and lamentations, come out to bid him a broken-hearted farewell.

Greatcoat covering his nightshirt, nightcap bobbing on his head, Caddy Crawford unbarred the door of the ale-house and, with no more than a grunt by way of greeting, handed out half the ticket that Tom had purchased in advance. The tavern-keeper waited just long enough for the four-horse coach to come to a halt at the tavern door, then, stepping to the pavement's edge, he gave the driver's lad the other half of Tom's ticket and with a surly 'good morning' waddled back indoors.

'Up or down?' the coachman asked.

'Down,' his boy replied.

'Is that all your luggage, sir?'

'It is,' Tom said.

'Take it inside wi' you then, for there's plenty room to spare.'

The boy hopped down and opened the door.

Tom thrust his valise into the coach and with a foot on the step and a hand on the rail, paused for one last glance in the direction of Thimble Row. Then, letting his breath out, he touched his fingertips to his lips and blew a kiss into the air in the hope that it might somehow find its way to Rose Hewitt.

'Got to hurry, sir,' the boy informed him.

Tom hauled himself into the damp, dark interior and heard the door slap shut behind him. He pushed his valise along the floor with his foot and, groping, searched for a seat.

'Why, sir,' said a voice, 'that's my knee you have your hand upon.' He snatched his hand away quickly, though the sensation of silk and satin remained on his palm. 'I do not think you would find it comfortable,' the voice went on. 'Do you have a flint in your pocket?'

The coach rocked into motion. Tom braced himself with a hand against the roof. 'I do have a flint in my pocket. Madam, where are you?'

'Here,' said the voice.

A gloved hand caught his sleeve and guided him down to the padded bench. He was suddenly enveloped in a cloud of perfume; a sharp, aromatic fragrance, not at all flowery. He reached into his pocket, fished out his tinderbox, clicked it open and scratched the flint against the steel. The spark ignited the loose little pile of wool and wood shavings in the base of the tin and quickly blossomed into a shapely flame.

Tom covered the flame with his hand and rose to his feet. Legs wide apart, he found the candle-holder on the wall, lifted the funnel and touched the flame to the wick. The tinderbox grew hot in his hand. He blew hard into it to put it out before he looked down.

She was directly beneath him, framed by his legs; a small, sharp-featured woman with huge brown eyes and a rosebud mouth that registered amusement – interested amusement, Tom thought. Glancing round, he realised that they were alone in the coach and would remain so until the horse-change at Gartmore where, with any luck, they might breakfast together. He dropped the tinderbox into his greatcoat pocket and, still standing over her, swept off his bonnet.

'Tom Brodie, madam,' he said, 'or is mademoiselle?'

'It is madam,' she answered. 'I am a widow, recently bereft.'

'I'm sorry to hear it,' he said, and resisted the temptation to pat her hand.

He liked the way she stared up at him, admiring his poise. She was rather young to be a widow, he thought, for unless the shadows flattered her she could not be a day over thirty, and if the cut and quality of her clothes was anything to go by, she had not been left penniless by her late lamented.

'Would it be forward of me, madam, to ask by what name I may call you?' Tom said. 'It seems that we'll be together for some while an' have already dispensed with formality.'

'Christina,' she said. 'Mrs Christina Goddard, or, if you prefer the old style, Mrs Andrew Goddard.' She offered her hand. Tom shook it, and, with the coach lurching again, seated himself at her side. She administered a thorough scrutiny and, to his relief, did seem put off by the shape of his nose.

She smiled. 'I'm so glad, Mr Brodie, that you're not some promiscuous old farming fellow with no manners and too high an opinion of himself. It's uncomfortable enough to take passage on an early morning coach without having to parley for one's honour.'

'Your honour, Mrs Goddard, is safe with me.'

'What are you, sir? A sea captain heading for Greenock, perhaps?'

'Certainly not a sea captain, no. Ministerin' to the land is my vocation.'

'Oh! You have an estate in Ayrshire, do you?'

'In a manner of speakin'. My brother has a property near Hayes.'

'I have an estate, too, a small estate in the vicinity of Perth,' Mrs Goddard told him. 'A meagre six hundred acres, but I am at a loss to know what to do with it.'

'Have you no children, no sons?'

'None.' She pouted for half a second. 'I have an uncle in Dumfries and I have travelled there to seek his advice. I passed a miserable night in Ayr and I am sure that I will spend another such in Glasgow. May I ask where you are bound, Mr Brodie?'

'Glasgow,' Tom said, without hesitation. 'May I enquire what sort o' advice your uncle gave you?'

'He advised me to employ a factor, an honest, experienced fellow to manage my holdings.'

'To look after your needs in general, do you mean?'

'Precisely,' Christina Goddard said. 'But where, I ask myself, may such a man be found?'

'Who knows?' Tom said casually. 'Who knows?' And let his hand, quite accidentally, wander to her knee once more.

At first it seemed that Henry had lost interest in Hawkshill. He moped about the yard doing very little for a day or two while his mother raged at him to stir himself and, in the quiet of the stable, shed tears for her wee lost laddie who might, or might not, be on his way to a sugar plantation on the far side of the world. It was left to Betsy to feed the sheep and cattle and attend the horses and ponies.

Friday came and went, and Saturday, too, without word from Tom; no letter of explanation or farewell. Neville Hewitt did not come charging up the hill, however, bellowing accusations so it was safe to assume that Tom had not eloped with the flax manufacturer's daughter after all.

On Sunday Betsy accompanied Agnes to church while Henry stayed home. He admitted to Betsy that he could not bring himself to spread the story that Tom had gone off to Jamaica when at any moment his brother might come strolling home, broke and impenitent, like the prodigal son.

Agnes harboured no such doubts. When the merchants of gossip convened around her at the kirk door, she told them the truth as she knew it: that Tom had gone abroad to earn a decent living and had left Henry to tend Hawkshill. Bold though the ladies of Hayes might be they were not so bold as to enquire of Mrs Brodie just how many fatherless bairns Tom had left behind or which fair maid might have another little Brodie nestling in her womb. They did give Betsy a good going over, though, and whispered at her swaddling coat which, in the opinion of some harridans, might hide a multitude of sins or, more likely, just one.

A week passed and then another. Shaking off his depression, Henry tackled a second ploughing of the small field and, with Betsy manning the cart, strewed the furrows with a healthy dressing of manure.

It was the wrong time of the year for hiring fairs and there were no spare hands to be found in Hayes. Henry put word about that Hawkshill was in search of a resident cattle-man and even rode over to Johnny Rankine's in the hope that the old man might have a servant to spare. But Johnny was no help to Henry who he considered no measure of a man, a measure that in Johnny's book equated with an unquenchable thirst for hard liquor and a willingness to mow anything in skirts. Betsy gathered that the meeting had ended with wild accusations but Henry refused to elaborate on exactly what had been said or tell her that he had lost his temper with Rankine in defence of her good name.

The first indication that winter was not over yet came in the last few days of February when dry cold gave way to howling gales and torrents of icy rain.

Betsy and Henry trudged out to the moor to round up the tups from the heather and drive them to shelter in the fold with the lambing ewes.

The fold by now was a quagmire of black mud churned up by the hooves of the restless ewes. The wind tore through the branches overhead and tossed in all directions the straw that Henry had brought to stiffen the ground. Cheeks stinging and nose running, Betsy gathered as much loose straw as she could, chasing it down along the wall, and trampled it into the fold to give the sheep a firmer footing and a decent bed to lie on. By three o'clock the sky was as black as pitch, a great dark curtain of cloud stretched across the horizon and, inch by inch, crept over the rim of the moor.

'By God, it's snow,' Henry said. 'God, not another spring like last year.'

Betsy was coated in fragments of straw, her nose dripped, her lips were cracked, and her hands were frozen.

Poor Henry was in no better state, his boots caked like elephant hide, his torn old coat flapping furiously about his legs, his mouth turned down like a fish on a hook. He leaned into the teeth of the wind, and the sheep leaned into him. He held out his hand, palm up, and caught the first granular snowflake. He opened his hand, peered at it and, looking round, said, 'It is snow, Betsy, isn't it?'

Holding herself steady with her forearm, she picked the grain from his hand with the tip of her tongue. She looked this way and that while pondering taste and texture, then gravely announced her verdict.

'Aye, Henry, it's snow.'

He stared at her blankly for a moment, then, giving her a push, burst out laughing and chased her through the mire and over the wall and, with the hard little flakes falling thick and fast, caught up with her and pinned her against the gable of the barn. He lifted his hand in a gesture that was almost foppish and she obediently wiped her nose on his sleeve just before he kissed her.

'For two pins, Betsy McBride,' he said, 'I'd marry you.'

'I haven't got two pins.'

'What have you got?'

'Chilblains an' chapped lips.'

'Is that the best you have to offer?'

'No,' she said, 'but the rest's my secret.'

Then, with a fierce gust of snow swirling around her, she ducked under his arm and, with Henry following close behind, scurried for the door of the cottage that Agnes had flung open to welcome them.

231 9/4
585 1/12